Once Upon a
HIGHLAND
CHRISTMAS

By Lecia Cornwall

Once Upon a
HIGHLAND
CHRISTMAS

LECIA CORNWALL

AVONIMPULSE
An Imprint of HarperCollinsPublishers

Excerpt from *An Heiress for All Seasons* copyright © 2014 by Sharie Kohler.

Excerpt from *Intrusion* copyright © 2014 by Charlotte Stein.

Excerpt from *Can't Wait* copyright © 2013 by Jennifer Hopkins. This novella originally appeared in the anthology *All I Want for Christmas Is a Cowboy*.

Excerpt from *The Laws of Seduction* copyright © 2014 by Gwen T. Weerheim-Jones.

Excerpt from *Sinful Rewards 1* copyright © 2014 by Cynthia Sax.

Excerpt from *Sweet Cowboy Christmas* copyright © 2014 by Candis Terry.

EPub Edition DECEMBER 2014 ISBN: 9780062328489

Print Edition ISBN: 9780062328496

10 9 8 7 6 5 4 3 2 1

To the readers of this book—
may every Christmas find you merry, bright,
and surrounded with the ones you love.

Prologue

Craigleith Castle, nineteen days before Christmas

"COME ON, FIONA—it's the season for magic," Lady Elizabeth Curry said to her Scottish cousin, pressing a small bundle of dried herbs into Fiona MacGillivray's hand as they knelt by the fire in the library of Craigleith Castle. Elizabeth held up her own herbs. "See? Like this—wrap a lock of your hair around the bundle, say the words, and toss it into the heart of the fire!"

Fiona stared at the crumbling gray leaves in her palm and wrinkled her nose at the pungent scent. "Are you sure this will work? I'm not English. Besides, magic can work in ways you don't expect. Auld Annie says—"

"Auld Annie!" Elizabeth scoffed. "What could she know of true love? She must be a hundred years old if she's a day."

Fiona glanced at the door, but it remained shut. "Annie has the sight," she whispered. "And she knows more magic than anyone. Why, I once saw her heal a ewe with just—"

Elizabeth sniffed. "This is about true love, not sheep. Come on. What can it hurt to know?" She drew a pair of sewing scissors out of her pocket and raised her eyebrows.

Fiona regarded her cousin's eager face, golden in the firelight. The rest of the room was filled with the thickening shadows of a winter afternoon. Night fell early in December, and Annie had predicted winter would come sooner than usual this year. "Shouldn't we be outside in the woods, dancing around a bonfire or something?" Fiona asked, holding very still as Elizabeth carefully snipped one of her curls.

"It's freezing outside!" Elizabeth protested. "Why can't it be in an earl's library?"

"Did the spell say so? Annie says a spell must be done properly, or it can go wrong," Fiona said. Elizabeth's brow crumpled for a moment, then cleared.

"What could possibly go wrong? It's not as if it's black magic. The spell says you must gather the herbs of midsummer, dry them, tie them with a lock of your hair, and burn them on the feast day of St. Nicholas. That's today. As long as the words come from your heart, then your wish is sure to come true."

Fiona closed her hand tight, and the scent of lavender rose to rival the peat smoke from the fire. There was nothing threatening about a wee bit of lavender. Still, she hesitated. "You go first," she said.

Elizabeth tossed her bundle into the fire. "Show me my true love, and send him to me by Christmastide," she said fervently. The flames pounced on her offering, flared with a hungry whoosh, and devoured the tidbit.

The girls leaned in, looking for a sign in the flames. "D'you see anything?" Fiona whispered.

Elizabeth screwed up her face and squinted. "Nothing that could be mistaken for anyone's true love. Throw yours."

Fiona wrapped her hair around the bundle. She took a breath and flung it into the heart of the fire. "Show me my true love, and bring him to me—" She hesitated. "Does it have to be by Christmas? Why can't it be by spring, or even next summer, perhaps?"

Elizabeth sighed in exasperation as the fire finished its second treat. "It's burned up now, so you'll have to wait for spring."

There was a sudden roar from the wind outside, and the windows rattled. The gust slipped under the door and swept down the flue, making the room suddenly cold. The chimney gasped and sucked hard on the fire, making the flame hiss and leap, drawing it upward, and breaking off sharp red sparks that clung to the soot for a moment and twinkled before being carried away on the icy breath of the wind. The fire sighed and sank back, subdued, and the flames fluttered nervously.

The girls looked at each other, their eyes wide. "What was that?" Elizabeth said. "What did it mean?"

Outside, the wind howled again, high and wild. Fiona pulled her shawl around her shoulders and rose to light the candles, driving the shadows back into the corners, where they hid behind the settee and the chairs. Elizabeth went to the window. "My, but the weather changes suddenly here in the Highlands. It wasn't snowing a minute ago, was it?"

Fiona looked. The snow *had* started suddenly, and frenzied white flakes were rushing across the brown landscape, driving toward the castle to dash themselves against the windows and stones with icy fury, clattering like the claws of an angry creature that desperately wanted in. Fiona's gut clenched. There hadn't been a single cloud in the sky an hour ago. She glanced at the fire again, but it burned sedately in the hearth, oblivious to the sudden storm raging outside. She swallowed. The herbs, and the spell . . . surely it was impossible.

Elizabeth stared out the window, hypnotized by the thickening flakes. "The snow—it's Christmas magic! Look, the garden is almost covered already!"

Fiona went to sit beside her cousin. The first snowfall was always beautiful, and magical—as if folk had forgotten what snow looked like over the seasons. Surely that's all it was.

She stared, mesmerized as the snowflakes danced intricate patterns in the air.

Show me my true love, and send him to me by Christmastide.

Outside the ancient walls of Craigleith, the sparks joined the snowflakes in a frenzied waltz around the castle's pointed tower in the thickening twilight, once, twice, and again.

Then they flew away across the moor, chasing the wind.

Chapter One

Craigleith Moor, nineteen days before Christmas

How DREADFUL IT was to freeze to death on the day before your own wedding.

Alanna McNabb looked around her and realized she was lost. Worse, a storm had suddenly blown in. Less than an hour ago—or was it two? —the sky had been clear, if gray as lead, and she'd been walking through hills dusted with the barest hint of snow, like a wedding cake delicately sprinkled with powdered sugar. Then wind and snow had tumbled over the lip of the mountains with remarkable ferocity, blotting out the earth and the sky and descending upon Alanna like a malicious ruffian bent on mischief.

The gale tore her bonnet off and tossed it away, slapped her cheeks raw, and twisted her cloak around her legs, making it almost impossible to walk, even as it drove her onward.

Landmarks disappeared behind a thick white curtain, and she felt the first thin edge of fear. This was supposed to be a short stroll in the hills, a chance to think, to let the brisk wind clear her mind and allow her to come to terms with tomorrow's events. Back at Dundrummie Castle, her wedding gown—pale blue—hung ready in her dressing room. The cooks were in a flurry, baking cakes and pies for the wedding breakfast. Her mother was preening in her mirror, putting the finishing touches on her own dress for the event, and her groom, the Marquess of Merridew, was on his way.

He would arrive at Dundrummie Castle this very afternoon, and she must be there to greet him. She looked around again at the blank white world. Would he worry if she was late? She drew a breath, felt the wind snatch it from her lungs, freeze it upon her lips, and knew she was going to be very late indeed. He might be irritated at the delay, or angry, or afraid. She had no idea how her fiancé would react, since she barely knew him. She turned, and the wind turned with her, spinning in a circle around her, binding her, refusing to let her escape. Surely if she retraced her steps, went back the way she'd come, she'd be home before anyone knew she was gone. But which way was it?

The snow was so white it hurt her eyes. The frigid air froze in her nose and throat. She had no idea which direction she was going.

Her mother would worry, once she got over her annoyance with her middle daughter for going out in the first place. Aunt Eleanor would pace the floor, her walking stick thumping the flagstones as she waited for Alanna to return. Her youngest sister would imagine the worst—as if there was worse that could be imagined. Her family would whisper that Alanna was not one for impetuous behavior, which made disappearance all the more shocking.

Her brother Alec and his wife, as well as her older sister, Megan, would not be attending Alanna's wedding. They'd have no idea she was lost. She doubted Alec even knew about the hastily planned wedding, and her sister was in England, equally oblivious, newly married herself. Alanna felt the lack of Megan's company keenly, but if Megan had stayed—well, there was no point in dwelling on that. What was done was done, and Megan, at least, was happy. Deliriously so.

One of them might as well be.

Alanna tightened her grip on her hood, fighting the storm for control of it. The wind bit through the thin leather of her gloves, made her fingers useless stumps. Her feet stung inside half boots meant for much lighter outings than this, and the cold crept through her cloak like a thief. She had never been so cold.

How much farther? She couldn't recall how far she'd come. She'd walked out through the orchard, up into the glen, past the loch and the ruins of old Glen Dorian Castle. She'd climbed a steep path and had stood for a moment, breathless, to look at the view. The hills had been spread out around her, and the waterfall tumbled down into the glen , silver lace against the brown landscape, like a bridal veil. She'd turned away from that thought, refused to look, walked on when she should have turned back. Had the clouds been gathering even then? She'd left the roar of the falls behind her as she'd reached the moorland. The wind had been brisk but benevolent, cleansing.

It wasn't kind now. It had turned angry, sharp tongued, and merciless. Panic flared in Alanna's breast, a small flicker of useless heat. Surely if she looked hard enough through the snow she'd see Dundrummie Castle in the distance, and be safely home in a few minutes. If not, someone would come out to look for her. She scanned the white world hopefully, seeking the dark figure of a rescuer, but she was entirely alone. She suppressed a gasp of dismay.

How foolish—she'd purposely left the castle without telling anyone she was going out. Mama would have stopped her, saying there was too much to do before Lord Merridew's arrival. Eleanor would have insisted that someone accompany her, just in case of—well, *this*. Her younger sister, Sorcha, would have wanted to come too, and she would have babbled incessantly, when Alanna wanted to think. Of course, thinking was no use at all. There was no way out of it—the wedding, she meant. Or the storm.

Oh, she was cold. The snow had reached the top of her boots, slipped inside to freeze against her ankles, gnawing her skin with sharp, icy teeth. How much farther? Surely such a sudden, terrible rage would blow itself out quickly enough and die away, like a tantrum. She listened for a change in the whine of the wind, a softening, but it screeched on. She blinked, felt the weight of ice on her eyelashes, rubbed it away and pushed back the urge to cry, since tears would only freeze.

She trudged on. Safety was just over the next hill—or was she in a glen? It was impossible to tell. Her cloak was crusted with ice, the hem stiff and scratchy against her legs, snagging her stockings, shredding them. Fear rose, more menacing now, and she fought the urge to panic. She gulped a deep breath and tasted snow, felt the chill invade her lungs, form a cold ball in her belly. She could barely open her eye against the force of the driving snow stinging her face.

The world was as opaque as linen, or new milk.

Or a shroud.

"Hello!" she called out. The wind snatched the word and flung it away. "Please," she begged. The gale took that word too. She bent forward, forced her way, step after step, the snow creaking and whining under her feet, the wind tearing at her clothes.

Alanna didn't see the gully. It was as white as everything else—but suddenly she was tipping sideways, sliding, unable to stop herself from falling down the frozen slope. She screamed as she hit something sharp and hard and came to a jarring stop. Pain shot through her knee, filled her body with agony, and made her pant as her heart hammered against her ribs. There were sharp rocks lurking under the fresh snow. They peered up like jagged teeth from where her fall had uncovered them. It could have been much worse than a bruised knee. "Lucky," she whispered.

She lay still, staring up at the sky, as white and heartless as the earth, lost in shock and pain. She reached her hand down to where pain radiated from her left knee, but her frozen fingers were useless. She raised her hand and stared at the blood on her glove. She swallowed hard.

Cut then, at least. Or was her leg broken? She tried to move it, felt the instant stab of pain, and cried out.

The world dissolved from snow to white-hot fire. She felt a bubble of hysterical laughter fill her chest. Surely this would delay the wedding. Or would it simply make her bruised and battered and ugly on her wedding night? Her mirth died. She tried now, as she had for days, to imagine Merridew above her, in her bed, his body against hers. She felt only dread.

Up—she must get up, keep going. She gritted her teeth and tried to rise. White hot agony forced the breath from her lungs, and she fell back. Perhaps the injury *was* worse than she'd thought, or maybe she was simply mired in a deep drift of snow. She would have to dig herself out, force herself to her feet, and continue on. She looked around, trying to get her bearings, but there was nothing, no one. The world had disappeared. She bit her lip, fought tears, and set a hand over her heart to still the terror that threatened to choke her. She was so cold, and so tired.

She lay back. She just needed a moment to rest, and then she would get up and find her way home. Above her, the snowflakes rushed toward her, silver on white, hypnotic. They tickled as they settled on her skin, a gentle caress. Alanna shut her eyes.

Just for a moment, she'd rest. Then she'd get up and find her way home.

Chapter Two

Craigleith Castle

FIONA STARED OUT the window with a frown, marveling at the ferocity of the wind-driven snow. It had come on like an invader, rushing across the moor, over fences and outbuildings, before hurling itself against walls and windows of the castle. The stones shook but held fast.

Beyond the wall that surrounded the garden, Fiona could not see anything at all. It felt as if the rest of the world had been swept away, leaving Craigleith, and only Craigleith, on the surface of the earth.

She wrapped her shawl tighter around her shoulders and shivered as she leaned forward to breathe on the windowpane and rub a hole in the gathering frost. Her brother Iain, Laird of Craigleith, was out in the storm somewhere. He'd gone to take one of Annie's potions to Illa MacGillivray for her sore joints. Knowing Iain, he would stop to check on everyone between Illa's holding and the castle, Fiona knew, just to be sure no one had need of anything the laird could provide. He took kindness and duty very seriously—more seriously than his own needs. He'd give away the shirt off his back if he thought someone else had need of it. She hoped he had not done so, not today, in the storm.

Iain would have gone out even if he'd known the storm was coming, refused to stay safe himself when others were depending on him. Soon, the people of Clan MacGillivray would have to do without him, for he had bigger responsibilities elsewhere as the new Earl of Purbrick. He hadn't said so, but Fiona knew he was worried how the folk here would manage when he'd gone south to Shropshire, in England.

She glanced over at her cousin. Elizabeth was dozing by the fire, bored and sleepy, a book open but unread in her lap, not worried about a thing. She had no idea how afraid Fiona was—for Iain out in the storm, for an unknowable future in England, and for the storm he faced here, inside the walls of Craigleith.

She glanced out the window again, looking for her brother riding homeward, but the moor was empty. Truly, there was nothing to worry about. Anyone would be pleased and honored to offer her brother a hot meal, a dram of whisky, and a bed for the night out of the storm. It was Highland tradition to do so, be the man a stranger or the familiar figure of Laird Iain MacGillivray. Still, this storm felt different. The snowflakes glittered like crystals, and the wind seemed to be muttering something she couldn't quite hear, sighing a spell, wrapping it tight around the castle.

The door of the library opened, and Fiona leaped to her feet, hoping it was Iain. She felt her heart drop into her stomach at the sight of Elizabeth's sister, Penelope. Fiona watched her twenty-year-old cousin saunter across to the fireplace to warm her hands, sparing Fiona a single dismissive glance before glaring at Elizabeth.

"What are you two doing?" Penelope demanded, her blue eyes narrowing with suspicion.

"Nothing now. We were casting love spells, but they didn't work," Elizabeth said. She sat up and reached into her pocket, and held out another bundle of herbs, her palm flat under her sister's chin, the way one fed an apple to a horse that might bite. "Why don't you try, Pen? I saved a bundle for you. You wrap the herbs with a lock of your hair and say the words."

"What words?" Penelope demanded, taking the bundle from her sister and turning it between her fingers suspiciously. She held it to her nose and made a face.

"You must say, 'Show me my true love, and send him to me by Christmastide,'" Elizabeth said eagerly.

Penelope turned her hand sideways and let the herbs fall to the rug. "What nonsense!" She ran a hand over her lush blond curls. "Why would I ruin my hair for that? I already know who my true love is, and he's here right now. I don't have to wait for Christmas."

Fiona crossed her fingers behind her back. "Has my brother proposed to you, then?"

Penelope flushed and stuck her nose in the air. "No, but it won't be long—and it will happen well before Christmas. Iain and I will be married in England next spring, and I will be the new Countess of Purbrick."

Fiona swallowed more dread. Marrying Iain would

also make Penelope the lady of Craigleith. Poor Iain, and poor Craigleith. Elizabeth bent to retrieve the little parcel of herbs as Penelope turned back toward the fire, shoving it into her pocket with a mutinous look.

Fiona wondered if the spell could send someone away by Christmastide too. She wished her English kin had never come to Scotland at all—though she liked Elizabeth, who was far more fun and far less sharp-tongued than her mother and older sister.

To hear Aunt Marjorie tell it, marrying Penelope was the smartest thing Iain could do. He was a Scottish laird—a *mere* Scottish laird, and therefore far inferior to an Englishman in Marjorie's opinion—but Iain had recently inherited the English earldom of Purbrick from his great-uncle, and hard on the heels of that surprising news had come Aunt Marjorie and her daughters. They'd arrived at Craigleith Castle in a fancy coach bearing the Purbrick crest, and tumbled out onto the doorstep, complaining of the smell of the Highlands, the cold, the rain, and the ramshackle condition of the castle itself, demanding to see the Earl of Purbrick at once. It had taken some time to understand they'd wanted Iain.

When he'd appeared, Lady Marjorie and her daughters had dipped low curtsies to him. They had come to help, Marjorie said, giving Iain a smile that had reminded Fiona of the fearsome stuffed wildcat that graced the castle's ancient hall. Marjorie had promised to teach Iain all the English manners and customs he'd need before he went south to take up his new responsibilities. Aunt Marjorie had made the offer as if Iain had no manners at all. She had barely even glanced at Fiona when Iain introduced her. She'd simply declared that a good English governess would soon mold Fiona into a proper young lady, though nothing at all could be done about her unfortunate limp. It hadn't been unfortunate until Aunt Marjorie arrived.

Fiona did not wish to be molded into anything other than what she was, and she thought Iain's manners were just fine. In fact he was the kindest, smartest, bravest man she or anyone else at Craigleith knew.

Then over dinner on the very first night of their visit, Aunt Marjorie had suggested—insisted, really—that Iain marry Penelope. Penelope would be a helpmeet to him, and make the perfect countess, since she'd been raised at Woodford Park, the magnificent principal residence of the Earl of Purbrick. Penelope had batted her lush golden lashes and smiled sweetly at Iain. For a long moment, Iain hadn't said a word, but he was a man who thought carefully before he spoke or acted. He'd had the good sense and diplomacy to suggest that they must know each other better first, in case Penelope found that he was not to her taste as a husband. He'd said nothing of his taste for Penelope, kept his expression carefully blank, so even Fiona didn't know what he truly thought of his simpering cousin. Even now, a fortnight after Penelope's arrival, Fiona still had no idea. Iain was unfailingly polite, of course, but the expected proposal had not been made.

The delay had simply made things more awkward. At every opportunity, Aunt Marjorie had thrown Penelope at Iain, dressed up like a princess, batting her eyelashes and pushing out her bosom. It was a chilly time of year in Scotland to be exposing that much flesh.

"Iain's had plenty of time to propose, if you ask me. Maybe he won't," Elizabeth said now to her sister. Penelope stepped forward, quick as a cat, and pulled her sister's hair.

"Of course he'll propose. Why would he not?" She sent a sharp look at Fiona, who had the sense to stay silent. "I'm beautiful and charming. Every man I meet falls in love with me. Iain will too. You'll see—he'll fall at my feet and beg me to marry him."

"When?" Elizabeth asked, moving safely out of reach before baiting her sister further.

Never, Fiona hoped.

"Very soon," Penelope insisted, drawing her fashionable cashmere shawl around her shoulders. "Put more wood on the fire. This miserable excuse for a castle is so drafty. There must be holes in the walls the size of my head."

And her head was just as dense as any of the stones that made up the castle walls, Fiona thought. She crossed the room and added an extra turf to the fire, because guests were always treated with honor and kindness in a Highland home, even if they weren't particularly kind in return. In her opinion, Penelope Curry would be the worst choice of wife Iain could possibly make, and he deserved better—much, much better—someone as kind and gentle and brave as he was.

Fiona couldn't resist a test. "What will you give to Iain as a Christmas present, Penelope?" she asked. "Perhaps that will convince him you're the right lass—lady—for him."

"A Christmas present?" Penelope looked shocked. "Do you do that in Scotland?"

"Aye, we do."

"What will he give me?" Penelope asked.

Fiona raised her eyebrows. "Christmas is about *giving* gifts—at least here in Scotland."

Penelope raised her chin. "Well then, what would he like?"

"Something from the heart," Fiona said, sure Penelope didn't have one.

"Such as?" Penelope asked, frowning now.

Fiona kept her tongue behind her teeth and smiled. If Penelope didn't already know, hadn't spoken with the man she wanted to marry enough to know what he liked and disliked, then Fiona couldn't—wouldn't—help. She was knitting her brother a scarf with wool she'd carded, spun, and dyed herself. He would make her something with his own hands as well, as he did every year: usually something carved from wood

The door opened again. Fiona looked up hopefully, but it was Auld Annie.

"Don't servants knock in Scotland?" Penelope said.

"Don't young folk respect their elders in England?" Annie shot back. She glared until the English girl looked away first.

Annie sniffed the air. "I smell meadowsweet, lavender, and yarrow," she said, and pinned Fiona with a sharp gaze. "What kind of spell?" she asked in Gaelic.

"A love spell," Fiona replied.

"For that one?" Annie asked, sliding her eyes over Penelope.

Fiona shook her head. "For Elizabeth and me," she said, and Annie cackled.

"You're too young for that yet, lass." She cast a look at the fireplace. "What did you see?"

"Nothing really. Sparks," Fiona said, and Annie crossed to look into the hearth.

"Speak English, and put more fuel on the fire while you're there," Penelope ordered, but Annie ignored her.

"Just sparks? Something brought the snow," Annie continued in Gaelic. "I didn't foresee it was coming, and Sandy's elbow didn't ache the way it usually does when the weather's set to change."

She got close enough to the flames to burn the arisaid she wore, and the fire lit up the muted colors of the Mac-Gillivray plaid—orange-red, teal, and green. She pointed a boney finger at the hearth. "Ah! You see that string of soot, just there, hanging from the grate?" she said in English Elizabeth rushed over to look as well.

"Is it an omen?" Elizabeth asked. "Is it true love?"

"It means we're going to have a visitor," Annie said. "Soon, too."

Fiona looked into the old woman's firelit eyes, saw the flame reflected in the dark depths, as if it burned inside Annie, and felt the thrill of magic rush through her limbs.

"The snow will bring someone to our door," she said, leaving the fire and moving toward the window. She frowned. "Iain has been gone since morning. I told him to hurry back, but it's near dark, and he's not home yet." She looked out at the blank whiteness of the park. Fiona felt her heart rise in her throat. The storm was a bad one, and if Annie of all people was worried—

But Annie turned to her and grinned. "No need to be

afraid, Fiona. I see nothing ill happening to the laird, and Iain knows these hills like the back of his hand. He'll take shelter till the storm breaks, and no harm will come to him."

But Fiona knew how easy it was to get lost on the moor in winter, to lose the track and wander off into the wilderness. If the landmarks were blotted out by the storm . . . Fiona refused to think of it. Annie squeezed her hand, her gnarled fingers remarkably strong.

"You can sleep soundly, lass. All will be well," she soothed, her gaze boring into Fiona's.

"When will dinner be ready? Is there any chance of tea?" Penelope asked. Annie sent her a sharp look, but Fiona grasped the servant's arm before she could voice the rebuke Fiona knew was hovering on her tongue. Fiona wondered if Annie could turn Penelope into a newt or even a toad. Now that would make a perfect Christmas present for Iain. She hid her smile at the idea.

"Come, Annie, I'll help you and Seonag with supper," she said.

"In England, ladies do not assist the servants," Penelope said as they reached the door.

Fiona sent her a pinched smile. "In case you hadn't noticed, we're in Scotland, cousin, and likely to remain stuck here until all this snow melts again."

Now there were cries of dismay and concern, and Fiona shut the door as Penelope and Elizabeth rushed to the windows to watch the storm rage.

Chapter Three

Craigleith Moor

IAIN MACGILLIVRAY PULLED his plaid up around his face against the force of the wind. The snow was driving sharp needles into his skin as the storm grew steadily worse. Odd, he hadn't seen it coming. The day had started out bright enough, even if his mood wasn't. He'd ridden out across Craigleith Moor, lost in thought, and he hadn't been paying attention to the heavy pewter clouds boiling up over the hills, bearing down over the other side, until the sky fell on him and took his breath away.

His valiant garron plunged onward through the snow, heading for home and the warmth of the stable, but the castle was still more than an hour away, too far in this weather with the chance of losing their way in the snow-blasted hills. Landmarks were disappearing, and the afternoon looked more like twilight. Soon there'd be nothing to guide him at all.

Ewan MacGillivray's cottage was closer, though Iain knew he'd find no welcome there. Ewan had been dead and buried since the spring, and the cottage lay empty.

Still, it was shelter, and he'd be safe until the storm passed. He'd take that gladly.

There was one good thing about the weather—it meant he had a reprieve. He had intended to propose to Penelope tonight, since he could see no way around it. He was only doing it for Fiona's sake, and because it was expected of him, not because he loved Penelope, or wanted her. That, he hoped, would come in time.

The storm howled in his ears, raged with a ferocity that surprised even him, and he'd grown up in the Highlands, spent twenty-seven winters here—well, twenty-six, since he'd spent a year in England. He'd decided then that he'd take the Highlands, even in weather like this, over England any time, but it was no longer his choice. He had new responsibilities, and an English title he didn't want.

He set his heels to the garron's broad flanks and bent low over the horse's neck. "Not far now, lad—just over the hill," he said, patting the horse's shaggy shoulder, thickly matted with snow, but the horse shied, and Iain caught the reins and steadied the beast, looked to see what had frightened it.

Something lay in the snow, red on white. A wolf's kill, perhaps? But wolves were scarce in the Highlands, hunted almost to extinction. He pulled the plaid away from his face and looked more carefully. A fold of red cloth fluttered in the wind like a flag, and his heart stopped. He could make out the shape of a body, half buried in the snow. He slid off the garron, his heart in his throat.

Falling to his knees, he touched the icy shoulder under the cloak. The figure didn't move. He frowned, and turned the body over, bracing himself, expecting to find someone he knew.

He pushed the red hood away and looked down. His belly turned to water. He didn't know her, but whoever she was, she was beautiful. She was as pale as ice, her lips darkened to blue. Her eyes were shut, and long, ice-tipped lashes lay frozen against her cheek. Dark hair framed her face, soft, like spun silk, held in place by a headdress of ice. She looked like an angel.

He bent closer, leaning in to check for signs of life. He felt for a pulse at her throat, found a faint beat. "Lass?" he said, but she didn't respond. The garron regarded the scene silently, blocking the wind.

Iain unwrapped his plaid, felt the wind bite through his coat. He wrapped her in the thick wool and picked her up, bundling her against his chest, but she didn't wake. She was cold as death already, he thought grimly. He scanned the horizon for the cottage. It lay half buried in the snow a short distance away, but he could see the line of the roof, the lone window peering at him with a one-eyed squint. He began to walk toward it, knowing the garron would follow.

"We'd best get inside," he said to the horse—and to her, if she could hear him. He looked down at her face again, more like a marble tomb effigy than a living woman. "Where the devil did you come from?" he asked softly.

At the cottage, he kicked the door open and carried her inside. He carefully laid her down by the hearth and covered her with his plaid. She lay unmoving, ash-pale and cold and all but lifeless. He tugged off her thin gloves. Her hands were delicate, her nails lavender blue with cold. He rubbed them between his palms, but she didn't wake.

He had to start a fire, get her warm. "Wait right here," he instructed her, though she hadn't shown any signs of leaving. Quite the opposite. He bundled the plaid more tightly around her, and for good measure he took off his coat and laid that on top of her as well.

He put kindling in the hearth, found a basket of dry moss and twigs, and fed the fire until it caught, lifted, and glowed in the dark blue shadows of the empty room.

He hurried out to find the peat that would be stacked in the lean-to, out of the weather. He led the garron into the shelter, rubbed the worst of the snow and ice away from the animal's thick coat, and pulled down some hay for him. Iain's teeth were chattering by the time he'd finished. He loaded his arms with peat and hurried back around the edge of the cottage, full into the jaws of the wind, gasping as he balanced the stack of fuel and opened the door.

The lass was still lying by the hearth, exactly where he'd left her. Her face was ice-white against the bright colors of his plaid. He fed the fire and muttered a prayer in Gaelic as he laid his fingers against the pulse point at her neck again. The beat of her heart was fragile and faint, but it was there. In the dim snow-light inside the cottage, he could see the delicate blue veins under her skin, like an egg held up to the light. The snow on his shirt began to melt, and he shivered. It was nearly as cold inside as it was outside. Iain turned to kneel by the hearth.

His fingers shook as he added more twigs, then the

peat, looking over his shoulder again and again at the woman, willing her to live, to wait for the heat to reach her. He blew on the newborn flames, watched as they turned orange and the blaze grew strong and steady, crackling with life and heat.

He heard a soft sigh and turned. Now that was good sign, wasn't it? But her face remained still. He touched her cheek, but it was still more like marble than human flesh. "Lass?" he whispered again, but there was no reply. The ice on her hair and skin was beginning to melt, and the droplets turned to diamonds. She glittered in the firelight, beautiful and still, asleep, or beyond sleep.

He carefully unwrapped the plaid that covered her, and unfastened the cloak beneath. She was wearing a fine woolen gown, green and soft as summer grass, though the fabric around her neck was wet and almost frozen where the snow had crept down the neck of her cloak. Iain frowned, felt fear creep through him. How long had she been out in the storm? If he hadn't come this way, had turned aside and tried to make it home to Craigleith, or had taken a path even a few dozen feet to the left or right . . . he swallowed.

"I need to get you out of your wet clothes, lass, get you warm, check for injuries," he murmured, though he knew she couldn't hear him. He cupped her head in his hands, checked her skull for bumps, or cuts, or blood, and found none. Her hair was coming loose from the braid that bound it, and the dark waves spilled over his fingers like silk. He took a breath as he reached for the pearl buttons that ran up the front of her gown from waist to collarbone.

He unbuttoned them and opened the garment. She did not leap up and rail at him for his audacity. She remained still, and he let his eyes fall on the slopes of her breasts. Her skin was ice cold above the lacy edge of her undergarment. He gently lifted her, cradled her in his arms as he loosened the sleeves of her gown, then slid it off her shoulders and down to her waist.

He did his best to keep his gaze clinical, but whoever she was, she was lovely. He didn't doubt that some man was going out of his mind with worry at this moment. He glanced at her left hand. There was no wedding band, but that didn't mean she wasn't someone's wife. He ran his hands down her arms, checking for injuries. There were bruises aplenty, but nothing was broken. He felt for the pulse in her wrist when he reached it, and chafed her hands between his own again, scowling at the fire, willing it to blaze hotter. He laid her down, cradled in a fold of his plaid, and slid his hands over her ribs to a waist that he could span with his hands, finding no hurts there. Her shift was made of fine linen, tied with satin ribbons and embroidered in delicate whitework. She wore no stays, and she needed none. He swallowed and averted his gaze from the pale shadow of her nipples beneath the garment. He concentrated on sliding the gown down over her hips and along the length of her legs, noted that the sodden skirt was torn and stained with blood, and he gritted his teeth, fearing what he might find.

He drew a sharp breath at the sight of her left leg. A long, shallow gash ran along the side of her knee, bounded by dark bruises and raw scratches. The cold had kept the swelling at bay, prevented it from bleeding much. He sent her an apologetic glance as he ran his hand over the limb. She groaned softly, almost inaudibly, as he touched her injured knee, her brow furrowing. Iain murmured an apology for the pain he knew he must be causing her, but her head lolled again, and she made no further sound as he checked for broken bones. He sat back with a sigh and wiped his brow. Despite the cold, he was sweating. At worst, her knee was probably sprained. It would hurt like the devil when she woke up—if she woke up.

Iain pushed that thought away. Her injury needed to be cleaned and bandaged. When she woke, it would start to swell. He had nothing with him for pain, hadn't expected to encounter anything worse than Illa MacGillivray's complaints about her aching joints. He'd left Annie's soothing salve with Illa, and he'd have to make do now, help the lass as best he could. He untied her half boots and peeled away the shredded, bloodied remains of her stockings. Where the devil had she come from? She's had a hard road of it. . . .

He covered her respectably with his plaid from thigh to throat and left her long enough to fetch a bucketful of snow. The wind outside was bitter, froze the perspiration on his skin with a single gust. He filled Ewan's old kettle and put it over the fire, not taking his eyes off her as he waited for the water to warm. He murmured an apology as he exposed her injured limb once again and dipped his handkerchief into the warmed water, using it to clean the wound. The fabric grew cold as soon as it touched her icy limbs. He worked quickly, then soaked the cloth again and bound it carefully around her knee. It needed a proper poultice, and ice to keep it from swelling, but he dared not chill her any further.

He frowned. She still hadn't woken. The fire had taken the edge of the chill off the room, but her limbs were waxen, her body unmoving ice. He added more peat to the fire and draped her clothing on the rope that was strung between the rafters, leaving it to dry. He checked her again. Her skin was still cold as death, her breathing shallow, her pulse a whisper under her skin. She still hadn't opened her eyes. He stroked her forehead, patted her hands, willed her to wake, but she did not.

Iain drew a deep breath. There was only one thing for it.

He swallowed hard as he reached for the ties of his shirt, began to undo them. "I hope you won't mind very much when you wake, lass. I'll have you know I'm not the kind of man who takes advantage of situations such as this, but I have to get you warm, and there's only one way I know of to do that. We've got the fire, and my plaid, and ourselves. The storm is terrible, or I'd find proper care for you, and proper company, but for now—" He pulled his shirt over his head. There was no gasp of surprise or outrage at the sight of his naked chest.

He pulled off his boots, put them next to the fire, beside hers, and began to open the buttons on his breeches. What if she woke now, at this very moment, and saw a half-naked man standing over her? No doubt the shock of that would warm her quick enough. He turned away, finished the task of undressing as discreetly as he could, and hung his garments over the line next to hers.

Naked, he opened the plaid and slid in beside her, gasping at the coldness of her body against his flesh. Under the covers he carefully untied the ribbons of her shift and slipped the straps of the garment off her shoulders. He worked it down the length of her body and away, taking care to keep her covered and to not look at what his hands were revealing. But his fingers brushed over her breasts, flitted across her taut stomach, skimmed her hips. He didn't need to see her to know she was beautiful.

Iain blessed the fact that he was a gentleman, even as he cursed the fact that he was a man, and she was bonnie. He tossed her shift over the line as well, next to her gown, then dove back beneath the covers, cold himself now. He suppressed a curse as he pulled her limp body into his arms. She was cold as death, the chill radiating from her limbs to fill his own, freezing him instantly. He gritted his teeth and wrapped himself around her, careful of her injured knee, surrounding her with his body heat, wrapping the thick softness of his plaid around them both. His teeth began to chatter in her ear, but she didn't notice. Would he wake up next to a corpse? He'd do his damnedest not to let that happen. He lay against her, willing the heat and life of his own body into her. He tucked her icy cheek into the crook of his shoulder and laid his fingers on the side of her neck, monitoring her pulse.

"You're safe now, lass. Live," he whispered in her ear. "Don't give up. Stay with me." Her heart kept beating, her body drawing warmth and comfort from his own, and Iain closed his eyes.

Beyond the sturdy stone walls, the storm raged on

through the night, and slowly he felt her grow warmer, soften against his, soaking up his heat. She curled closer still, pressed her bottom into his groin, her back against his chest. She was soft, sweet, and her curves fitted perfectly to his. The last time he'd spent a cold winter night curled under a plaid with a bonnie lass . . . his body reacted as any healthy man's would, holding a naked beauty in his arms on a cold December night. Iain gritted his teeth and willed the erection away, trying to ignore it as he concentrated on keeping her warm and alive.

He listened to the guttural chanting of the wind as it circled the sturdy stone cottage, looking for a way in. They were safe here. Still, it was going to be a very long night.

Chapter Four

Eighteen days until Christmas

ALANNA MCNABB WOKE with a terrible headache. In fact, every inch of her body ached. She could smell peat smoke, and dampness, and hear wind. She remembered the storm and opened her eyes. She was in a small dark room, a hut, she realized, a shieling, perhaps, or was it one of the crofter's cottages at Glenlorne? Was she home, among the people who knew her, loved her? She looked around, trying to decide where exactly she was, whose home she was in. The roof beams above her head were blackened with age and soot, and a thick stoneware jug dangled from a nail hammered into the beam as a hook. But that offered no clues at all—it was the same in every Highland cott. She turned her head a little, knowing there would be a hearth, and—

A few feet from her, a man crouched by the fire.

A very big, very naked man.

She stared at his back, which was broad and smooth. She took note of well-muscled arms as he poked the fire. She followed the bumps of his spine down to a pair of dimples just above his round white buttocks.

Her throat dried. She tried to sit up, but pain shot through her body, and the room wavered before her eyes. Her leg was on fire, pure agony. She let out a soft cry.

He half turned at the sound and glanced over his shoulder, and she had a quick impression of a high cheekbone lit by the firelight, and a gleaming eye that instantly widened with surprise. He dropped the poker and fell on his backside with a grunt.

"You're awake!" he cried. She stared at him sprawled on the hearthstones, and he gasped again and cupped his hands over his— She shut her eyes tight, as he grabbed the nearest thing at hand to cover himself—a corner of the plaid—but she yanked it back, holding tight. He instantly let go and reached for the closest garment dangling from the line above him, which turned out to be her red cloak. He wrapped it awkwardly around his waist, trying to rise to his feet at the same time. He stood above her in his makeshift kilt, holding it in place with a white knuckled grip, his face almost as red as the wool. She kept her eyes on his face and pulled her own blanket tight around her throat.

"I see you're awake," he said, staring at her, his voice an octave lower now. "How do you feel?"

How *did* she feel? She assessed her injuries, tried to remember the details of how she came to be here, wherever here might be. She recalled being lost in a storm, and falling. There'd been blood on her glove. She frowned. After that she didn't remember anything at all.

She shifted carefully, and the room dissolved. She saw stars, and black spots, and excruciating pain streaked through her body, radiating from her knee. She gasped, panted, stiffened against it.

"Don't move," he said, holding out a hand, fingers splayed, though he didn't touch her. He grinned, a sudden flash of white teeth, the firelight bright in his eyes. "I found you out in the snow. I feared . . . well, it doesn't matter now. Your knee is injured, cut, and probably sprained, but it isn't broken," he said in a rush. He grinned again, as if that was all very good news, and dropped to one knee beside her. "You've got some color back."

He reached out and touched her cheek with the back of his hand, a gentle enough caress, but she flinched away and gasped at the pain that caused. He dropped his hand at once, looked apologetic. "I mean no harm, lass—I was just checking that you're warm, but not too warm. Or too cold . . ." He was babbling, and he broke off, gave her a wan smile, and stood up again, holding onto her cloak, taking a step back away from her. Was he blushing, or was it the light of the fire on his skin? She tried not to stare at the breadth of his naked chest, or the naked legs that showed beneath the trailing edge of the cloak.

She gingerly reached down under the covers and found her knee was bound up in a bandage of some sort. He turned away, flushing again, and she realized the plaid had slipped down. She was as naked as he was. She gasped, drew the blanket tight to her chin, and stared at him. She looked up and saw that her clothes were hanging on a line above the fireplace—all of them, even her shift.

"Where—?" she swallowed. Her voice was hoarse, her throat as raw as her knee. "Who are you?" she tried again. She felt hot blood fill her cheeks, and panic formed a tight knot in her chest, and she tried again to remember what had happened, but her mind was blank. If he was— unclothed, and she was equally unclothed—

"What—" she began again, then swallowed the question she couldn't frame. She hardly knew what to ask first, Where, Who, or What? Her mind was moving slowly, her thoughts as thick and rusty as her tongue.

"You're safe, lass," he said, and she wondered if she was. She stared at him. She'd seen men working in the summer sun, their shirts off, their bodies tanned, their muscles straining, but she'd never thought anything of it. This—he—was different. And she was as naked as he was.

"May I have my clothes?" she asked.

"Oh—of course." He grabbed her shift, handed it to her. Her cloak slipped a little, revealing the jut of a male hip bone, the flat plane of his belly before he hitched the fabric back to his waist. He was tall—his head was nearly touching the roof beams above him, but that might be a trick of the eye, since he was standing, and she was flat on the floor. He had red hair that glinted in the firelight like polished copper. The stubble of the beard on his cheeks shone too, making him look gilded, almost magical. Was he real? She shut her eyes, opened them again, but he didn't disappear.

He reached for her gown as well, dry and warm, if badly torn, and set it beside her on the plaid.

"If you need my help with—" he began, but she sent him a glare and snaked one hand out from under the cover to drag her clothing inside, bundling it for a moment against her belly, watching him warily. Even that small effort was exhausting.

She watched as he took his shirt off the line and, with careful maneuvering, traded that garment for her cloak, covering what was necessary. Then, with one hand, he hung her cloak over the line to create a makeshift curtain between them.

All she could see now were his ankles, well-shaped and sinewy, and his feet, long and white against the hearth-stones. He snatched his breeches off the line, and she watched one foot rise, then the other, as he drew them on. The soft hush of the cloth was intimate in the tiny room. Then he stood there, his feet still, and she realized he was offering her time to dress too. She clutched the plaid to her breasts, pulled her shift over her head, then her gown, and reached underneath to right the ties and buttons. Her fingers felt thick and awkward, and she managed to knot the ribbons of her shift, but the buttons on her gown were impossibly small, and she couldn't fasten them. She gave up, held the two halves of her gown tightly over her breasts and stared at her boots, sitting near the fire next to his. Her stockings were nowhere to be seen.

His hand emerged from behind the makeshift curtain, grabbed for his boots, put them on. "I'll need to go out and check the garron. It will give you time for, ah—whatever is necessary. I'm close enough to call if you should need any help." Alanna felt a gust of cold air as he opened the door, then shut it firmly behind him. The silence was deafening.

She pushed away the plaid and tried to rise. Her leg rejected the idea at once, and her head agreed. The rest of her limbs were as thick and slow as her fingers. She looked at the bandage that covered her knee—a handkerchief, by the looks of it. There was a monogram done in awkward stiches, blue thread against white linen—I.M. She untied the knot and winced. The scratches were deep and ugly, long claw marks left by the ferocious storm, savage as a mountain cat. The bruises were like shadows on snow, bronze and black, and her knee was twice the size it should have been.

The door opened again. She flung her gown down over her naked leg, but the garment was torn from hem to knee, and it didn't cover anything at all. Her buttons were open as well, and she had to make a choice. She grabbed the edges of her bodice and held them together in her fist.

He stood and stared at her injured leg. He was wind tossed and cold, his skin flushed. He met her eyes. "The storm has stopped for the moment, but it looks like there'll be more snow before very long. Can you travel?" He came closer, holding out his hands as if to show he had no weapon, and no evil intent. There was snow in his hair, and it began to melt, the drops shining like gems, making a halo around him, as if he were an angel, or something else otherworldly. Was this heaven? Had she— She forced her mind into order. Her leg wouldn't hurt if this was heaven, and it wouldn't be snowing, or cold, surely.

"I think—" she began. Her voice was thick, and she could not recall what she wished to say. She swallowed as he knelt beside her.

"I should check your leg," he said, his tone apologetic. "May I?"

How polite he was, and there was nothing but kindness in his gray eyes. She nodded, knowing she could hardly fight. He shifted the folds of her gown, exposed as little of her flesh as she could. His hands were gentle, almost soothing, his long fingers dark and sure on the whiteness of her skin. She gasped at the pain, and he winced.

"It's not broken. I checked for other injuries—"

She stared at him. "You did?"

His skin flushed again, but he met her eyes. "It was necessary, lass. I found you in a bad way. How did you come to be out in the storm?"

She felt tears sting her eyes. "I got lost," she said. He dipped the handkerchief into a bucket of cold water, wound it back around her knee. The cold shocked her. "I.M.—is that you?" she asked through gritted teeth.

"Iain MacGillivray," he replied, and raised his brows expectantly.

"Alanna McNabb," she replied. "Where am I?"

"Craigleith Moor. Where were you going?"

She shrugged, and it hurt. "I wasn't going anywhere in particular, just walking," she said. "I wanted to think, so I went for a walk. My mother must be wondering where—" Her eyes widened. Her wedding. How could she have forgotten about that? She looked at him. "How long have I been here?"

"Just the night," he said. "Where did you come from?"

"Dundrummie."

"Dundrummie?" He looked at her in stunned surprise. "That's twelve miles away! That must have been some problem."

"Problem?" she asked.

"You said you went for a walk to think. That usually suggests a problem that needs considering."

She tried to rise but sank back, gasping, her limbs refusing to obey.

"Oh, lass—Alanna—you'd better take it slow."

He scooped a hand behind her shoulders and knees, and picked her up like a child. For a moment she was clutched against the broad warmth of his chest before he carefully set her on the bench by the fire. The room faded to spinning black dots, and he held onto her for a moment, his hand around her waist, steadying her.

"I must get back to Dundrummie at once," she managed.

He poured hot water into an earthenware cup, added whisky from a flask, and pressed the cup into her hands. It was warm, and she wrapped her palms around it. "Not today. The blizzard has made Glen Dorian impassable. You'll come to Craigleith Castle. Your knee needs proper attention, and Annie can see to it. We'll get word to your family as soon as we can, let them know you're safe, but not today."

Alanna felt tears fill her eyes. "But today is—it's my wedding day!"

His brows shot up into his hairline. "Your—" She saw the wheels turning inside his head. "You ran away!"

She tried to straighten her spine, didn't have the energy. Every inch of her body ached, and tears threatened. She clung to her unbuttoned bodice and glared at him. "Of course I didn't."

"You walked twelve miles in a blizzard to *think*, and you very nearly—" he began, but she sent him a fierce look.

"I will disappoint my mother if I am not there."

His brows quirked again. "Your mother? What of your bridegroom?" he asked. His eyes roamed over her, his appreciation plain. "I mean, he's sure to be eager—that is, *disappointed*—" He paused as she folded her arms over her breasts and gaped at him, felt hot blood creep into her cheeks.

"You saw—*everything*?"

He flushed again and looked apologetic. "I only did what was necessary. You were ice cold, near to— I had to get you warm, my skin to yours. Nothing else occurred. Your bridegroom will have nothing to complain of, save the fact you'll be late for your wedding."

She stared at him, her body tingling at the very idea that he, and she, had . . . *oh dear*. She felt her cheeks grow very warm. But he had saved her life. She raised her chin. "Thank you," she said in a formal tone, wondering if it was the right thing to say under the circumstances. She stared at the spot on the floor where they'd spent the night. Together. Naked.

He turned away and opened his saddle pack. "I'm afraid there's naught for breakfast save an oatcake or two. I've a flask of whisky, if you want it for the pain, but Annie will have something better to give you."

"Who is Annie?"

He grinned at her as he handed her an oatcake. "Auld Annie MacIntosh—she's been at Craigleith forever. She heals injuries and ailments, tells stories, and even keeps the laird in line."

"Muira," Alanna murmured, taking the proffered oat-cake, her fingertips brushing his, sending sparks flying up her arm. "We have Muira McNabb. She does the same for us." He really did have a lovely smile. She looked away and nibbled on her breakfast, unable to manage more than a mouthful.

"I'm sorry to insist on haste, given your injuries, but the storm has cleared for the moment, and the sky doesn't look promising. We'll have more snow before the day is out. We'd best get you back to Craigleith, where you can rest properly. You'll be among friends, Alanna. There's nothing to fear."

What choice did she have? She could hardly walk a dozen miles back to Dundrummie, even if she had any idea of the way. She watched as Iain MacGillivray shrugged into his coat and knelt before her. "May I?" he asked. He looked as if he were asking her to dance, his hands extended, his face expectant. Then he pointed to her chest. "Your buttons. It's cold outside."

She blushed and dropped her hands, felt his fingers brush the skin of her chest and throat. It was a shockingly intimate sensation.

"Not to worry—I used to do this for my sister when she was small," he said, giving her the kind of reassuring smile one gives a frightened child.

"How old is she?" Alanna asked. His head was inches from her own, and she smelled the clean sweetness of the wind in his russet hair. It looked soft and thick, and if she leaned forward just a little, she could rest her cheek against it . . .

"Fiona's fifteen now, a woman grown," he said, looking up from his task, bringing her back to the present. His eyes were gray, fringed with copper lashes. She pictured Sorcha, her own younger sister, just twelve, and not quite a woman grown. Sorcha would be worried. They all would be—her mother, her aunt, even Graves, the English butler, and Jeannie, Aunt Eleanor's maid. Guilt formed a ball in her chest. She should never have left Dundrummie at all.

Iain MacGillivray turned away to pick up her boots. Her stockings lay inside them, and she noted the bloodstains and the gaping holes in them, remembered the violence of her fall, the pain of landing hard on her knee. She swallowed. She was lucky, then. The stockings were beyond rescue, but she had been much more fortunate. She let her eyes move over Iain MacGillivray yet again. If not for him— He must have seen her blanch, for he gave her a smile and stuffed her tattered stockings into his pocket, out of sight. She felt her heart thump against her ribs. He really did have a marvelous smile, was the kind of hero a lady dreamed about.

"Can you wear your boots without your stockings?" he asked. "We'll find you another pair at Craigleith." He knelt at her feet, a knight-errant, and cupped his warm hands behind her heels, setting each foot on his lap, one after the other. He grimaced as he pushed her boot onto her injured left side. She gritted her teeth, did her best to be brave, to stifle the cry of pain, but she could see by the way his eyes darkened that he knew it hurt, was sorry to cause her discomfort.

He wrapped her cloak around her shoulders, fastened it, and scooped her off the bench. The world shifted as he lifted her. She tightened her grip on the lapels of his coat and met his eyes. A rush of breathlessness filled her, and she put it down to light-headedness. No one had ever carried her before—well, aside from Alec, her brother, when she was very small.

Surely if Alec was here now, he would be as kind and as careful with an injured stranger as Iain MacGillivray was. Yet she could never mistake this man for her brother. His touch, as polite as it was, was different, made her feel unsettled, more aware.

"You must be a wonderful brother," she murmured, and his laugh vibrated through her chest.

"You can ask Fiona about that."

The snow was blinding after the dark warmth of the cott. The cold sucked the breath from her lungs, flung it into the leaden sky in a cloud, and made her gasp.

Iain MacGillivray set her carefully on the garron's sturdy back, and she gripped the creature's coarse mane, concentrated on holding on as the horse swung its shaggy head around to look at her with friendly curiosity. The beast made no complaint as Iain mounted behind her and settled the plaid around them both, binding her into a cocoon against his body. It was warm and intimate.

"Comfortable?" he asked as they set off, the snow squeaking under the garron's hooves.

"Yes," she said, though she wasn't. She had never been so comfortable, and yet *uncomfortable* too, in all her life. She was wrapped in a stranger's plaid, her bottom resting between his thighs—thighs that had been naked against hers throughout the night. She could feel his heart beating against her back, and his breath fanned over her cheek.

Her knee ached like the devil was gnawing on it, but he held her safe, enclosed in the circle of his arms as he held the reins with casual ease. She had never been this close to any man before now—not even Merridew, her bridegroom. But she had met him just twice, and since he had come to court her older sister on both visits, she wasn't sure those meetings counted at all. He'd barely even looked at *her*, the second sister, the spare. . . . She felt her cheeks flame despite the cold. The garron trudged on across the blank white landscape, eager for home.

"There's Ben Laggan," Iain said, pointing out a gray mountain wearing a thick shawl of fresh snow. "Glen Dorian and Dundrummie are on the other side. You must have come through the pass there." He pointed again, but she could see nothing but snow. "It's blocked now."

"How far is it to Craigleith?" she asked. She pictured a cottage like the one they'd just left, snug and warm, his wife at the door . . . and his sister, of course. Did he have bairns as well? Her cheeks flamed again at the thought of facing his wife, telling her that she had spent the night naked in her husband's arms. Would she believe it had simply been necessary? Alanna wasn't sure *she'd* believe such a tale, not when a man looked like Iain MacGillivray.

"About four miles," he answered her question. "It won't take long. We'll be there in an hour. Sleep if you want."

She sat up straight, as she'd been taught. She'd not give Missus MacGillivray anything more to fret about, and she most certainly could not sleep on a strange man's chest, or on a horse. But perhaps she'd close her eyes for just a moment against the dazzling brilliance of the snow.

IAIN FELT HER body relax into his as she fell asleep, warm this time, a soft, sweet weight in his lap, and he shifted her more comfortably against his chest so her cheek rested on his shoulder. He looked down into her face. Her lips and cheeks were pink now, but there were dark smudges under her eyes—soft hazel eyes, he recalled, wary and wide and beautiful. She needed a bowl of Seonag's nourishing broth, a comb, a bath, a proper bandage for her injured knee, and hours of sleep, but he'd still never seen a more beautiful woman. He might not have peeked beneath the covers, not even once, or looked above her knee, or below her shoulders, but his body knew what hers felt like, the slender curves, the softness of her skin. And now, the angle of her bottom against his groin and the movement of the horse were proving to be arousing in the extreme. He kept still, not wanting to wake her, or alert her to his condition. She belonged to another man, a man no doubt pacing the floor before the altar, burning to have her back again, to marry her and bed her properly before his own hearth. Iain felt a rush of jealousy and tightened his grip on her shoulder for a moment before reminding himself that she did not—could not—belong to him. Their paths led in different directions—his to England, hers to Dundrummie village, and her wedding. He wondered about her husband. Was he a crofter, a blacksmith, a baker, perhaps? Whoever and whatever he was, he was a lucky man indeed.

He turned his eyes up to the glowering sky and concentrated on counting the garron's steps.

They could not reach Craigleith quickly enough.

Chapter Five

Dundrummie Castle

"WHAT DO YOU mean you can't find her?" Lady Devorguilla McNabb, the dowager countess of Glenlorne, demanded, eyeing Dundrummie's half-frozen gamekeeper with suspicion. The man had been out for hours, was flushed with cold and exhaustion, but he hadn't found Alanna. "She didn't just disappear!" Devorguilla insisted.

It was too soon to imagine that anything truly unfortunate had happened to her middle daughter, or to consider that Alanna might have run away, or even eloped to avoid her wedding. Alanna was sensible and obedient. She wouldn't do any such thing. Devorguilla bit her lip and looked at the clock. Still, Alanna had been gone all night, and it was nearly midmorning. Fortunately, Lord Merridew had not yet arrived, no doubt delayed by the weather himself. How could she explain that Alanna was missing on her wedding day, especially after Megan had eloped to avoid marrying his lordship only a few short months earlier? The poor man would begin to suspect that Devorguilla's daughters weren't grateful to be marrying an English marquess. Devorguilla clenched her fist. She would not let that happen. Alanna must be found.

She watched as her sister-in-law, Lady Eleanor Fraser, pressed a dram of whisky into the gamekeeper's hand. "Come get yourself warm by the fire, Jamie, and tell us what you know."

"No one saw her after noon yesterday, my lady," Jamie said, shaking his head. "Jeannie said she saw Lady Alanna out in the orchard, dressed in that red cloak of hers, walking among the trees. That was before the snow began." Devorguilla saw the worry in the man's keen eyes as he shook his head. "There's no sign of her now. The storm has covered any tracks she might have left. We've had a lot of snow, and there's another storm coming." He rubbed his elbow. "This one will be worse than yesterday's—I can feel it in my bones."

"Go out again," Devorguilla insisted, ignoring the puddle the man was leaving on the floor as he thawed out. "She must be found. Did you check everywhere—the lodge, the village inn, the old castle at Glen Dorian?" Was Alanna hiding somewhere, sulking?

"Several times, my lady," Jamie said. "We've got everyone in the village looking for the lass as well. We're all worried about her." He twisted his cap in his hand and looked at Eleanor.

"Go and get some soup in the kitchen and warm yourself," Eleanor said and sent him out.

Devorguilla paced the carpet. "First Megan runs off and handfasts with Lord Rossington, and now—" She felt a frisson of irritation replace concern in her breast. "It took me *weeks* to placate Lord Merridew, to show him that if he couldn't have Megan, then Alanna would do just as well. And now this—will all my daughters disappoint me?"

Eleanor went to the window and scanned the orchard yet again before turning to face her sister-in-law. Devorguilla could see by her expression there was still no sign of Alanna, and her heart fell.

"Well, since Merridew isn't here, I have no doubt he has been delayed by the storm as well," Eleanor said. "There's still time to find Alanna before he arrives. I'm sure she's safe. It's the custom in the Highlands to offer welcome and shelter to travellers, and someone will have taken her in." She met Devorguilla's eyes. "Of course, this means there's still time to invite Alec and Caroline to the wedding, weather allowing. Alec will eventually find out his sister is getting married, and he won't be pleased that you left him off the guest list. If we delay the ceremony for a week or two, we can have a Christmas wedding. That, and it will give Merridew and Alanna a chance to get to know each other a little better."

Devorguilla frowned, twisted her fingers together under Eleanor's scrutiny. "Alec is the Earl of Glenlorne now, and he has enough to do there without bothering with my affairs. Alanna is my concern."

"She's his sister, and he loves her. He wants what's best for her as much as you do," Eleanor said. "He'd want to be here, you know that. And he is her guardian."

Devorguilla raised her chin. "And I'm her mother! Lord Merridew is what's best for Alanna. He's titled and willing, and Alanna agreed to his proposal."

Eleanor folded her arms over her chest. "She agreed to *your* proposal. You're afraid Alec will refuse to allow the match, aren't you? He'll ask Alanna if she loves Merridew, and she'll say no."

Devorguilla colored and turned to pace the floor. "Love! What difference does that make? Of course she loves him—or she will eventually."

Eleanor shook her head. "That wouldn't be good enough for Alec, and it's not good enough for anyone else but you. Merridew is marrying Alanna's dowry."

"So? She'll be a marchioness, and then a duchess someday," Devorguilla countered.

"Does that matter to her? She's a sensitive soul. A title won't make her happy. She only agreed to marry Merridew because you insisted. She's afraid of disappointing you."

"The way Megan did?" Devorguilla said. She knew what was best for her daughters—English titles, power, position. They couldn't have that in Scotland. Here, they'd always be second best.

Eleanor grinned. "I'm proud of Megan. She chose the life she wanted, the man she loved. That's exactly how it should be. She still married an English earl, and isn't that what you really wanted?" Eleanor asked.

"Not when she could have had a marquess!"

Eleanor rolled her eyes. "Aren't you just a little bit more concerned about whether Alanna is safe or not? She's not stubborn and willful like Megan. Alanna wouldn't run away. She may be in trouble."

Devorguilla shrugged and studied her manicured hands, clasped them to hide the fact they shook. "Of course I'm worried, but you said it yourself, someone will take her in if she needs help."

Eleanor sighed. "I hope you're right. 'Tis a terrible thing to press a young girl so far that she'd run away into a snowstorm." She headed for the door. "I think I'll go and see if we can organize another search before the storm closes in again."

Devorguilla watched Eleanor go, then went back to the window, looking for her daughter among the bare trees of the orchard. She leaned her head against the glass and hoped Alanna was safe. Merridew would surely be here very soon, and he'd want to see his bride.

Chapter Six

Craigleith Moor

THE WIND CARRIED the scent of tobacco smoke to Iain before Sandy MacGillivray came into view. Iain smiled when he saw Craigleith's gamekeeper riding toward him over the snow.

The old man's frill of white hair floated around his bonnet like a cloud, and he grinned, showing both his remaining teeth as their garrons drew even. "Good day, Laird."

Sandy regarded the bundle in Iain's lap for a moment. If he was surprised to see Iain carrying a woman wrapped in his plaid, he didn't make any comment. He merely nodded. "Auld Annie said I'd find you right about here this morning—and she said the signs pointed to a visitor coming to Craigleith. I suppose this must be she."

Iain chuckled as Sandy fell in beside him. "What did Annie use this time? Dreams, scrying?"

Sandy squinted. "She saw it in the ashes yesterday, and again today in the bannock batter." His eyes fell on Alanna again. "Is she hurt?"

"Yes, and asleep for the moment. She got lost in the storm. We spent the night in Ewan's cott. She injured her knee," Iain said, offering the short explanation of things.

Sandy gave Iain a manly grin. "A night in Ewan's cott, eh?"

Iain thought of holding Alanna's icy body against his own through the night, willing warmth and life back into her limbs. It hadn't been even remotely romantic. Still, he'd woken this morning, and she'd been warm and soft and curled against him like a lover. He'd never gotten out of bed so fast in his life. He looked down at her now, sleeping like the dead in his arms. But she wasn't dead. He'd saved her. He pulled a fold of his plaid tighter around her face to keep out the cold, and Sandy chuckled at the gesture.

Iain glowered at him. "She was unconscious. All night."

Sandy waggled his brows. "Och, aye, just as you say, Laird. Still, your Sassenach won't like this, especially if this lass is bonnie. Is she? I can't tell with her wrapped so tightly against your heart."

"Penelope is hardly my Sassenach. She's my cousin, just here to visit." *And yes, Alanna McNabb is bonnie indeed . . .* His hand tightened on her shoulder, possessively, unwilling to share her, even with Sandy.

Sandy puffed his pipe, his white eyebrows winging toward the edge of his bonnet. "As you say, Laird, as you say," he said again. "It's just that you're the only one who believes that. We'd better hurry home," Sandy said. "The storm won't be long in coming."

Iain held his tongue and almost sighed with relief when

Craigleith Castle came into view. The sickly yellow-gray storm light loomed behind the sturdy square tower and its pointed roof. Snow clung to the weathered stones, giving the castle a speckled appearance. It looked magical, and as always, he felt a sense of contentment and pride at coming home. Would he feel that in England, at Woodford Park?

They rode into the bailey, to the kitchen door. It swung open as they brought the garrons to a stop, and Annie stood in the doorway regarding Iain fondly as he slid off the horse with Alanna still in his arms. She didn't bother with a greeting. "Our visitor, no doubt. Bring her inside out of the cold," she commanded, standing back, pulling her arisaid closer against the chill. She cackled softly as Iain carried Alanna over the threshold of his home like a bride. He sent the old seer a quelling look. Alanna was a bride indeed, though not his. This was to have been her wedding day, a joyful occasion, but at Craigleith she was just an injured stranger. Poor lass.

She woke and looked up at him in surprise, her hazel eyes widening, her lips parting. Iain's breath caught in his throat, and he forced a smile. "We're here, lass—Craigleith."

"There's a fire in the kitchen—I'll tend to her there," Annie directed him, and Alanna glanced at her. "Annie MacIntosh, this is Alanna McNabb," Iain said and set Alanna carefully on the bench near the fire. She clung to his shoulder a moment, and he had the urge to keep hold of her, but he stepped back, his body cold where she'd lain against him. Alanna looked around at the curious eyes regarding her—Sandy, his daughter-in-law Seonag the cook, and wee Janet, Seonag's eldest daughter. He introduced them, and Alanna smiled at each one in turn, as if she was glad to know them. They beamed right back at her as if they were all simple and had never seen a pretty lass before this moment. Iain frowned at them over the top of Alanna's head, but they didn't take the hint. They stayed right where they were, staring. Alanna folded back the plaid from her hair and blushed.

"Why, aren't you a bonnie lass!" Annie said, peering at her. She looked at Iain with a grin. "This will set the cat among the pigeons, Iain, you mark my words, and neither one of us needs the sight to ken that."

Iain ignored the comment and leaned on the mantel, loathe to leave Alanna, even in Annie's gentle care. Annie poured a cup of whisky, went to the cupboard, and took out a pot of herbs. She put a generous pinch into the cup, added some honey, and took a poker out of the fire to stir the brew. The whisky hissed and bubbled, and she pressed it into Alanna's hands. "You drink that down while it's hot," she instructed.

Alanna looked at the faces around her. Was the pregnant woman with her sleeves rolled high on her arms Iain's wife? She had eyes only for Alanna, it seemed, and had barely looked at Iain. Alanna was glad he stayed, stood close by, leaning against the fireplace.

They did not look unkind—far from it—but they were staring at her. She supposed she was a dreadful mess, her hair uncombed, her clothing wrinkled. Her face heated, and she looked around the kitchen. It was big and homey, and it reminded her of Glenlorne, where she'd grown up.

There was the same scrubbed wooden table, the same pots and pans and bundles of drying herbs, the same kettle hanging over the fire, and the familiar scent of fresh baked bread and hot soup. She felt tears prick her eyes.

Seonag MacGillivray made a soft sound of sympathy and caught Alanna's hand. She patted it and called her a poor wee lass to be caught in such terrible weather. She rested her other hand, flour-coated, on her pregnant belly.

Wee Janet smiled and leaned against Sandy MacGillivray, introduced as her grandfather. Sandy MacGillivray regarded Alanna with a fond smile, his white hair orange in the firelight, the color it must have been in his youth.

Annie MacIntosh studied her even more carefully than the rest, her eyes dark and shiny amid deep wrinkles and crags. Alanna had the feeling Annie could see right inside her skull and read her thoughts. She was aware of Iain behind her, resisted the urge to reach for his hand. She straightened her spine instead and looked down into the amber brew in her hands. The cup was soothingly warm against her palms, and she sipped it. The honey soothed the whisky's burn and the bitter edge of the herbs. The hot liquid made her limbs light and warm. As everyone leaned in to watch her, she wondered what was in the brew, but Annie smiled reassuringly, just the way Muira might have done if Alanna had been home at Glenlorne. "That's it, lass."

The door burst open, and a young girl hurried through the door and flew into Iain's arms. Alanna noticed she limped. "You're back!" the girl said as he wrapped her in a hug and kissed the top of her head. "We were so worried—

well, I was," the girl said, pulling back to look up at Iain. "Annie said you'd be fine. Was it the storm that kept you out all night?"

"Yes. We were forced to spend the night at Ewan's cott, but all is well," Iain said.

The girl grinned. "Well, you're here now, and safe. Annie says there's another storm coming."

"More of the same—snow, wind, and cold. Winter's early this year, and fierce," Annie said, and made a sign against ill fortune.

"Come and meet our guest," Iain said, his hand on the girl's shoulder. "Alanna McNabb, this is my sister, Fiona MacGillivray."

Fiona's eyes widened. "Annie said we should expect a visitor. How do you do?"

Alanna smiled. "I'm pleased to meet you." She had no chance to say more than that as Annie bent over her leg.

"You'll turn away now, Iain, and Sandy, out you go too, old man. This isn't for your eyes," Annie instructed, her gnarled hands on the hem of Alanna's skirt.

Alanna looked up at Iain. He was looking back at her, his eyes shadowed with the fire behind him. She wished he would stay. Did propriety matter now? He'd seen far more than just her injured knee—he'd seen *everything*. He'd stripped her of her clothing, held her naked body against his own, kept her warm and safe. She felt heat rise in earnest now.

"I'd better see to the garron. I'll leave you in Annie's capable hands," he said and gave her a reassuring smile. So he was a groom here at Craigleith, perhaps, and likely used to healing horses with injured legs, which explained his care of her. She watched as he left the room, and felt strangely alone without him, though she'd only known him for a matter of a few short hours—did all the hours she was unconscious count? She supposed in this case they most certainly did, but still, he was a stranger. Yet it felt as if the light and heat went out of the room when he left it. Perhaps it was because he'd rescued her. Perhaps it was because he was the tallest, handsomest man she'd ever seen. Perhaps it was the fact that he'd saved her from a fate *almost* worse than death: If she were at Dundrummie at this very moment, she would be reciting the wedding vows that would bind her for life to the Marquess of Merridew. Iain MacGillivray had given her a reprieve from that. She felt gratitude bloom in her breast.

Annie laid a wrinkled hand on Alanna's cheek. "You're flushed like a summer rose. I feared you were fevered, but you're not." The old woman glanced after Iain, her eyes speculative. Alanna lowered her gaze.

"I'm well, I think, except for my leg."

Annie moved the tattered edges of her skirt away.

Janet gasped at the sight of her injuries, and Seonag made a sound of pity. Fiona pointed. "That's Iain's handkerchief!" she said in a half whisper. "The one I embroidered with his initials last Christmas."

Annie cackled. "Perhaps we needn't have sent him out after all. I trust he was the one that bandaged you up in the first place?"

Alanna felt more fiery blood fill her cheeks. She pictured his naked body in the firelight, the sensation of his strong hands on her leg, the way he'd held her on the horse, the ease with which he lifted her, carried her. She kept her eyes on her leg. "Yes, he was the one who bandaged it," she said. "Is it as bad as it looks?"

Annie probed carefully and squinted before replying. "Sprained and swollen, bruised and scratched too, but not broken. No wonder Iain was carrying you about the way he was. He'll be carrying you for a few days more."

"Oh, no, I'm sure that won't be necessary. I can manage," Alanna said. "I really can't stay here for so long as that. I am grateful for your kindness, but I must get home."

"Where's that?" Annie demanded as she poured hot water into a bowl and added a handful of herbs. She mixed them with her hands.

"Glenlorne—well, Dundrummie," Alanna said. She suddenly wanted nothing more than to go home to her brother, and Muira, and the people she loved—not that she didn't love her mother, or her aunt Eleanor, but she decidedly did not love the Marquess of Merridew. She felt fresh tears sting her eyes.

"Och, lass, don't cry. You'll be fine. We may be strangers now, but we're good, kind folk, and Iain . . . well, there's no better man than Iain," Seonag soothed, laying a reassuring hand on Alanna's shoulder.

Annie spread the warm poultice on Alanna's knee, her fingers gentle. The strong summer smell of the herbs filled the air, another reminder of home. "You'll need to stay put," Annie said firmly, but not unkindly. "You mentioned a healer named Muira—I've no doubt at all that she'd tell you the same."

"What of the Laird of Craigleith?" Alanna asked. "I should speak to him, ask his permission—"

Annie looked surprised, and Seonag chuckled.

"But Iain is the Laird of Craigleith. Did he not introduce himself properly?" Annie asked.

"We did not—talk—very much." Alanna swallowed, and Annie cackled again.

"My brother is also the Earl of Purbrick in England . . . well, he's going to be. The old earl was our great-uncle, and he died this past autumn. Iain will go to England in the spring and take up his duties there," Fiona said.

An earl? Alanna swallowed. And she'd imagined him to be a tacksman or a stable hand. She should have known of course, by the confidence in his eyes, the innate attitude of a man in charge. Yet everyone here was at ease with him, and he had a way of making even a stranger feel comfortable and safe.

Annie made a sour face. She uttered something dark under her breath in Gaelic about Sassenachs, and Fiona clasped her hands together anxiously.

"My brother's an earl too," Alanna said quickly. "A Scottish one—the Earl of Glenlorne."

Fiona's eyes widened. Annie's brow unfurled at once, and her eyes twinkled. "An earl's sister?" She began to laugh, her mouth wide to expose her missing teeth. "Aye, you will indeed set the cat among the pigeons," she said cryptically. "Wait until the ladies upstairs meet you, my lady!"

"Ladies?" Alanna asked.

"Sassenachs," Annie whispered the word again, her lips pinching.

"My aunt Marjorie and my cousins Lady Penelope and Lady Elizabeth, from England," Fiona explained. "Elizabeth is very nice . . ."

"Och, they expect English food, English manners, and an English Christmas. I wonder if they realize that this is Scotland they're in," Seonag said. "And they're determined to give our laird lessons, teach him how to be English—as if Iain MacGillivray could ever be mistaken for an Englishman! They can take him out of the Highlands, I say, but they will not take the Highlands out of Iain."

Alanna knew all about lessons in English manners, language and customs, and felt sympathy for the laird. Was it worse if one was a man? Her own mother had decided long ago that her daughters would marry English lords. She had raised them to make their debuts in London, had hired English tutors, governesses, maids, and even an English butler. When Alanna married the Marquess of Merridew and took her place as an English Marchioness, every aspect of her Scottishness would be hidden or banished. Even the lilt of Alanna's accent would be crushed after many hours of correction. Well, almost crushed. They could never entirely take the Highlands out of *her* either.

She tried to imagine Iain MacGillivray walking into an English drawing room, tall and redheaded, broad-shouldered and tanned, his plaid across his shoulders, his hair windblown. No, Seonag was right—no one would mistake Craigleith's laird for an Englishman. He was as different from an Englishman as eagles were from blackbirds. At least the Englishmen Alanna had met.

"Then I should perhaps pay my respects to Lady Mac-Gillivray," Alanna said.

"My mother has been dead for many years," Fiona said, misunderstanding.

"She means Iain's wife, I believe," Annie corrected her, and Fiona blushed.

"Oh! He isn't married. There isn't a Lady MacGillivray," Fiona said.

"Yet," Annie muttered under her breath, and Fiona hid a frown.

Alanna didn't ask what that might mean. She watched as Annie bound her leg in strips of clean linen, sat back, and wiped her hands on her apron. "There now. You'll need a bit of quiet and a long sleep. I'll go get Iain, have him carry you upstairs. Sit for the moment, and finish the draught I gave you. Fiona will keep you company."

Alanna felt her face flame. "I don't wish to trouble Ia—the laird," she said. He wasn't just her rescuer anymore—he was the master of this place, a man with responsibilities, and better things to do. She began to rise. She hadn't realized she was so tired, or that her knee was so very sore. The room dissolved, and Annie set a hand on her shoulder and pressed her back into her seat.

"Iain won't be troubled in the least. I've seen him lift heifers heavier than you, carry them a mile across rough pasture. 'Tis best if you rest. Wee Janet, go and get the warming pan, and take it up to the green bedchamber."

Fiona's eyes widened. "The green chamber? But that's—"

"Whisht!" Annie said, snapping her fingers. Silence fell, as if by magic. "Go on now." Wee Janet went at once.

Alanna stared into her cup. It was the herbs—and the whisky—that had made her sleepy and weak, made her mind move more slowly than usual, made her content to sit and drowse by the fire. She stared at the grayish bits of herbs that swam in drunken circles in the whisky, let them draw her into the brew. Perhaps it *was* a magic potion, something to make her forget Merridew, and dull duty, and her mother's lofty ambitions. She put the cup to her lips and drank it to the dregs, wishing she could sleep until spring, wake at home in her own bed at Glenlorne, with the marquess long gone. She looked into the empty cup. She could see his face—Iain's, not Merridew's. It was a very nice face. She rubbed her eyes and sighed. She looked up to find Annie watching her with a keen expression.

She felt the thump of her heart against her ribs, the whoosh of light-headedness and heat that swept through her.

"Are you all right?" Fiona asked from far away.

Alanna grinned at her. "Oh yes, thank you, I'm very well," she said, as she'd been taught—polite, ladylike, and gracious. To her ears, she sounded like she was speaking from the bottom of a very deep well. She grinned, resisted the urge to laugh out loud. There would be no wedding today. She had a reprieve, even if it was only a short one.

She sobered. She would take a brief nap, she decided, and then she would ask for pen and paper, or borrow a cart and horse, or even a garron. Would she go to Dundrummie or Glenlorne? One was west, one north. She shut her eyes.

Dundrummie was much closer, and she *had* promised.

Her mother would surely be beside herself by now, especially after what had happened with Megan. She could not elope, or handfast with a handsome stranger, as her sister had done, or fall in love. Lord Merridew was waiting for her at Dundrummie, and she must honor her pledge to marry a man she did not love.

Chapter Seven

IAIN PICKED UP the garron's shaggy hoof and began to pick out the compacted snow. As he did, he considered the problem of Alanna McNabb—for she certainly was a problem. He tried to free his mind from the image of her sitting in the cott, her dark hair a seductive tumble around her face, naked except for his plaid, her lips parted, her eyes wide at the sight of him, as naked as she was.

He shook his head and concentrated on the garron's hoof. No, he hadn't looked under the plaid, but he had hands, and legs, and— He picked up the next hoof.

He'd done what was necessary, nothing more. Any man would have done the same. She could have died otherwise.

But she'd lived, and she was sitting in his kitchen, being tended by Annie and his sister, late for her wedding.

Her wedding. Iain frowned. She said she hadn't been running away. Still, she'd chosen to take a twelve-mile stroll in a blizzard on the eve of her wedding. It didn't make sense.

Perhaps there had been a lover's quarrel, but what man wouldn't come after a woman like Alanna McNabb?

"It's none of my concern who she chooses to marry," he said aloud, and the garron cast a curious glance at him. He picked up the next hoof and wondered what Alanna would tell her betrothed about the events of last night, and if the man would understand. If it were him, he would not want to share a woman like Alanna, not even for so innocent a reason.

"She was not running away," he murmured, and the garron looked at him again. "Or so she said."

In other circumstances, if she'd stayed put at Dundrummie, tonight would have been her wedding night, and she would have been tangled under the covers with her husband, and for a far more pleasant purpose. He found he didn't like the idea at all. He felt an instant of . . . what? Possessiveness? Jealousy? It wasn't his right—Alanna McNabb did not belong to him.

As soon as the weather allowed—tomorrow, perhaps—he and the faithful garron now leaning his heavy foot on Iain's knee would make the journey to Dundrummie Castle to inform her anxious bridegroom that Alanna was safe, unharmed, and awaiting him at Craigleith. She would not be able to travel comfortably for a few days, and it was better that she remained here. *Would* the man understand that Iain had only done what was necessary? Would *he*?

"Not for a moment," he told the garron, shaking his head.

Then there was the problem of Penelope. He had intended to propose to her last night, and instead . . . it had been a reprieve, nothing more. He would have to ask her, and he knew it must be soon. "Duty," he muttered. How he hated the word. And it was a terrible reason to marry someone. Penelope deserved better than that, surely.

"Who are you talking to?"

Iain looked up to find his cousin Penelope leaning over the edge of the stall, watching him. He hadn't heard her come in. They would be betrothed now, this minute, if the storm had not kept him away. He could ask her now, of course. He looked at her expectant face and his tongue stuck to the roof of his mouth.

"Just the garron," he said, moving on to the last hoof.

"*Horse*," she corrected him. "In England we say 'horse,' not 'garron'—and English earls don't muck out their own stables. As Earl of Purbrick, you'll have servants for that at Woodford Park."

Purbrick. Iain made a face she couldn't see. He couldn't even say the word Purbrick properly, remembered how his English cousins had mocked his pronunciation of the word when he'd visited Woodford Park as a boy, had beaten him for his Scottishness. His mouth twisted. That was long before he—or they—ever thought he'd inherit the damned earldom. No man would dare to try to beat him now—not physically, anyway. They could still mock him, though he hardly cared for his own sake. Fiona, though—gentle, shy, crippled Fiona—would feel every slight, every insult. He'd need to be vigilant and protective, shield her from hurt.

"I don't mind working," he said to Penelope. "What can I do for you?" It wasn't like his highborn cousin to venture out of doors on a cold day. To his knowledge, she hadn't left the castle since her arrival nearly three weeks earlier, not even for a stroll in the garden. *She'd* never get lost in a blinding snowstorm . . .

"Nothing really." She pulled her cloak around her throat. "It's cold," she said. "Is it always so cold in Scotland?"

He couldn't resist a grin, which he hid by turning to look for a brush. "No, sometimes it's rainy, or windy, or dark. The summers are lovely, though." He applied the stiff bristles to the garron's coat, ran his hand over the creature's supple muscles.

She came around the edge of the stall, stood closer to him. He could smell her perfume, even over the darker odors of the stable. "Well, maybe they are, but we won't be here then. You'll have to get used to English summers— boating on the river, picnics, strawberries . . . Do you like strawberries, Iain?"

He met her eyes, as blue and sultry as the summer sky in any country. Alanna's eyes held all the colors of the Highland landscape. Strawberries—he forced his mind back to the topic at hand. "Doesn't everyone like strawberries? We grow them here too."

"Oh, I doubt they're as sweet as English berries!" She edged closer still, put her hand on his arm. He glanced at her. She was wide-eyed, her lips parted, inviting a kiss—or a marriage proposal. He felt his stomach knot. She was waiting for him to speak, and all he had to do was say the words. She would agree. She'd been told she must.

He looked away instead.

"You'd best be going back indoors, where it's warm— there will be more snow before long," he said.

Her brow crumpled. "My boots will be ruined! They're handmade!"

"Fine as they are, they're hardly fit for the snow or the stable," he said as he caught her arm, guided her away from a pile of manure she was about to back into, and let go. He felt nothing when he touched her—no desire, no longing, and certainly not love. "Perhaps Annie could find you some sturdier footwear, and you could save those boots for England. You need a warmer cloak too."

She ran a gloved hand over the fine blue wool of her stylish garment, lavishly embroidered around hem and hood with twining pink roses. It was more a costume than protection from any kind of weather worse than a light English mist. "Don't you like this cloak? Mama says the color matches my eyes exactly. Do you agree?" She leaned toward him, her eyes wide, her face inches from his own, and licked her lips.

Iain stared into the blue pools, and she stared back at him. She was waiting for him to kiss her. He didn't want to. He *should* want to. His aunt Marjorie was right—Penelope would make the perfect countess. She was born to the role, and he was not. Perhaps if he did kiss her, he'd feel differently. He swallowed and began to lean in, but the door opened and a blast of cold air swept snow into the warmth of the stable. Penelope spun, and Iain stepped back.

"I hope I didn't interrupt anything," Annie said, glancing at Penelope, who retreated to lean against the wall, her arms folded over her thin cloak, her blue eyes full of ice. Iain felt relieved by the interruption. He looked at Annie expectantly.

"I just came to tell you that the lass will do well enough, Iain. She needs rest, of course, but there's nothing broken. She'll stay here with us for a few days to mend. Will you come and carry her upstairs?"

Iain immediately dropped the brush and wiped his hands.

"What lass? Carry her where?" Penelope demanded.

"Och, did you not think to mention our guest, Iain?" Annie scolded him. "The laird found a lass lost in the snow. Forced to take shelter in a humble cott for the night, they were, all alone."

Penelope's face reddened dangerously, and her jaw dropped. Her eyes swung on Iain, hit him like an arrow.

"Annie," Iain warned.

Annie merely grinned and held out his handkerchief. "Here's your handkerchief back." He stuffed it into his pocket as she turned back to Penelope. "Her poor leg was all cut and bashed. Iain bandaged her up with his own linen, just here—" She indicated a place higher on her thigh than the wound had been, and he watched Penelope turn a deep shade of plum.

His cousin tossed her head. "It was some silly child, no doubt. Is that not what a 'lass' is in Scotland?"

Annie cackled. "Och, she's no child. She's a woman grown, and a beauty. She'll not be walking for a day or two, so Iain will need to carry her. Not that it will be any hardship. She's as light as a snowflake by the looks of her. Is she, Iain?"

He didn't answer. Penelope's blue eyes boiled. Iain had no doubt she was warmer now. "Can she not walk on her own? What room is she in?" his cousin demanded.

"The only one suitable for an earl's sister—the green chamber," Annie said.

Iain's heart lurched. That was his room. Alanna would fill his bed . . . he forced himself to concentrate.

"An earl's sister?" he asked.

"Aye, did she not tell you? Her brother is McNabb of Glenlorne," Annie said.

"Who's he?" Penelope demanded, looking from Iain to Annie and back again.

"We didn't talk much," Iain admitted. *An earl's sister?*

Penelope gaped at him, her blue eyes like saucers. "You didn't talk much? All night? Then just what did you do?"

Iain pushed past her and opened the door. "Just what was necessary," he growled, and headed out into the cold wind. The snow had started again, and so had the trouble. He'd have a word with Annie later, once he'd settled Alanna—*Lady* Alanna—in his bed. He frowned into the gale. Not his bed—her bed. For now. He'd sleep in the old tower, alone.

He stalked into the kitchen and heard a trill of laughter. Sandy was seated near the fireplace with Alanna, his old eyes besotted, his smile fey as a lad's as he gazed at her. The light caught Alanna's dark hair, limned it like a halo, brought out streaks of copper in the glorious tangled length of it. Iain's breath caught in his throat, and his footsteps faltered in the doorway. Penelope crashed into his back.

Alanna glanced up at him. Her smile faded, and a blush rose over her cheeks at the sight of him. It made something turn in his chest, and he swallowed.

Sandy glanced up as well, but his grin only grew broader. He got to his feet. "I was just having a wee word with the lass." He stuck his thumbs in his belt and puffed out his chest. "Since I'm Craigleith's gamekeeper, I wondered what she'd like me to fetch in for her supper—a nice grouse, perhaps, or a coney for a pie, I thought."

Annie folded back her snow-covered arisaid. "You haven't been the gamekeeper for nigh on ten years, Sandy. You can't see to aim the gun. You'd better get Logan to ask her."

Sandy looked crushed. "I taught that boy everything I know, and I can still set a snare good as I ever could, woman."

Annie quirked an eyebrow. "Logan may be your son, but he's a man grown with four bairns of his own, not a boy—and nor are you, old man. What the lass needs is a good nourishing broth. Go and see if you can snare a chicken in the henhouse," Annie ordered, and the old gamekeeper stalked out of the room, grumbling.

"Good day," Penelope said, slipping past Iain to stand in front of him. She took Alanna's measure with a sweeping glance. "Allow me to welcome you to Craigleith. I'm Lady Penelope Curry."

Alanna smiled and held out her hand. "I'm Lady Alanna McNabb," she said in perfect English. "Please forgive me for not getting up and making my curtsy."

Ian couldn't take his eyes off her. She was an earl's sister who spoke perfect English, and obviously understood English manners. What else didn't he know about her? *Everything.*

"You can curtsy all you like later on, once you've had

some sleep. Iain?" Annie said, and Iain stepped past Penelope to gently lift Alanna off the bench. She did weigh less than a snowflake. She put her arm around his neck, though under Penelope's eyes she was stiff, her cheeks rose pink. Better than chalk-white, he thought. She was warm now, smelled of herbs and whisky, and the faint scent of his soap clung to her as well, no doubt carried to her from his plaid. It was like a stamp of ownership. Alanna looked up and colored like a sunset when their eyes met. Her mouth lay inches from his own—such lush, perfect lips. Now this was a woman he wanted to kiss . . . he glanced at Penelope, saw the simmering speculation in her eyes, the tightness of her jaw.

He turned and headed down the kitchen corridor, and out through the great hall toward the staircase. His footsteps rang on the stone floor, and Penelope's lighter footsteps were clipped and sharp. Annie rushed ahead, offering a kind of tour as he strode through the dining room and along the hall, babbling the history of Craigleith and the Clan MacGillivray in Gaelic.

Iain wasn't listening. He was aware of Alanna in his arms, and of Penelope following. His cousin's eyes were fixed between his shoulder blades like a spike. He felt a moment's irritation. He'd given her no reason to be jealous, and they were not betrothed yet. He was doing what was necessary, and nothing more. Still, he felt a twinge of guilt that he was enjoying it so much, the feeling of Alanna in his arms, the scent of her skin. She was listening to Annie, her eyes drinking in his home, and he followed her gaze, saw it as she did. Craigleith had stood for some four hundred years. When his English father had married his Scottish mother, he had added a new wing. On one side of the hallway, the walls were old stone, hung with dirks and targes and Lochaber axes. There were doors that led to the old armory and knight's quarters, and stairs that led upward to the tower and the solar. On the opposite side of the hall, the walls were paneled in polished oak. Doors led to a very English library, a small salon, and a grand dining room fit for an English king, should one ever dare to venture so far north again and was of a mind to drop in for supper at Craigleith.

He was proud of his home. Was Glenlorne grander? He wondered about her fiancé's home too. Alanna was a lady, not just a simple Highland lass who'd gotten lost while out looking for her cows. She was used to finer luxuries than she would find here. Would he have treated her differently last night had he known? An interesting question, that. Not that he had an answer to it.

Annie opened the door of his bedchamber. Iain drew a breath as he carried Alanna over yet another threshold, this one more intimate than the last. His clothes and belongings still lay where he'd left them, on hooks and over the chair and on the chest in the corner. A stack of books stood on his desk by the window. His bed was freshly made, the sheets warmed, and Annie turned back the blankets invitingly. A fire burned in the grate. Alanna stiffened in his arms. "Oh, but this is obviously someone's room—"

"'Tis Iain's, but he doesn't mind," Annie said before he could say it himself. "You'll be most comfortable here."

Iain carefully deposited her on the bed, and she looked up at him. "Where will you sleep?"

The question rattled through his brain, shot to his groin. He imagined tumbling into bed next to her, both of them warm this time, wide awake, and . . . he shook the thought off and stepped back, clasped his hands behind his back.

"Craigleith has other rooms."

"The lord's chamber is free, Iain. You could sleep there," Penelope said.

He still thought of it as his father's room. He had left it untouched and uninhabited since Lord Anthony Marston MacGillivray death nearly ten years ago. Iain preferred this room, since it was less grand, less English. Even his father, who had built his apartments in the image of the grand English manors he'd grown up in, had preferred to sleep in his bride's simpler apartments.

"The tower will do me just fine."

Annie looked at Alanna as Iain set her down on the bed and stepped back at once. "He refuses to move into the lord's chamber until he's wed."

"Then it's certainly appropriate now," Penelope said, and came forward to slip her arm though his. Her hand was like a talon on his sleeve, sharp and possessive.

Iain watched Alanna's eyes slide over Penelope's hand. She understood at once—he saw that in her eyes. He kept his gaze flat as he detached himself from his cousin and began to gather his things.

Annie was watching him like a curious bird, and he wondered what she was thinking. He sent her a warning look and went to the door. He glanced back at Alanna. She sat on his bed looking wan and tired, and his heart went out to her. He had the damnedest urge to lay his hand on her brow, check for fever before he tucked her between the sheets, settled her on the pillow, and closed the drapes.

"Rest well, Lady Alanna," he said and bowed crisply before fleeing along the hall.

Penelope followed him. "Would she not be more comfortable at her own home? Annie should not have troubled you. There are servants who can tend to her, and if she needs a doctor, then surely one can be found for her."

Iain gritted his teeth. "It is a Highland custom to welcome travellers, to see that they have what they need. In this case, she needs kindness and care and rest. Annie can see to her health."

"I could ask my mother's opinion, of course," Penelope said. "She'd know best what to do."

He stopped so suddenly that she nearly crashed into his back again. "Not here, Penelope. Not in Scotland. This is my home, and as Laird of Craigleith, I will decide. I'm glad to help the lass—the *lady*—if she needs it. She is my guest, as you are."

Penelope blanched. "Oh, but I'm more than that, Iain—" she began, but he turned down the corridor that led to the old part of the castle, and the tower. He could—*should*—stop walking, turn back, drop to his knee, and ask her. But he glanced back at the door of his bedchamber, firmly shut now, with Alanna inside, and the words stuck in his throat yet again.

"I'll see you at supper, Penelope," he said instead.

"Iain?" she called after him, and he stopped.

"Yes?"

"What would you like for a Christmas present?"

A Christmas present? He turned to look at her. "That's not necessary," he said. "You're a guest."

"Oh, but I could be more—so very much more," she reminded him again. "Did you know my room is just steps down the hall from the lord's apartments?"

She looked hopeful, her blue eyes wide. Another opportunity to propose dropped into the well of silence that yawned between them. "I'll be quite comfortable in the tower," he said and climbed the stairs two at a time, leaving her standing there watching him.

Running away, perhaps, just like Alanna had. He tightened his jaw and kept going. Of course he wasn't.

No doubt his cousin would head straight for his aunt's room. Together mother and daughter would plot the next step in his capture, decide how to bring him to his knees—or one knee, he supposed. They'd think him stubborn, backwards, but he was in fact only careful, both of his feelings and Penelope's. Still, he knew he *must* come to terms with it, find a way to speak the words.

But not now—In a day or two, perhaps. Once Alanna McNabb had gone.

Chapter Eight

"ELIZABETH, WAKE UP!" Fiona shook her cousin awake.

"What time is it?" Elizabeth demanded. "It can't be past dawn."

Fiona wondered if everyone in England slept so late. "It's nearly ten o'clock. It's just dark outside because of the weather. Iain's back safely, but you won't believe this—we have a visitor, just like Annie said."

"Who? Is it your true love?" Elizabeth grunted, covering her head with the blanket. Fiona pulled it back again, all the way to the bottom of the bed, and her cousin curled into a ball and shrieked at the room's chill.

Fiona folded her arms over her chest. "Not my true love, but somebody's, perhaps. She's pretty, and young, and she's an earl's sister."

Elizabeth's eyes opened at last. "Truly? Where on earth did she come from?"

Fiona grabbed the pillow and hugged it to her breast. "She was lost in the snow, and Iain rescued her. Isn't that romantic?"

"Yes," Elizabeth sighed, sitting up, her eyes glowing now. "Who is she?"

"Her name is Alanna McNabb. Annie says she's sure to set the cat among the pigeons," Fiona said.

Elizabeth frowned. "What pigeons?" Fiona raised her eyebrows and waited for her cousin to figure it out. "Oh! You mean Penelope. Penelope Pigeon," she giggled.

"Aye," Fiona said with a sly grin.

"She's pretty?"

Fiona sighed. "Yes, very."

"Dark or fair?"

"Dark hair," Fiona reported.

Elizabeth sighed. "Oh, well then. The English prefer blonds, or so mama says—well, she tells Penelope that, since she's the family beauty, and I have mousy hair. What about her eyes?"

"She has two of them," Fiona quipped.

"The color, silly."

"The color of the Highland hills on a frosty morn, golden brown and silver all at once," Fiona said.

"Pen's are plain blue. Is she plump or thin?"

"Slender, but still—" Fiona rolled her hands in front of her own flat chest. Elizabeth's eyes popped. "She has pretty legs, too, well, the one I saw was pretty, despite the cuts and bruises. She got hurt in the storm, and Iain carried her all the way home, and—"

"He *carried* her?" Elizabeth clasped her hands to her breast. "How far?"

"All the way, of course—miles and miles, wrapped in

his plaid and his handkerchief, the very one I made him last Christmas."

Elizabeth tilted her head. "His handkerchief? Is that some kind of a Scottish custom?"

Fiona remembered the way her brother had looked at Alanna, his eyes soft. Her eyes had been soft too, and neither one of them seemed to be able to look elsewhere. "I don't know," she said slowly. "If it is, I think I'm too young to understand the full importance of it."

"Oh, but we *have* to know!" Elizabeth got out of bed and hurried to the wardrobe. She pulled out the gown she'd worn the day before and rummaged through the pockets. "There's still one left—" She held out a bundle of herbs like the ones they'd thrown into the fireplace. "Can we get a lock of her hair?"

Fiona stared at her cousin. "Don't be daft. We can hardly go up to a guest—an injured guest—and ask her for a lock of her hair, now, can we?"

"Why not?" Elizabeth asked. "Perhaps we could get it while she wasn't looking."

"She'd think we were both daft!"

"Don't you want to know?" Elizabeth asked. "What if she's Iain's true love, sent by magic in time for Christmas?"

Fiona felt a tingle rush through her body. *Was she?* She shook off the feeling. "If you'll recall, the spell didn't work for us, Lizzy. What makes you think it will work for her?"

She recalled the roar of the sparks as they rushed up the chimney, the wind's reply, the suddenness of the storm, and felt a tingle rush up her spine again.

"What if it *does* work this time?" Elizabeth insisted. "Don't you think it's odd, the two of us casting spells, asking for a true love by Christmas, and then she appears, wrapped in your brother's plaid—and his handkerchief?"

Fiona sobered. "And Annie did see that we'd have a visitor, and here she is. But what if we do see something in the flames? That will indeed set the cat among the pigeons."

Elizabeth giggled. "Yes, it will, won't it? Penelope will be livid. It's going to be such fun!"

Chapter Nine

"HERE'S THE CHICKENS, Annie," Iain said as he laid three birds on the kitchen table. Sandy had caught a goose, which Iain had returned to the fold. Sandy crossed to the fire to light his pipe and settle by the hearth.

Seonag crossed the kitchen, poked the birds, and grinned. "Fine and plump, too. How's the goose fattening up? I trust he'll be ready for Christmas dinner?"

"I didn't think to ask," Iain said with a smile. Seonag looked ready to burst with her fourth babe. Annie predicted the child would come before Christmas, and there was a lively pool of wagers as to the exact date of the happy event. Logan was as proud as a father could be, and though Sandy complained that the cottage he shared with his son's family would be even noisier with the newborn child's cries than it was now, he too was delighted.

Annie folded her arms over her chest and leveled a sharp look at Iain. "Do you mean to keep her?"

"The goose?" Iain asked, though he knew well enough

whom she meant. Sandy and Seonag looked at him with the same question in their eyes.

"Not the goose—the lass, Lady Alanna McNabb."

"Aye," said Sandy from his seat by the fire. "In the old Highland tradition a stray cow or a stray lass is fair game. She's a pretty thing, and when she's back on her feet, she'll make a fine and fetching wife."

Iain folded his arms over his chest and stared Annie down. "That she will, since she's betrothed to someone else—almost married, in fact."

"Almost is a long way from is," Annie said and turned her hand to helping Seonag pluck the chickens.

"We don't steal our brides anymore. We're civilized folk," Iain reminded them.

Sandy rubbed his bearded chin. "My grandfather stole his wife. She was a Fraser lass. He'd gone a-reiving for a cow, but she wouldn't let go of the beastie's halter, so he brought her home right along with it. He would have returned her—the lass, not the cow—but she declared herself in love with him and insisted on staying. He hand-fasted with her to give her time to think it through and change her mind, but then he fell in love with her too."

"The lass upstairs seems like someone a man could very easily fall in love with," Seonag said, pulling feathers while keeping one eye on Iain. He kept his expression flat.

"Och, aye. She's a bonnie wee thing," Sandy agreed. "I'd keep her."

Annie sent him a sharp look. "Not you—Iain."

"I've told you that I intend to—" Iain began, but Annie held up a feather-covered hand.

"Oh, I know, the Sassenach. She—they—expect you to marry her. But the omens aren't favorable."

"What do the omens say about the McNabb lass?" Sandy said, leaning forward.

Iain made a sound of frustration. Making a success of Purbrick was what mattered. Did they not understand? "Omens won't build a new roof for this castle, or add new cattle to the herds in the spring," he said.

"They won't keep you warm at night either," Annie said.

Iain swallowed, remembered the icy chill of Alanna's flesh against his. She'd warmed, though, become a soft, warm, feminine weight in his arms. Every time he thought of her, tucked up in his arms, or his plaid, or his bloody bed, other images rose—lusty, improper ones. He clenched his fists against such thoughts. "I will do what's necessary," he growled. "My duty is to this place and my people—all my people." Even so, the thought of Penelope in his bed, even warm and willing, left him cold.

"Stubborn," Annie muttered.

"The lass is spoken for. It isn't magic or omens that brought her here—it was misfortune. When the weather allows, we'll see she gets safely home for her wedding."

Annie reached into her pocket. "I forgot—she wrote a letter, just in case it can be delivered. She said she couldn't sleep until it was done, knowing her kin will be fretting about her."

"Is it a love letter?" Sandy asked.

"It's addressed to her brother, Glenlorne," Annie said, dropping the folded note on the table. "Makes no mention of her betrothed at all. Odd she wouldn't write to *him*, whoever he is, don't you think?"

Iain stared at the letter, the corners adorned with white feathers from the chicken, like an imitation of angel's wings. Omens indeed. "You didn't read it?"

Annie shrugged. "I may have glanced at it. It isn't sealed."

Sandy got to his feet and picked up the letter. "I'll take it through to Jock MacIntosh's farm. He's planning to go and visit his daughter, storm or no, to see his first grandchild born. Her man Connor can take it on to his folks at Loch Rain when he goes with the news of the birth. Someone will take it on from there until it gets to Glenlorne. Her brother will know she's here, and safe."

Iain nodded. "Good."

"You could ask a ransom for her. She's bound to be worth a good number of cows," Sandy suggested.

Iain rolled his eyes. "We will tell Glenlorne that his sister is welcome here at Craigleith until the weather breaks—no ransom."

"Perhaps she'll be with us for Christmas then," Seonag said eagerly. "The weather looks truly terrible."

"It will get worse as the days pass," Annie said softly, as if she knew.

Iain shook off the thought. "Christmas is still weeks away. No doubt she'll be gone by then." *Gone, married, forgotten.*

Annie pursed her lips. "Maybe yes, maybe no. The signs suggest the snow will grow deeper still, keep us here." The feathers floated around her head like a snowstorm, and Iain felt a guilty twinge of hope that neither he nor Alanna would be able to go anywhere. He was as bad as old Sandy.

Annie pointed to the ceiling. "Will you go up and check on her, Iain? I don't want to leave her alone too long, in case she needs something. She can hardly get out of bed and call down the stairs, now, can she? I've got the chickens to pluck, and the soup to make, and the bread won't bake itself, and Seonag should stay off her feet."

Seonag cast a wide-eyed glance at Annie. "Why? Is it time? I don't feel anything yet . . ."

Annie ignored her. "'Tis the lass I'm worried about. The babe will come when it comes."

Iain thought about opening the door of his room, looking down at Alanna in his bed—not that he hadn't been imaging that very thing all morning. "It's hardly proper for me to go up," he said stiffly. "What about Marjorie, or Penelope? Where's Fiona?"

Sandy snickered. "Proper? You spent the night in Ewan's cott alone with her."

Annie cast the old gamekeeper a quelling look. "Proper or not, someone must look in. Lady Marjorie is still abed, and your Lady Penelope looked like she'd strangle the lass in her sleep if she got the chance. Fiona could go, I suppose, if I can find her, but she'll drive Alanna daft with her chatter," Annie said. "Just have a wee look, Iain, and I'll be up as soon as I'm done here. It's part of being a good host, and you said yourself you take your duties seriously."

"A quick look, then," Iain said, feeling a very foolish and ill-advised anticipation of seeing Alanna. "I'll come back at once and let you know if she wants anything."

"Of course," Annie said, waving him out of the kitchen. "Just do whatever you think is necessary, Laird."

Chapter Ten

THE DOOR CREAKED as it opened, and Fiona stopped on the threshold and gripped Elizabeth's arm, both of them wincing at the noise. They peered into Iain's room—well, Alanna's room for the time being. Alanna didn't move, appeared to be fast asleep.

"There she is," Fiona whispered.

"I can see that," Elizabeth said as she crossed the room on tiptoes. "Oh, she's like the Sleeping Beauty, all pink and white and lovely," she gushed. "That's a story about a princess who is put under a terrible curse by an evil fairy. She must sleep until her true love comes to wake her with a kiss."

"Is that true, or is it just an English story?" Fiona asked in a whisper.

"German, I think, and of course it's true. Things like that happen all the time. Well, not to me, but to princesses."

"She isn't a princess," Fiona said. "She's an earl's sister."

"But perhaps she has noble blood in her veins, going back long generations, a connection to a king, and—"

Fiona pinched her cousin. "She's sure to wake up if you keep prattling on."

"Did you bring the scissors?" Elizabeth asked.

"I thought you brought them," Fiona whispered back. "Shouldn't we ask her first?"

"She's asleep, and it would be rude to wake her," Elizabeth insisted.

"But it's fine to cut her hair off?"

"Just a little lock of it. She has plenty."

Fiona sighed and handed her cousin the small pair of sewing scissors from her pocket. "Be careful," she said.

The two girls leaned over the bed, and Elizabeth raised the scissors.

IAIN PAUSED OUTSIDE the door of his chamber—Alanna's chamber—and listened for sounds inside. He raised his hand to knock, and paused. He pictured her in his bed, her dark, auburn-streaked hair spread across his pillow, and remembered the way that hair had felt like silk against his naked chest. He swallowed, leaned his head on the door, and knocked.

FIONA JUMPED BACK in horror as someone knocked. Elizabeth dropped the scissors and kicked them under the bed.

"What are you two doing here?" Iain asked when his sister opened the door. He glanced at Alanna first, then at the two of them. Fiona held her breath. "Is she . . ."

"Sleeping," Fiona whispered. "We were just checking

on her." She watched as her brother crossed to the bed and put the back of his hand on Alanna's brow, checking for fever. "Why are you here?" she asked him.

"Hmm?" He seemed mesmerized by Alanna's sleeping face. "Oh, Annie asked me to see if she needed anything." He withdrew his hand, clasped it with the other one behind his back. "She'll be up directly, of course."

"Of course," Elizabeth said.

Iain turned away, went to the bookshelf in the corner, and took down a book. "If you two can stay, then I'll go," he said.

"Oh, no—I've got things to do, and Elizabeth does as well," Fiona said quickly, and grabbed her cousin's hand. "Come on."

She shoved Elizabeth out of the room and shut the door.

"What did you do that for? We could have got her hair if you'd sent him away," Elizabeth complained.

Fiona set her hand on her cheek. "I don't think we need the hair after all," she said. "Did you see his face?"

"His face?" Elizabeth scrunched up her own. "What was wrong with it?"

Fiona sighed. "Never mind. Come on."

"Where are we going?"

"To see Annie."

Chapter Eleven

ALANNA WOKE TO find Iain MacGillivray sitting by the fire again. This time he was fully clothed, and reading a book, as civilized and correct as you please, but the fire-light still glinted off the copper of his hair and sculpted his cheeks to masculine perfection and outlined the breadth of his shoulders. What would it be like to always wake up and find him near? The idea made her breath catch and her stomach flip. "Will you always be here when I wake up?" she asked, and immediately felt foolish for voicing the thought out loud.

He looked up and met her eyes, then set the book aside and rose. "I . . . Annie's busy downstairs. She sent me to look in on you. Do you need anything?" He laid his hand on her forehead, then pulled back. "My apologies. I used to tend Fiona when she was sick as a child. Not that you're a child, of course." He sat down again, back by the fire. It was his room, his chair, yet he looked ill at ease there. That was her fault, she realized.

"And?" she asked.

"And what?"

"Do I have a fever?"

He swallowed, and she watched his throat bob. "No. Annie's a very good healer, and you're young and strong." He swallowed again, and she saw the shadow pass through his eyes. "You're safe now, and you'll be well again soon."

Alanna gripped the edge of the thick blankets that covered her. "I almost died, didn't I? How foolish."

He held her gaze. "But you didn't, and that's what's important."

"Because of you. I owe you my thanks, my lord."

"Just Iain will do, and there's no need for thanks—I only did what was necessary."

"Necessary," she parroted, and blushed, remembering the way she'd woken to discover both of them naked, with only a plaid between them.

He flushed. "I mean that I wasn't taking advantage of you because of the situation. It was necessary to warm you, and for that you—and I—had to be—"

"Naked," she murmured.

He rose again and went to the window, pulled back the heavy drape and looked out. Alanna could see nothing but white. "You were cold as ice, deeply unconscious. It's the best way to warm a body. Ask Annie."

"Thank you," she said again, unsure of what else to say. Safer to change the subject. "I see it's still snowing."

"Aye," he said. "I'm afraid you'll be here a few days more. Annie says she can't recall so much snow coming so quickly. We'll try and get your letter through to your kin. Are you fretting about your wedding?"

Her wedding. She'd forgotten that. Almost. "Oh—yes, of course," she managed, and suddenly hoped the snow would keep right on falling and never stop, that she would have to stay here forever, and never have to wed Merridew at all. "You as well—when is your wedding day?" she asked.

"Mine?" He looked surprised.

"Lady Penelope is very pretty."

"Oh." He gazed out the window again. "I suppose she is. She's my cousin. My English cousin. We've only just recently—" He stopped. "Why did you write to your brother instead of your betrothed?"

"I just thought of him first," she said. She hadn't realized how much she missed her brother, and Glenlorne itself, until she'd picked up the quill. And hadn't Iain told her that the way to Dundrummie, through Glen Dorian, was impassable? Alec would find a way to get word to her mother—if her letter reached him, of course. She felt a sharp pang of guilt that her family had no idea what had become of her, might be thinking the worst. She was causing them tremendous pain and worry. She should have stayed put, and not—

"*Did* you run away?" Iain turned away from the window and was leaning on the sill, fixing her with a sober, gray-eyed gaze.

She felt her skin heat. Of course she hadn't. Not really. She'd just gone out for a walk. But the truth was that she hadn't been able to make her feet turn, walk back to Dundrummie, knowing she must face Lord Merridew, and marry him. It had seemed so much easier to just keep moving forward, heading away from—everything. Good heavens, she *had* run away. There was no other explanation for it. She lowered her eyes to the blanket, stared at the soft green wool. "I most certainly did not run away!" she said aloud. "I gave my word, and my mother is counting on me."

He folded his arms over his chest. "Your mother? You've mentioned your mother and your brother. What of your fiancé?"

"He's English."

"Like Penelope."

"Yes," she said. Though Merridew was not young or good-looking. Nor was there love, or even admiration, as there was between Iain and his intended. She felt a moment of envy. Lady Penelope would have Iain, and she would be the one to wake up next to him every morning. "I just went for a wee walk to get some fresh air before . . . he . . . arrived." She couldn't bring herself to speak his name, not in front of Iain MacGillivray, her rescuer, her hero.

He folded his arms over his chest. "A dozen miles in a blinding snowstorm is hardly a wee walk. You're fortunate to be alive."

She felt irritation chafe, heat her skin, and she pushed the covers back slightly, tried to sit up. "Is it so hard to think that I simply lost track of time, and the storm caught me unawares, made me lose my way? Is there anything wicked in that? Shall I thank you again? I truly am grateful, my lord earl."

"Just Iain," he said again. His brow furrowed. "Is that my shirt?"

She'd forgotten she was wearing it. Annie had given it to her as a makeshift nightgown when she'd taken Alanna's own clothes away to be cleaned and repaired. She shifted. The homespun linen was soft against her breasts. She folded her arms over her body. "Um, yes. Annie gave it to me, just until she can return my gown. I did not mean to impose."

"No, you look quite fetching—I mean, you're welcome to wear it." He looked stricken as he backed toward the door. "I should find Annie, tell her you're awake—" He bumped into the chair next to the desk, caught and righted it before it fell, and found the door. He set his hand on the latch. "I'll go then, send Annie up, tell her you're—" He swallowed, probably realizing he was repeating himself. She made him nervous, and that made her nervous. Her tongue stuck to the roof of her mouth, and she could only stare back at him.

She watched as he opened the door and darted through it with a final nod of farewell. She lay very still and stared at the door. No man had ever made her feel the way Iain MacGillivray did, unsure in her skin, breathless, nervous. Perhaps it was circumstances, the aftereffects of the storm, and her injury, or the fact that he'd saved her life. Just that. She wished she could be certain. She sighed, settled deeper into the bed, and closed her eyes. She would think about this tomorrow, when she was not so befuddled.

IAIN LEANED AGAINST the wall outside the door and put the heel of his hand against his forehead, trying to banish the image of Alanna McNabb wearing his shirt, in his bed, her hair spread in a wanton, sexy tumble across his pillow. And under that shirt, she was as naked as she'd been at the cottage. He forced his mind to turn, do an about-face, away from danger. What would Penelope look like wearing his shirt? He couldn't even imagine it. He'd had the damnedest desire to touch Alanna, to lay his hand on her forehead again, to stroke her cheek, see if it was as soft and warm as it looked, though he already knew it was. She'd lain in his arms all night, and she was soft as a rose petal everywhere. All the places his shirt now covered.

Surely he was under a spell. He wasn't immune to a pretty face, wasn't a green lad when it came to women. But no woman had ever affected him the way Alanna did— and she was right, he was betrothed to Penelope, well, almost.

And she belonged to another man.

He turned away from the door and stalked down the stairs to the library, where he took out the accounts. He needed an hour or two with numbers, dry figures, time to grapple with the job of trying to spread too little money over too much need. That should take his mind off Alanna McNabb.

The woman who lay in his bed, wearing only his shirt.

Chapter Twelve

LADY MARJORIE CURRY sighed as she sipped her tea in bed. She was the daughter of the sixth Earl of Purbrick, the widow of a viscount, and the last in the long line of Marstons that had sadly ended with her uncle—well, there was still Iain, of course. His name was *supposed* to be Marston, not MacGillivray. Her grandfather, the fifth earl, had had three strapping sons, and the future appeared set for the powerful Marston family. But in just two generations, the male line had dwindled down to just one person, Iain, more Scottish barbarian than English gentleman. It was a terrible shame.

If her uncle had had married a stronger wife, a woman capable of breeding more than a single sickly boy who'd died in childhood, and if his brother had not died young, and if her own brother had not gone off and married a Scottish laird's daughter for love and took the name of his wife's clan—MacGillivray—and begotten a strong, healthy son, Marjorie would not be here, in Scotland, at this moment. She made a face and set her teacup down.

She would be home in England enjoying better tea, at the very least.

But she was the last Marston, and this was her duty. With her uncle in his grave, she had been forced to make this trip, to take things in hand, as it were. She glared at the cup and saucer on the tray. Even the cup itself was a poor thing, plainly made for utility rather than beauty.

Like Iain MacGillivray himself—ordinary and rough around the edges, even if he was useful. It was up to her to mold Iain into the next Earl of Purbrick, even if that was the last thing either of them wanted.

Marjorie added another spoonful of sugar to the pallid tea in hopes of improving it, sipped again, and grimaced. A *Scot* as the Earl of Purbrick. It still seemed impossible, and she'd had nearly three months to come to terms with it. They would be the laughingstock of the English aristocracy if she couldn't make this—him—work.

She gave up on the tea. She had not set eyes on Iain MacGillivray since he was a green, half-grown boy, brought by his father to visit his English kin at Woodford Park. He'd filled out since then, was handsome, and at least looked the part, thanks to his English blood no doubt—and that was fortunate, since Penelope would have to marry him. Still, she fretted, a handsome face was no guarantee of a man's honor.

Penelope's father had been fine looking indeed— breathtakingly so. He'd also been cursed with a fondness for brandy and gambling. Viscount Aldridge had lost his fortune twice over while in his cups, and he'd died young, just after Elizabeth turned two, which had been more of a relief than a great sorrow. Upon his death, his title had passed to a distant cousin, who'd neither known his predecessor's widow and her two young daughters, nor wanted them in residence at his new home. Marjorie had packed up her daughters and returned to the elegant sanctuary of Woodford Park, where her uncle had been more than happy to welcome her home and make her his hostess.

Marjorie had hoped—expected—that her uncle would make provisions for Penelope and Elizabeth in his will, leaving them enough for decent dowries at the very least, but the sixth earl had left nothing at all to the girls, or to Marjorie. Without dowries, the girls could not hope to wed men of power, wealth, and stature. Pretty as Penelope was, her beauty alone would not make the kind of match Marjorie wanted for her daughter. And without a financial legacy of her own, Marjorie would also be consigned to rot in a small cottage somewhere out of the way, forgotten.

She wished now that she had not dismissed her young Scottish nephew as a worthless bumpkin when she'd met him all those years ago. She could have cultivated a friendship— or at least an acquaintance—with the boy who was now going to be her salvation.

He hadn't yet proposed to Penelope. He must, of course, be brought to the point, forced to it, if necessary. She smoothed the frown lines away from her brow. Penelope was exceedingly pretty, and raised to be a countess. It baffled Marjorie that Iain had not dropped to his knees and proposed the moment he'd met his lovely cousin. There was not another woman at Craigleith who could be considered even remotely attractive—not when compared with Penelope. Marjorie had assumed the man would be all too eager to take such a fine lady to wife, but he was proving remarkably stubborn about it, or perhaps he was just slow. Marjorie had hinted to her daughter—sharply— that if Iain would not come to the point, then Penelope must do whatever was necessary to make him propose.

She was determined that before Iain set foot inside Woodford Park's hallowed halls, Penelope would be the next Countess of Purbrick.

Penelope need only give birth to a strong, healthy son, and her duty would be done. Iain looked more than capable of breeding healthy boys. Marjorie would carefully raise her grandson to be the next earl—a proper *English* earl.

She laid a finger against her cheek and smiled. There was so much to be done, so many things to take charge of. There was Christmas, first of all—they would have a proper English Christmas, not the bannock-and-bagpipe slapdash kind of thing the folk here were no doubt accustomed to.

And before the wedding vows were said, Marjorie planned to insist that Iain change his name back to Marston. She imagined the wedding invitations, stating that Lady Penelope Curry would wed the esteemed Earl of Purbrick, Lord Iain Marston. Or better still, he might be coerced to use the English version of his Christian name too, become John Marston, a proper English name no one could find fault with.

She nibbled on the edge of her toast, then tossed it back on the plate in disgust. Rough brown bread was all they seemed to have here. How she missed fresh, warm white rolls, served on a bone china plate with strawberry preserves and thick English cream.

The door burst open. Marjorie opened her mouth to scold the invader for failing to knock, but she stopped at the sight of Penelope's stricken face.

"Darling girl, whatever is the matter?" She'd instructed Penelope to encourage Iain to kiss her. Surely the man hadn't *insulted* her, taken it too far, or not far enough.

"Iain brought a woman home," Penelope said, and Marjorie felt a sharp stab of anger in her chest.

"A woman? What kind of woman?" A doxie, perhaps, or a mistress?

"He found her in the snow, lost on the moor, injured," Penelope said. She folded her arms over her bosom and stuck out her lower lip like a mutinous child.

Marjorie sighed. "Some local woman, I assume, a Highlander." She let her lip curl on the last word.

"She's a *lady*," Penelope said.

Marjorie's brows shot upward. *A lady*? "Scottish or English?"

"Scottish. But her brother is an earl."

Marjorie clenched her fists under the bedclothes, but she forced her face to register flat calm for the moment. "Is she plain or—" She couldn't say it.

Penelope looked at her hands, studied her ringless finger. "Oh, she's pretty. Iain carried her here, through the snow, wrapped in half his clothing."

"Half his clothing?" Marjorie set the tray aside. "What on earth does that mean?" Penelope shrugged. "Don't shrug, dear," Marjorie said. "It's common, and a countess is never common."

Penelope clasped her hands at her waist, raised her chin, and squared her shoulders. "She was wearing his plaid, and his handkerchief was tied around her knee. She was hurt, you see, needed help."

"Oh." Marjorie felt relief course through her veins. "It's of no matter, then. Have you kissed Iain yet?"

Penelope's lip stuck even further out, making her look most unkissable. "I tried, but—"

"But what?" Marjorie prompted.

"What am I to do, throw myself at him, force him to kiss me?"

If that's what it takes, Marjorie thought. "He's a quiet man. Perhaps he's shy," she said aloud instead. Or maybe he was stubborn, or unutterably stupid. Marjorie gave her daughter an encouraging smile, reached out to squeeze her fingers. "You must do more to encourage him, smile, flirt, compliment him, draw him out—"

"He doesn't seem shy with *her*," Penelope huffed. "In fact, everyone here is treating it like it's some kind of magic that she appeared out of the snow."

Marjorie frowned. "Magic? Don't be silly. These are simple folk. They see magic in everything, divine the future from visions seen in bread dough or in the shape of clouds. I'm sure Iain is just being polite or kind to this strange woman. I understand it's a Highland custom to offer visitors anything they want or need. It's some sort of code they live by."

"Even his bed?" Penelope asked.

The tea turned into a whirlpool in Marjorie's belly. "His bed? Was he in it with her?" She kept her tone flat, incurious.

"No," Penelope said. "He intends to sleep in the tower until she's gone. Still—"

Marjorie sighed. "I'm sure there's nothing to worry about. No doubt she'll be leaving very soon, going back where she came from. You simply need to try a little harder with Iain. Some men require more convincing than others, must be shown what they want, led to it. Flatter him, charm him," she began again, but the door opened again and Elizabeth barged in, her eyes bright.

"There's a visitor!" she said. Marjorie frowned at her youngest daughter. Her hair was half-combed, her gown plain, her face pink with mischief. Would the child ever learn manners and decorum?

"Penelope was just telling me about her," Marjorie said in a bland voice.

"She's so pretty, and Fiona says she's nice too," Elizabeth babbled.

Penelope rubbed her temples. "Do be quiet," she said.

"What else do you know about her, Eliza?" Marjorie asked, as Elizabeth sat on the edge of the bed and eyed the uneaten toast on the tray.

"Well, she's the sister of the Earl of Glenlorne, and she's betrothed. She got lost in the storm on the eve of her wedding, which was supposed to be today, and Iain found her and saved her life. If he hadn't seen her in the snow, she would have frozen, been lost forever. Isn't that romantic? They were forced to take shelter in an empty cottage for the whole night. Her leg is hurt, and Iain has to carry her. Auld Annie says she weighs less than a snowflake, and she's here by magic."

"Magic again?" Penelope demanded.

"Annie says the snow brought her—or she brought the snow. I can't remember which. Fiona says Christmas is the time of year for magic here, though it seems to me that most days are magical in Scotland. Are you going to eat your toast, Mama?"

"You'll get fat," Penelope said.

"Who is she betrothed to? Who is this Earl of Glenlorne? Is he anyone important?" Marjorie demanded.

"I don't know," Elizabeth said to both questions, shrugging. Marjorie didn't bother to scold *her* for the gesture.

"Well, at least she's betrothed," Marjorie said, looking at Penelope, who slumped in a chair by the fire, pouting. "There's no need to worry then, is there?"

Elizabeth smirked. "Maybe there is—Fiona says she's never seen Iain look at any woman the way he looks at her."

"And how exactly does he look at her?" Penelope asked.

"Like there's no one else in the room, or even in the whole world, but her."

Penelope gave a moan of dismay, but Marjorie held up her hand. "He's simply concerned about her health, perhaps. You said she was injured. Iain is a—" She swallowed bile. "A kind man, a good *laird*, and that is all. We must do our part as well, and see that she is comfortable while she's here. Penelope, you will befriend her, and find out about her betrothed. If he has not been sent for, that should be done at once. Play the hostess, act the part of the chatelaine of Craigleith. Make your position entirely clear."

"What good will that do?' Penelope asked.

"You will convince her that Iain is spoken for, that he belongs to you, is head over heels in love with you."

"As far as I know she isn't blind," Elizabeth said.

"What's that supposed to mean?" Penelope demanded, her blue eyes narrowing on her sister.

"It means she'll see that Iain is not head over anything with you." Elizabeth defiantly snatched the toast and crammed it into her mouth even as she dodged Penelope's swat.

Marjorie got out of bed and headed for the dressing room, ringing for her maid. "Go and change your dress, Penelope. Put on something fetching."

"What's wrong with the one she has on?" Elizabeth asked.

"It needs to be grander, more stylish," Penelope said.

Marjorie smiled. "Precisely. We must leave our visitor—and Iain—in no doubt as to who is lovelier, better dressed, more suitable as a wife and countess, just in case," Marjorie said.

"Do you believe she's here by magic, Mama?" Elizabeth asked.

Marjorie glowered at her younger daughter. "Of course not—don't be ridiculous, Elizabeth. Go back to your room and comb your hair, and you can put on a better gown as well. We must all present an image of English pride and superiority. An English title always takes precedence over a Scottish one. We must make that clear to everyone."

Elizabeth's cheeky smile faded at the prospect of changing her clothes.

Marjorie considered what to do next. "I will go and speak to Iain, see if there's anything we need to worry about. We will bring him to the point before Christmastide, and most certainly before we return to England. You will be charming, flirtatious, and you will do whatever it takes to win Iain, do you understand, Penelope?"

"Yes, Mama," Penelope said.

"Anything?" Elizabeth asked, her eyes widening.

"Anything," her mother and her sister insisted in unison.

Chapter Thirteen

"OH, MY DEAR nephew, I just heard the dreadful news. Are you quite well?"

Iain looked up from the accounts as his aunt entered the library. Her dress was more appropriate for a stroll in a London park, or tea with royalty perhaps, than for a cold, snowy day in Scotland. The heavy scent of her French perfume instantly filled the room.

"Good morning, Aunt," he said, and crossed to add more peat to the fire, knowing his English kin found the weather cold here—both inside and outside the castle. When that was done, he turned to face her. "What news would that be?" he asked. Had Penelope decided she did not wish to marry him after all? That wouldn't be dreadful to him.

"I was informed that you were out all night in that terrible storm, rescuing some silly local girl who managed to get herself stuck in the snow. I hope you didn't catch a chill."

Ah, so that was it. If he were to die, who would inherit

Purbrick then? He leaned on the mantel. "She's not a local girl at all. She came quite a way, was lost."

"How thoughtless of her," Marjorie said, leveling her lady-of-the-manor stare at him. He knew that look. It meant there was another lecture coming. "Penelope would never be so unthinking. Well-bred English ladies do not do such foolish things."

"Then English ladies must check the weather a dozen times a day before setting out anywhere," Iain said, keeping his expression flat, unreadable, and coolly polite, reminding himself that she was a guest in his home, and unfamiliar with Scottish customs. "Winter storms can come over the hills very suddenly, catch even seasoned travellers unawares."

"There was some mention she had to be carried," Marjorie said, as she opened a basket of embroidery and took up her needle. She was always working on something, yet it was not at all clear what use the finished piece would serve. Worse, she had insisted that Fiona must learn such needlework as well, since she could not be expected to learn to dance, or walk like a lady with her limp.

"Lady Alanna fell. Her knee is sprained, but there's no lasting harm, fortunately."

His aunt pursed her lips. "Is that her name? Alanna? There was no need to explain in such detail how she was injured. Ladies in England do not speak of—such things—in company." Iain wondered how they discussed anything at all, with rules against so many perfectly ordinary topics. "And in England, no true lady would have inconvenienced you so. It won't happen again. You will have servants to see to such inconsequential matters."

Servants again. Did everyone expect he would be content to live in luxury and never lift a finger again once he arrived at Woodford Park? It was not his way. Iain clasped his hands tightly behind his back and gave her a bland smile. "Whether Lady Alanna was found by a servant or myself, her care and welcome at Craigleith would be the same."

"I understand she is to be married very soon," his aunt said, changing the subject slightly. She was very well informed, as usual.

"Aye," he said, and felt his shoulders tense. He clasped his hands tighter still. This was it, the reason she'd sought him out, had worked the topic round to betrothals and marriage.

"I daresay her family, not to mention her betrothed, must be stricken with sorrow at her disappearance. She must be allowed to go home at once."

Iain recalled the conversation he'd had with Annie and Sandy about keeping Alanna. He frowned. "It's not a matter of allowing her to go, Aunt. She isn't a prisoner. She is unable to travel. She needs rest, and a few days for her leg to mend."

Marjorie looked horrified. "But she arrived without even a chaperone. Surely you can understand that if she's truly a lady, and she stays here much longer, her reputation will be irreparably tarnished. Or some might suspect she fled from her own wedding, and she'll get a reputation as a jilt. Or it might be supposed she eloped with someone other than her betrothed. The potential for scandal and gossip of the most damaging kind is looming with every hour she's here. And not just for her, Iain—for you, as well."

There might be scandal indeed if it became known that Alanna spent the night naked in his arms, as innocent and necessary as that had been. He kept that piece of information to himself and smiled at his aunt. "You need have no fear. Those are English rules. No one here will see anything but a young woman's misfortune, and they will understand that the situation was tempered with kindness." Iain nodded toward the window, where snow still fell thickly against the panes. "Lady Alanna will be here with us at Craigleith for a wee while longer. Her family will certainly understand, and there is no one to spread gossip, of course."

Marjorie's cheeks grew red, and she drew her lips tight as she pulled the thread through the fabric. He'd won that round, or so he thought when she changed the subject yet again. "This room is so chilly, Iain, elegant though it is. Penelope had some ideas just this morning on how it could be improved, made warmer and brighter, more fashionable. I mean, the draperies alone . . . well. Of course, when you marry Penelope, she will help you improve this place—if you want to fix it, of course. Purbrick includes four manors, and Woodford is considered to be one of the most beautiful homes in England. Once you see it, you may never wish to come back here at all. Or you could convert it to a hunting lodge, spend a week or two here each year."

Iain looked around his library. His father had hired one of England's premier architects to help design the new wing of Craigleith. True, the furnishings and window coverings had not been changed since, but a home was more than bricks and mortar and fashionable damask draperies, more than grand paintings and wide lawns—it was the people, and the land that had been theirs for five hundred years. There was no improving on the view across the hills, or the sight of the sky reflected in the black surface of the loch, or the heather in bloom. Isn't that what windows were truly for?

He reminded himself that he wasn't just responsible for the MacGillivrays of Craigleith now. The people and lands of Purbrick—all four estates—were also his to care for. He took that responsibility every bit as seriously as he did his duties at Craigleith. It felt like a weight between his shoulders, and he saw the doubt in the eyes of Marjorie and Penelope when they spoke of his role as earl. Would it be so different? He knew how to manage Craigleith, but he hadn't been raised to be an English earl, or the owner of great estates, as Marjorie had pointed out to him more than once since she'd arrived here.

As if she could read his thoughts, Marjorie sighed and shook her head, regarding him with a frown, as if she doubted he would be capable of handling such a lofty responsibility.

"It's not just the refurbishment of Craigleith you'll need to consider, but this place, even this room, simply shows how much you'll need a wife who can help you with English customs and manners, who can make introductions to the right people for you. You are an English earl now, and you must learn to act the part," she admonished him yet again.

"When the time comes," he said. He turned to face the fire, watching the flames. He saw Alanna's face there, not Penelope's.

"Really, Iain—that time is coming faster than you think," Marjorie warned. "We'll leave Scotland after Christmas, as soon as the weather breaks. You'll hardly have time for a stop at Woodford itself—a few days at most—before you must go to London and find a tailor, a bootmaker and . . . well, you'll need absolutely everything. It will be good to have someone by your side to advise you, don't you think?"

"I trust I'll have servants for that," he said sarcastically, aware that in her eyes, his scuffed boots and homespun shirt were as shabby as the curtains. His aunt and cousins had done nothing but wistfully long for the small army of servants they were used to. He wondered if they'd ever had to do anything at all for themselves. He hadn't considered he'd have to go directly to London, spend long weeks there. He'd thought to stop in Edinburgh with Fiona, show her the sights of the Scottish capital before going south to the English one.

"A wife will be of far more help than a valet or even the best man of affairs, Iain. And you'll need an heir as soon as possible—and you'll definitely need a wife for that, a lady of impeccable pedigree. You can't afford to delay." She looked at him expectantly, as if she expected him to fall to his knee at this very moment and propose to Penelope through her.

But Iain had a stubborn streak—one his mother always swore he'd inherited from the English side of the family.

He was used to being the one in charge, and he meant to keep it that way. He didn't doubt he'd need help once he crossed the border, but for now he would keep his own counsel.

"I appreciate your advice, Aunt, but I'm used to making my own decisions," he told her yet again.

"Of course you are," she said in a singsong tone, as if she were placating a truculent child. "It's just that—well, the English will see you as a foreigner, and an outsider, especially if you haven't got the right clothes or the right manners. We're your family. Who better to guide you through these difficult days? And you'll want Fiona to benefit from her connection to the English aristocracy, won't you? With guidance, a proper education, and a little polish, she might make a sound marriage despite her infirmity—far better than she could hope for if she remained here."

Her infirmity. Would the English be so cruel as to dismiss his sister as dull or stupid because she limped? Iain thought of what he could give his sister in England— pretty clothes, books, an education—and felt a twinge of guilt at his reluctance to follow Marjorie's directives. Fiona deserved all that and more.

Marjorie prattled on, her eyes on her needlework. "You'll enjoy the London Season—there's so much gaiety and fun, so many parties and balls. Of course, Penelope is certain to be beset by suitors and admirers once the Season starts. It would be a shame if she had to refuse dances and the usual pleasures a young lady looks forward to because she's waiting—hoping— for a particular proposal. You know you simply need to ask, and we can make the arrangements at once. Penelope is most amenable to being the next Countess of Purbrick."

He noticed she didn't say a word about whether Penelope wanted to be his *wife* as much as she wished to be his countess. Did she love him? He did not love her, and he needed time to know if he could eventually come to feel that emotion for her. His parents had loved each other passionately. Scots tended to marry for love, and he had hoped to do so himself, once the right woman appeared. For a fleeting instant, he thought of the woman upstairs— Alanna, not Penelope—and pushed the thought away. She was spoken for. He felt a knot of regret in his chest and willed it away.

Marjorie had continued on with the conversation without him. "We could announce your betrothal here at Christmas, plan a spring wedding in London, and have a grand summer party at Woodford Park to celebrate your nuptials. Just think, a new earl, a grand wedding, it would be the perfect way to start your new life, to show you are willing to fit in."

What about a wedding here, at Craigleith? He knew better than to suggest it. "I will consider it," he said instead, politely, patiently, as he had a dozen times over the past weeks.

"Good," his aunt said, tucking her needlework back into her workbox. "If you'll excuse me, I must go and see the housekeeper and instruct her about the plans for Christmas. It will be an English Christmas of course, but I think you will find our—your—celebrations quite delightful, and your people will soon grow accustomed to the English way of doing things."

Iain opened his mouth, then shut it again. Marjorie was going to instruct the housekeeper? He supposed she meant Annie, or perhaps Seonag. He hoped she meant Seonag, because instructing Annie on how to do anything in the English fashion was sure to result in disaster. And as for Christmas, there were traditions, celebrations that went back through generations of MacGillivrays. No one was going to give those up, when they looked forward to them all year. Not for all the estates in England.

He considered stopping Marjorie, warning her of the dangers of Annie's temper, of her devotion to the old ways. But which side would he take? What could he say, now half English and half Scot? No one would be happy. He stayed where he was as his aunt swept out of the room, a sense of purpose in her blue English eyes, eyes that were so like her daughter's.

Iain stared out at the snow and wished he'd never inherited the damned English title.

Chapter Fourteen

Dundrummie Castle, seventeen days before Christmas

"I ASSURE YOU, my lord, Alanna is most willing—eager, in fact—to marry you."

Lord Wilfred Esmond, Marquess of Merridew, sat in the salon of Dundrummie Castle and frowned at Lady Devorguilla McNabb, his future mother-in-law, across the tea table. He scanned her lovely face and looked for some evidence that she was lying to him.

It had happened before. Lady Devorguilla had informed him that her older daughter, Megan, was willing to marry him as well, until the young lady proved her mother's confidence misplaced by eloping with the Earl of Rossington instead.

"My lady, if Lady Alanna has not followed her sister's lead and eloped with someone else, then where precisely is she? I expected my bride to be here to greet me when I arrived—especially if she is as eager as you say. Yet now you tell me she is 'delayed.' What precisely does that mean?" The snow had delayed his arrival by two days. He had expected to find his bride dressed and ready for the wedding, even if he was a day late for the ceremony, but she was not even here. It didn't suggest eagerness to him.

Devorguilla smiled at him, and Wilfred tightened his grip on the tumbler of whisky in his hand. The dowager countess of Glenlorne was a lovely woman, and looked far too young to be the mother of three grown daughters, including his fiancée. Devorguilla McNabb had a remarkably good figure, flashing green eyes, and a knowing look that stirred a man's imagination—even an imagination as limited as his own. Wilfred shifted and hoped that the daughter proved as interesting as the mother.

He could only hope, because he had almost no recollection of Lady Alanna. He'd barely glanced at her, hadn't spoken more than a half dozen words to the chit in the few times he'd been in her company, since he'd expected to wed her older sister. Lady Megan had been a beauty indeed.

It had been Devorguilla who had suggested he marry Alanna when Megan ran away to avoid his suit. He assumed she was pretty, though what she looked like paled in consideration of the generous dowry she'd bring him, and that was what mattered most. He watched his lovely hostess as she babbled an explanation, her cheeks flushed becomingly.

He sighed and sipped his whisky, having rejected the countess's offer of tea. It was ever thus—gentlemen with titles must marry for money, and the young ladies with the best dowries married the loftiest titles. Cash trumped beauty on both sides.

"Alanna was caught in the storm while out taking

charity to some of the local folk. She has always been so kind and caring, as I'm sure you know."

He didn't care one whit what the girl's hobbies or interests might be. Her duties were to restore his fortune and breed an heir.

"The weather must have caught her unawares—storms can come suddenly in the Highlands, my lord," Devorguilla continued. "No doubt she is staying with friends until the weather improves. We have had two days of heavy snow already."

Wilfred set his glass down and leveled a sharp look at his future mother-in-law, who was at least five years younger than he was. "Yet I managed to get here."

Devorguilla immediately lifted the lid on the decanter and refilled his glass. "Yes, of course—but even you were a day late for the wedding, my lord. You only arrived this morning."

"Because I wished to be here," he insisted. "I made every effort." Actually, it was his coachman who'd made all the effort. Wilfred had stayed inside his plush coach with heated bricks at his feet, lounging under thick eiderdowns, sipping brandy and eating sweetmeats.

Devorguilla gave him a beguiling smile. "And I'm sure Alanna is also making every effort to return as quickly as possible as well. As much as it is a Highland custom to offer shelter and assistance to travellers in need, it's also a Highland custom to respect the weather."

He sipped from the refilled glass of whisky. Did anything warm so well as good Highland whisky? The smoke curled through his veins pleasantly. "But your older daughter—" he began, but Devorguilla gave him a reassuring smile that warmed him almost as much as the whisky did. "Megan is impetuous. Alanna is sensible, sweet natured, and deeply honored to be your bride. I have every expectation that she'll walk through that door in the next minute and apologize profusely."

They both glanced at the doorway, but it remained empty. He raised an eyebrow and looked back at Devorguilla. The clock on the mantel ticked a nervous drumbeat.

The countess let her lashes sweep down over her eyes, then bit into her lush lower lip. "If I were Alanna, I'd be counting the moments until you made me the happiest woman on earth," Devorguilla added, her voice an octave lower, and as smoky and potent as the whisky.

He looked at her with interest. "Would you?"

She smiled. "Of course. You must be aware of your charms without my needing to describe them. Your good looks, your noble nature, your devastating wit . . ."

He was forty-six and balding, with a large mole on his nose. He was widely regarded as the most humorless man in all England. He looked more deeply into the countess's green eyes, seeking subterfuge, and found only admiration. His chest swelled. Perhaps he could afford to wait a day or two after all.

"Alanna has not said anything of my . . . charms," he said.

Devorguilla tilted her head. Her golden hair gleamed in the light of the fire. "Oh, but she is young and shy."

He leaned forward. "While you, dear countess, are a woman of experience."

A blush bloomed over her high cheekbones. "Not that much experience, my lord. I was only seventeen myself when

Alanna was born. Women marry young in the Highlands, and we choose men of distinction and maturity, such as yourself."

"You flatter me, Countess." Perhaps she did, but he liked it.

Her smile spread like a slow seduction. "Do call me Devorguilla, my lord."

"Then you must call me Wilfred."

"It will be my pleasure, Wilfred."

"Lovely," he murmured, wondering when he'd last heard his given name on a beautiful woman's lips. "May I say you look more like Alanna's pretty sister than her mother?" He preferred older women, actually. They were experienced, knowledgeable in bed, and they understood how to please a man. Virgins were for marrying, but women like Devorguilla McNabb were for pleasure.

She didn't simper at his compliment. She looked him square in the eyes for a moment before she lowered her lashes again in a long sweep. "There you see—you are very charming indeed, Wilfred." She set her cup down. "What shall we do while we await Alanna? Perhaps a hand of cards, or a game of chess?"

She said the word as if chess meant another game entirely, and Wilfred got to his feet and held out an arm to his lovely hostess.

He helped her set up the chessboard on a table in front of the fire, their fingers brushing.

As the snow fell outside, the glamorous dowager Countess of Glenlorne poured him another brimming glass of whisky and smiled, and he didn't give the weather or his missing fiancée another thought.

Chapter Fifteen

Craigleith, seventeen days before Christmas

SANDY SHOOK THE snow off as he entered Jock MacIntosh's snug cottage the morning after Alanna McNabb's arrival at Craigleith. "I'm glad to still find you here. Any news from your daughter?" he asked as he hung his plaid by the fire to dry. Jock's wife nodded a wordless greeting and poured him a dram of whisky before going back about her work, knitting something, no doubt for her new grandchild.

"No, but the babe is due to come anytime now. I promised her I'd bring her mother to help, but the storm's delayed us. We'll go today, snow or no snow." Jock said. "If the babe gets time to be born amidst all the blethering the pair of them will be doing, it will indeed be something to see." His wife sent him a scowl and tossed another stitch over her knitting needles.

Sandy chuckled. "You make it sound as if you've no interest a'tall in seeing your first grandchild. I'm waiting on the arrival of my fourth. I like bairns best when they're old enough to hold their tongues and give a man some peace."

"You can no more resist a new babe than I can, Sandy MacGillivray," Jock's missus scolded.

Jock grinned. "Each grandchild is a blessing at our age. Auld Annie says this one will be a boy, so of course I'm interested. And I don't share a cott with my daughter, so I won't have to have my sleep interrupted a dozen times a night like you will." He lit Sandy's pipe, then his own. So what brings you out on a day like this?"

Sandy stretched his feet to the fire to warm them. "I've come to ask if you'll carry a letter when you go to see your daughter. I assume your son-in-law will be making the journey to Loch Rain to take the news of the birth to his own kin. Perhaps he could take the letter that far, and find someone to take it on from there."

"Aye, and gladly, but who are you writing to?"

"Not me. There's a lass at the castle. Iain found her lost in the snow and brought her home. They were forced to stay the night at Ewan's old cott because the storm was so bad. He came back yesterday morning holding her in his arms, wrapped up safe in his plaid, wearing his handkerchief as a bandage."

"Is that a fact?" Jock asked, his eyes bright. He rubbed his stubbled chin. "Does he mean to keep her?"

Sandy sighed. "He says not, but she's a bonnie wee thing, pretty as the hills on a fine summer morn."

"Then who's he writing to?"

"Not him—her. She has a brother at Glenlorne, wants him to know she's here and safe."

"I remember a time when it wasn't necessary to send

a letter to say that. Everyone would know she was safe," Jock mused.

"It's the Highland way," Sandy agreed.

"And Iain—there's no better laird than Iain MacGillivray." Jock raised his mug to the man, and Sandy raised his as well, drained his cup, and rose.

"Well, I'll not keep you. Travel safe, and give my best to your lass and her husband when you see them." He handed over the letter, and Jock took it.

"Connor will find someone to take it from Loch Rain. We'll be back by Christmas, or maybe not, if the wife has her way. It won't be easy to part my May from the little one."

"Or you, old man," May said, not looking up from her knitting.

"A fine Christmas to you and yours," Sandy said, nodding to May and clasping his old friend's hand before heading back out into the snow.

Chapter Sixteen

Craigleith, sixteen days before Christmas

"COME IN," ALANNA said as she pulled the covers up to her neck and held her breath, wondering if it was Iain knocking on the door.

"Am I disturbing you?" Fiona MacGillivray asked. "Annie sent me up with some clothes for you, and a comb and some hair ribbons, if you're well enough to come down for dinner. Your own dress is torn, and Seonag's stitching it, since she does the best needlework of anyone here at—" She realized she was babbling and colored as she fell silent.

Fiona looked like a feminine, pretty version of her brother, with the same red hair and gray eyes. "Thank you," Alanna said with a smile, pulling herself up on the pillows. She'd been in bed for two days, and she was indeed anxious to get up.

"It's one of my dresses, but it isn't as fine as yours," Fiona added, laying it over the back of a chair. "You must be used to much nicer clothes than this."

"Not really," Alanna said. "Well, not until my mother insisted I'd need fancy clothes to wear in England, that is."

Fiona's eyes widened. "Is it truly so different there? I've seen how Elizabeth and Penelope dress. Penelope changes her gown four or five times a day, and each one has matching shoes and shawls and bonnets. Each outfit is for a different activity—like tea, or callers, or theater parties. Even if those activities aren't ever going to happen here, she says good manners must be observed no matter where we are." She twisted her hands together. "I think it will be difficult to get used to doing nothing but changing my dress all day when I get to England. I doubt I'll remember the difference between a morning gown and a tea dress." Her voice dropped to a whisper. "Penelope says the English don't tolerate mistakes, especially—" She shrugged. "I limp, you see. I'd rather stay here, at Craigleith, but Iain must go to England, and I can't let him face it alone."

Face what? Was he nervous, afraid, as anxious as she was? Alanna swallowed her surprise. Iain MacGillivray was a man, strong, brave, and kind. Surely he wouldn't be afraid of anything. Like she was. Alanna gripped the folds of his shirt under the covers. "Is he—looking forward to going to England?"

Fiona's face scrunched. "Oh, he puts a brave face on it, but I don't think so. He visited England once before, when he was much younger. He didn't like it."

"Why didn't he like it?" Alanna asked, her heart climbing into her throat, the familiar feeling of anxiety rising in her belly.

"He wouldn't say, and I was just small. What's England like?"

There were rules, strict ones, or so Alanna had been

taught. As a foreigner, her smallest slip would be noticed and magnified, inciting gossip and scandal. As a marchioness, she would be under constant scrutiny. She swallowed a lump of sheer terror and forced a smile for Fiona's sake, the same way she did when placating her own younger sister.

She'd already solved the problem of which gown for which activity, so she could help Fiona with that at least. She intended to label every dress in her wardrobe. "I suppose there are always things to get used to in a new place, but I've been told that England has many good things as well, like parties and balls, and new sights to see." She fervently hoped that proved to be true.

Fiona bit her lip. "I think I'd like that. Not the balls, since I can't dance, but the sights. What have you seen?"

"I've never been there either," Alanna admitted. "I only know what I've been told." She felt the familiar ache in her stomach at the idea of marrying Merridew. "I suppose I'll find out once I'm married."

Fiona's jaw dropped. "Your fiancé is English?"

Alanna managed another smile, but it felt stiff. "Yes, just like your brother's—"

There was another knock at the door, but this time it opened before Alanna could bid the visitor to come in. Lady Penelope regarded her from the doorway with a cool smile that did not reach her eyes as she scanned the room like a bird of prey.

"Hello, Penelope," Fiona said, her smile fading.

"What are you doing here?" Penelope asked her young cousin.

"I came to bring Alanna one of my dresses to wear until hers is repaired." Alanna watched the English lady's eyes flick over the warm russet wool of the gown on the back of the chair.

"I see. I understand your gown was torn somehow," Penelope said, color rising in two spots over her cheeks. Alanna wondered what Iain had told her.

"I fell, I think," she said. "In the storm."

"You don't remember?" Penelope asked.

"No, not a thing. I recall the storm, and then I woke up in the cottage with—" She paused as Penelope's frown intensified. "I am most grateful for the care Iain and everyone here at Craigleith has shown me," Alanna said in careful English. "Thank you," she said. Penelope was going to be the lady of Craigleith soon enough, and as such, Alanna owed her as much of a debt of thanks as she did Iain.

"You're quite welcome to the dress," Penelope said, as if the gown belonged to her, and not Fiona. "Fiona's things should do you well enough. I'm sure you're more used to Scottish clothes, and I doubt anything of mine would fit you." She smoothed a hand over her more generous curves. Alanna was slender, but the comparison to Iain's fifteen-year-old sister stung. "I just came to see if you need any assistance. I'm sure you're anxious to be on your way home," Penelope said, as if she expected Alanna to leap out of bed—Iain's bed—and leave Craigleith at once. She raised her chin when Alanna remained where she was.

It seemed the safest thing to do, given that Alanna was still wearing Iain's shirt.

"I understand your wedding plans were interrupted by this unfortunate incident," Penelope said stiffly. "Is your intended a local lad? Perhaps he could be summoned here."

Like a shepherd, or a gamekeeper, perhaps? Alanna's incautious temper flared at the condescension in Penelope's tone.

"Oh, he's not a Highlander, if that's what you mean. He's English," Fiona said before Alanna could reply.

Penelope's eyes widened, and interest replaced suspicion in her eyes. "English? How on earth—I mean, how did *you* come to be betrothed to an Englishman?"

Alanna held Penelope's eyes. Was she suggesting Alanna wasn't worthy of an English lord, wasn't pretty enough, or smart enough? She lifted her chin.

"He's a marquess," she said. "The Marquess of Merridew. Perhaps you know him, being English yourself?"

Penelope's jaw dropped, and her voice rose an octave. "A marquess? *You're* going to be a *marchioness*?"

"Yes. And my sister is married to an English earl—Lord Rossington. And my brother, the Earl of Glenlorne, is married to the sister of the English Earl of Somerson."

"*Kit* Rossington?" Penelope gasped, and put a hand to her lush bosom. "But every lady in England wants to—" Her jaw snapped shut.

"Indeed," Alanna agreed with the unspoken sentiment. Rossington was handsome and very rich, a prime catch, sought after by many women who'd hoped to be his bride, but he had chosen Megan. Alanna wondered if the surprise in Penelope's eyes meant she found Scottish ladies more worthy of her respect now.

"I hadn't even heard that Rossington had married," Penelope murmured, her face scarlet.

"My brother is worth a dozen marquesses," Fiona murmured in Gaelic, folding her hands over her chest and glaring at her cousin. Alanna smiled at her.

"Of course he is," she whispered back, also in Gaelic.

"Speak English," Penelope demanded.

"I said I'm sure Alanna's marquess is very charming," Fiona said and gave her cousin an acid smile. "But Iain is better still."

Penelope's chin rose again, and she looked around the room. "Yes, of course," she unknowingly parroted Alanna, sounding far less convinced. "But an English marquess . . ."

As far as Alanna remembered, Merridew was not charming in the least. He wanted a healthy young wife with a large dowry. Her mother wanted a title for her daughter. It was a match made in a counting house, rather than heaven. But while Alanna's opinion of her future husband's charms did not matter to him or to her mother in the least, they mattered very much to Alanna.

As a child, she had imagined marrying a handsome prince, being swept away over the hills and glens on a white horse, to a castle by a shining loch, where they would live happily ever after. Dreams didn't always come true, it seemed.

"No wonder you speak such good English," Penelope said. "You've been taught, I suppose." She ran her hand over the fine wool of Fiona's waiting gown. "So tell me, have you any other unmarried sisters?"

"Just one," Alanna said.

Penelope looked relieved.

"She'll be making her debut soon, in London, of course." It was a lie. It would be years yet before Sorcha was old enough to wed. She was letting Penelope provoke her. "She's the prettiest of all of us," she added, knowing Sorcha might well be, someday.

"Oh," Penelope's lips pursed miserably. "And who else do you know in England? Any dukes, or princes, or the Queen, perhaps?"

"No one, really," Alanna admitted.

"Good—" Penelope sighed in relief, then colored at Fiona's gasp at her rudeness. "I mean, it will be better not to know *everyone* before you even get there. There must be some surprises."

"I'm sure everyone will want to know Alanna," Fiona said, her smile kind as she looked at her guest.

"Where are Lord Merridew's estates? I'm sure my mother knows, of course," Penelope said.

"Kent, I believe."

"Woodford Park is in Shropshire. Is that close to Kent?" Fiona asked.

"No," Penelope said. "The chances of our meeting again are very remote."

"Unless we're all in London," Fiona said. "Elizabeth says everyone goes to London."

"Not you," Penelope told her. "You'll be kept in the nursery with Elizabeth at Woodford until you're old enough to be introduced to polite company. Of course, you'll need to learn proper manners and correct English before that can happen, and even then—" She looked pointedly at Fiona's damaged leg.

Alanna watched Fiona's smile fade.

Fiona turned to Alanna, hiding the sparkle of her tears from her cousin. "Will you help me learn, Alanna?" she asked in Gaelic. "At least a little, so I don't embarrass Iain."

"Yes, of course," Alanna said. Fiona smiled wanly, her fear evident. Alanna had learned to hide her fear. It would be the first thing she'd teach Fiona.

Penelope moved toward the door. "I really must go. I'm sure Iain is looking everywhere for me. The poor man is lost without me. I'm helping him learn all the little things that will make him a success in London. Since you have everything you need, I'll leave you to dress. I can see you aren't used to having the assistance of a proper lady's maid, or I'd offer you mine."

Alanna held her silence, and so did Fiona. Alanna watched Iain's betrothed leave the room as quickly as she'd come, and let out a breath she hadn't known she was holding.

"Iain's manners are just fine," Fiona said, glowering at the closed panels. "I think he should be teaching *her* some manners. She will be the wife of a Scottish laird, after all. She has refused to learn one single word of Gaelic, not even a greeting, or how to say please or thank you."

"I'm sure Iain will help her when the time comes," Alanna said diplomatically. Lady Penelope was very beautiful, despite her sharp tongue, and surely Iain must love her very much.

She must look like a hag by comparison. She sat up and began to comb her tangled hair, doing her best not to wince at the snags. "What would you like to know?" Alanna asked.

"I would like to know how to speak better English. Elizabeth says everyone will laugh at my accent and my foreign ways. I don't think anyone would ever laugh at you, Alanna. I wish I didn't limp so, but I can't help that. I think I'd like to know how to look at people the way Penelope and my aunt Marjorie do, make them feel as if I am much more important than they are."

Alanna set the comb down. "But that's no way to gain friends. You must learn to show people that you are kind, and pleasant company, and that you think they are important to know."

Fiona smiled. "That's just what Iain would say."

Alanna smiled at Fiona and patted the bed. "Come and sit beside me, and I'll show you how to do your hair in an English style."

She combed Fiona's dark red hair and coiled it into a simple, sleek style the way she'd been taught, wondering yet again just how she was ever going to fit in as Marchioness of Merridew.

Chapter Seventeen

"OH, MAMA, THERE ought to be a law!"

Marjorie turned as Penelope burst into her room. Marjorie was changing her gown for dinner with the help of her maid, and she noted first that Penelope had not yet dressed for dinner. Then she saw that Penelope was wringing her hands, her face tear-stained. She sent the maid out of the room with a wave of her hand.

"There's a handkerchief in my top drawer. Calm yourself before your complexion turns blotchy. What law are you talking about?" Marjorie demanded, sitting down at her makeshift dressing table and regarding her own face in the ancient-looking glass.

Penelope threw herself on the bed. "A law that Scottish ladies can only marry Scottish men and Englishmen can only wed Englishwomen!" Penelope said, rubbing her eyes with the monogrammed square of fine Irish linen.

"And where would that leave you with Iain?" Marjorie asked calmly.

Penelope sniffed. "Oh. I hadn't thought of that."

Marjorie picked up her hairbrush and regarded her daughter's reflection in the dark mirror. "Then what were you thinking?" she asked. Sometimes Penelope could be a trifle slow to explain herself.

"Did you know she—Lady Alanna—is betrothed to the Marquess of Merridew?"

Marjorie's jaw dropped. She regarded her daughter's reflection in the glass. "Wilfred Esmond—that Merridew?"

"And her sister is married to the Earl of Rossington."

Marjorie's surprise deepened. "Kit? I didn't even know he was married."

"Well, he is. And her brother—the Scottish earl—is married to the Earl of Somerson's sister."

Marjorie set the brush down and turned to gape at her daughter in disbelief. "But Charlotte Somerson is a dear friend. She didn't mention a thing."

"And *she'll* be a marchioness, a waif dragged out of a snowdrift, wrapped in a plaid! It's mortifying," Penelope continued, rolling her eyes.

Marjorie blinked. "She's certainly a very well-connected waif."

"She will have precedence over me should we ever meet in England. Her sister will be my equal as a countess. She and her sisters have stolen all the best gentlemen in England, right out from under our noses!"

Penelope was twisting the handkerchief as if it was Alanna McNabb's neck. Marjorie rescued the fragile cloth before her daughter shredded it. Penelope got up and paced the room instead.

"A lady does not pace," Marjorie reminded her. Penelope stood still and folded her arms mutinously.

"I wonder how Wilfred met the sister of a Scottish earl," Marjorie mused, still stunned. "And why would he marry her? I wonder if his mother knows?"

"What does that matter?" Penelope asked.

Marjorie studied her manicured nails. "Perhaps Wilfred will come to fetch her here. It would be nice to see him again. His mother and I were dear friends once." They'd been fierce rivals, in truth. "The two of us and Charlotte Somerson all made our debuts in the same year. Charlotte won Somerson, of course, and Jane married Wilfred's father, the Duke of Lyall, and I wed your father." Her lips twisted. Aldridge had been the handsomest man Marjorie had ever seen, the most charming, the prime catch that Season. Lyall and Somerson were stodgy, ordinary men, if rich and titled. The night Marjorie accepted the charming, handsome, and youthful Aldridge's proposal, she'd thought she'd won the game, made the best marriage of all. But Aldridge had spent her dowry within a few short years and died, leaving her with nothing. And now her daughter must wed a Scot, while the chit upstairs would win a far bigger prize in the wedding game.

"Why can't *I* have a marquess?" Penelope whined.

"You'll be a countess, my dear," Marjorie said. Without a dowry, Iain was the best Penelope could do. Yet now her daughter would never be satisfied, not when Alanna McNabb had a marquess.

"She'll be a duchess someday!"

Marjorie considered. When she realized she was twisting the handkerchief herself, she tossed it on the dressing table. She didn't point out to her daughter that Lady Alanna wasn't anything but a Scottish earl's sister as of yet. Betrothed didn't mean married. She clasped Penelope's clammy hands in her own. "Go and get dressed for dinner, my dear. I understand that Lady Alanna is feeling much improved and will be joining us this evening. I'm anxious to meet her. I had no idea she was worth my notice."

"But she is?"

Marjorie smiled. "Oh yes—now she is. Wear your pink silk this evening."

She watched her daughter go, and turned to her writing desk.

Chapter Eighteen

"DID YOU GET some of her hair?" Elizabeth rushed across the library as Fiona came in.

Fiona bit her lip. "I managed to get a few strands from her comb." She held out her palm, and Elizabeth squinted at the dark strands of hair in Fiona's palm. They glinted copper in the candlelight.

"That isn't very much," Elizabeth said.

Fiona closed her hand protectively. "How much do you think we might need? This was all I could get, short of pulling out a handful. She's so kind—I just couldn't." She patted her coiffure.

Elizabeth drew the bundle of herbs out of her pocket with a sigh. "This won't be easy with just three hairs."

"Are you sure we need to do this at all? What if her true love really does arrive before Christmas?" Fiona asked.

"What if he does?" Elizabeth blinked.

"He's a marquess—an *English* marquess," Fiona whispered.

Elizabeth's eyes widened. "Truly? How on earth did

she—" She took a breath. "Well, perhaps he'll ride in like a knight on a charger, dressed in shining armor, and sweep her up into his arms."

"A garron would be better in all this snow, and he'd better wear something warmer than armor," Fiona said.

Elizabeth folded her arms and sent her cousin a sharp look. "Like a MacGillivray plaid and a handkerchief?"

Fiona looked mutinous. "Iain is twice as good as any marquess," she said again.

"He's only an earl," Elizabeth said. "But what does that matter? It's destiny that matters, and true love. Don't you want to know?" She beckoned for the hair, and Fiona opened her hand.

"Just be careful not to drop them," Fiona warned, holding her breath.

They were so intent on winding the hairs around the bundle that they didn't hear Annie enter the room until she spoke right beside them. "What are you two up to?"

Elizabeth yelped in surprise, and the bundle of herbs flew into the air. Annie reached out a hand and deftly caught it. "What's this? More magic?" She put the herbs to her nose and sniffed. "The same spell as before."

"It's not for us, Annie. It's for—"

Annie folded her arms over her chest. "For Iain and the lass upstairs. You want to know whether your spell has brought her here for him."

"Or if he'll marry Penelope," Elizabeth said.

"Yes," Fiona said, hoping even more now that that wasn't going to happen.

Annie looked at them both, one after the other, her

eyes bright and sharp, her expression unreadable. "Did your sister cast the spell?" she asked Elizabeth.

"She wouldn't do it. She's certain Iain will propose by Christmas."

Annie stuck her nose in the air and waved her hand. "Then what do you need magic for? What will be will be," Annie said.

Fiona put her hand on Annie's arm. "Please, Annie. I saw the way Iain looked at Alanna when he carried her upstairs."

"What way?" Annie demanded.

"Different from the way he looks at me, or you, or even Penelope. I've never seen him look at anyone quite like that before, as if he'd forgotten every sensible thought in his head, or he'd lost something."

"Or found it," Annie said.

Elizabeth sighed. "I have a spaniel who looks at me with complete adoration when I rub his ears—was it that kind of look?"

Annie and Fiona frowned at her. "No," they said in unison. Elizabeth looked disappointed.

"Then how?" she asked them.

"Iain's not a dumb beast, for one thing. He's a man," Fiona said.

"How is that different?" Elizabeth asked.

Annie patted Elizabeth's arm. "You'll know soon enough, lass."

"What about now, and Lady Alanna?" Elizabeth asked.

"There isn't time now," Annie said. "It's almost time

for supper, and Iain's gone up to fetch her downstairs. Besides, the lass really should cast the bundle into the fire herself, or the spell won't work."

"But it was the spell that brought her here, wasn't it?" Fiona argued. "And the storm . . ."

Annie's smug expression faded, and she looked into the fire for a moment.

"What do you see?" Fiona asked her breathlessly. She'd seen that look in Auld Annie's eyes before—as if she could see the past, the present, and the future all in one moment, as if she was reading it in the air before her eyes, or listening, or watching something happening, something no one else could see or hear. Annie's head cocked to one side, like a bird's, and the firelight reflected in her eyes. "Annie?"

Annie turned slowly, as if she was waking from a long sleep. "Jock MacIntosh has a new grandson," she murmured.

Elizabeth frowned. "Who's Jock MacIntosh?" she asked, but no one answered.

Annie put the bundle of herbs into Fiona's hand with a sober look and folded her fingers over it. "Put it away, lass. Best leave magic out of this."

With that, Annie turned on her heel and left the library. The girls hurried after her, begging for more, but Auld Annie's lips were tightly sealed.

Chapter Nineteen

IAIN TOOK THE stairs two at a time. He had promised Annie he'd fetch—escort—Alanna down to the dining room for dinner. She'd slept for most of the last two days, but Annie had assured him that was perfectly normal, that Alanna was mending and there was nothing to fear. "The roses are back in her cheeks, and the swelling is going out of her knee," was all she'd told him before continuing on with her chores. Did Annie expect he'd forget about her, be content to leave her to the womenfolk, closeted in his bedroom?

That should have been the way of it, perhaps, but he'd thought of nothing else but Alanna in the three days since he'd found her. He dreamed of her face, white as the snow, her lips rose red and soft, surrounded by sparkling crystals of ice—an ice maiden, ready to be woken and revived by a kiss. He woke alone in the tower room, reaching for her, desire making him breathless, with the wind laughing at the window.

When he was awake, he saw her face in the frost patterns

etched on the windowpanes of the castle, remembered the curves of her body when he looked at the sinuous snowdrifts that reclined over hills and walls and the black branches of trees. He saw the reflection of her eyes in the fire. In three short days, Lady Alanna McNabb had become an obsession.

He paused outside the door of her room and drew a deep breath before he knocked, and waited for her to bid him enter.

She was sitting in a chair by the fire, with a book in her hand—his chair, his book. Her eyes were expectant, shining as she met his gaze. Her hair gleamed in the firelight, dark shadows and bright copper, elegantly braided and coiled up behind her slender neck. She wore one of Fiona's gowns, red wool trimmed with dark green ribbons. Not an ice maiden at all. She looked soft, sweet, and right, as if she belonged here in this castle, this room.

His castle, and his room. His mouth dried.

He was aware he was staring, and she was waiting for him to say something. "I came to see if you're ready to come down for supper."

She got to her feet a trifle awkwardly, holding the back of the chair. He crossed to take her elbow and steady her.

She was inches from him now. He could smell the soft scent of the heather soap Annie made, so familiar, yet exotic on this woman, tantalizing. Had he ever noticed it before? He was noticing it now. He swallowed, felt his whole body warm.

She blushed, looking up at him. "I'm all right—just stiff from lying in bed for so long. I'm not used to doing so."

He let go at once, stepped back, clasped his hands

behind his back. "Of course. If you were home, you'd be married by now, a new bride." He could have bitten his tongue in two. If she were his bride, she'd spend longer than two days in bed and get no rest at all.

Her skin flushed again. "Oh—of course. I was actually thinking about being home at Glenlorne, with my brother and his wife, and my sisters. There's always so much to do at this time of year. I've never spent a Christmas away before. My brother's wife is expecting her first child in the spring, and it will be a very happy Christmas for them."

"There's still time to get you home," he said.

She shook her head. "His lordship—my fiancé—wishes to spend Christmas at his home in England."

His brows rose. "In England? Your intended is English?"

She swallowed before nodding. "Aye. A marquess."

He felt his brows shoot upwards.

"Are you impressed? You needn't be. I didn't mean—" She shrugged, and he detected a hint of bitterness in her tone.

"It's not that . . . I simply imagine English marquesses are as rare as wolves in the Highlands."

She forced a smile that didn't meet her eyes. "Yes. I suppose I'm just—"

"Lucky?" he supplied.

She didn't reply to that. She lowered her eyes to stare at her hands. "We'd better go downstairs," she said instead.

"Shall I carry you?" he asked, his tone stiff.

"No, I can walk, though I will limp, like—" She bit her lip.

"Like Fiona," he finished for her, scanned her face, looking for mockery, disdain. There was only interest.

"Has she always limped?"

He felt the familiar anger in his breast, that people judged his sister as daft or slow because of her infirmity. He considered not replying, but she waited. "No. Fee had an accident as a child. She fell down the steps of the old tower, and even Annie couldn't get the bone to set straight again. The stones are worn and dangerous after centuries of use. No one is allowed up there now—just me. Shall we go?" He held out his arm, and she slipped her hand under his elbow.

"Fiona is afraid she'll be mocked in England," she said as they set off slowly, accommodating her injured leg.

"Yes. I considered leaving her here when I go south, but she won't hear of it, insists on coming with me. It might be for the best. She deserves opportunities, the best education, pretty clothes, like other girls."

"And she can't have that here at Craigleith?" she asked.

"There are doctors in England." And there he would be an earl, with power and money to pay them. He glanced down at Alanna. "Don't tell Annie."

"I'm sure Annie would simply tell you that Fiona is a lovely young woman just as she is."

"Of course she is. No one thinks anything of her limp here in Scotland. They've learned to look past it, see Fiona as she truly is. But I've seen the way Marjorie and Penelope look at her, how they talk to her. I couldn't bear for others in England to treat her that way—crippled, useless, and foreign." The way they'd look at him, as well. He felt her fingers tighten on his arm, press slightly. Instinctively, he placed his other hand over hers, a soothing gesture, but who was soothing whom?

"It will simply take time to get used to a new place, new customs," she said, "and you'll be there to protect her. They—the English—aren't entirely different from us."

"You say that as if you have recited it a hundred times."

"Yes," she whispered. "Probably more."

"Anxious about your own welcome, my lady? But you'll be a marchioness."

"Still," she murmured. "It will take time to think of it as home, to see new people as family."

They reached the top of the stairs, and she paused and took a breath. "This could take some time," she said, looking down.

"Not at all." He bent and put his hands behind her knees and around her shoulders, swung her into his arms. The soft weight of her breast settled against his chest, and she put her arm around his neck and whooped in delighted surprise at his speed as he hurried down the steps, laughing. "I used to carry Fiona down the stairs like that after her injury. She was afraid of steps for a long time after the accident."

Alanna sobered and looked into his eyes. "But she got over it, didn't she? You helped her do that. How?"

"I stopped carrying her. I took her hand, made her walk."

"You made her feel safe."

"She's brave and she's smart."

They reached the bottom of the stairs, and still he held onto her, unable to force himself to set her on her feet. She reached up and laid her fingers on his cheek, and the touch went through him like lightning. "She'll still be brave and smart in England."

He scanned her face. "Who will make you feel safe and brave?"

He saw emotion pass through her eyes, fear perhaps, before she swept her lashes down like a curtain. "Me?" she asked. "I—"

"There you are," Penelope said, stepping out of the shadows. "We've all been wondering if perhaps Lady Alanna was still indisposed after all." Her narrow gaze took in Alanna's arm around his neck, her face inches from his, noted their whispered conversation. Iain watched as color rose across Penelope's features like a tide of dye and her jaw tensed.

"Perhaps we could find you a pair of crutches," she said to Alanna, her tone tart. "So Iain need not be inconvenienced every time you wish to come down the stairs."

Iain felt Alanna stiffen in his arms, watched her smile fade. "And yet it is not inconvenient at all. It is my pleasure to assist you," Iain told her. He should have put her down, but stubbornly he carried her past Penelope, striding down the hall and into the dining room. He heard the heels of Penelope's stylish high-heeled English slippers rap a sharp and angry staccato as she hurried to catch up. He lowered Alanna gently, kept one hand on the small of her back until she steadied herself. Only then did he step back, ignoring Penelope's glare.

ALANNA HELD HER breath as Iain swept through the doorway of the dining room. Conversation died as they entered, and every eye widened at the sight of her in her host's arms. The women at the table stared silently as Iain set her down. She gripped the back of her chair. She squared her shoulders, forced herself to smile, to look at ease.

"I don't believe you've met my aunt yet. Lady Marjorie Curry, this is Lady Alanna McNabb."

Lady Marjorie looked like an older version of Penelope, elegant and well dressed. She regarded Alanna down the length of her patrician nose. Alanna dipped a curtsy, hid a wince as her knee objected to the rules of etiquette. Lady Marjorie inclined her head regally, taking in the details of Alanna's simple dress. Marjorie, Penelope, and Elizabeth wore silk. Alanna and Fiona wore fine wool.

"Thank you for the loan of your gown, Fiona. It fits perfectly," Alanna said, and she watched Fiona beam. She was wearing white wool, with a soft woolen shawl against the chill.

"You look pretty in red," Fiona said as Alanna took her seat.

Penelope sat on Iain's right-hand side, across the table from Alanna, watching her with cool curiosity.

Her gown was pale blue, worn with a collar of pearls— like Alanna's wedding dress, still awaiting her at Dundrummie. It reminded her that Penelope, too, would soon be a bride. Iain's bride.

"Your dress is lovely—the pale blue silk suits you very well."

"Thank you," Penelope said through tight lips, as she wasn't sure if the compliment was genuine. It was.

"I understand this whole unfortunate incident has

made you late for your wedding. Dear Wilfred must be beside himself," Lady Marjorie said.

"Wilfred?" Alanna asked, baffled.

Lady Marjorie put a hand to her throat. "Why, yes—the Marquess of Merridew's Christian name. Penelope, did you not say she was betrothed to Lord Merridew?"

Alanna swallowed, feeling her skin heat as every eye at the table turned on her. She had never heard Merridew's Christian name before.

In fact, her gaff only served to emphasize that she knew nothing about him at all.

"Are you a friend of—Wilfred's?" she asked, trying his name on her tongue for the first time. She felt Iain's eyes on her hot face and didn't dare look at him.

"I know his mother very well indeed. I'm sure she must be perfectly enchanted with you, my dear. It's about time dear Willie married. The duchess says so in every letter she writes to me. How did you find Her Grace when you met her?"

Willie? If Alanna could not think of Merridew as Wilfred, then "Willie" was even more impossible. Would he expect her to call him by the pet name, or stick to "sir" or "my lord"? She realized she was gripping her napkin in a stranglehold and forced herself to let go.

"I have not yet met the duke and duchess," Alanna said quietly. "We were—are—to travel south immediately after the wedding, weather permitting."

"I see," Lady Marjorie said and looked down her nose again, suspicion and doubt clear in her eyes.

Alanna could have cheered when Seonag and Wee Janet

entered to serve the meal. The thick stew smelled delicious to Alanna after days on broth and fortifying draughts of goat's milk and strong ale. She smiled at Seonag and asked her in Gaelic about the babe, knowing Lady Marjorie was still regarding her with keen interest.

She was rewarded with a wide smile, and Seonag flushed with pleasure. "Annie says it will be only a few days now," she whispered back, and moved to serve Penelope. Iain's betrothed made a face at the simple fare.

"In England, we'd have roast beef, and turtle soup, or roasted pheasant," she muttered.

"Oh, we enjoy pheasant here, too, and venison, and beef. Just not every day," Fiona said.

Alanna watched as Seonag filled her glass with red wine. "I also hear that you are related by marriage to Kit Rossington," Lady Marjorie said, her gaze pinning Alanna to her chair. "His sister, Lady Arabella Collingwood, is another dear friend of mine."

"Lord Rossington recently married my older sister," Alanna murmured. She felt Iain's steady gaze on her flushed face.

"And the Earl of Somerson is kin to you by marriage as well?" Marjorie asked in a marveling tone.

Alanna was strangling her napkin again. She took a sip of wine. "Lord Somerson's half sister Caroline is married to my brother."

Silence fell over the room and Alanna glanced at Iain, read the surprise in his eyes. He had gone from thinking her a simple Highland lass to discovering she was related by marriage to half the English aristocracy. She was still a simple Highland lass. She raised her chin, desperate to change the subject. She'd grown up as the daughter of a penniless clan chief. The Glenlorne McNabbs had had pride and not much else. When her brother inherited the title, he came home and made careful investments and improvements that made Glenlorne prosperous again. It was due to hard work, not birth or marriage. There was love between Alec and Caroline, and between Kit and Megan as well, for that matter, and that had nothing at all to do with money or title. Only Alanna's marriage was different.

She looked at her plate, bit into fresh bread, savored the delicious rabbit stew, and knew she could never call Merridew Willie, even after—The bread crumbled in her grip, fell into the stew, and she felt an instant of panic fill her chest, making it difficult to swallow, or to smile. The idea of a wedding night with a stranger made her blush anew, sent dread cascading through her limbs. She set her spoon down.

"Are you well, Alanna? You're flushed. I could call Annie—" Fiona began, noting her blush.

"No, I was just thinking of . . . Christmas," she said quickly.

"*Nollaig Beag,*" Fiona said in Gaelic, then grinned, her eyes lighting like Christmas candles. "It's my favorite time of year."

"It is rude to speak a language not everyone at the table understands," Marjorie scolded her niece. "You will have to remember that when you're at Woodford Park. Best to start now, I believe. In fact, I have decided that we shall follow English Christmas customs here this year, since we are all soon to be English."

Fiona's face fell, and Alanna felt indignation rise. She looked at Iain. His hand was clenched on his spoon, his knuckles white. He was looking at Fiona's stricken expression.

"We have traditions here in Scotland—and at Craigleith—that have stood for centuries," he said. "There will be time enough to learn English ways."

"Still, would you deprive us of our traditions?" Marjorie asked, her lips pinched. "When you're in England next year—"

"Then I shall respect those traditions," he said. Tension crackled in the air.

"Perhaps a combination of the two," Alanna suggested. "The new and the old."

"And just how will we do that?" Penelope demanded.

"Well . . . do you bring in evergreens in England?" Alanna asked.

"Of course," Penelope said. "On Christmas Eve, we go out and cut boughs, collect holly and mistletoe, and decorate the great hall at Woodford Park."

Fiona looked hopeful. "We do the same here. We tie them with the MacGillivray plaid. What about a *Cailleach Nollaigh*? Do they do that in England?"

"What is that?" Elizabeth asked. "Is it something to eat?"

"It's a Yule log. It is carved with the face of Cailleach, the winter hag, to keep her—and the cold winter—at bay. It brings warmth and joy and luck. Iain carves it, and the face is so real, you'd swear she was among us. He is very good with his knife," Fiona said proudly. "He makes such wonderful things."

"We have Yule logs in England. The men of the household go out and find an ash tree. They take turns chopping until it falls, and then they drag it home. It's set alight on Christmas Eve and burns for the whole twelve days of Christmas," Penelope said. "It's mostly fun for the common folk and the servants." She looked at Iain with a bland smile. "As Earl of Purbrick, no one will expect you to chop down trees, Iain, or carve them. There's a woodsman for that, and a carpenter, and their assistants."

"It is a tradition I enjoy, and I believe I'll continue it. Here at Craigleith everyone participates in the Christmas preparations, not just servants and common folk. The men tie ropes to the *Cailleach Nollaigh* and pull it around the house three times before it comes inside. The children ride on the log. It is a test of strength and time of fun."

"Everyone laughs until they fall off," Fiona said, her face bright again. "We have a party in the great hall on Christmas Eve, and invite all the MacGillivrays to come. There's piping, dancing, and merriment all night," Fiona said, her eyes shining.

"We used to attend a ball at old Lord Wellbridge's estate when I was very young," Marjorie said, her tone wistful. "They played the fiddle, not the pipes, and the punch was spiked with rum. The traditions wasn't carried on after Wellbridge died, and my uncle wasn't much of a one for Christmas celebrations after his wife and son died."

"You'll enjoy the party here, Aunt Marjorie," Fiona said. "We'll teach you to dance Highland reels."

Marjorie's brows shot upward. "You dance, Fiona?" she asked in surprise.

Alanna watched the joy fade from the young woman's eyes. "I watch, mostly," she said.

"But you join in when you can," Iain said.

She looked at him with a sad smile. "When you carry me, let me stand with my feet on yours. Surely I'm too old for that this year," Fiona said, her cheeks crimson.

"And it will certainly be out of the question in England," Marjorie added.

"Fiona says it is perfectly acceptable for me to dance if a lad asks me. She says everyone dances, even if they haven't made their come out yet," Elizabeth chirped.

"Don't be ridiculous. You are three years from making your debut, Elizabeth. You will sit in the corner and keep Fiona company, along with the rest of the children, and you will go upstairs to bed when the infants retire at nine o'clock," Penelope said cruelly.

Alanna forced a laugh. "Oh, but no one sits at a Highland party or goes to bed early. Everyone dances, and no one minds the old folks with their gamey hips, or the bairns with short legs, or the lame, like me," Alanna said, looking at Fiona. "Fiona and I will dance together, hold on to one another for balance."

Fiona laughed, and Iain sent her a shadowed look of speculation.

Penelope looked horrified. "Bairns—you mean children? You let children attend the party? It should be a formal event for the quality folk, a ball. Surely the servants and common people can have their own celebration in the barn in the village, the way they do at Woodford. No, I must insist. It will be a formal affair, and Iain and I will open the festivities with a waltz. We shall hire proper musicians, too."

"No one here knows how to waltz, Penelope," Iain said flatly. "And I think you'll find the MacGillivrays are all quality folk, when you've met more of us. Donal MacGillivray has been playing the pipes for our feasts and gatherings since his father died. His father played before him, and his father before him."

"It would be a dreadful insult not to have Donal play this year," Fiona said.

"And a shame to miss the chance to hear such an esteemed piper," Alanna added.

Iain smiled at her. "As Sandy would say, Donal could squeeze tears from a stone with his laments."

Alanna felt a wave of homesickness, thought of Niall McNabb, Glenlorne's piper.

"Perhaps you'll still be with us for Christmas, Alanna," Fiona said hopefully.

"Oh, but that's many days away yet. Will you keep dear Wilfred waiting for so long?" Marjorie asked.

The mention of dear Wilfred was like a wet blanket on Alanna's merry mood.

Annie brought in the whisky and set the pitcher on the table with a thump. "It may not be a case of keeping her betrothed waiting—whether she stays or goes may have more to do with the weather. Sandy is back from visiting Jock, Iain. He says the pass through Glen Dorian is still closed, and there's more snow coming. Odd, but much of the rest of the hills are free of snow. It seems Craigleith is enduring its very own spate of bad weather."

"What does that mean?" Penelope demanded.

"It means that even though Dundrummie is less than twenty miles away, to get there we'd have to take a much longer journey around the glen to get there—nearly sixty miles," Iain explained.

"Dundrummie, is that where you came from?" Marjorie asked.

"My aunt lives there, yes, and my mother. My wedding was to have been—will be—at Dundrummie," Alanna said.

Marjorie made a moue of sympathy. "Then poor dear Wilfred is trapped there, without you?"

Alanna nodded, the movement jerky, imagining her betrothed red-faced and angry at her absence, the way he'd been when Megan had run away. Would he stay, wait for her? Her dowry was worth waiting for, at the very least. "I suppose he is," she answered Marjorie's question. "My mother and aunt will keep him company until I return."

Annie grinned at her from the doorway as she went out. "*Is blianach Nollaid gun sneachd,*" she said in Gaelic.

"And what does that mean?" Penelope asked again.

"Nothing fearsome," Alanna said. "It means Christmas without snow is poor fare."

Fiona grinned. "Then this will be a very jolly Christmas indeed."

Chapter Twenty

IT SEEMED THAT the English side of the family did not spend time with the Scottish half after the meal. Or perhaps, Alanna thought, it was because she was here, a stranger, making things awkward. Tension hummed in the air throughout the rest of the meal, and it was a relief to leave the dining room at last.

Alanna managed to walk as far as the bottom of the stairs, with Marjorie and Penelope watching her closely, as if they were assessing the severity of her injuries.

Fiona took her arm and the two of them made their way along the hall to the foot of the stairs together, chattering about Christmas. Iain followed. Alanna could feel his eyes on her back like a touch. He'd scarcely said a word at dinner.

"I'll carry you up," he said as they reached the bottom step.

"I'm quite able to manage—" Alanna began, but the look in his eyes brooked no argument. He swung her into his arms and began to climb, aware of everyone watching them.

"Perhaps if I had a cane, or a crutch—" Alanna began, but he silenced her with a look.

"The stairs are dangerous," he said. "It's no bother, if that's what worries you. Or is it something else?"

Something else? Alanna wondered what it could be. He kept his eyes on the stairs, his jaw tight.

"I'll be in the library, Iain," Penelope called after him.

"I'll say good night. I have some letters to write," Marjorie said.

Elizabeth and Fiona disappeared.

"I can walk from here," Alanna said when they reached the top step.

"As you wish, my lady." He set her down, clasped his arms behind his back, and walked by her side. "You didn't tell me you were related to half of England."

"Not quite half—a quarter at best," she quipped. He didn't smile. "Does it matter?"

"It's like entertaining royalty. We might have chosen a more impressive suite of rooms, served a more lavish meal," he said, his tone sarcastic.

"I shall remember to properly introduce myself next time I'm rescued from a storm, or be sure to carry an annotated list of my family connections in my pocket at all times, just in case," she replied tartly. "Perhaps I simply should wear a sash showing the various coats of arms. It would make an interesting conversation starter."

"At least I understand now why you're marrying an English lord—a marquess, wasn't it? It appears it's a family tradition."

She felt anger nip at her. "Said the English earl, betrothed to the English lady."

"Touché," he said softly. "But I'm not betrothed to Penelope."

Alanna felt hot blood fill her face. "I assumed that you were. I apologize." She watched a dozen emotions cross his face—guilt, pride, and a touch of fear.

"She—that is, I expect that soon . . ." He let the thought trail away. Alanna hid a smile. Could it be possible that Iain MacGillivray hadn't the courage to ask for Penelope's hand, that he was shy or nervous, or afraid she might reject him? She wouldn't—in fact, Alanna could well imagine Penelope dragging Iain McGillivray to the altar by the hair in her eagerness to marry him. She had certainly hinted broadly that Iain belonged to her, that they were soon to wed.

They had reached the door to her room—his room. She set her hand on his arm. "I'm sure Lady Penelope will welcome your proposal, my lord, be very fortunate to marry you," she said encouragingly as she looked into his eyes. He stared back at her, his eyes in shadow, his expression unreadable.

"And do you feel fortunate to be marrying your marquess?"

She dropped her gaze. "Of course," she lied. "Wilbur is very—" Her mouth moved, but no word came out to describe him. She couldn't think of one. Iain put his finger under her jaw and lifted her face, made her meet his eyes.

"I thought I heard Marjorie call him Wilfred, not Wilbur."

She swallowed. "Yes, that's right—Wilfred. Willie. Lord Merridew," she babbled, mortified at her mistake.

He looked at her for another long moment, his expression bemused. Then he smiled and stepped back, releasing his hold on her chin, as if he'd decided something, had come to a conclusion. Alanna's heart clenched. Now, she thought, he'd go down to the library, drop to one knee before Penelope, and propose. She felt jealousy flit across her nerves.

"Good night, my lady," he said, and bowed to her as if she were a queen.

She automatically dipped a curtsy. She winced at the pain in her knee, rose, and fumbled for the latch. She stood for a moment and watched him stride away from her before she scurried inside and shut the door behind her.

IAIN STOOD AT the top of the stairs. He could still go downstairs to the library, find Penelope, and propose. This time, the words wouldn't stick in his throat. He would look her in the eyes and simply . . .

It wasn't Penelope's eyes he imagined.

Still, it must be done. He stomped down the stairs. A moment was all it would take, and it would be over, the future secured. He stopped at the bottom of the steps, his hand on the wall. He stood at the junction of his home, the place where the ancient Scottish half of the castle joined the new English wing his father had added. The two sides of the hall couldn't have been more different— stone versus polished panels of oak. Comfort and luxury versus raw shelter and defense. Two worlds connected in this spot, each with its own values, its own traditions. He stood in the center of the hall, stared down the length of it toward the double doors that opened into the great hall. Halfway along, the library door stood open a crack, and warm candlelight leaked out over the cold stone floor.

He stared at the crack. Penelope was inside, waiting for him. He swallowed again and moved to stand before the door. Behind him was the door that led to the solar. He glanced at the ancient iron ring instead of a polished brass latch.

Iain reached for the iron ring, listened to the door creak open. He shut it behind him.

The solar had once been his mother's favorite sitting room. He used it as his study and for wood carving now, a workshop, since the light was good. He crossed to a wide table that stood by the windows, lit a lamp and hung it on a hook. For a moment, the light swung over the table, casting shadows, making them dance over the curled wood shavings on the surface. He lit a second lamp, set it on the table, picked up a knife and a block of wood, fragrant pine, and began to carve. The feeling of the knife biting into the wood, the act of shaping it in long, sure strokes, the warmth of it in his hands, the dry, sharp smell soothed him.

He was making a Christmas present for Fiona, an angel, and he put Penelope and proposals out of his mind for the moment, watched the angel take shape, wood shavings curling around his fingers.

"Wilbur," he muttered, flicking the curls away. He grinned down at the faceless, half-formed angel. "She was obviously running away."

But why?

Chapter Twenty-One

Duncorrie, fifteen days before Christmas

CONNOR FRASER GREETED his parents-by-marriage at the door of his cottage, welcoming them in from the cold with a broad grin. "It's a braw wee lad!" he told them, and was enveloped in his mother-in-law's joyful hug before she rushed inside to see her daughter and newborn grandson.

Jock stepped inside and unwound his plaid. "It was a fearsome journey through all the snow, but worth the trouble. Mind you, the storm doesn't seem to have reached you here. Not a day's travel from Craigleith, and there's barely a sprinkle of snow on the ground here."

"Still, it's cold enough," Connor said. "Come and meet your grandson and have a dram to warm yourself and wet the baby's head," Connor said. "Now you've come, and we've had a meal together, I'll set off to see my own kin in the morning and tell them the news."

Jock gripped his son-in-law's shoulder. "Good lad. We're not the only grandparents who'll be waiting for the news. By the way, can you take a letter, pass it on to someone heading toward Glenlorne?" Jock asked.

"A letter? Who is it you know at Glenlorne?" Connor asked, his brows rising into his dark thatch of hair.

"No one at all. It's for Laird Iain—he found a lass lost in the snow and brought her home with him. Her brother is at Glenlorne."

Connor poured two cups of whisky. In the box bed in the corner, his Isla was cooing like a contented dove over the babe with her mother. He waited while Jock admired the child, commenting on the babe's fine solid weight in his arms, and opening the blankets to count the bairn's fingers and toes, ignoring the objections of the womenfolk that the child would catch cold. May took the babe from her husband's arms, rewrapped him, and sent Jock back to Connor.

"So who is this lass? Does the laird mean to keep her?" Connor asked.

Jock sighed. "I haven't seen her, but I hear she's a lovely wee thing. Sandy MacGillivray told me Iain chased her down like a fine hind, and kept her through the night. He brought her back to Craigleith over his shoulders, wrapped in naught but his plaid and weeping into his handkerchief."

"There'll be a wedding then," Connor said, sipping his whisky.

"Or a ransom," Jock added. "Or perhaps he'll give her back if she doesn't suit him."

"I'd keep her if she's as bonnie as you say," Connor said, whispering so his wife wouldn't hear.

"That's just what I'd do," Jock agreed with a wink, and let Connor pour another measure of whisky into his cup. "Once there's a child, all will be settled right enough, and the lass will be as tame and content as a fine cow."

"As is the Highland tradition," Jock agreed. "Tradition is a fine thing, where women and cattle are concerned."

"Helps a man make sense of them both," Connor agreed. Jock's wife came to stir the stew that bubbled over the fire and sent them both a sharp look of disapproval, because that was tradition too, when it came to making sense of men and keeping them in line.

Chapter Twenty-Two

Loch Rain, fourteen days before Christmas

THERE WAS A celebration at the home of Connor Fraser's family. Even if the proud father had not brought the blessed grandchild with him to visit, the news of the babe was welcome enough.

"How big is he?" his father asked. Connor held his hands apart a good two feet and received a nod of approval.

"And so heavy we can scarcely lift him," Connor bragged. "He'll be a fine man when he's grown."

"Like his father," Connor's mother beamed at him. "Does he feed well, cry loudly?" His aunt nodded her approval of the question.

"Sounds like the bagpipes wailing across a broad glen on a clear day, and he feeds like a lusty sailor," Connor said with colorful enthusiasm. His cousin, a lad of just sixteen, looked bored.

Connor took the letter out of his pocket and nudged the lad. "I've a job for you, Farlan."

"What is it?" Connor's mother asked, snatching the letter.

"A letter that needs delivering. It's going all the way to Glenlorne, but if you could take it part of the way, to Cairnforth, maybe, then ask someone to take it on from there—" Connor knew the blacksmith at Cairnforth had a pretty daughter, and Farlan sat up eagerly.

"Aye, I'll do it," the lad said at once.

"Now who do you know at Glenlorne?" his aunt asked, setting her hands on her hips. She took the letter from his mother and read the address. "Alec McNabb? Isn't the chief called Alec? How do you know the chief of the McNabbs, Connor?"

"Och, no, not me. I'm carrying the letter as a favor for Jock MacIntosh, who promised Sandy MacGillivray he'd pass it on. There's a lass at Craigleith who's trying to get word to her kin at Glenlorne."

"A lass?" his mother asked. Everyone leaned in, even Farlan. "Is she pretty?"

"Jock says she's the loveliest lass in the Highlands," Connor said. "The Laird of Craigleith himself found her while he was out walking in the hills, stalking a fine deer for Christmas. He found her instead and fell madly in love with her. He caught her up in his plaid, gagged her with his handkerchief, and carried her home to his castle."

Connor's family stared. "Is that a true tale?" his aunt asked.

"As true as it came to my ears," Connor said.

"Maybe she's an enchantress, or Cailleach herself," Farlan said. "There's snow at Craigleith, isn't there? There's almost none here."

The womenfolk gasped. "But Cailleach's a crone."

"She could be whatever she wanted, couldn't she, if she's magical?" Farlan asked, rubbing his beardless chin.

Connor rolled his eyes and broke the spell with a laugh. "Laddie, you've been listening to too many of the *seannachaidh*'s stories. Why would an enchantress be writing letters? She'd just fly where she wanted to go, or cast a spell. Jock said she was naught but an ordinary lass."

Everyone looked disappointed. "But beautiful, you say?" Farlan asked.

"Aye," Connor said.

"*Enchantingly* beautiful? Does the laird intend to keep her? If she's not spoken for, then I might go to Craigleith, see her for myself."

Farlan's mother boxed his ears. "You'll do no such thing. You'll take the letter to Cairnforth, find someone to carry it on to Glenlorne, and you'll go this very day."

Farlan colored and rose to his feet, grumbling. "Fine, but if I find a beautiful lass in the snow on my way there, I won't be home for supper."

He stuffed the letter into his pocket, wrapped his plaid over his shoulders, and slammed the door behind him.

Chapter Twenty-Three

Craigleith Castle, thirteen days before Christmas

THE LIBRARY OF Craigleith Castle was a pleasant place to spend an afternoon, Alanna thought. The shelves were stocked with an excellent collection of books, all well read by the looks of it, which was as it should be. She had grown up with a limited supply of books, and had devoured the ones she did have over and over again. She could indulge her desire to read now, of course, and did. She hoped that Lord Merridew's home had a library.

Tired of being alone in her room, Alanna had found her own way down the stairs, moving slowly, using a fireplace poker to lean on. She felt like a crone, the Cailleach herself perhaps, hobbling over the hills and glens of Scotland on ancient bones. She'd found her way to the library, looking for company, or a book at least.

She'd found Fiona and Elizabeth sitting by the fire, sewing.

They jumped up as Alanna entered the room, and hid their work behind their backs. Then Fiona's face lit with pleasure at the sight of Craigleith's guest. "Hello. We were afraid you were Seonag. We're sewing for her new baby, for Christmas. Well, and for other folk, too. Can you sew? I mean, you needn't feel you must, but I'm woefully behind this year. I've been working on Iain's Christmas present," she said. She glanced at the door. "Did Iain carry you down?"

She was chattering nonstop, and Alanna smiled.

"No, I made my own way. My leg is feeling much better." She set her makeshift cane aside and took a place on the settee.

Elizabeth dipped a curtsy. "Good afternoon, my lady."

Alanna smiled at her. "If you call me Alanna, may I call you Elizabeth?"

Elizabeth grinned. "Yes, of course—I mean, aye, of course."

"Elizabeth wants to learn some Gaelic," Fiona said. "I've been trying to teach her."

"*Fàilte*," Elizabeth said, meaning welcome.

"*Tapadh leibh*," Alanna replied. "That means thank you. Why do you wish to learn Gaelic?"

Elizabeth sighed. "My mother says that I shall be very difficult to marry off, being plain and plump and a trifle dull-witted. I thought if I did not wed, I should like to come here, to Craigleith, and live out my days here, sewing for the clan and learning magic from Annie."

"I think you're very pretty indeed," Alanna said. "My mother says the same things to my sister Sorcha. Sorcha has freckles on her nose and unruly curls, and she prefers roaming about the hills barefooted with her skirts tucked up instead of wearing pretty clothes and sitting in the schoolroom. She's hopeless at sewing, or any of the other ladylike accomplishments my mother thinks are important—but Sorcha will grow up to be the family beauty."

"How can you tell?" Elizabeth asked, twining a blond curl around her fingertip, her blue eyes on Alanna's.

"She loves to laugh, she's kind to everyone, and she doesn't care a whit what people think of her. She just needs to grow into her looks, for the beauty is already there, inside."

"Oh," Elizabeth breathed, her eyes widening with delight. "How wonderful. Perhaps I have an inner beauty waiting to come out."

"Like a butterfly," Fiona said. "One day you'll spread your wings, step out onto the dance floor at your London debut, and dazzle everyone."

"So will you," Elizabeth said. "Maybe we can make our come-out together."

Fiona's eyes fell to her stitches and she shook her head. "I don't know," she said. "I can't dance, and my English is laughable. Penelope said so, and Aunt Marjorie says she can't understand a word I say. I can sew, but I'd hardly call a shirt for an infant a ladylike accomplishment."

Alanna felt indignation curl in her breast at the harsh criticism. "Then we shall practice. The English tutor my mother hired put pebbles in my mouth, told me to speak around them, as if they weren't there."

"Did that work?" Fiona asked.

"Not at all, though it might help with Gaelic."

The girls laughed.

"Say 'How do you do,'" she instructed Fiona.

"How d'you do?" Fiona said, adding a lilt.

"She said 'doo' instead of 'do,'" Elizabeth said.

"But she said the words as if she was genuinely glad to meet me. That will make the person she's meeting notice the sentiment, not the accent, and be pleased indeed." At least Alanna hoped that was true. Her own accent refused to yield to pebbles or hours of instruction. It remained as an underpinning to her speech, like a homespun shift under a silk ball gown.

"Oh, I see," Elizabeth said, beaming at her cousin. "It does sound charming, doesn't it? It makes one want to lean in, listen more closely."

"Is it the same for men?" Fiona asked, her brow furrowing.

She meant Iain, of course. Alanna thought of Iain's mellow voice, the soothing sound of it, comforting, sensual and rich, like warmed whisky. The familiar heat that invaded her limbs whenever she was in his presence, or even when she merely thought of him, flooded her body even now, and he was nowhere in sight. "I'm sure it is," she assured Fiona.

"You have a way with people, Alanna. Your marquess must love you very much. Is it a love match?" Elizabeth asked. "I mean, if it isn't rude of me to ask."

Alanna felt her skin prickle. "I—" She swallowed. "I am very pleased to accept your—his—proposal of marriage." She said it just the way she'd practiced it, over and over again, until there was no accent at all and she could say the words without tears, or panic threatening to choke her. She looked up, met Fiona's eyes, saw the question there, and forced a smile. "May I help with some of the sewing?"

Fiona dropped her gaze to the linen shirt in her lap. "Of course. Children are always growing out of things, or wearing them out. By the time hand-me-downs reach the littlest ones in a family, there's nothing left. My mother would make new things for the very youngest ones, give them at Christmas, so they would have something brand-new to call their own."

Alanna smiled at her kindness. "I can see the wisdom in that. I wore my older sister's castoffs when we were children, and I hated it." She had grown up in Megan's shadow, the middle child, forgotten, always second in line for clothes, attention, and affection. Now, once she married Merridew, she would outrank her sister, who was a mere countess. She would be first at last. And yet, Merridew was still a castoff—he had wanted her sister before he'd wanted Alanna. She was still less worthy than Megan, even in marriage.

She shut her eyes for a moment. She wanted something—someone—who was just for her, who wanted her above anyone else, perfect, not second best.

She swallowed the bitter thought, chose something pleasant to think about. It was Christmas. If she were at Glenlorne now, she would be helping Muira and her sisters plan Christmas surprises for the folk there, and for each other. Since she could not be there, she would help here, in the company of strangers—nay, new friends. She smiled as Fiona put a tiny garment into her hands. She looked at the careful stitches that had already been added to a little shirt. The linen was soft, had been washed in lavender and heather to make it smell sweet. She threaded the needle with blue thread instead of white and began to stitch tiny flowers around the collar.

"Oh my," Fiona said. "That's lovely. You didn't say you were so skilled."

"My tutors despair of the way I paint, and I cannot play the piano or sing. Sorcha sings like an angel, and Megan collects stories. But they can't sew. That is my talent," Alanna said proudly.

"I am quite good at knitting," Elizabeth said. "But my mother says it's a skill better suited to peasants and old women. I'm ham-handed when it comes to any delicate work."

"Would you like to knit a blanket or two?" Fiona asked. "There's some red wool in the basket."

"How festive!" Elizabeth enthused and picked up her needles. "My mother and Penelope would have fits if they knew I was knitting for ordinary folk."

"But it's charitable, and kind, and so much appreciated, especially as a gift. Why would anyone mind that?" Alanna asked.

"Oh, Mama's charitable—she directs the servants at Woodford to make up baskets for distribution to the poor."

Fiona looked at Alanna. "We tend to do it ourselves here in the Highlands. We call them handsels. I help Annie and Seonag make preserves and bake Yule cakes, and then Iain and I go out a few days before Christmas and visit everyone, take gifts, and invite the clan to the party on Christmas Eve. We see that no one wants for anything we can provide."

"It's the same at Glenlorne," Alanna murmured. "My sisters and I would pack the handsels and make the rounds in the village."

"May I help this year?" Elizabeth asked. "I would like to."

"Of course—the more hands, the lighter the work. It makes everyone happy and merry, and sets the mood for the festivities."

"It's very different, the way folk are with each other here, than it is in England, isn't it?" Elizabeth asked. "I mean, the way you treat your servants—they're more like family."

"They *are* family," Fiona said. "They're all MacGillivrays, like Iain, and me. Annie took care of me when my mother died—Iain too."

Elizabeth leaned forward. "Does she truly have magic?"

Fiona's expression turned solemn. "Aye. She saw a crown and ring in the fire even before Iain knew he'd inherited Purbrick. She saw Alanna's arrival as well."

Alanna glanced up.

"Can she tell my future, see what will happen to me?" Elizabeth asked.

"It isn't like that," Fiona said. "She sees what she sees. She doesn't tell folk bad news, or try to stop it happening unless she's sure she can."

"We have Muira McNabb at Glenlorne. She's a healer, a cook, and she sees things in the flames of the fire, or the sky, or in her own mind from time to time. We've learned to believe her, and to love her the way the MacGillivrays love Annie."

The door opened. There was a flurry of hiding half-stitched garments under cushions and in the folds of skirts, but it was only Sandy, bringing in a basket of peat. He carried it to the fire with a sober expression.

"Seonag had the bairn this morning," he said. "It's a wee lad, just as Annie said it would be, healthy and strong. Lungs like a piper."

"How wonderful!" Alanna said, and Fiona rose and kissed the old gamekeeper's weathered cheek.

Sandy sighed. "Wonderful? There won't be a moment's peace in the cottage. The wee one will be wailing all day and night. A man needs his sleep."

Fiona smiled. "You can sleep here in the castle, Sandy. There's plenty of room."

He looked at her in surprise. "What, and leave my family?"

"We'll go and visit Seonag this afternoon," Fiona said. "We'll bring some sweeties for the children. That should keep *them* quiet at least."

Sandy looked pleased. "They'll be glad of the visit. Seonag's proud of her bairns, loves 'em all. Logan too."

"No wonder you don't want to be anywhere else," Alanna said, and he looked at her with soft eyes.

"The wee lad is my fourth grandchild, and I love him well. I'll teach him to hunt if the good Lord gives me a few more years on this earth." He bid them good day and left, and the needlework resumed.

"Who'll cook now?" Elizabeth asked.

"Wee Janet, of course, and Annie and I will help," Fiona said. "If I know Seonag, she'll be back in a day or two, fussing about the Christmas baking, checking up on things, with the babe happy as a wee piglet in a basket by the stove."

"You'll help out, in the kitchen?" Elizabeth said to her cousin. "Mama would be horrified!"

"Then we shan't tell her," Fiona said. She looked at Alanna. "Are things truly so different in England, people so separate from one another?"

"So I've been told," Alanna said.

"But you'll be a marchioness. Surely you'll be able to do things just as you wish," Fiona said.

"I will do as my husband directs." She'd been told that, too. An English wife, even a marchioness, was obedient and uncomplaining. She did as her husband thought best in all things without argument or demur. Alanna was already sure she'd burst if she could not express an opinion, make her own decisions on things. Would he choose her clothes, her friends, her books?

"I wonder how many times a day a marchioness must change her clothes. Mama says it's at least four times for a countess," Elizabeth said. "More, if there's a busy schedule on a given day."

"What does a countess—or a marchioness—do all day?" Fiona asked. "Especially if the servants do everything for her?"

The girls looked at Alanna. Her mouth dried. "Well, as it's been described to me, I shall confer with the housekeeper each morning, discuss my schedule of activities, advise her what my . . . h-husband . . . is doing that day, and approve her menus for luncheon and dinner. The cook, of course, will already know what his lordship likes to eat, and there will be little reason to make changes to her suggestions. I shall write letters in the morning, or read. I shall take lunch, then stroll the grounds or ride out a short distance with a groom if I am in the country, or take a carriage ride through the park if I am in London. Then I shall pay calls, or wait for others to call on me. I will rest before supper, and dress for whatever the evening plans are—a ball, or party, or a trip to the theater, then bed, then up the next day to do it all again." Even as she recited the expected agenda of her days, she didn't think she could bear it. Once she conceived Merridew's heir, she would retire to the country to await the birth. The cycle would continue the same way year in and year out.

"The parties sound like fun," Elizabeth said. "Penelope made her debut last year. She was out dancing every night and slept half the day away. We were called home, of course, when my great-uncle took sick, and Penelope was furious that her Season had to be interrupted. Now she'll be married by the start of next Season, of course, and her flirting days will be over."

"Doesn't she want to marry my brother?" Fiona asked, her lips pinched. "She'll not find a better man, no matter how much she flirts."

Elizabeth concentrated on her stitches. "Maybe not, but if she had a bigger dowry—or any dowry at all— she'd have her choice of any man she wanted, earls, marquesses . . . even dukes."

Alanna kept her eyes on her work.

"What about love?" Fiona asked. "Doesn't she want to fall in love?"

Elizabeth giggled. "Mama says love has nothing to do with marriage. Marriage is about position, and power, and security—especially security, if you're a woman."

"It's different here in Scotland, then," Fiona said and looked at Alanna. "Do you love your marquess, Alanna? You never said." She asked the dreaded question again.

Alanna's tongue knotted itself around her tonsils, and the familiar lump of dread filled her chest. "I—" She paused, thinking carefully. "I understand he is a fine gentleman, much admired in England, and I have hopes—"

Fiona's jaw dropped. "You don't love him?"

"I do," Alanna managed. "I mean, I will, I'm sure." She stabbed her finger with the needle, winced, and sucked the digit. She would try, at least, to love him. She was certain he did not love her. She was merely a convenient substitute for her sister. Had he loved Megan?

"My mother loved my father. He loved her so much that he changed his name to MacGillivray for her so her father would allow him to wed her, and he promised to live in Scotland forever, and that his children would bear the MacGillivray name. I should like to be loved like that," Fiona mused.

Alanna suppressed a sigh. So would she—oh, so would she. Longing filled her, and her toes curled in her shoes. Iain MacGillivray's face came to mind, standing by the fire, wrapped in nothing more than her cloak. She shifted, winced at the twinge in her injured knee.

"Are you in pain?" Fiona asked at once. "Shall I fetch Annie—or Iain?"

"No." Alanna set aside her needlework and rose, giving

the girls a brave smile. "I'm just tired. I think I'll go and rest for a little while."

IAIN FROWNED AT the carving in his hands. The angel was beautiful, the lines of her body and her gown were graceful and elegant. Her wings curved softly over her head.

It was the face he was having trouble with. The expression was sweet, ethereal, and angelic indeed, but it was Alanna's face, the way she'd looked when he found her in the snow under a halo of frost. It hadn't been what he'd intended. He stared at the features that had appeared as if by magic under the delicate strokes of his knife.

There'd be questions asked if he gave this Alanna-angel to Fiona at Christmas. Why hadn't Penelope's face appeared under his knife, or Fiona's own lovely features, or even their mother's face? This angel's distinct features could not be mistaken for any other woman's. It was Alanna. He wrapped the figure in a cloth and opened a drawer. Then he put the little angel inside, took another block of wood, and began again.

ALANNA RETRIEVED THE fireplace poker and made her way across the library slowly, gently refusing offers of assistance from the girls. Surely walking would help her heal, allow her to regain her strength. She must go back to Dundrummie, face her responsibilities, prepare to travel to her new home in Kent. She could not stay here at Craigleith.

She reached the door, gave Elizabeth and Fiona a smile as she went through it. She shut it behind her and leaned on it a moment, catching her breath.

A door opened across the hall and Iain emerged. For a moment they stood and stared at each other. He took in the fireplace poker and frowned. She noted the wood shavings in his hair and the fragrance of pine that clung to him. He smelled like Christmas, and she smiled faintly.

"I hope that poker isn't a weapon," he said.

She raised her chin. "I'll have you know it's not a poker at all. It's my walking stick, and I am doing very well with it. My leg is almost healed. I shall be ready to dance a gay Highland reel by Christmas Eve."

He rubbed his chin thoughtfully. "Well, if it's a walking stick you need, I have a better one than that," he said. He opened the door at his back again, then took her arm and escorted her into the space beyond.

Alanna looked at the well-worn table covered with curls of wood and sawdust. It smelled sweet in this room, warm. A half-carved angel stood on the bench, and she limped across to pick it up. Only one wing and the rough shape of her arm and gown had emerged from the wood. The lines were fluid and graceful, the shape lovely. The face was still a blank flat plane. "Did you make this?" she asked in surprise.

He moved to stand next to her, looking down at the carving in her hands. "It's a Christmas present for Fiona. I make her one every year. Not always an angel—I made dolls for her when she was a child, and wooden animals."

"How wonderful," she said, running her fingers over the warmth of the wood.

"She couldn't run with the other children, you see. So I carved friends for her out of wood, playmates to pass the days."

She regarded him carefully, but his eyes were on the angel, his expression soft.

"She's very lucky," Alanna said.

"Is she?" he asked. "How will she fare in England? She's too old for toys now."

"She worries about you as well," Alanna said. He met her eyes.

"And do you worry for yourself?"

She set the angel down. "You and Fiona will have each other," she said. "I daresay I shall manage."

He leaned on the bench and folded his arms. He had sawdust in his hair, she noticed, and she curled her fingers against a longing to brush it away. "You said that perfectly, my lady marchioness, in flawless English—'I daresay I shall manage.' I have no doubt you will. You will, of course, have your marquess." His expression was slightly admiring, as if he thought she was brave, ready, capable of facing an unknown future. She tried to feel as brave as she apparently looked, but she felt bitterness fill her mouth, part fear, part regret. She changed the subject.

"I liked to receive books for Christmas when I was little. My mother despaired that so much reading would make me cross-eyed."

"It didn't," he said, looking into her eyes.

She lowered her lashes. "It will be a very different Christmas this year," she said. "And from now on, as well."

"It will indeed," he agreed soberly.

"Oh, but it needn't be so different next year. You could introduce a few Scottish customs in your new home. No one would dare to refuse you, my lord earl."

He regarded her with a slight frown. "Do you think it will truly be that easy? Will your husband—the marquess—allow you to make changes?"

She had no idea. "I . . . don't know. But Penelope will surely—"

He took a step closer, picked up her hand. "Are you afraid, Alanna?" he asked.

She scanned his face, wondered for a moment what he meant—Marriage? England? Being in charge of her husband's home? Yes, to all those. She swallowed and nodded. "Are you?"

"Deathly," he murmured. She squeezed his fingers. His hand was warm, safe, familiar.

"I wish—" she began, and stopped. What did she wish? That she could marry Iain instead? That was impossible. She had spent hours daydreaming about her own future, wishing then, too, for a home, love, a husband like Iain. Instead, Merridew awaited her.

He brushed her hair back from her brow, his fingers soft on her skin. He let them linger on her cheek. "You're beautiful, Alanna," he said.

She read the admiration in his eyes, and something more—longing perhaps, a wish like her own that things could be different than they were, that the future held something better, something hopeful and bright instead of fearful.

She looked at Iain's mouth and wondered what it would

be like to kiss him. Would it be wrong to do that now, just to see how it felt to kiss a man you admired, desired, before she was forbidden from kissing anyone at all besides Lord Merridew?

She didn't hesitate. She threw herself into his arms, her mouth mashing against his. She did not have very much experience with kisses. None, really. Iain made a sound of surprise as her lips bumped his, and he gripped her shoulders. Then his mouth softened against hers, and his arms came around her, pulled her tight against his chest, and he kissed her back. Awareness shot through her body, made her tingle everywhere. Was it always this way between a man and a woman? Would Merridew's touch do this to her? She felt as if bubbles were coursing through her veins, popping in the most remarkable places, her nipples, low in her belly.

She wanted more, made a soft sound in her throat, need and demand, and he obliged. His thumb pressed gently on her chin, opening her mouth. His tongue stroked the inner surface of her lower lip, and she gasped at the delicious intimacy of that. He slanted his mouth over hers, thrust his tongue deeper, and she felt a moment's surprise. Was this how kisses worked? She liked it. Very much. She wrapped her arms around his neck, tangled her fingers in the silk of his hair, let her tongue meet his, pressing closer. She stood on her toes, her breasts pressed against the hard muscles of his chest, his arms enfolding her, surrounding her. She moved her hips, shifted them a little against his body, wanting—
He pulled back.

"We should stop," he said, breathless.

She looked into his eyes. The gray was gone, subsumed into the black. He was breathing hard, and she could feel his heart beating against hers. He leaned forward, laid his forehead on hers, his eyes closed, stroking her hair with shaking hands. She tried to kiss him again, to press her mouth to his again, but he caught her arms, untangled her, stepped back. "God, Alanna—" He moved to the other side of the table. "I didn't bring you here for that," he said, "but damned if I can remember now why we came in here."

Alanna clasped her hands. "I apologize," she said. "I kissed you. I didn't intend to." But she didn't truly regret it. Then she remembered that he was betrothed—or almost—to Penelope, and she belonged to Merridew. Hot color filled her face. He must wonder what kind of wanton, wicked, dangerous creature he'd let into his home. She turned away, moved toward the door.

"Wait." He stopped her as her hand closed on the latch. "A walking stick. That's what I meant to find. I was making one for old Ewan MacGillivray, but I didn't finish it in time. It was his cottage we stayed in, the night of the storm." Alanna felt her cheeks grow warmer still. Her heart still pounded against her ribs, her lips tingling, the taste of him on her tongue. She watched as he searched the shelves, cool and unaffected. He found the stick and held it out to her with a smile. She took it from him and felt the jolt of awareness, of desire, as their fingers touched. She heard his sharp intake of breath. Not quite so unaffected, then.

"Thank you," she said, moving her fingers away from

his, closing her hand on the wood. She concentrated on looking at it, not really seeing it, all too aware that he stood before her, close enough to kiss again. She couldn't move, nor did he. Instead she waited. Would *he* kiss *her* this time? Her mouth watered.

"Do you need help going up the stairs?" he asked at last, his tone flat, calm, and she imagined how it would feel if he carried her now, after the kiss.

"No," she said quickly. "I can manage. Thank you for the stick."

She turned and fled, going through the door as quickly as she was able, racing down the hall and up the steps as fast as her wounded knee would allow, more afraid that he would *not* chase her than that he would.

She reached the sanctuary of her room and shut the door firmly. She was surrounded by his presence here, his belongings, his scent. Her breath caught in her throat, and sharp longing shot through her body. She pressed her hand to her lips.

She'd kissed him, and he'd kissed her back.

Now she knew how it felt to kiss a man you admired.

It hadn't made it better. It made it worse.

Chapter Twenty-Four

IAIN LEANED ON the bench and stared at the door after Alanna left. He'd kissed her.

He shouldn't have. She belonged to someone else, and he hadn't the right. Actually, she'd kissed him. He grinned. He'd been surprised when her mouth met his. It had been an unskilled kiss, a first kiss.

He licked his lips, tasted her still. He paced the room, hard as a bloody pole, wanting nothing more than to go after her, throw open the door to his room—her room—and do it again. This time, he wouldn't stop.

The door opened, and he looked up eagerly, his heart rising, expecting, hoping it was Alanna.

It was Penelope. She stepped inside and looked around the room. If she'd arrived five minutes earlier, she'd have found Alanna here, in his arms. He swallowed and ran his hand through his hair, dislodged sawdust, wondered if she'd seen Alanna leaving.

Penelope made a face and stepped back. "You're covered in dust! Whatever are you doing? You poor man—

you won't have to clean stables or chop wood or rescue wayward peasants at Woodford."

He held up a hand to stop the familiar insistence that he would be idle, unnecessary. "So you've said—there are servants for that. But like working with my own horses, and I'm carving a Christmas gift for my sister. No servant can do that. And Alanna—*Lady* Alanna—is hardly a wayward peasant." *She was an angel.*

Her eyes lit. "Presents? Are you making me one?"

He swallowed. He hadn't considered it. "Of course."

She came forward eagerly, her eyes flirtatious, intimate. She laid her hand on his arm, crowded closer. "What is it? May I see? I promise to act surprised."

He forced himself to stay where he was and not move away, pasted on a smile he didn't feel. He should touch her, cover her hand with his, *kiss her,* but he found he could not. "That's not how Christmas works," he murmured. "The surprise is better if it's not feigned."

"Oh, but I'm a very good actress," she said and stepped closer still, batting her lashes at him. Her eyes were as blue as the loch at high summer, her perfume heady and sweet. He stared down at her and realized to his horror that her eyes had closed. She was rising on her toes, her lips puckering.

He ducked.

He couldn't kiss her now. Not after kissing Alanna. Penelope nearly fell on her face as he moved out of reach, and she gripped the edge of the table to steady herself, stared at him in disbelief. He snatched up the half-finished carving, the one Alanna had admired minutes ago, and held it out to Penelope. "This is what I'm making for Fiona. What do you think?"

Her lips were still puckered—pinched, really, and her eyes had darkened now—the loch before a storm. She let her gaze fall on the figurine, but she made no move to touch it.

"That's it? Well. I hope you're going to give me something more interesting. At Woodford, I have a collection of rare porcelain dogs. Wood is so—well . . ." She let the thought trail off.

"Then what would you like for your Christmas gift?" he asked, and he could have bitten his tongue in two.

She laid a finger on her chin and raised her eyes to the rafters. "I don't know. I will inherit the Purbrick jewels when—if—we marry. Are there any MacGillivray jewels?"

He had his mother's wedding band, and her betrothal ring, set with an amber cairngorm in gold. It was simple, and Scottish in design. He tried to imagine slipping that ring onto Penelope's finger.

"No," he said. "No jewels. My father wanted to buy a necklace for my mother one Christmas, went all the way to Edinburgh for it, but she chose to purchase books for the library instead. He gave her books every Christmas after that, because that's what made her happy." He recalled in that moment that Alanna had said books had always been her favorite Christmas present as well.

Penelope recoiled, as if she feared there was insanity on his side of the family tree. "How very odd," she managed. "I suppose all those books are at least good for Fiona, being unable to walk properly or dance, or hope for—"

He scowled at her, and she had the grace to stop talking. She blushed. "I mean, she's very sweet, but that limp . . ."

Alanna called his sister brave, charming. She saw beyond Fiona's infirmity. Penelope hadn't even looked. He felt anger burn through his chest, checked it. Instead, he crossed to the door and opened it. "If you'll excuse me, I have things to see to," he said firmly, waiting for her to go.

She hesitated. "Oh, but I came to ask you what you wanted for Christmas. There's a mere fortnight left before Christmas Eve."

What did he want? *A way out.* He shut his eyes. "There's nothing I need."

She sauntered toward him, smiling seductively. There was a long curl of planed wood clinging to the fringe of her shawl. "But what do you *want*?" she asked, her voice an octave lower.

Iain swallowed. Now was the moment—he only had to say, *You. I want you to marry me, and be my countess.* He took a deep breath, clenched the door latch tighter, and licked his lips before speaking.

But he could still taste Alanna's kiss. He ran his hand through his hair, smelled her heather-scented soap on his hands. He closed his mouth with a snap. Penelope tilted her head expectantly, raised her eyebrows, blinked at him, wordlessly giving him permission.

He couldn't.

"I must go," he said and left the room, leaving Penelope standing by the table, knowing she was staring after him in disbelief. He didn't stop until he reached the stable and the quiet, undemanding presence of the horses.

PENELOPE STARED AT the doorway. What the devil was wrong with the man? "Books, instead of jewels?" she said to the empty room. "How ridiculous." Iain would not find her so easy to please. One could not dazzle a man with a book. A book did not reflect the sparkle of diamonds and sapphires in a woman's eyes. She could not walk into a room and draw the envious stares of every person there with a *book*. If he gave her a book for Christmas, she'd use it to hit him over the head and knock some sense into him.

What *would* he give her for Christmas? She had promised to act surprised. She looked around the room. The stone walls radiated chill, and she drew her shawl tighter. Aside from the carving bench lined with knives and saws, blocks of wood and wood shavings, there was nothing to see. Penelope noticed the drawer and smiled. Of course. He'd hide his gift if he wanted it to be a surprise. Just a little look couldn't hurt, could it? It would make it easier to feign anticipation and delight if she knew. She opened the drawer, saw the little linen-wrapped bundle.

She held her breath and unwrapped it.

Chapter Twenty-Five

ANNIE WATCHED THE laird stride through the kitchen without a word to anyone, heading toward the stable. She exchanged a look with Wee Janet. "The laird's in a hurry," Janet said.

"Aye," Annie replied, turning back to cutting carrots. Iain had fled to the stable the night his father died, when he was a boy. She'd found him curled up in the hay, pretending not to cry. He'd gone there after Fiona's accident as well. He would stand in the shadows amid the peaceable company of the garrons and the milk cow and think—or worry. Not that he shared his thoughts with Annie or anyone else—he was a quiet man who kept his own counsel. And he had a lot to think about. Annie sniffed the air as he passed. Heather. The Sassenach wore lavender.

She stared at the doorway and smiled.

"What are you grinning at, Annie?" Wee Janet asked.

"The cat," Annie murmured. "And the pigeon."

"The cat's outside somewhere, isn't she?"

"She's wherever Iain is, I'm thinking," Annie replied, tapping her forehead, and she smiled again.

Chapter Twenty-Six

ALANNA SAT BY the window of her room and stared out across the moor. The world was tucked up under a fine thick feather quilt, white satin embroidered with the tracks of rabbits, the bold black lines of the bare trees. Their bony branches pointed accusingly at the sky and the mountains, blaming them for the snow. The tops of the distant hills kept their noses in the air, remained aloof, gray and proud against the clouds, daring them to shake down more snow, to just try and bury them if they thought they could.

She could see the barn and byre, and the cluster of houses that formed the village, just down the hill from the castle.

She was trying to read, but the words kept dissolving on the page, and all she saw was Iain's face. Her lips still buzzed from the kiss they'd shared. It had been a very nice kiss, memorable indeed. It would be the kiss against which she measured all other kisses. She forced her thoughts away from that idea. Her hand, her kisses, her body, belonged to the Marquess of Merridew. Had it been only five days since she'd left Dundrummie? It felt as if she'd been away for a lifetime, had come to another world, another time, where Merridew didn't exist.

But he did, and he was waiting for her. If she had not gone out for that walk, gotten caught in the storm, she would be travelling through England at this very moment with her new husband, on her way to spend Christmas with her esteemed in-laws, the Duke and Duchess of Lyall. They'd be complete strangers to her, and she to them. Her heart lurched. Christmas shouldn't be spent among strangers. She'd have Merridew—would he feel like less of a stranger after they had consummated their marriage? She repressed a shudder. But she had made a promise, she reminded herself again.

A knock at the door surprised her, and she stared at the panels for a moment before she bade her visitor enter. What if it was Iain? What if he wanted to kiss her again? She would not—should not. Not again. "Come in," she said, her voice husky. She put a hand to her hair, smoothed a wayward strand back behind her ear, and bit her lip.

Penelope opened the door and, as usual, swept the room with a suspicious glance before she entered, as if she hoped to catch Alanna doing something she shouldn't be.

Like kissing Iain MacGillivray. Alanna felt her cheeks heat. This time, she was indeed guilty. She resisted putting her hand to her lips. Was it possible to look at a woman and know she'd been kissing a man? She got to her feet and dipped a curtsy, ignoring the pull of pain from her knee. "Good afternoon, Lady Penelope."

Penelope blinked at her, her eyes narrow. "I was wondering if you'd heard from your family as yet—or Lord Merridew."

Alanna swallowed. "No, not yet."

"Surely you're anxious to leave this place, go home, marry him." She clenched her teeth on the last word, spat it out like a curse.

Did she know about the kiss? Alanna clutched the book against her chest and wondered if she should apologize. What would she say, that it had been a mistake? Not to her.

Penelope's eyes fell on the book. "You're reading a book," she said, making it an accusation. "I suppose you love books."

"Very much. This is poetry. Robert Burns. Have you read his poems?"

Penelope's expression stayed hard, and she ignored the question. She folded her arms over her lush breasts. "Tell me, if you had to choose a Christmas present, would you choose jewels or books?"

Alanna swallowed. Was this a test? As Marchioness of Merridew, she could have both, she supposed. She wouldn't have to choose. "I think—" She looked at Penelope, noted the fine wool of her gown, blue, to match her eyes, and the expensive cashmere shawl, embroidered with summer roses—and noticed the delicate curl of the wood shaving hanging from the fringe, like a decoration, or a signal. Alanna felt her stomach knot. Had Penelope been in the solar before or after her? Had Iain kissed her as well?

"Books or jewels?" Penelope asked again.

"Um—books," she said, wishing she were in the library at Glenlorne, curled up in her favorite chair by the fire, safe, where the only adventures were the ones written on the pages.

Penelope's face bloomed redder than any rose, and she unfolded her arms. For a moment, Alanna wondered if Iain's cousin meant to hit her, but Penelope's manicured hands clenched at her waist instead. "I'd choose jewels. Diamonds, rubies, sapphires . . . even if one is disappointed in love, the jewels never lose their sparkle, do they?" She stroked her skin, as if the jewels already lay upon her white bosom.

"I suppose not," Alanna murmured.

"Do you have a betrothal ring from Lord Merridew?" Penelope asked.

Alanna stared at the curl of wood. It would fit perfectly around a lady's finger. "Um, no. He was to bring it with him to the wedding, present it to me the night before we married. I suppose it's at Dundrummie."

Penelope stretched her naked left hand before her, stared at it, and smiled. "The MacGillivray betrothal ring has a sapphire as big as a pigeon's egg. It's too heavy to wear every day, of course, so I keep it locked away. I shall wear it at Christmas, let everyone see it." Her eyes glowed. "It will be official then, and everyone will know."

Alanna's chest tightened. So Iain had asked Penelope to marry him. Her heart dropped to her ankles even as she forced herself to smile. It made her jaw hurt. "I'm sure it's a lovely ring indeed," she managed. "You'll make a beautiful bride," she added, parroting the words she'd heard so often from her mother, her aunt, the seamstress, and every other person at Dundrummie. Their smiles hadn't reached their eyes. No one at all expected her to be truly happy, it seemed.

"Thank you." Penelope preened like a contented cat, full of cream. "Now, we should see what we can do to get you back to your own groom for your own wedding as quickly as possible. You'll be his Christmas present, safe and sound."

Christmas had always been Alanna's favorite time of year. She suddenly wished that her wedding could have been at any other time of year.

She felt more like Merridew's Christmas dinner than his present.

Chapter Twenty-Seven

Twelve days before Christmas

ANNIE STARED INTO the embers of the fire and blew on them. She watched the banked fire open a sleepy red eye and glare back at her, awaiting her bidding. It was after midnight, and the kitchen was quiet and empty.

Annie was gathering herbs for Seonag's new bairn—elderflower and holly, to be made into a tisane to wash the child, to ensure protection from evil. She tied bundles of hawthorn and mulberry leaf together too, to place in the wee one's cradle to ward off sorrow. It was a happy task.

In a few days, she would begin to gather the herbs she needed for *Nollaig Beag,* blend them, and brew potions to make folk merry on Christmas Eve—meadowsweet to steep in wine, elfwort to add fragrance to the fire and bring joy and love.

Her hands hovered over the rows of pots and jars, and she wondered if she'd need extra holly and ivy, for purposes other than decoration. That was up to Iain, of course. Holly crowned a bridegroom, and ivy his bride. To hear the Sassenach ladies talk, Iain would be betrothed to Lady Penelope by Christmas.

Or not.

She thought of Alanna McNabb, one of their own, a Highland lass, gentle, kind, and lost. Annie's hand moved on along the row. Perhaps mistletoe, to encourage kisses, or lavender, to draw her true love to her side—whichever man she was fated to wed—and bring joy, peace, and healing. She liked the lass but dared not meddle in things that fate had already decided. Still, when Annie thought of how Iain looked at Alanna, and how she looked back at him, her heart swelled.

Her fingers dipped into a pot of cedar. She crushed it between her palms, inhaled the bright, earthen scent. Still, she hesitated as she stood before the fire. Cedar enhanced the sight. If she dared, she could look into the flames, see what lay in store for Iain.

She made a soft sound and put the cedar back into the pot. She must not cast spells, especially love spells, now. What if they went wrong? It could be that the fates intended for Iain to wed Penelope, and for Alanna to wed her Sassenach lord.

She frowned. But why bring them together, and set the cat among the pigeons now, if that was so? She pursed her lips and reached for the cedar again, gathered several other herbs too, and crouched beside the fire. It wouldn't hurt to take a wee look. Iain's fate would touch everyone at Craigleith, after all. "His happiness is our own, and our joy is his," she murmured, meeting the flames eye to eye.

She opened the first jar and tossed a handful of twigs and leaves onto the fire. "Cedar, for clear sight," she murmured. The flames leaped. She opened another pot. "Juniper, to attract love to this place." She added mistletoe next. "To strengthen magic." If, of course, magic was at work here. She considered the pot of starwort and shook her head. It was for the most potent love spells and might not be needed. Yet. Fiona and her English cousin had perhaps already begun things with their silly love spell. Annie had no doubt that at the very least they had managed to call down snow from a clear sky, and that snow had brought Alanna McNabb to Craigleith in Iain's arms. What was next, what awaited Iain?

She cocked her head and watched as the flames digested the herbs, waited for a sign. What was it the lasses had said? *Show me my true love, send him to me by Christmas.* She murmured the words now, but the flames burned sedately, calmly, guarding their secrets. "Come now," Annie coaxed. "You can do better than that."

The door of the kitchen burst open, hit the wall with a bang that shattered the silence. Annie spun, her hand on her heart.

Alanna stood there, out of breath, leaning on her walking stick, her eyes filled with panic.

"Annie—there's fire in the village. The barn is ablaze," she said. "Sandy came upstairs to Iain's room to wake him. I sent him up to the tower."

Iain was right behind her, still pulling on his clothes. His shirt was half buttoned, and he was pushing his arms into his coat. "There's a fire," he repeated through grim lips. He glanced at Alanna before he looked at Annie. "You'll stay here," he ordered tersely, and dove through the door, letting in a gasp of cold wind.

Annie stared after him. "I'll get blankets ready," she

murmured, feeling dread fill her breast. They'd need bandages too, if there were burns, shrouds if it was worse. She glanced at the fire and frowned. The omens hadn't shown her this, or she'd mistaken the signs, had been looking in another direction. She ran a hand over her wrinkled cheek, felt the ache of age and fear in her bones. She saw—or imagined—the worst, people burned or killed, animals lost, the harvest stores gone.

Alanna was reaching for a cloak, her eyes wide, her expression determined. She stuffed her bare feet into a pair of heavy boots that sat by the door. "I'll go and help," she said and hurried out, limping. Annie didn't stop her. For a moment she couldn't move.

Sandy stumbled into the room, his face white and drawn. There were smudges of soot on his hands and clothes, a burn on his wrist. Annie took his hand, looked at the injury. "What happened?" she asked.

Sandy shook his head, and she watched his face crumple. It was bad, then. Very bad indeed. Her heart crumpled in her breast. "I didn't mean any harm," Sandy said, his voice thin with age and shock. "It's the bairn—he cries at night, keeps me awake. I only wanted some peace and quiet. I went to sleep in the barn, and I fell asleep with the lantern burning—" He grimaced, but squared his shoulders. "I got the beasts out, at least, and sounded the alarm. Then I came to get Iain."

"You old fool," Annie muttered. "You old fool."

Chapter Twenty-Eight

THE ORANGE GLOW climbed into the starless sky, pushing back the night. Iain urged the garron toward the village, his heart in his throat. Sandy had shaken him awake where he'd finally fallen asleep, sitting in a chair in the library, a book in his hands. He'd paced the floor of the tower for hours, unable to rest, then prowled the castle. He'd been thinking of Alanna, her kiss, her body, her face, until he was half mad with longing. He'd stood in the hall outside her door, considering what might happen if he opened it, went inside.

If he'd been in the tower, or the solar, or his own bloody bed, he would have seen the flames. It had taken Sandy precious minutes to find him. Now, he could see by the height of the flames that there was no way to stave off disaster.

The villagers—MacGillivrays, MacIntoshes, and Frasers, men, women, and children—were watching for him to arrive. They came running toward him through the smoke, half dressed, panicked, with soot on their faces.

The garron skittered, fearful of the rush of bodies and the roar of the flames, so Iain slid off the creature's back and looked around.

His heart sank as he took in the situation. It wasn't just the barn—the wind had driven the hungry sparks toward the cottages too, where they burrowed into the thatch, took root, and flared to life, until the fire was devouring all in its path. Four cotts were already aflame, and the rest were in danger of catching as well.

The barn was a birdcage of blazing timber, lost. He looked around for anything that might have been saved, sacks of grain or barrels of salted meat, but there was nothing. At least the cattle were out, and the sheep. They stood in the shadows, bawling at the smoke and heat, their eyes rolling white in their heads. Dogs circled the flock, barking, adding to the mayhem.

Women stood in the snow, bewildered and numb with shock. Children were crying, babies wailing. Iain counted the faces, identified who was here, and who was not. Logan was here, and Seonag and the children. Her newborn babe was bound against her breast, and the others clung to her skirts. Old Lottie had her hand to her mouth, and the fire lit the tracks of tears on her cheeks as she watched the home she'd lived in all her life burn.

"What do we do first, Laird?" Logan asked. "The barn—"

Iain shook his head. "It's too late. Soak the cottages," he said to the men struggling to draw water out of the well, directing them toward the houses, away from the barn. The heat was all but unbearable. He looked at the frozen loch, cursed the cold. "Chop a hole in the ice," he ordered. "Find more buckets." Folk rushed to obey, less fearful now they had something to do, a purpose, a leader.

Screams rose as the barn caved in, and Iain spun to watch as great timbers that had stood for centuries were now defeated by the flames. He heard sobs, prayers, and curses in Gaelic. It could not be helped. He slithered down the icy bank to the loch, grabbed a bucket, filled it, handed it off, took another and filled that too, and carried it to the nearest cottage, soaking the thatch, returning for more. His clansmen followed, copied him.

He caught sight of a red cloak, a frail figure standing in the shadows, watching as the flames devoured Lottie's cottage. *Alanna?* He felt a moment of fear and then fury as he strode toward her. She shouldn't be here. Did she think he'd rescue her again, save her from fire the way he'd saved her from ice? With her injured leg, she could easily trip, fall, suffer burns, or worse. He muttered a curse. He hadn't time to see to her. He had a score of others to see safe and warm. He gripped her shoulder.

"Alanna, what are you doing here? Go back to the castle, and—" He turned her to face him and looked down into Lottie MacGillivray's white face, and at the faces of her grandchildren, all wrapped in Alanna's red cloak.

"The lass gave us her cloak, Laird, and went to help Seonag," Lottie said, pointing toward one of the burning cottages.

Iain swallowed. "Take the garron, Lottie, put as many bairns as he'll carry on his back, and go up to the castle," Iain ordered, and moved toward the cottage. He found

Seonag crouched in the lee of a stone wall, her wailing babe cradled tight against her breast, her other children clustered beside her. They looked up at him with wide eyes, shivering. He took off his coat and wrapped it around them. "Where's Alanna?" he asked. "Lottie said she was here."

"She was," Seonag said. "She helped me carry the children here." Seonag turned and counted her brood once more, touching each dark head, drawing them closer to her body and the scant protection of the wall.

She wasn't here now. Fear gripped him. "Go up to the castle with Lottie, Seonag, get the bairns indoors," he ordered. "Which way did Alanna go?"

Seonag shook her head, tears in her eyes. "I don't know. She made sure we were safe, and went to help."

How could a wee slip of a lass like Alanna, an injured one at that, help? What the devil was she thinking? Iain looked around him, searching for her.

But Alanna McNabb was nowhere to be seen.

ALANNA'S HEART CLIMBED into her throat as she looked around at the devastating fire. Smoke rolled across the snow like long claws, creating macabre shadows.

Folk screamed and prayed. Alanna had given her cloak to an old woman, but there were so many more who needed help. She could see Iain moving among his people. He'd taken charge, was everywhere at once, helping put the fires out, and doing his best to prevent any more cottages from catching fire. But the wind fanned the flames, pushed them onward, and above her, the sky thickened with more snow.

There were people in the cotts still, despite the danger, unsure and afraid to leave their homes. They had to. She knew that, had seen the devastation of fire before.

She helped Seonag with her bairns, led them to a place of shelter, out of the wind and safe from the flames. A mother only had two hands, and one was wrapped around the newborn child. Alanna gave her hands to the others, and they clung to her, let her lead them, see them safe. "Thank you, my lady," Seonag said. "Your poor leg—"

Alanna gritted her teeth and ignored the ache in her knee. It wasn't so bad. The cold numbed it, and she needed two good legs now, and wits, and courage. She remembered a fire at Glenlorne, a single cottage only, but no one inside had woken until it was too late. She looked around. Four—no, five now—cottages were burning, while a sixth smoldered, on the brink of falling prey to the flames. The folks passing buckets from hand to hand had not yet noticed. She grabbed a bucket, filled it, and hobbled toward the cott. She threw the water at the flames with a growl, heard the fire hiss as she slowed it, injured it.

She heard a warbling cry, a thick grunt. Someone was still inside. Alanna's heart climbed into her throat. She went to the door, threw it open.

"Hello?" The room was filling with smoke, even if the flames had not yet appeared. It was a matter of minutes.

"Here!"

Alanna scanned the room, saw an old man on his knees,

his arms around a prone figure wrapped in a blanket. He looked up at her, his eyes streaming in the smoke.

"It's my Nessa—she won't budge," he said with tears in his eyes. "She doesn't like the cold and won't go outside."

Alanna pictured the ancient man's ancient wife, stubborn and fearful, refusing to leave her home, unwilling to admit that tragedy was about to strike. "We've got to convince her," Alanna said.

"Och, she's as stubborn as any woman. Help me put a rope around her flanks," the old man said.

Alanna gaped. A rope? She blinked, trying to see the woman through the smoke. The figure under the blanket grunted rudely.

"Nessa?" Alanna knelt, laid a hand on her broad back. "We must go. Your cott is on fire."

Nessa squealed a wordless objection. "Now, Nessa, don't be difficult. 'Tis time to go," the old man said.

He handed Alanna the end of a rope and drew back the blanket.

Alanna stared. A very large pig lay on the floor, panting unhappily. The creature regarded Alanna with a baleful glare and refused to budge.

"She won't do a thing if she doesn't know ye, lass," the man said. "You'd best introduce yourself."

Alanna cast a quick glance at the back corner of the room, where the smoke was thickest, and growing thicker still. Even now, hot sparks were eating their way through the thatch, looking for a way in. There was little time. She looked at the old man and saw tears in his eyes. "We have to go," she said urgently.

He shook his head. "I can't leave without Nessa."

Alanna swallowed. He'd die if he stayed, and so would the pig. She turned to the creature. "Nessa, I'm Alanna McNabb," she said, and wondered if she should shake the beast's trotter or curtsy. The pig showed no sign of being glad to know her, but the old man's brows shot up to join the thin white thatch of his hair.

"The laird's lass!" he said. "Lost in the snow, you were."

"Yes," Alanna said, though she was hardly the laird's lass. Nessa grunted and sat up, fixing Alanna with a look of interest. The old man quickly slipped the rope over the pig's head and around her vast neck.

"I'm Donal MacGillivray, the piper, and this is Nessa," the man said.

"Pleased to meet you both, but we must go right now." Alanna said. The smoke in the corner was thickening, blacker now. "

Donal rushed to open the door, and tugged on Nessa's lead rope.

The pig lifted her nose to the cold air for a moment. Or perhaps it was the scent of fire, but she refused to budge any further

Donal hauled on the rope, but he was a mere fraction of his pet's size. Alanna got behind and pushed on Nessa's wide backside, trying to get her through the door. The pig sat down and shut her eyes, blocking the doorway.

There were tears in Donal's eyes as he let the rope go slack, and he shook his head. "I can't leave without Nessa and my pipes," he insisted, shaking his head. "You'd best go, save yourself, for there's no life for me without them."

Alanna coughed. "Where are your pipes?" she managed. Her eyes stung and her knee ached.

"In the chest, by the far wall. I can't get past Nessa to get to them, and if she won't go out, and I can't go in, we won't be going anywhere at all," he said stubbornly.

Alanna looked over her shoulder and felt fear creep into her breast. The chest stood where the fire was gnawing at the thatch. There was already a hole, and sparks nibbled the ragged edge of the furze, like red lace. Any moment, with the next puff of wind, the flames would roar to life.

She looked around the cramped cottage and realized that she was trapped. Nessa blocked the doorway.

Panic rose in Alanna's chest. Unless the pig shifted, or she could climb over her with her injured leg, she was in great danger. Fire this time, instead of ice. Which was worse? Desperately, she shoved at Nessa's bottom, but the sow refused to move. Alanna could hear the crackle of the flames as they took hold of the roof above her head.

"Look—Donal's cottage is about to go up," Seonag said to Iain, pointing. "I didn't see him or Nessa, and you know he won't leave without Nessa, Laird."

Iain looked up the narrow lane that led to the piper's cottage. The roof was smoldering, sparks glittering wickedly in the thatch. In a moment, the fire would gather itself, rise, and catch. He had minutes to find Donal before that happened. It would not take long for the roof to cave in. Iain's heart climbed into his throat. If the old piper was inside—

He began to run. Donal appeared in the doorway, waving frantically. "Laird, thank the Lord you've come. The lass is trapped inside, and Nessa, too."

The lass? Alanna was inside? Iain shoved past Donal.

"Alanna?" he called into the smoke. "Where are you?"

"Behind the pig, pushing," she said, her voice husky with smoke.

He looked over the back of the huge beast and saw her. Her eyes were wide in her soot dark face. She was shoving with all her might, determined to save the damned pig.

"Pull on the rope," Iain ordered Donal. He put his arms under the pig's shoulders and forcibly hauled the great stubborn beast out of the cottage. She squealed at the snow, but Donal threw a blanket around her, then knelt in the snow beside her, using his skinny body to protect his pet from the wind. To Iain's surprise, Alanna didn't come out. "The lass—" Donal began, but Iain was already plunging back into the smoke, just as the flames came to life with a hungry whoosh.

"Alanna!" The fire lit the interior of the cottage like an image of hell. Iain took a breath and dove in. The smoke was so thick he could barely see her. "What the devil are you doing?" he demanded, following her. Flames were crawling along the walls, reaching for her as she walked—limped— boldly through the middle of it, going the wrong way.

She grabbed a moth-eaten plaid from the bed and wrapped it over her head.

"Alanna!" He grabbed for her shoulder, but she eluded him, rushed toward the flames, not away.

She dropped to the floor in front of a chest, the fire

mere inches above her head, deadly sparks falling around her. She threw back the lid and rummaged inside, coughing. She cried out and Iain lunged forward, scooped a hand around her waist, and hauled her back against his chest just in time. The flames roared down the wall, reaching for her. Alanna let out a god-awful squall, and then a long moan, but Iain ignored the noises and carried her outside.

"Are you hurt?" he asked as he set her into the snow. She shook her head, but bent double, coughing, and the terrible moaning continued.

"My pipes—you've got my pipes," Donal said, reaching for the bagpipes in Alanna's hands. He took them from her and cradled them in his arms, then crouched beside the pig and regarded his home. "Now it can burn. What's most precious is safe." He looked at Alanna, and Iain saw tears in Donal's eyes. "I owe you my thanks, lass."

Alanna straightened, gave the piper a smile. Still, Iain noticed her hand shaking as she brushed back a lock of hair, rubbed her hand over her soot-stained face. The flames lit her skin to gold under the black and flamed in her eyes. Iain felt his breath catch in his chest. She glanced up as it began to snow, blinking at the icy flakes

Folks paused to look up at the snow. The barn and the cottages still burned, but the flames hissed as the snow thickened. The wind worked for them now, snuffing out wayward sparks.

Iain looked around at the destruction. His clansmen, some only half dressed, everyone filthy, stood blinking at the ruins of their homes. He felt his chest clench, felt fury and helplessness. It was gone, all of it, a village that had stood here for hundreds of years. He would not be here to rebuild—he had responsibilities that would tear him away. Who would manage it for him?

He spun on Alanna, determined to take out his anger on someone. "Are you completely daft? I told you to stay put. Do you ever do as you're told?"

For a moment she stared up at him in surprise. "Yes, Laird, I do as I'm told. Always in fact. At least until now." She folded her arms over her thin gown, raised her chin. "I like it better this way."

Now what did that mean? Iain stared at her as she stepped around him and went to Donal's side.

"Donal, can you play your pipes now?"

Donal's bantam chest puffed like the bag of his pipes. "Of course I can."

"Then pipe the clan up to the castle," she said. "They need shelter, something to warm them."

Iain gaped at her. She was filthy, her hair covered with soot and snow, sleep-tousled. Yet she stood tall, wrapped in Donal's old plaid, threadbare and singed. She turned to him. "I mean, with the laird's permission, of course."

Iain swallowed a lump in his throat. He'd thought her lovely before. Now, calm despite the terror of the situation, with her eyes shining through soot and dirt, she was the most beautiful woman he'd ever seen. He could see the same thought in Donal's eyes, and even in the eyes of the damned pig. The sow leaned into Alanna with a sigh, and Iain caught her arm, mindful of her injured leg, and drew her against him protectively. He nodded to Donal. "Tell Annie to feed everyone, keep them warm."

"Aye, Laird. But what about Nessa, and the cows and sheep?" Donal asked.

"Put the children on them, let them ride," Alanna suggested.

Iain looked at her. She didn't need him to rescue her. She was doing the rescuing now. "Good idea," he said. She bent to scratch Nessa's head, as if the sow was a faithful hound, and helped Donal tie the pig's lead rope to his waist so she would follow him as he played his pipes.

"Come then, Nessa," Donal said, and set the chanter in his mouth. The pipes called the first bright notes, cutting through the wind and the snow. Folks turned, looked at him as he began to march up the lane between the smoldering cottages, the pig at his heels.

They began to follow him, and Iain swung the children up and placed them on Nessa's back. Lads herded the sheep into line, and the cows behind them, and the whole village set off across the moor toward the castle.

Iain stood amid the ruins with a handful of men and looked around. There was nothing left to save. The snow fell harder, faster, melting on still-hot timbers, ending the fire's brief reign.

"What will we do now, Laird?" Logan asked him. The other men stood behind him, their gazes hollow, full of worry, as if Iain had all the answers, could somehow *fix* this, make it right, give them everything. He clenched his fists at his side. But that was his responsibility, as Laird of Craigleith and Earl of Purbrick. It was his duty to make everything right, no matter the cost to himself. He'd be gone from here in the spring, spread between Shropshire and London and Craigleith, stretched too thin. He felt the full weight of all that responsibility crush the air out of his lungs. All the doubts he'd faced over the past months, since inheriting the English title, crept up, and he had no answer to give the anxious men around him. What *would* they do? It was the dead of winter. They could not rebuild in the snow, and the stores of grain and hay that had been lost would have to be replaced somehow. They'd need seed for spring planting.

Alanna stood in the shadows, watching him, waiting, having set the last child on the back of a cow and sent her off.

He felt her eyes on him like a touch. He met her gaze across the little distance. She stood with her shoulders straight. There wasn't any worry in her gaze. There was confidence, encouragement, and hope, as if she knew he was capable of this, believed he could do anything.

Iain squared his shoulders and looked each man in the eyes. "There's nothing more to do now. We'll go up to the castle and get warm, then see what's to be done in the morning."

"It *is* morning, Laird," Logan said grimly. "We won't be able to do anything until spring, if you ask me."

Dawn was indeed creeping over the horizon, gray and somber, like an old woman with a heavy pack.

"What we need is a miracle," Niall MacGillivray said, shaking his head, looking at the remains of his cottage.

"Then it's a good thing it's the time of year for miracles, isn't it?" Alanna said, loud enough for all to hear.

For a moment, they stared at her as if she'd spoken a

foreign language. She gave them a beguiling smile, her eyes bright with hope.

Logan MacGillivray smiled back.

Niall looked relieved.

Will Fraser squared his shoulders. "Aye," he muttered.

Iain felt his own chest swell. "Let's go," he said, and they began to walk toward the castle.

He crossed to Alanna and took her arm. "Your knee?" he asked.

"I'm fine," she said, though her jaw was clenched to keep her teeth from chattering. He noted dark rings under her eyes that had nothing to do with soot.

"Take this, my lady," Logan said, and handed her his plaid. Iain wrapped her in it, over top of Donal's, then scooped her into his arms.

"You'll rest when we get back to the castle," he commanded.

She looked mutinous. "There'll be a lot to do. Food, and beds—"

"Baths," he said, looking down at the smudges on her cheeks. She blushed under the dirt.

"Don't worry, lass. You look just fine," he said, and she met his gaze, let her eyes fall to his mouth. He watched her swallow, wondered if she would kiss him again. He wanted her to, very much. He began to lower his lips toward hers.

She turned her head away. "We shouldn't," she said. "Penelope—"

He let out a sigh. Penelope. "She isn't here," he said. Not in his head, or his heart. That place was already occupied.

Chapter Twenty-Nine

SANDY MACGILLIVRAY HOVERED by the kitchen door as folk began arriving from the village. Tears left tracks in ash-stained faces. Everyone was cold and exhausted and too stunned to do more than shuffle into the room and collapse, wordlessly holding loved ones and the few possessions they'd managed to save.

He felt guilt in his chest, a pain in his heart, and he counted everyone as they arrived, praying that no one had died because of his foolish mistake.

The laird was the last to arrive, following his people, as soot-stained and dirty as everyone else. In his arms, wrapped in a MacGillivray plaid yet again, was Alanna McNabb, likewise stained and rumpled. Sandy caught Iain's sleeve. "Is everyone safe?" he asked.

Iain gave him a curt nod, and Sandy met the scorn in the laird's eyes, felt shame. Tears stung his own eyes as he stepped back.

He watched as Iain set the lass carefully on her feet. She didn't collapse, though she was tired and dirty. She began to move among the bewildered folk who crowded the kitchen, helping Annie and Fiona and Wee Janet, handing out warmed ale and broth, as if she belonged here. Folk looked up at her with gratitude in their eyes. Sandy marveled. She was a stranger, yet she was taking care of the MacGillivrays when it was their duty to take care of her, their guest.

Shame and despair filled Sandy's breast, and he slipped farther back into the shadows. It was his fault, all of it. Cottages lost, food stores and supplies, gone. How would they make it through the winter? And in the spring, with Iain gone to England, how would they survive at all?

He felt a hand on his shoulder, and she pressed a warm mug into his shaking hands. "Drink this," Alanna said. "Everyone's safe, Sandy—even Donal's Nessa."

He could see the piper's pig stretched on her side by the fire. He felt a tear crawl down his cheek. "'Twill be a sad Christmas now," he said. "And a hard winter, and I'm to blame for all of it. I didn't mean any harm."

"Of course not," she said. "Everyone will have to make the best of it."

"How?" he asked, looking up at her. "Seonag makes wine for Christmas, preserves berries, makes Christmas cakes. It's all gone, burned up. I daresay the Christmas cheer of all the other folk is gone too. Even their livelihoods are lost—tools and supplies and belongings—and their homes. There won't be enough hay to feed the beasts, or enough grain to last through the winter, let alone for spring planting."

Alanna's expression was grim as she looked around the

room. She put her hand on his arm. "Sandy, I have an idea, but I need your help. I cannot ride with my knee injured, or I'd go myself. My brother Alec will help, I know it, and gladly. Can you ride to Glenlorne, ask him to send what might be needed for a few months? He's kind, like Iain, a good man. He won't say no." She swallowed. "Tell him I'd consider it a wedding present."

He looked at her, hope swelling in his breast. "'Twill take me two or three days to get there, but I can go. I can be back by Christmas too." He put his thumbs into his belt. "I might stop and hunt on the way back, bring home a stag for a feast—" She bent forward and kissed his wrinkled cheek.

"Thank you, Sandy," she said. "You're very brave. We'll keep it as a surprise, shall we?"

Suddenly he felt brave. He nodded, strode out of the corner without a word to anyone, and went to the stable. He mounted a garron and rode out into the snow, just as the daylight straggled over the horizon. He huddled into the warmth of his plaid, thankful the wind-driven snow was at his back, following him, pushing him onward. He paused to frown at the yellow pall of smoke that rose over the village.

The lass had given him a task, a way to redeem himself for his mistake, and he would not fail her, or his clan, again.

He thanked the heavens for the day Lady Alanna McNabb had arrived at Craigleith. It was a lucky moment indeed.

He set his heels to the garron's flanks and rode on.

"Seonag's family and the baby can have my room," Fiona said, organizing things. "I'll share with Elizabeth."

Annie nodded. "And we'll put Lottie and her daughter in Iain's room."

Fiona made a face. "But that means Alanna will have to share with Penelope."

"Or one of them will have to share with Iain," Annie muttered under her breath, and glanced at the fire again. The sight had never let her down before. Why now, tonight? She looked around. But no one was watching or blaming her—they were staring in wonder at Alanna McNabb. The lass looked as if she belonged here, as soot-stained and busy as everyone else. Perhaps she did.

There was no sign of the Sassenach who wished to be Lady of Craigleith. Annie's lips pursed tight for Iain's sake. She looked up as the Sassenach's maid came into the room, no doubt here to fetch hot water and make up the breakfast trays for the idle ladies above stairs. The maid stopped short and looked around her in shock. "What on earth?"

Annie's grip tightened on the ladle in her hand. "Breakfast in bed will have to wait. Try tomorrow morning," she said tartly. The maid colored and fled. No doubt she'd march up and tell Lady Marjorie, and she would sweep downstairs to scold Annie personally. Annie made a sign to ward off evil and served another bowl of soup.

"The beasts, Iain—where shall we put them? Is there space in the stable?" Logan asked. "The wind is picking up, and they'll need shelter."

"The old armory will do. There's a door that leads

straight out to the yard, but that's Annie's storeroom," Iain said. "Annie?"

"'Twill be as you decide, Laird," Annie said. "It can't be helped, though it is an inconvenience." She looked pointedly at Donal, who put his hand on Nessa's flank protectively.

"Not Nessa," Donal said anxiously.

"She can't stay here," Annie said, setting her hands on her hips. "Unless she wants to join us for Christmas dinner."

Donal glared at her. "Nessa's not for eating! Would you eat a fine hunting dog, an old friend?"

"It may come to that," Annie grumbled.

Iain and the men went out, and Annie and Donal glared at each other over Nessa's pink belly.

Alanna stepped between them. "The children are so sleepy now the worst is over. Perhaps we could take them to the library, let them rest there. Wee Janet was wiping noses and mopping sooty cheeks as fast as she could."

"That's a fine idea. They're just underfoot here in the kitchen," Annie replied.

Alanna smiled at Donal. "Perhaps Nessa can come too," she said. Annie smiled. It wasn't the solution she would have chosen, but it would do.

The piper rose gratefully. "Of course, lass."

"Once the bairns are tucked up in the library, the rest of you can go into the hall," Annie announced. There were so many people, so much to see to. It was like the old days, when the castle was full of Iain's grandfather's clansmen and their families. Iain's father had preferred a less chaotic home. It felt good to have people in the old place again, especially so close to Christmas.

She turned toward the fire once again and poked it, looking for a sign, but she saw only more snow and a future yet uncertain.

ALANNA SETTLED A dozen children on the settees and chairs and on the rug before the fire. Nessa took her place among them on the hearth like a beloved dog, and went to sleep with the little ones curled around her. They looked up at Alanna expectantly.

"Why don't you tell them a tale, lass?" Donal said. "They've heard all of mine."

"I shall tell you a story that I heard when I was a child. It's one of my favorite tales for Christmas," she began.

"Is it true?" one child asked.

"Of course it is. All the very best stories are true ones," she promised. "As long as you believe in magic, that is. Do you?"

The youngest ones nodded, though the older ones looked skeptical. "Close your eyes and try your hardest to believe."

She told them a tale of magic, and Christmas. Before long, the fearful excitement of the fire, the warmth of the room, and the sound of her voice lulled everyone to sleep, including Donal.

Alanna looked up to find Iain standing by the door, listening. He'd washed his face, but his clothes were still stained with soot and mud. He needed shaving and sleep, and probably a meal. Alanna was tired enough to sleep for a week, and needed a bath herself. Still, his eyes were roaming over her face, appreciation clear in the gray depths. She felt blood rise to her cheeks.

She looked away, down to the child who had fallen asleep in her lap, a wee girl with red curls. "I didn't hear you come in. Is everything all right?"

"Everything is fine—well, as fine as it can be, given the situation. There are beds ready for the little ones upstairs, though I suspect they'll all wake up and want their breakfast soon. We might as well leave them to sleep here for the time being."

He came across the room, leaned against the fireplace mantel, and looked around at the sleeping children. "Seonag's grateful to you for seeing to the children. She has her hands full with the new bairn, and Wee Janet and Fiona are helping Annie. Lottie is telling everyone how brave you are. I daresay the story of Lady Alanna and the piper's pig will become a favorite Christmas tale in years to come."

"I'm not so very brave," she said. "I hope you didn't come in here to tell me that. Have you slept?"

"When everyone else does," he said. "I'm looking for Sandy, actually. Have you seen him?"

She bit her lip. "Do you intend to punish him? It was an accident." Iain was a proud man. Would he welcome help from Alec? She hadn't thought about it. She had plunged in, done what seemed right at the moment. It was an unfortunate habit she had, trying to fix what was wrong between people she loved.

The firelight caught in the creases of Iain's frown as she deflected his question. "People could have died."

"But they didn't. Everyone is safe. Cottages can be rebuilt. If Sandy hadn't sounded the alarm, then it would have been worse."

"He's the villain here, not the hero," Iain said.

"Oh, but it might have been anyone—"

"Do you see the good in everyone so easily? If you do, you're a remarkable woman indeed, Alanna McNabb," he said softly.

She felt her heart climb into her throat. "I was brought up to be the one—well, Megan was the family beauty, the one who told stories, but her temper was fiery indeed. Sorcha was the adorable one, always into trouble, but easy to forgive."

"And you?" he asked.

"I was the one in the middle. I made peace when Sorcha stole Megan's ribbons, made things right again when Megan—" She closed her mouth. She was the useful, dutiful McNabb sister, the one who did as she was told, did her best to please everyone, even at the expense of her own happiness. What would Megan have done last night, or Devorguilla? She looked at the frown on Iain's face. He was wondering too, no doubt—not about her kin but about his own.

"Poor Penelope. She's a stranger here, not used to Highland ways. I daresay she needs—wants—a chance to help, a task, and she'll surprise you . . ."

He folded his arms over his chest. "*You* surprise me. These aren't your people either. And yet, even injured—"

She looked at him fiercely. "But they are my people. Lottie MacGillivray might have been Morag McNabb, from Glenlorne village. Sandy might be Leith Rennie, our gamekeeper, his cottage lost in the fire. How could I not help? I miss them all, love them, see them in the faces and words and deeds of the MacGillivrays." She felt tears fill her eyes, the horror of what might have happened filling her chest.

He knelt beside her, wiped her tears away with the pad of his thumb. "So brave, and yet you ran away." He held up a hand when she opened her mouth to deny it again.

"Whether you're willing to admit it or not, you don't want to go to England, do you, and marry Lord Wilbur?"

She closed her eyes. "It's Wilfred, and I gave my word, promised." How often had she recited those words in her mind? They sounded less noble spoken aloud, a weak reason to marry any man.

"Promises can be hard to keep when regrets crowd in," he said.

"I am told that you can grow used to anything if you wish to do so. It won't be so bad." She met his eyes, saw the doubt there, but not for her—why would he worry about her? She recalled what Fiona had said, that she feared Iain didn't want to go to England, dreaded it. She put her hand over his, squeezed. "It won't be the same for you, Iain. You'll be an earl, and Penelope is beautiful. She'll make a good countess—" Perhaps by reassuring him, she might reassure herself, make it bearable. Touching him, even his hand, just made her regret worse.

"Don't pity me," he said, mistaking her intent.

"But I—"

He withdrew his hand and went back to the fire, stared into the flames, his expression harsh, his fist clenched on the mantel. "I never expected to be an English earl. I hadn't heard from my English kin for years, not since my father died, never thought I would. I thought my life was here at Craigleith, doing my best to be a good laird, a good husband and father when—if—the time came for it, and I told myself that I'd be content with that." He swallowed, his throat bobbing, gilded golden by the firelight. "And yet—" He paused.

"And yet?" she prompted.

"And yet there are possibilities that come with this, the chance to do more, be more. An opportunity to build things, change things, to help Fiona make a life for herself, and find out what I—" He turned to look for her, his hands clasped behind his back. "What I want, what I'm capable of," he finished.

She smiled. "You're a remarkable man, Iain MacGillivray. You're a fine laird, and you'll be a finer earl."

"What if I'm wrong, and Marjorie is right? What if they won't accept me, a Scot, as the new Earl of Purbrick?" He ran his hand through his hair and shook his head. "I've practiced the damned word over and over again, and I still can't say it properly. Poor-breck."

She smiled softly. "I like the way you say it. It sounds like a warm, inviting place instead of—" She looked away. "My aunt Eleanor says you need to start as you mean to go on, show folk from the outset who you are."

"And how will you begin?" he asked. "The moment you

step out of your carriage, Lord Merridew's bride, the eyes of his people upon you. How will you begin?"

She took a deep breath. It would begin long before that moment. She had thought it would be enough to simply do as she was told, to don her wedding gown and speak the vows that would bind her to Lord Merridew. She hadn't considered the moment Iain had thought of, the instant she would truly become a marchioness, a wife, the mistress of a great estate.

She bit her lip. She should have begun by saying no when her mother insisted she take Megan's place.

"I think I wish I could start again," she whispered.

"Perhaps you already have," Iain replied. "Perhaps that's why you ran away, came to—"

The door opened before she could reply, and Penelope came in, freshly bathed and elegantly turned out in frothy pink muslin, her hair artfully styled. Her placid expression instantly shriveled as she looked at the children, then at Iain and Alanna, and her nose wrinkled with distaste. "What's going on here? There are people everywhere. I hear animal noises across the hall, and the smell is dreadful. Why are these children here?"

"There was a fire last night," Iain said, not bothering with "good morning," his tone sharp. "Did you not hear the commotion?"

"Of course I did. Elizabeth woke me. I assumed the tenants would handle it on their own. They would have in England. No one would think to wake their betters for a simple fire in a cottage."

"Six cottages, and the barn," Iain corrected her. "If

such a thing ever does happen at Woodford or any other Purbrick estate, then I will expect to be woken, insist upon it. I will be the one to see to it, no matter how many servants I have," Iain said. Penelope shut her mouth with a snap, but she glared at him indignantly.

"It made the people feel less afraid to have Iain there," Alanna said soothingly.

Penelope made a moue of distaste. "Your face is dirty."

Alanna resisted the urge to run a hand over the soot stains on her skin, the tangles in her hair. She raised her chin. "Aye, I need a bath, no doubt."

Iain turned toward her. "Shall I carry you upstairs?" he asked, and Alanna heard Penelope's strangled gasp, though he ignored it. She felt her whole body heat now. She'd made the disagreement worse.

She glanced at the child in her lap. "Better to carry the wee ones, I think, put them to bed."

"Perhaps they could sleep here a while longer. It's warm, and quiet," Iain said, lifting the little girl off Alanna's lap carefully and laying her down on the settee next to her sister. The brush of his hands on Alanna's sent sparks flying through her veins. He turned to his cousin—his fiancée—and said, "Perhaps Penelope could stay and watch them."

But Penelope frowned. "Me? I think not. If there's another room, then by all means they should be taken there. Surely they are all old enough to walk. They don't need you to carry them, Iain. Nor does Alanna. This is the only decent room in the castle for their betters, since there is no proper salon. Shouldn't these urchins be with their parents, their own kind?"

Iain straightened. "My kind, you mean?"

Penelope looked startled.

"My kin, my clan."

"Not mine," Penelope said.

"No, not yours," he agreed. The tension in the room was so thick it hurt to breathe.

Alanna rose to her feet. "But surely—" A sharp look from Iain warned her to be silent. They were not her clan either.

Seonag came in, carrying the babe in a fold of plaid against her chest, fast asleep. "I came to see if the little ones were hungry. There's porridge ready for them, but I see they're asleep. Best to let them rest, since there'll be chaos when they wake up again."

Penelope glared at the woman. "You will keep them out of the way, is that clear?" she ordered, drawing herself up. "They are not to bother their betters. I—" She cast a quick glance at Iain. "—we do not wish to see or hear them."

Seonag blinked at her. Alanna saw the cook's eyes slide to Iain, then to her, but she kept silent, her expression flat. Iain silently glared at his wife-to-be and said nothing.

"Yes, my lady," Seonag said at last, an edge to her voice. "We'll see to it at once, just to please you." She turned to Alanna. "Annie has a bath ready for you upstairs, Alanna, and—"

"*Lady* Alanna," Penelope interrupted. "There must be some rules here, some deference."

Alanna limped across the room and squeezed Seonag's hand. "Thank you. I'll go up at once. I'll be back to help once I've changed my clothes."

"You'll go to bed and sleep," Iain snapped. He shut his eyes. "You've done enough," he said more gently. "More than enough."

He strode past his betrothed without a glance and scooped Alanna into his arms. She could feel the anger in every line of his body, though his touch was careful. She lay as stiff as a block of wood in his arms. He paused at the door. "Do you know how to make tea, Penelope?" he asked.

Penelope glared daggers at him. "Of course not."

"Then I suggest you might wish to learn if you want anything to eat this morning," Iain said and strode out of the room.

Chapter Thirty

Dundrummie Castle, eight days before Christmas

DEVORGUILLA MCNABB STARED out the window, across the orchard. Snow blanketed the trees, made everything soft and white and lovely, offered the anticipation of Christmas.

But she wished it were foggy, or raining, or any other form of weather that better suited her mood. She wondered where Alanna was, felt pain in her chest, pressed the heel of her hand to it. It had been eleven days since she'd disappeared. She looked across at the desk, where she'd left the letter she'd begun writing to Alec, her stepson. She'd started the same letter a hundred times over the last two days. How did one break such dreadful news? She was still hoping that Alanna would return and make the note unnecessary. Her heart dragged in her chest. The maids were whispering about snow-filled gullies, sharp rocks, the killing power of cold and snow. They passed her with pity in their eyes, as if there was no hope left.

Devorguilla turned away from the desk again, rubbed her temples.

She couldn't think of that now, the fact that Alanna might be— She swallowed and looked across the orchard again, hoping to catch a glimpse of Alanna's red cloak among the bare black trees. She rested her forehead on the glass, felt the cold seep into her skull. Was this her fault?

Devorguilla had been ashamed and furious when Megan had eloped, rejecting Merridew. She had thought—*known*—that she was doing the right thing for her daughters, marrying them to the loftiest English title she could find. They would outrank their brother, be richer and better than if they remained in Scotland. Had she been wrong?

Merridew was upstairs, still asleep, though it was nearly noon. He viewed Alanna's disappearance as an inconvenience, but nothing more. He was happy enough to sit and drink Dundrummie's cellars dry while he waited for his bride. He showed no interest at all in joining a search party. Eleanor had wondered yesterday if he would sit at Dundrummie until Sorcha was old enough to marry him if Alanna didn't return.

Devorguila closed her mind to that terrible possibility. Somewhere, Alanna was safe—she must be. Devorguilla could see now that perhaps the marquess wasn't the best choice of husband for her middle daughter, any more than he'd been for her eldest. He was pompous, self-centered, and opinionated. He had never had to work for anything in his life, including his bride. She should have made him win Alanna, prove himself, but she could see now that Wilfred Esmond was not that kind of man. He wasn't much of a man at all. Better Alanna had married the gardener— No, she didn't mean that. It's just that she had imagined the kind of life she wanted for herself and had decided it would be best for her daughters. She had schemed and planned and lied to achieve it, and at what cost?

Alanna was missing, and Megan had run away. Upstairs, Sorcha was in tears, refusing to eat, pleading to be allowed to go home to Glenlorne.

Devorguilla couldn't go back to Glenlorne, not now that she'd failed. How Alec would gloat. She couldn't bear it. Nor could she bear losing Alanna, her gentle, shy, kind, clever daughter. Devorguilla had barely taken notice of Alanna until she was gone. She'd stood in the shadows behind Megan, waiting for her turn in the spotlight. Would she have liked a Season in London? Devorguilla hadn't asked her. She sighed and crossed back to the desk, sat down and picked up the quill, her hand shaking, and began again. *Dear Alec...*

Jeannie appeared in the doorway. "My lady, there's a man to see Lord Merridew. He has a letter for him."

"He's still asleep. Have him leave the letter and go."

"He said he was told to wait for a reply, to offer the marquess transportation if necessary."

Devorguilla felt her heart constrict. She dropped the pen and rose. "You'd better ask him to come in," she said.

He was covered with snow, his face red with cold, his heavy redingote marking him as a coachman. He looked at the fire longingly.

"Jeannie, have the cook prepare a meal in the kitchen— hot soup, ale." She turned to the coachman. "What news have you?"

"I've come with a letter for Lord Merridew, if he's here."

"Who sent you?" Devorguilla asked, her back stiff, not daring to hope that it was news of Alanna. The servant was English, not a Scot. Perhaps Merridew was being called back to England, though the coachman wasn't wearing Merridew's colors, or the Duke of Lyall's.

"I come from Lady Marston, who is presently staying at Craigleith."

The name meant nothing to her, but curiosity bloomed in her breast. "I see. The marquess is unavailable at the moment. May I convey your message to him?"

Eleanor hurried into the room. "I heard there's a visitor—is there news of Alanna?" she asked, looking at the man eagerly.

"I came from Craigleith Castle," the man said again. "Lady Marston—"

"Craigleith?" Eleanor put a hand to her heart. "Why, it's scarcely fifteen miles from here. Is my niece there? Lady Alanna McNabb?"

The man nodded. "She is, my lady."

Devorguilla felt her knees weaken with relief. She sat down on the settee.

"Is she safe, injured, ill?" Eleanor asked, advancing on the servant, peppering him with questions.

He shifted from one foot to the other, his heavy boots leaving a puddle on the rug. "Everything is in Lady Marston's letter," he said. "Addressed to Lord Merridew."

Eleanor frowned. "Young man, my niece has been lost for eleven terrible days. We've had no word at all, have been out of our minds with worry. This lady is Alanna's mother. We have no intention of waiting until his lordship deigns to rise from his bed to hear what you have to say. Tell us what you know."

He scanned the faces of the two women before speaking. "Please," Devorguilla said.

"She's safe," he began. "The Laird of Craigleith found her lost in the snow, carried her home. Her leg is injured, but otherwise I believe she's well."

"The laird? Iain MacGillivray?" Eleanor asked.

"Aye, he's Earl of Purbrick as well now."

"Purbrick in England? What happened to Bertie Marston? He was the last earl of Purbrick I knew of," Eleanor said.

The coachman pointed to the black armband on his coat. "His lordship died a few months ago, and Lord Iain is the new earl."

"Where is my daughter now?" Devorguilla asked. "Why haven't you brought her home?"

The coachman shook his head. "I was just ordered to bring a letter to his lordship, the Marquess of Merridew. It took me a week to get here, since I had to come the long way around because of the snow."

Devorguilla's "Was she unable to travel?" and Eleanor's "How badly was she hurt?" came out at the same time.

The man looked at them with a plea in his eyes. "I only know what I was told to relate to his lordship."

Eleanor folded her arms over her breast and stared at him. "Nonsense. You're a servant. You hear everything, know everything. What's happening at Craigleith?"

He slid his eyes from one lady to the other, and swallowed. "The laird found the lass—the lady—in the snow. He brought her back to the castle wrapped in his plaid. They bound up her leg, and she's in his bed. That's all I know of things," he said.

Devorguilla felt rage rise. "In his bed?"

Eleanor raised an eyebrow, and the coachman blushed. "Do you intend to tell Lord Merridew that?" She crossed and pulled the bell. "Graves will take you down to the kitchen. There will be hot food waiting, and a bed. We'll be ready to accompany you back to Craigleith first thing in the morning."

"But—" the coachman began, then stopped when Eleanor held out her hand.

"Give me the letter and I'll see the marquess gets it."

The coachman handed over the letter with a quick bow. "Thank you, my lady."

"Give it to me," Devorguilla said, but Eleanor clasped the letter to her bosom and waited until the door was closed behind the servant before she crossed to the sewing basket in the corner and took out a needle and thread.

"What on earth are you doing?" Devorguilla asked.

"Finding out what Lady Marjorie Marston has to say to the Marquess of Merridew about Alanna," she said, then slid the thread behind the wax seal and worked it back and forth gently. The seal popped up.

Devorguilla crowded closer to her sister-in-law. "What does it say? Is she safe?"

Eleanor scanned the note. "Lady Marjorie wanted Merridew to know that Alanna was at Craigleith. Lady Marjorie is there with her own daughters. She suggests that he come and fetch Alanna at once. Apparently Marjorie knows his mother, the Duchess of Lyall, quite well. It looks as if they're old friends, since the letter is addressed to "'Dearest Willie.'"

"Dearest Willie?" Devorguilla said. She could not picture Lord Merridew as anyone's Dearest Willie.

"Indeed," Eleanor said, grinning. She warmed the wax, resealed the letter, and rang the bell. "Take this up to his lordship's room if you would, please, Graves. Tell his valet it's time his lordship was out of bed."

The butler accepted the letter and bowed.

"No doubt you've heard by now from the fellow who brought this that Alanna is safe," Eleanor added.

Graves offered a real smile. "There could not be more welcome news, my lady."

"We'll be travelling to Craigleith tomorrow to see for ourselves. Pack a hamper, Graves. Make sure there's a bottle or two of the MacIntosh whisky. It's Christmas, and we owe Laird MacGillivray a great debt. Fill it with all Alanna's favorite treats too. Devorguilla will tell you what they are."

Devorguilla felt heat rise in her cheeks. She had no idea. She racked her brain. Alanna was quiet, she read books, she liked—her mind was a blank. "Gingerbread," she said.

Surely everyone loved gingerbread, especially at Christmas.

Chapter Thirty-One

Craigleith Castle, eight days before Christmas

"GINGERBREAD IS THE only Christmas treat I dislike," Alanna said to Fiona as they made up yet another bed for their guests and passed the time asking each other questions.

"Seonag makes wonderful shortbread, and her treacle cake is—" Fiona hesitated, rolling her eyes, searching for the right words. "*O cruit mo cridh*—the harp of my heart," she said poetically. " I suppose we'll need to make much more this year, since everyone will be here. And we'll still have to take handsels to the folk who live outside the village. They'll come for Christmas Eve, of course, but Iain and I usually take parcels of cheer to them a few days before Christmas."

"We did the same at Glenlorne," Alanna said. "My sisters and I would help Muira with the baking, then we'd pack it all up, eating as much as we packed. The cart was hitched up, and we'd sing as we rode through the village. As we visited each cottage, folks would come along, dropping in on friends and neighbors with us, and we'd all come back to the hall, and drink warmed wine and whisky, too, and make a party of it."

"Why don't you come with us this year?" Fiona said. "I'm sure Iain wouldn't mind, and it would be—"

Alanna lowered her eyes, concentrated on plumping a pillow. "I think Penelope should be the one to go with Iain," she said.

Fiona's smile faded. "Oh. Of course."

"She will be his—" Alanna could not make her lips form the word *wife*. "—Lady of Craigleith."

Fiona moved on to the next cot, flicking the sheet over it with a sharp crack. "She probably won't wish to come. It's cold, and there's snow. It must be summer all year round in England—at least it is to hear her tell it."

Alanna forced a smile. "Then we won't have to worry about weather like this when we get there."

Fiona bunched the sheet in her hands and stared wistfully at the white linen. "I'll miss the snow. *Is blianach Nollaid gun sneachd*. Christmas is indeed poor fare without snow."

"Then we must enjoy it while we can. Let's go out and play in the snow with the children. Or we could slide on the ice on the loch," Alanna suggested.

Fiona gave her a sad smile. "I've never done that. My leg, you see—I could never keep up with the other children. I suppose it will always be so. In England I won't be able to keep up with the other young ladies, either, will stand out as a—"

Alanna grabbed Fiona's hands. "Don't say it! I limp as badly as you do at the moment. Let's go out anyway—we'll hold each other up. The children need to get outside before they drive everyone mad with their running around. Come on—it will be fun."

Fiona's fragile smile reappeared, and she nodded. "I'll get my cloak, and we'll find plaids for the wee ones."

Chapter Thirty-Two

IAIN RAN HIS hand through his hair, dropped the pen, and rubbed his eyes. He sat in the privacy of the tower room—one of the few places in the castle that was private and quiet now that the rest of the place was full. His rule forbidding anyone but himself to climb the treacherous stone stairs remained law.

He was looking over the accounts, wondering how he would find the money to rebuild the cotts and the barn. It looked hopeless unless there was money available once he got to England that could be diverted to assist Craigleith. As yet, he had no idea what his English estates earned, or what they required. Marjorie said there were competent stewards at each estate, and a man of affairs in London. That gentleman had been the one to write and inform Iain of his uncle's death, and his inheritance of the title.

He had managed Craigleith without outside help for a decade. He had hoped to continue, keeping his Scottish holding separate from his English lands.

A thump rattled the windowpanes, surprising him,

and ink spattered across the page. Iain crossed to look outside. Lads with snowballs, no doubt, rowdy and tired of being indoors. He'd have to find tasks for them, or some kind of occupation. One more thing to manage . . .

To his surprise, it was two women who were throwing snowballs. They were surrounded by a crowd of laughing, red-cheeked children, all looking very happily occupied indeed, and engaged in the task of pelting the women with snow. He recognized Alanna at once—she wore her red cloak, and she had the aim of a champion stone putter.

The sight of the other woman stopped his breath in his throat. She moved less surely, but she still held her own.

Fiona.

He had not seen her play rough games—ordinary childhood games—since before her accident. What if she fell? He should go down, stop the mayhem, make sure she was—

But then she turned, and he looked down into her flushed, laughing face. Iain felt a shock rush through him. Fiona did not play with other children. She did not run, or climb. Her leg made her awkward and slow. She worried she'd ruin the fun of games or races for the others if she tried to join in. She sat out willingly. He'd always allowed her to make that choice for herself, had never encouraged her to try.

He felt as if he was watching a miracle unfold. Fiona was throwing snowballs, her limp as pronounced as ever. She and Alanna linked arms and hurried across the lawn, supporting each other—Fiona using her strong left leg, Alanna her right. The pair of them dissolved into laughter and fell time and again, but his sister's face was radiant. So was Alanna McNabb's.

He stared down at her in amazement. She'd somehow taken a disaster and made it feel like a holiday. The children would remember this day far longer than they would remember the fire. He blinked. The wind picked up her cloak and sent it flaring up and out behind her.

Like angel's wings.

A snowball caught her in the chest and she fell back, laughing, breathless. He wished he was there, basking in the joy of her company, smiling and flushed like the children who piled on top of her.

He had never met a woman like Alanna McNabb, though he'd hoped to someday. When he'd imagined the kind of woman he'd want for a wife, a partner, a lover, he'd pictured someone like her. His heart clenched in his chest. No, not someone *like* her—*her*, Alanna.

His hand clenched on the windowsill. But it was too late.

Chapter Thirty-Three

Cairnforth, eight days before Christmas

FARLAN FRASER SIPPED his ale and looked around the inn. He was feeling pleasantly tipsy, and he'd managed to steal a kiss from Breanna McNabb, the blacksmith's daughter. He'd promised to return in the spring and ask her father for work, if his own father was willing as well, of course. For the moment he was drunk and in love, and the only task he had before he turned his steps for home was to see that the letter in his pocket was passed on.

He'd found a ferryman at the inn, and surely such a man knew everyone's business, and where they were travelling. "Can you take a letter on toward Glenlorne for me?"

The ferryman looked at the battered note in Farlan Fraser's hand and sipped his ale. "Aye. I can take it as far as the inn at Loch Ramsey. Someone there is sure to be going on to Glenlorne."

"You have my thanks," the lad said and raised his tankard to the ferryman.

"Letter to your sweetheart, is it?" the ferryman teased, making conversation on a cold winter's night.

Farlan felt his cheeks heat, which made the old boatman's grin wider.

"Och, she's not my sweetheart. She belongs to MacGillivray of Craigleith. He went a-reiving, and caught her in the snow. He carried her home bold as you please, slung over his shoulder, and he means to keep her. This letter is just to tell that to her kin at Glenlorne."

"I trust the laird is satisfied with her and wants to seal the bargain, then," the ferryman said. "She must be a beauty."

Farlan leaned in. "I've heard she's the bonniest lass any man ever set eyes on. The laird was struck dumb the moment he set eyes on her, knew he had to have her for his own. It's all done, if you know what I mean, except telling her kin."

The ferryman grinned. "Lucky MacGillivray," he said. "He'll have a warm bed this winter."

"And riches," Farlan said, then tapped his forefinger on the letter. "The MacGillivray is writing to find out what goods the lass will bring to the match. I hear he expects cattle, land, and gold . . ."

The ferryman whistled. "All three? She must be some lass."

"All three," Farlan confirmed. "And I hear she's worth every coin."

The ferryman sipped his ale and looked around at the curious faces that had drawn in to listen to the tale. "Here's to us all finding so fine a lass in the snow."

The tankards clinked, and warmed ale ran down the chins of every man there.

Chapter Thirty-Four

IAIN WAS DOWNSTAIRS when Alanna and Fiona came inside. They leaned on each other's arms, counted their steps aloud, and walked as straight and perfect as a pair of princesses.

Fiona fell out of step when she saw him waiting, and she hurried toward him, hugged him.

"Oh Iain, we've had such fun," she said. "Come out with us tomorrow—Alanna says we can clear a patch on the loch and slide on the ice—she does it all the time."

He looked over her shoulder at Alanna, who was unwrapping her cloak, her cheeks pink, her eyes bright. His mouth watered to kiss her again. "Well, not all the time," she said.

"I think I'll go and tell Elizabeth, see if she'll come too." Fiona bussed her brother's cheek, her lips cold as ice, and went away humming a tune.

Iain stared at Alanna. "She hasn't played like that since she was a wee child, before the accident. It never occurred to me she might miss it. I never thought to ask her."

She smiled. "It was just as much fun for me. I haven't thrown snowballs since my sisters and I used to do so. Alec would clear off the loch—before he left home, of course—and we'd pull each other around on the ice." She looked wistful for a moment.

"Watching you play gave me an idea," he said. "For Fiona, something that might help with her limp. A Christmas present." Alanna's eyes widened. "I mean, I'm not saying there is anything wrong with Fiona the way she is."

"Of course not."

"It's just that watching the two of you walk together, I thought perhaps if Fee had a special shoe, one that added height on her weak side, then she could walk straight."

Alanna clasped her hands. "She could even dance," she said.

"Or walk into a room without people knowing that she limped," he said.

"They won't judge her on sight," Alanna continued. "They will want to know her, and when they see how kind, and clever, and wonderful she is, they won't care if she limps."

"Yes," he said.

She laid her hand on his sleeve. "It will mean the world to her." The smile she gave him meant the world to him. God, he could get lost in the depths of her eyes.

Iain stared at her, sobering. His throat dried. He wanted to kiss her. She must have read the emotion in his eyes. She blushed and stepped away, busying herself with folding her cloak in quick, nervous motions.

"How will you do it?" she asked. "I mean, it will be an easy thing to add a wedge to her boots. But dancing slippers are thin, delicate things."

"I—" His brain had stopped working for the moment, and he couldn't think of anything but Alanna. She stood waiting for an answer, an intelligent response. "Thank you," he said instead. "For being kind to Fiona."

"Oh, but that's an easy thing to do," she said. She moved to pass him, but he caught her arm.

"Still," he said. He could smell her soap, and the scent of wind in her hair, see the colors in her eyes—copper, silver, and bronze. His mouth watered, and he leaned in, heard the soft gasp she gave, half anticipation, half fear, perhaps. His lips met hers, soft and cool, and he restricted himself to just that, a single, chaste peck. "Thank you," he said again, and forced himself to let her go.

She smiled up at him, looking at him as if he could move mountains. A peck wasn't enough. He swore softly under his breath and pulled her close, pressing her into his arms, determined to kiss her properly.

But just as their lips were about to meet, there was a sudden crash, and two children raced between their knees, chasing a cat.

"Where'd that cat come from?" Iain asked. Alanna laughed and stepped back, and the spell was broken.

Chapter Thirty-Five

Glenlorne Castle, seven days before Christmas

ALEC MCNABB, EARL of Glenlorne and Chief of Clan McNabb, watched his wife packing handsels for the villagers.

Caroline never failed to take his breath away when he saw her, and now her red hair glowed in the firelight as she taught Muira and the undercooks how to make English Christmas treats. Muira had been certain that no self-respecting Scot would appreciate lemon tarts and almond biscuits, but she'd been proven wrong. The scent of almonds still hung in the kitchen, and Alec leaned forward to snatch one of the still-warm cookies from the plate, putting one arm around his wife's swelling belly. "Do you think everyone will like them?" she asked anxiously.

"Aye," he said, and swooped in to kiss her.

"I know it will be a different Christmas without your sisters here," she said. "Muira has given me a list of Glenlorne traditions. I'm to learn to make a proper black bun. She declared my first attempt as too English. What do you suppose that means?"

"Too much brandy," Muira said, passing by to collect cookies for the next handsel.

Alec grinned. "I've not had black bun for years, not since I left for England."

"Thank heaven—then you won't be able to tell if it's not quite right."

Muira sent him a sharp look, and Alec laughed. "One never forgets Muira's black bun."

"Oh," Caroline said, her face falling.

"Not to worry. You could take the villagers lumps of coal and stale bannock and they'd still be pleased to see you on the doorstep." He laid his hand on her belly. "Especially now."

She put her hand over his. "I've heard a dozen tales about the night you were born, Alec—all about the number of stars in the sky, or the dreadful rainstorm, or the hot noonday sun."

"Muira will know the true tale. She was there."

"Then I shall ask her. Now help me wrap the rest of these biscuits," Caroline said. "I thought we could send a basket to Dundrummie."

Alec sobered. "I think Alanna and Sorcha would like that very much."

"I wish they were here."

Muira came in bearing a bundle of herbs, adding it to the small bowl on the table. "Meadowsweet, for adding to the Christmas bowl to make folk merry," she said. She sniffed the air.

"Almonds?" Alec guessed, identifying the odor, but Muira shook her head.

"Nay—visitors," she said. "Coming with news."

Caroline smiled. "You're remarkable, Muira. Is it good news?"

Muira cocked her head like a bird. "It's not good, and it's not bad. We will have to wait and see. I'll put the kettle on to heat."

Chapter Thirty-Six

Craigleith Castle, six days before Christmas

"EVERYONE HAS GONE MAD!" Penelope said to her mother. They stood at the window of the library watching children and adults alike playing in the snow. From across the hall, distant animal sounds—cattle mooing and sheep baaing—leaked through the door of the armory. "Can you imagine anything of this sort occurring at Woodford Park?"

"I think it looks like fun," Elizabeth said, her nose pressed to the glass.

"Don't be ridiculous." Penelope pinched her sharply.

Elizabeth cried out and flounced out of the room.

Marjorie gazed out at the mayhem. Everyone was laughing, throwing snow, and no one seemed to mind a bit when the snow slid down their backs or hit them square in the face. Iain was in the thick of it, beset by a gaggle of children, peasants all, and he allowed them to climb on him as if he was one of them instead of a laird and an earl. Marjorie sighed. She would need to have a word with him about propriety and the importance of keeping his distance from the lower orders. Such behavior would never do at Woodford, or any other civilized place. And it was just as bad inside the castle—noisy children racing everywhere, women gossiping in the great hall and in the kitchen. Not a one of them had the manners to rise, or even lower their eyes, when their betters entered a room. She and Penelope could scarcely leave their room without curious looks following them, or children trailing them, asking impertinent questions. And the baking and cooking—every female in residence seemed determined to create her particular Christmas specialty. The house smelled of spices and sugar day and night. Marjorie had to admit that was pleasant at least, and it did put one in the mood for the Christmas festivities.

How odd these people were. They'd lost their homes and their possessions in the fire, but they were as merry as monkeys. Perhaps they had no sense. Or perhaps it was something—or someone—else entirely.

"Look at her. This is *her* doing," Penelope complained, and Marjorie followed her daughter's baleful glare to where Lady Alanna McNabb was throwing snowballs like a ploughman.

"You would think nearly freezing to death would make her more wary of the cold," Marjorie mused, watching the girl. She also noted that Iain had scarcely taken his eyes off her. She did look fetching with her cheeks pinkened by the cold, soft tendrils of her hair loose in the wind, her eyes bright.

"I wish she—" Penelope began, but Marjorie cut her off.

"Don't say it! It's bad luck to ill-wish someone."

"You sound like Auld Annie," Penelope grumbled. "Everyone seems to think it's magic that brought her here. Why should an ill-wish not take her away again?"

Marjorie tried to imagine Alanna McNabb as the Marchioness of Merridew, presiding over a ball, or a *ton* dinner. Oddly, she could, even now, with snow in her hair. The girl had a natural, captivating grace, a way of making people like her. She glanced at Penelope, her eyes narrowed on her rival, her lip stuck out mutinously, her hands claws on her skirts. It was not a favorable comparison.

"You should be concentrating on Iain, my dear, not Alanna."

"She's been here for nearly two weeks. If she had not come, then I would be betrothed by now," Penelope said.

"You've nothing to worry about. She's spoken for. Why would she want a mere earl when she has a marquess in hand?" Because Iain was handsome, because he was one of her own kind, Marjorie thought. But it was more than that, something deeper, beyond mere attraction. There, it was in Alanna's eyes too, as they caught and held Iain's for just an instant too long.

A snowball hit the window, and Penelope screeched like a scalded cat. Elizabeth stood among the children and laughed, her face wide with it, her own cheeks pink. She stuck her tongue out and crossed her eyes at her older sister, then grinned. For an instant, Marjorie thought her plain younger daughter looked quite lovely, very festive, and happier than she'd ever seen her. She found herself smiling.

Magic indeed. There was surely something in the air

here at Craigleith, something heady and warm and wonderful, and Marjorie felt the thrill of Christmas anticipation in her breast. She hadn't felt it since she was a child. She felt as if miracles and magic were very possible. Perhaps even now, there was a way. Surely Merridew had received her letter by now and was coming to fetch his wayward bride. Iain could hardly refuse to give her up, now, could he? And that left Penelope, just as it was supposed to be.

She looked at Penelope and smiled. "Don't worry. I think we can count on everything working out just the way we hope, darling girl. Now go and change into something fetching, and when Iain comes in, be sure to smile."

Chapter Thirty-Seven

PENELOPE WATCHED IAIN come into the castle with Fiona and Alanna, surrounded by happy people. They looked like a family, a family she wasn't part of. Even Elizabeth was there, chattering and smiling. It made Penelope's stomach ache.

She pasted on a charming smile, caught Iain's arm in hers, and fell into step beside him.

She gave him a sultry grin, and he regarded her in surprise, but nothing remotely like love or desire kindled in his eyes. Instead, his smile dimmed. It was withering in the extreme. She smiled wider, squeezed tighter. "How kind you are to amuse the children, keep them out from underfoot," she gushed.

"They're not in the way," he said. "People here are used to having their children about. It's when they don't see them that they worry."

"It's quite the opposite in England," Penelope murmured, vowing that when she and Iain had children, they would be relegated to the top floor of Woodford Park with an army of nannies and governesses and kept out of sight until they were grown.

"You should have come outside, Penelope. It was such fun," Elizabeth said, unwinding her borrowed cloak, something made of thick wool, serviceable but most unfashionable.

Penelope gritted her teeth, managed to keep the smile in place. Her cheeks ached. "Oh, but it's so cold, Elizabeth dear. Has the snow stopped?" she said sweetly. Elizabeth blinked at her in surprise and didn't answer.

"For the moment," Iain replied instead. He was looking over her head at something behind her, and Penelope knew exactly what—who—it was. Alanna was helping the children pull off sodden woolens, directing them to hang them by the fire in the hall, but not too close. They were all smiles and sweetness with her.

"There will be biscuits later if you behave," Penelope called, and the children merely stared at her, their eyes solemn, as if she'd threatened castor oil and toadstools instead of sweets. Penelope forced a laugh, even as impatience rose. "Why, Alanna, you are so good with children. If you weren't engaged to a marquess, you would have made an excellent nanny."

She felt Iain's arm stiffen under her own, and she held him tight. Alanna's glow dimmed just a little, and Penelope felt a sense of triumph.

"Thank you, Penelope," Alanna said carefully, then turned away as one of the local men, an elderly fellow with a set of bagpipes cradled in his arms, entered the room. Penelope felt a sense of dread at the sight of them. She hated the bagpipes more than she hated . . . She watched Alanna's face light up once more, as if the Prince Regent had walked in. The old man turned to a puddle of mush under her warm smile. Was there a man born Alanna McNabb could not charm? How did she manage it? Penelope was prettier, better dressed . . .

"Are you ready, m'lady?" the old piper asked, beaming.

"Good morning, Donal," Alanna said. "How's Nessa?" Penelope bit her lip. Alanna knew the old man's name, and his wife's name too. She knew everyone's name. As if that mattered. At Woodford Park, they called all the footmen Michael, just so there was no confusion when one wanted something. Still. Penelope beamed at the man.

"Yes, how is Nessa? Is she the one I saw baking the lovely shortbread this morning? We had a lovely long chat—"

She stopped when she realized Iain was shaking. "What?" she asked. The old man was regarding her with undisguised surprise, and Alanna was trying to suppress a grin. Iain was red with suppressed laughter.

"I'd be very interested to see that, indeed, my lady," the old piper murmured.

"Penelope?" Iain leaned down to whisper in her ear. She sent Alanna a look of triumph until she heard what he had to say.

A pig? She felt her face color, was sure she'd catch fire under the heat of her blush.

"Penelope, I promised to teach the women some English country dances for the Christmas Eve party," Alanna said, her eyes as warm and kind as if they were friends, as if Penelope had not just made the mortifying mistake of suggesting she'd not only watched a pig baking shortbread but had also enjoyed a long conversation with the creature.

Penelope glanced at Iain. His expression was carefully blank as he regarded her. "Will you join us, Penelope?"

"Do come," Alanna said. "I'm still limping, and if I try to show them the polonaise like this, or a reel, we'll all be limping come Christmas Eve."

Elizabeth, damn her eyes, was still bent in two, laughing at Penelope's gaffe. Penelope clenched her fist. She knew every English dance, was considered an excellent dancer, and a much sought-after partner. Still, there was a whisper making its way through the crowd, smiles forming, giggles, and knowing looks, all falling on her like wet blankets. They were laughing at her.

Penelope raised her chin. If she did not help demonstrate the steps, they would be stuck with Alanna to teach them. She smiled to herself, picturing a roomful of lopsided Scots limping through English country dances. It would serve them right.

She sent Alanna a long look. "Perhaps Elizabeth can help you—though she's not very good at dancing." She watched her sister's grin fade. "Still, she's had the lessons, knows some of the steps. I'm afraid I have things to do, and it's nearly time for tea."

"As do I," Iain said. "And I have two left feet when it comes to dancing." He smiled at Alanna and bowed slightly. "I shall see you at dinner," he said to Penelope, obviously waiting for her to let go of his arm, but Penelope held on, moved with him, accompanying him down the hall, hoping Alanna McNabb was watching.

"We haven't had much of a chance to talk in the past few days, Iain," she said. He turned into the library, and a dozen pairs of eyes looked from their knitting. The conversation and the clicking of needles stopped.

"Good afternoon," Iain said, smiling.

"Hello, Laird. You should have knocked. You'll be spoiling Christmas surprises if you're not careful, walking in on folk unannounced," one woman said tartly.

Penelope bristled, waited for Iain to upbraid her for her presumption, but he grinned instead. "I'll leave you to it, then, Lottie." He backed out of the room, and Penelope followed.

"Where can I escort you, Penelope?" he asked politely, looking pointedly at her clinging hand.

"Where are you going?" she asked, batting her lashes.

"To the solar. I have things to do as well. Christmas is a busy time."

She had nothing at all to do. "Yes," she said. She remembered the angel, lovingly carved with Alanna's face. "Can I help you with anything?" she asked. She stepped closer, looked into his eyes. "Perhaps I could simply keep you company."

He closed his hand over her fingers, but only long enough to lift them off his arm, free himself. For an instant she considered throwing herself into his arms, pleading with him, but the flat, distant look in his eyes kept her silent. "No, but thank you, Penelope. I'll see you later."

She watched him walk away from her, felt frustration and fury and jealousy roll through her belly. She winced as the bagpipes gave a preliminary groan from the great hall before screeching into song. She picked up her skirts and fled up the stairs. She didn't stop until she reached the sanctuary of her room. Annie had asked her to share a room with her sister, to make space for more of the villagers, but Penelope had refused. She was the Lady of Craigleith, after all—well, almost—and she could see no reason at all to give up the privileges of rank for ordinary folk.

She opened her wardrobe, looked at the rows of gowns hanging there. Which one would Iain like best, find most enticing to the eye and the touch? She had a blue silk she was saving for Christmas, to be worn for the formal announcement of her betrothal to Iain. There was a demure pink satin, or a flattering, form-fitting green wool. She sighed. Did he care what she wore? He had not made one comment on her clothes, and she was used to being complimented, flirted with, and flattered. She crossed to the mirror and stared into the glass at her flawless face. He hadn't noticed that either. She paused as an idea came to her.

Perhaps he'd notice if she wore nothing at all.

THE EARL'S BEDROOM was just steps down the hall from her own room. Penelope opened the door and slipped inside.

It was as grand and fine as any room at Woodford Park, but Iain's father had been an English gentleman, the son of an earl, a man raised in luxury and refinement. She ran her hand over the polished oak posts of the bed and the fine damask of the bed curtains. The Turkey rugs were thick and soft, swallowing her footsteps. She sighed with pleasure.

Now, why would any man prefer to sleep in an ordinary room when this was his legacy, his right? Iain would probably opt to sleep in the stable at Woodford Park. She frowned. It was her duty to teach him, or so her mother said, to train him and mold him to be the kind of earl her grandfather and her uncle had been, lofty and full of consequence.

She looked down at the bed. The satin coverlet was smooth and soft. It was blue, her favorite color. She imagined sharing this bed—or the English equivalent—with Iain, and shuddered. She would endure his attentions, breed him an heir and a spare, and retire to her own apartments and lock the connecting door. She wanted to be a countess, and she accepted that came with certain duties attached, but beyond that, well, handsome as he was, she did not love Iain. She had never been in love with anyone, and she was beginning to doubt it was even possible. Marriage was a necessity, not a pleasure, for gain, not giving. She'd been raised on that belief.

It was clear to Penelope that if she wished to be a countess, she was going to have to force the matter. She ran her hand over the coverlet one more time and smiled.

Chapter Thirty-Eight

Glenlorne Castle, five days before Christmas

THE LETTER CAME as a surprise, to say the least. Worse still was the tale the bearer of the letter was telling when Alec walked into the room. The stranger was regaling Leith Rennie with a ribald tale about the Laird of Craigleith

Apparently, the laird had happened across a beautiful woman walking across the moor in the snow. Better still, she'd been driving two hundred head of fine Highland cattle ahead of her. Not one to miss such an opportunity, the laird had claimed the lass then and there, bundled her into his plaid, carried her back to his castle. He took her straight to his bed, where she'd been ever since.

Alec hadn't thought anything at all about the story until he read Alanna's note.

She wished him to know that she was safe, had gotten lost in the snow on Craigleith Moor, near Dundrummie, but was now at the very castle the messenger mentioned, under the kind care of none other than the Laird of Craigleith. *Kind care*? Alec had knocked the messenger on his backside.

Now, an hour later, he sat at the table reading the damned letter again and again while his wife applied a soothing salve to his bruised knuckles.

"We can't be sure the lass in the man's story is Alanna, Alec," she admonished. "It sounds like a made-up tale to me."

"Then it's an odd coincidence. Just how many women are wandering around in snowstorms on Craigleith Moor? Maybe this MacGillivray makes a habit of accosting females."

"Alanna didn't say she was accosted."

He waved the letter. "She says almost nothing at all. And that's not the tale the man who brought this tells. He says Alanna was kidnapped, carried off, forced to—" His mouth worked, but he could not find a suitable word, or at least one he could endure saying aloud.

"Nonsense. Alanna says nothing of the kind, and the letter is written in her own hand," Caroline reminded him. "Still, it is odd."

"Odd?" Alec turned a dangerous shade of red. "My sister has been stolen away by a madman, imprisoned in a castle, and—" He broke off again.

"No, I mean the part about the cows. The messenger said the lass was driving a herd of fine cows. Does Eleanor even keep cows?" Caroline asked. "Why would Alanna be herding cows in a snowstorm?"

Alec frowned. "I don't know. I haven't seen her for nearly four months. Until I got this letter, I assumed she was at Dundrummie with her mother, safe. None of this makes any sense."

Caroline put her hand on her husband's cheek. "Alanna is an intelligent, sensible young woman. I'm sure everything is fine."

"She's fanciful and shy," Alec replied. "And young." He made a fist, winced at the bruises. "I'd break any man who dared to harm her in two."

"You nearly killed the messenger," Caroline reminded him.

Alec strode toward the door. "I think it might be best if I go and find out for myself what's going on," he said.

"But where will you go first, to Dundrummie or Craigleith?"

Alec stopped in his tracks. "I meant the kitchen. If he's still here, I intend to question the messenger again."

SANDY MACGILLIVRAY PULLED the frost-stiffened plaid away from his face and stared down at Glenlorne Castle. It stood in a long, wide valley dusted with snow, the loch black and deep. A crumbling tower stood on the highest hill like a sentinel, overlooking all. The old place stared balefully at him, and Sandy set his heels to the garron's flanks. It had taken him six days of hard riding to get here, and the horse was as tired as he was. "The lass promised we'd find a welcome here," Sandy said and patted the beast's shoulder.

There were lights at Glenlorne, spilling warm yellow squares out across the snow, promising hospitality. He hoped the Earl of Glenlorne was as kind as his young sister.

He nearly collided with a man hurrying up the slope, bound tight in his cloak. The garron shied, and the man cried out when he saw Sandy.

"Ho there," Sandy said. "You're in a hurry, friend."

"To get away from a madman," the fellow said. "That's the last time I do a favor for any man. I offered to carry a letter, a simple enough thing. All it got me was a hard punch in the mouth."

"Are the folk here at Glenlorne not friendly?" Sandy asked, frowning.

"Not the laird," the man said. He pulled aside his cloak to show Sandy the bruise on his jaw. Sandy winced.

"The McNabb did that? The earl?"

"Aye," the man confirmed. "I gave him the letter, and while he read it I was enjoying a pot of ale, and telling a lad a fine tale I'd heard. Then all of a sudden the McNabb himself grabbed hold of me and hit me for no reason I know of."

"Perhaps he doesn't like tales," Sandy said. He wondered how the man would react to the story he had to tell.

"Not this one, though 'twas a good tale indeed."

"How'd it go?" Sandy said, none too anxious to arrive at Glenlorne now. He offered the man the flask from his pack, watched him drink deeply.

"Och, 'tis a bonnie tale. It seems the laird of a place called Craigleith stole a lass and five hundred—or was it six hundred?—fine cows along with her. She was so fair of face and form that he bound her hand and foot in his plaid and carried her to his castle. He refuses to give her up—or is it the cows he wants to keep? Either way, he refuses to return anything unless the lass's kin pay him a ransom in gold. He keeps the lass in a high tower, tied to his bed, clad in naught but a wee small handkerchief." He waggled his brows.

Sandy gaped at him. "Where on God's green—white—earth did you hear that?"

"At the local inn. There's a lad there who's writing a song about it."

Sandy was off the horse in an instant, his fists raised. He popped the stranger in the eye.

The man reeled. "What the devil did you do that for?"

"The MacGillivray is a good man, and the lass is a fine lady. I won't hear a word against them, d'you understand me?"

"Who the devil are you to care about a tale?" the stranger asked.

"I'm Sandy MacGillivray."

"MacGillivray?" The man recoiled, and his eyes widened. "Of Craigleith?"

"Aye. D'you know it?"

The man was stumbling away already. "I know enough to stay away from MacGillivrays and McNabbs," he said, stumbling backward. "You're all mad." He turned and fled.

Sandy looked down at the castle and imagined the earl inside it. Even if he was the most forgiving man in the world, the kindest, most understanding laird that ever was, as good as Iain MacGillivray himself, he wasn't going to like a story like this one. The lass was his sister, after all, a sweet and gentle lady.

"Tied to his bed? A wee small handkerchief?" Sandy

muttered. He took out his own generous kerchief and blew his nose. The garron snorted as if he didn't believe it either. And the lass—he blushed to think of how her reputation had been besmirched.

The only true part of the tale was the report of Alanna's beauty.

His heart quailed. He looked back up the track and almost turned the garron's head around to go back the way he'd come.

But Lady Alanna McNabb had done him a favor, given him a chance to redeem himself with Iain. All he had to do was face her brother.

He remembered the messenger's bruised jaw and swallowed.

"Still, I owe her a debt," he whispered. He cast his eyes skyward, said a quick prayer for mercy, and nudged the garron on toward Glenlorne.

Chapter Thirty-Nine

WHEN IAIN MACGILLIVRAY looked into the hall two hours later, the dancing lesson was still in progress. To be honest, it was more mayhem than dancing, with couples of every age and size crashing together, dissolving in laughter, having fun.

Alanna looked up to find him watching, leaning on the doorway, his arms crossed, his expression bemused. Lasses rushed across the room to take his hands and insist that he join the lesson.

Alanna wasn't dancing, since her leg still wasn't ready for such vigorous exercise, but she was demonstrating the steps with Elizabeth's help, and the English girl was having as much fun as anyone else. Alanna did not doubt that if Marjorie was anything like Devorguilla, Elizabeth was in for a long lecture about decorum and maintaining a strict and dignified distance from servants and tenants. She'd heard that lecture a dozen times and had ignored it whenever possible. The parties at Glenlorne were for everyone—laird and lady, gamekeeper and cowherd alike.

She sat next to the piper and watched as Iain partnered one lass after another, spinning each through the steps, making them blush and smile. He was a good dancer, but that hardly surprised her. He had a lean, athletic grace. Her breath caught in her throat, and her body warmed. He made a fine figure on the floor. Had she ever seen a handsomer man? His russet hair caught the snow light that poured through the high windows. Donal's pipes rang like Christmas bells, accompanied by laughter and clapping hands. How long had it been since she'd laughed like this, been this happy? Not since she'd left Glenlorne months ago.

Iain caught her eye and grinned as he spun his partner through the figures of the dance. Her heart leaped in her breast, and she could not help but smile back. He held his hand out to Fiona, who sat among the old folks, clapping the beat. She shook her head, sure her leg would make her clumsy. Alanna saw the wistful light in Fiona's eyes, the desire to dance. Iain bowed to her again, refusing to take no for an answer, and Fiona bit her lip and set her hand in his. Her brother swept her into his arms, lifting her off the floor. He twirled her through the air until she was laughing. He set her on the floor; she placed her damaged foot on his, and they danced smoothly around the floor. He returned Fiona back to her seat when the music ended. Alanna watched Fiona nod in her direction

"Ask Alanna." She read the words on Fiona's lips from across the room, watched Iain turn toward her.

Alanna felt hot blood rise in her cheeks as he crossed the floor, held out his hand, and bowed, offering a roguish smile by way of added encouragement. There was something in the depths of his eyes that took her breath away. She swallowed, hesitated, her fingertips curling on his palm, her heart hammering against her ribs.

"Up with you, lass," Donal said. "I'll play a reel."

She glanced around the room, saw everyone waiting, staring at the pair of them, their eyes expectant, and she clasped Iain's hand and nodded, felt electricity travel up her arm, warm her everywhere.

"Can you waltz?" he asked.

She looked up at him in surprise. "Yes, can you?"

His eyebrows rose. "I do get to Edinburgh from time to time."

"Of course, I didn't mean— Of course, I can't waltz now, with my knee—"

He lifted her in his arms, the way he'd done with Fiona, and held her against his chest. He spun her through the steps. She was aware of his arm around her waist, her breast pressed to his, his laughing gray eyes inches from her own. Close enough to kiss. She tightened her grip on his hand, curled her opposite hand on his shoulder, and wished the dance could go on forever.

She had only ever waltzed with her sisters, under the strict instruction of a dancing master. It had been tedious, mechanical, and dull. But with Iain it felt like flying, like— She dropped her eyes to his mouth. Dancing with him made her feel the way kissing him did. It made her imagine them together, naked under his plaid, both of them awake and warm this time. The light in his eyes turned serious, as if he was thinking the same thing, and his heartbeat quickened under her breast. His eyes dropped to her mouth, his smile slipping a little.

"We should stop," she whispered. "Donal isn't playing anymore."

In fact the whole room had gone silent, and they were dancing alone, surrounded by a ring of bright eyes and besotted grins. Iain set her carefully on her feet, held her until he was sure she had her balance, and Alanna felt her cheeks flame. She didn't want to let him go.

"I want to learn how to dance like that," someone said in a breathless voice, and everyone laughed.

Iain turned and bowed deeply over her hand, the way he might at a London ball, to a lady—or a marchioness— who had honored him with a dance. She bit her lip, but he squeezed her fingers until she looked at him.

"Come to the solar," he whispered for her ears alone.

Her mouth dried and she clenched her fist in the wool of her skirt. "I don't think that's a good idea," she managed, remembering the last time she'd been in the solar with him. Only now, she knew how it felt to kiss him, desire him. If she kissed him now, she wouldn't want to stop.

"I've got Fiona's Christmas gift partly finished, and I want your opinion," he murmured, and Alanna's face flamed again.

"Oh." She felt like a ninny. Of course he didn't wish to kiss her again—he had Penelope for kisses. Alanna had been the one to kiss him the last time. She'd practically thrown herself at him. Not practically. She unwound her fist from her gown, clasped her hands loosely at her waist, and forced a placid smile. "Of course I'll come." He nodded and left the room.

An hour later, when the dancers were exhausted and happy, Alanna knocked softly on the door of the solar. Iain opened it a crack and peered out at her like a spy. Would she always feel this unsettling sense of breathless excitement when she looked at him? Did it show? Oh, how she hoped it didn't show.

He stepped back to let her in, and she breathed in the scent of wood shavings, and of peat burning in the fireplace, and the familiar scent of Iain himself.

He lifted a cloth on the table to reveal a pair of Fiona's boots, one with a sole slightly thicker than the other. Alanna crossed and looked at it. It was still rough, but he'd hollowed out the heel so it wasn't too heavy or bulky.

He took it in his hand and turned it, running his thumb over it. "I'll smooth it out, paint it the same color as the sole of the other boot."

"It's perfect," she said, taking it, marveling at it.

"It may need some adjustments when Fiona tries it on. Here, for instance—" His hand touched the heel, brushed her fingers, and she felt a rush of longing pass through her. Her breath hitched in her throat, and she nearly dropped the boot. He stopped, but didn't move his hand. Instead, he moved his fingertips more firmly over hers, caressed her fingertips, her knuckles, her wrist. She shivered.

"I have been—happy—since you came to Craigleith," he said softly, standing inches from her. "You make me feel as if—well, as if being an English earl might not be such a terrifying thing after all, not if you—" She laid her finger against his lips, but his meaning was plain enough when he kissed it. "Why is it I can't be near you without wanting to kiss you?" he asked.

So it wasn't just her. Was her desire for him so easy to see, to read? She looked into his eyes, read his own need there, and her mouth watered. She closed her eyes, forced herself to think of Merridew and Penelope. Her heart clenched tight in her chest. They had both made promises to others. Penelope loved Iain. She must. How could she not?

Even if Alanna did not love Merridew, she loved her mother. Devorguilla had been devastated when Megan had eloped with Rossington. It had caused so much unhappiness, regret, and pain. Kissing Iain now, falling in love with him, would only cause more pain, if not for her, then for others, people she loved, people Iain loved. She shut her eyes and fought desire. How easy it would be to give in and take what she wanted, just this once.

She pulled away, shook her head, wrapped her hands around her body. "We cannot do this, Iain—*I* cannot do this. We've both made promises."

He came around the table, stood behind her with his hands on her shoulders. He kissed her ear. "What of desire?" he asked.

She tilted her head, gave him access to her throat. "What of honor and duty?" she asked.

His arms slid around to enfold her, draw her back against him. It felt good, right.

"What of destiny? Perhaps it was fate that brought you here to me."

Her heart ached, but she found the strength to move

away. "I don't believe in fate," she lied. She wanted very much to believe in it, along with magic, and true love, and happy endings. But she was betrothed to the Marquess of Merridew. He was her fate, not Iain MacGillivray. "I promised—"

"So you are willing to please everyone else, even if it means disappointing yourself. I see it in your eyes, Alanna."

"What do you see?" she asked, afraid.

"I see you, and I see myself there. You make it easy to imagine a different future than the ones we both expected a few weeks ago."

She shut her traitorous eyes, felt tears sting the back of them. "I wish—" she said, and stopped. Would it make it any better to say it aloud, would it change anything? Did a wish trump promises, expectations?

"What do you wish?" he asked, and the low timbre of his voice vibrated over her nerves, drew them taut. She wished she had never agreed to wed Merridew, that she was as brave as her sister, had dared to refuse his offer of marriage, even at the risk of disappointing her mother. She wished she had met Iain sooner. Much sooner. She clasped her hands together to stem the need to touch him. It wasn't enough. She thought of him in Penelope's arms, Penelope's husband, father of her children.

"I wish I had not left Dundrummie that day," she lied. "You are a very lucky man, Iain MacGillivray. Penelope will make a wonderful wife."

"Will she?" he asked, his tone flat.

"Of course. She's lovely."

"And will Merridew make a wonderful husband?" he asked.

Alanna swallowed. She couldn't answer that. Bitterness filled her throat. She backed toward the door. "I must go," she said. "I promised Annie I'd help her in the kitchen, and Fiona needs—" She had no idea what Fiona needed. She only knew she had to leave the room. "She'll love the shoes, Iain. You are—" Her tongue tripped on itself.

He tilted his head. "Wonderful?" he asked dully. "Honorable?"

She felt tears coming, and fled.

IAIN CAREFULLY WRAPPED the shoes and pushed them into the drawer of the workbench. He found the angel there, still wrapped in the square of linen. He took it out, stood it on the table, and regarded it. He ran a fingertip over the carved face—Alanna's face—and touched the wave of her hair, the curving wings. It would be all he had left of her when she went away, married her marquess.

He imagined the future. What if he did marry Penelope, and then someday he met Alanna again—Marchioness Merridew—by chance at a London ball? He would smile, bow, and make some bland remark about the weather, or the crush of people attending the party. They'd part as strangers. He shut his eyes. Were they more than strangers now?

He wanted Alanna McNabb as he had never wanted anything or anyone before. He looked into the angel's face, saw Alanna's sweetness, her soft smile. Damn duty and honor. What of desire, love? He turned the angel in his hands, letting the light fall on her face. He knew what he wished, what he wanted.

There was a knock on the door. His heart skipped a beat, expecting Alanna. Had she changed her mind? Wee Janet stood outside the door.

"Laird, Lady Penelope asked me to give you this." She held out a folded note with his name scrawled across the front. If she was curious about the contents, or surprised that Penelope had written to someone here in the same castle instead of just coming herself to speak to him, she didn't say. She went on her way, too busy, no doubt, to give it much thought. Iain broke the seal.

There is something I wish to discuss, the note said. *Come to the earl's apartments.*

It was simply signed *P.*

He held it in his hand and considered. What could she want? For weeks, he'd left her hoping for a proposal. She'd been waiting for him most patiently. He looked at the angel again, still standing on the table. He crossed and picked it up, wrapped it once more, and tucked it back into the drawer beside Fiona's shoes.

Iain turned his steps toward the laird's apartment—his father's rooms. What would his father do now, if he were here? Anthony Marston had married for love, changed his own name for the woman he loved, a Highland beauty with little to bring to a marriage with an English earl's youngest son. His parents had loved each other passionately, forged a new life together. His father had been lost when his wife had died.

Iain put the note into his pocket and turned toward the stairs. He'd made a decision. It was time to speak to Penelope.

Chapter Forty

ALANNA WENT TO her room, her heart aching. She paced the floor, thinking. There must be a solution to this. She could not possibly be in love with a man she could not have.

She was too sensible, too smart for that. Surely what she was feeling was something else entirely. Perhaps it was gratitude because Iain had rescued her and made her feel safe. But then, Alec made her feel just as safe, and it wasn't the same at all. Alec didn't make her heart pound whenever he walked into a room. And in truth, anyone else would have done the same if they had come upon her in the storm, wouldn't they? And yet she'd known this was different, that *he* was different, the moment she'd woken up, found him crouched by the fire, wearing her cloak for a kilt.

Maybe it was admiration. Iain was a fine and noble laird who did his best for his people. But that described a hundred other men as well . . . surely, a thousand. She didn't feel dizzy in the presence of her father's friend Laird

Melrose, and he was most beloved by his clan for his kindness. Her admiration for Iain was different from that. It was how he made her feel just by looking at her, as if she was different, perfect, not a second daughter, a shadow of her sisters, but first.

She felt intense love for her clan, and for her sisters, her brother, her mother, and her aunt.

Yet only Iain made her feel dizzy, unsettled, and breathless. She ached to touch him, to kiss him.

But he belonged to Penelope, would be her husband. Alanna shut her eyes.

She'd been shocked when Megan had run away, refused to wed Lord Merridew, had risked scandal and shame and the anger of her family for a man she barely knew. Alanna hadn't understood then. She understood now. Megan had been in love. Her mother was wrong—titles and fortunes meant nothing without love. But Devorguilla had grown up a poor Highlander's daughter with nothing but her looks to give her hope. She had married an earl, decided her daughters would never know the hardships, the fear of hunger and privation that she had known. And in Devorguilla's eyes, an English lord was better by far than a Scottish one.

Alanna recognized her feelings for what they were now. It wasn't gratitude or admiration or even fond regard. It was love. She loved Iain MacGillivray. Alanna pressed a fist to her midsection, felt the pounding of her heart. If this was love, it hurt.

She thought of her betrothal. Would she feel the same thrill when Merridew kissed her, or touched her hand? She swallowed. She knew she would not. When he touched her, she would close her eyes and think of Iain.

She crossed to the window. A bridal veil of frost clung to the windowpane. Her own veil would hide her regrets, her lack of enthusiasm as she met Merridew at the altar. Her heart would remain as cold and frozen as the snow. She wished— She swallowed.

She wished it could be different, all of it. She imagined her mother's shock and rage. If she did not marry Merridew, she would be disappointing so many people—even Lord Merridew himself, perhaps.

And still she could not have Iain. He was betrothed to Penelope. His clan, his kin, and his English tenants were counting on that match, the happy union of their laird and the perfect lady.

Alanna breathed on the windowpane, rubbed away a patch of frost, a hole in the veil. She peered across the windswept moor, white with snow.

She had stayed at Craigleith too long. She realized now it wasn't the snow or her injured knee that had kept her here. It was Iain.

And now it was time to go.

Chapter Forty-One

IAIN ENTERED THE sitting room of his father's apartments. The room was exactly the same as it had been when he had died, nearly a decade earlier. The furniture was English, gentlemanly, rich. The books were scholarly tomes on English history, husbandry, and politics. Iain supposed he should read them now. A cut crystal decanter stood on an elegant table near the window, glasses at the ready, waiting to be filled with the brandy Lord Anthony had preferred over whisky.

This room, filled with English comforts, was part of the wing that had been added to the castle when Iain's parents had married. His mother's rooms were across the hall, part of the fourteenth-century Scottish castle. His own room was in the old castle. Penelope, Elizabeth, and Marjorie were housed in the new part, in English rooms with English furniture.

He wondered why Penelope had asked to see him here, of all places. Perhaps she wished to offer him a lesson on how an English earl should live, as compared to a Scottish one. His own room was crammed with books, accounts, and simple furnishings, his belongings held in a chest built to hold the armor of a Scottish ancestor. He liked it there, felt more comfortable with his Scottish blood than the English, and he knew that would have to change. He must find a way to be both.

The door to the bedchamber was ajar.

"Penelope?" he called.

"Here," she answered, and he crossed the room, the colorful Turkey carpet absorbing his footfalls.

He opened the door fully, and his breath caught in his throat. Penelope was lying in his father's bed. Her blond hair was loose, spread across the monogrammed pillowcase, her cheeks flushed. She sat up and let the satin coverlet fall away from her creamy white shoulders—very naked shoulders.

Iain glanced around the room, noted the discarded garments that lay over the chair at the end of the bed. He felt dread climb his throat. He glanced at her again. She held out her hand.

"Come here," she said, her voice a low purr. She smiled at him, but it did not reach her eyes. They remained as hard and as cold as sapphires. "I thought you might like to unwrap your Christmas surprise a few days early."

He didn't move. She let the coverlet fall further, exposing her breasts. Two spots of hectic color filled her cheeks. Her chin rose defiantly. She didn't look like a woman in love. She looked like a woman who intended to get what she wanted. "Do you need help unwrapping it?" she asked.

He looked away. "Penelope—" he began.

"There'll be time for talking later," she said. There was a hard edge to her voice as she interrupted him, a touch of desperation, of anger, but no love or desire. He met her eyes, saw the fierce determination there. It took his breath away, but not in the way she expected.

"No, Penelope," he said. "I can't stay. I just came up here to tell you I can't marry you, that I won't be proposing."

Her eyes grew harder and colder still. She snatched the sheet and wrapped it around her breasts. "This is because of *her*, isn't it?" she demanded.

There was no need to clarify who she meant. Iain sent her a level look. "This has nothing to do with anyone else. This is about whether or not you and I would suit."

"Of course we would," Penelope insisted. "We're perfectly matched."

Iain looked around the room. "This was my father's room. He spent a fortune bringing the finest furnishings from London, France—even China. Still, he spent every night in my mother's room. He only slept here after she died. They married for love, you see. The tale was that he was riding through the hills, here in Scotland to do a spot of climbing, when he happened to stop at a castle to ask directions. Once he'd set foot over the threshold, met the laird's daughter, he never left again." He met Penelope's eyes. "Can you honestly say you love me?" he asked her.

The spots of color grew, and she looked away. "I'm sure I will grow to see you with a—fond regard—in time."

He shook his head. "Would that be enough for you? Haven't you ever wanted something more, something better? Something beyond what is expected of you?"

Her brow crumpled. "Whatever are you talking about? We would marry for power and position, not love. Love is for peasants because they haven't got anything better to look forward to. I was raised to be a countess."

"And if another man had inherited the title instead of me, another cousin, would you be sitting in his bed?" Iain asked.

She didn't answer, but her lips pursed tightly.

"You deserve a better man than me, cousin, someone you have more than a fond regard for. I hope you find love along with the title you're looking for, but it won't be my title." He turned to go. "I'll go now, and let you dress."

"Stop!" she said, and he turned. She had her arms folded over her chest. "It doesn't matter if we do this or not, Iain. All it will take is for me to tell my mother that you and I were in this room together, that you—" Her mouth worked, but she didn't say it. Her chin rose, her eyes commanded. "You will be forced to marry me. What do you say now?"

She let the sheet fall again.

"ANNIE, HAVE YOU seen the laird?" Alanna asked, coming into a kitchen full of the sweet smell of cinnamon.

"He's upstairs, in the old lord's quarters," Wee Janet said, stirring a pot of stew over the fire and turning to look over her shoulder at Alanna.

Alanna turned and left the room, climbing the stairs slowly. Her leg was healed, and it felt perfectly well now. Or almost. She winced as she took the next step up. Still, she would force herself to stand straight and tall before him.

She would thank the Laird of Craigleith for his kind hospitality, and she would tell him that she had decided the time had come for her to go. She would leave in the morning, ask if he could have someone take her even part of the way to Dundrummie. She hoped he would assign the task to someone else. Surely he had more important duties to see to, as well as the announcement of his betrothal.

She came to the double doors that guarded the formal apartments in the English wing of the castle. They were grand panels of oak with polished brass hardware. One door stood open, and she slipped into the room, stopping when she heard voices.

"That would condemn us both to a lifetime of unhappiness and mistrust. Do you want that?" she heard Iain ask.

"I don't care," she heard Penelope say, her tone cold.

Alanna saw Iain standing in an inner doorway, his back toward her. "No," he said, his voice firm.

Penelope let out a shriek, and Iain ducked as a pillow flew past his head. It landed at Alanna's feet, and she jumped back. Something far heavier followed the pillow, and shattered against the door. It swung open, and Alanna's eyes widened. She met Penelope Curry's angry eyes over Iain's shoulder. He didn't even realize Alanna was behind him. He was staring at Penelope.

Penelope was wrapped in a bedsheet . . . well, mostly. Alanna took in the sight of rumpled bedclothes, saw Penelope's discarded clothing, and felt her mouth dry. The blood drained from her body. For an instant she was unable to move. She felt—what? Heartbreak? It wasn't her right. Penelope and Iain had every right, every reason to— She saw triumph bloom in Penelope's eyes, watched her smile coldly, mocking Alanna.

The blood rushed back again, filled Alanna's cheeks, burning her with shame and humiliation. She had to get away before Iain saw her. She could not bear it if he turned now, saw her. She could not hide the hurt in her eyes.

But he had no idea she was there. His eyes were full of the sight of his intended, naked, in the bed they shared, would always share, as man and wife.

Alanna stumbled backward, tripped over the damned pillow, and flailed her way toward the door. She had to get out, had to leave. She felt tears blur her vision as she hurried down the hall. She didn't stop in her room—Iain's room. She had come to Craigleith with nothing at all, and she would leave the same way.

She hurried through the busy kitchen, took her cloak from the peg, and flung it over her shoulders. It was midafternoon, plenty of time to reach shelter somewhere, at one of the outlying farmsteads, an inn, or a shieling. Someone would help her travel on, reach Dundrummie or Glenlorne.

She paused by the door that led to the bailey. "Are we going outside to play?" she heard a little voice ask. She turned to find Seonag's daughter, Molly, just six, standing behind her.

"No, sweetheart, not today."

"Annie says it's going to snow," Molly said. "Can we build another snowman?"

"Tomorrow, perhaps—and Christmas Eve will soon be here, and then there'll be greens to gather, and the *Cailleach Nollaigh* to ride around the castle, and bring inside. Won't that be fun?" Alanna babbled, her heart thumping. She felt a wistful edge of regret that she would not be here, or anywhere warm and familiar, when Christmas arrived.

"And the party," Molly said.

"Aye," Alanna said. They would announce their betrothal on Christmas Eve, Iain and Penelope. Alanna was grateful she would not be here for that.

She smiled at Molly, hoped the child didn't see the tears in her eyes. "Annie was baking biscuits when I came through the kitchen. She might let you have one if you offer to help wrap them up and put them away."

She watched as Molly's eyes lit up and the girl hurried away toward the kitchen.

Alanna watched her go, then opened the door and slipped out into the cold.

A gust of wind sucked the warm breath out of her lungs, and Alanna pulled her cloak more tightly around her throat as she forged on into the snow.

Chapter Forty-Two

IAIN DIDN'T UNDERSTAND IT. In one moment, Penelope had gone from being furious, insisting that she would force him to marry her, to laughing like a loon the next. He didn't see the joke. *Was* she joking?

"Perhaps I won't insist you marry me after all. Maybe you're right. I could find a marquess of my own, or a duke, even. Then you would be the one to bow to me, cousin, my lord earl." She threw the words at him like insults. Then she descended from the bed like a queen wrapped in ermine instead of a sheet, her chin high. "Get out."

He hadn't needed a second invitation. He had no idea what had changed her mind. He just counted it as a Christmas miracle.

Iain went into the armory and looked down at the log that would become the *Cailleach Nollaigh,* a huge trunk of a pine tree, gnarled and knotted and fragrant. It was his task to carve a face into the wood, the face of the winter goddess.

He began to work, using hammer and chisel to remove

pieces of bark and wood. Around him, the sheep made soft, contented sounds, and the cattle chewed their cud and watched him work. They were tethered to hooks and pegs that had once held armor and weapons for Craigleith's fighting men, knights and champions of old, who had probably enjoyed many a Christmas party in the great hall, with the laird and his lady seated at the top table, watching the merriment. His clan would have to be content with just Iain yet again this year. Would there be questions? Many expected him to marry Penelope. But there'd be no announcement. He pursed his lips bitterly. There might have been if things were different, but Alanna had made it clear enough she intended to wed her marquess, and that was that.

He chipped away at the log and pictured her by his side on Christmas Eve. He'd dance with her, laugh, but that was all. There'd be mistletoe hung in the hall. Perhaps he could steal a kiss—one final kiss that would have to last him for the rest of his days. Then he'd return her to Dundrummie, to the arms of her betrothed.

The door opened and Annie came in, holding Molly's hand. He grinned, but Molly didn't smile back. He glanced at Annie, saw the worry in her eyes.

"Laird, Alanna's gone."

He rose to his feet, set the chisel down. "Gone? Gone where?" he asked, though he knew by the look in Auld Annie's eyes.

"She left an hour or two ago, perhaps longer. Molly saw her go, but she can't recall exactly when that was."

"I was eating cookies," Molly said in her own defense.

"Wee Janet said Alanna came into the kitchen, asked where you were. She sent her upstairs to Lord Anthony's chamber. Did she find you there?" Annie asked, her eyes sharp.

Iain didn't answer. He suddenly knew exactly what Alanna had seen. He'd tried to kiss her in the solar, and less than an hour later— He swallowed. Did she imagine him such a cad?

"It's going to snow, Iain. Another storm," Annie said.

He remembered finding her in the last storm. She's almost died. He rose, set the chisel aside. "I'll go after her. The snow won't have covered her tracks yet."

Annie tilted her head. "There's only one reason why a woman runs away if you ask me. She ran away from what she didn't want. Perhaps now she's running away from what she thinks she cannot have. Am I right? Is there something between you and Alanna? I can't read the signs. They've been hidden from me. If this is a spell, it's been laid by someone else's magic, not mine."

"There she is," Molly chirped, pointing. Annie and Iain spun to look. But Molly was pointing at the *Cailleach Nollaigh*.

Once again, without meaning to, Iain had carved Alanna's face into the wood. She looked out at them with a sweet, mischievous smile. He heard Annie chuckle softly, and she squeezed his shoulder.

"Never mind. The signs are all pointing one way now. You'd best go and find her."

Chapter Forty-Three

LORD MERRIDEW WRAPPED his cashmere scarf more tightly around his throat and straightened the rug that covered his knees. He looked out the window of the coach, but the landscape was blank, white and uninformative. He had no idea where he was. Devorguilla watched him from the seat opposite his own, her expression carefully blank. They'd been travelling at a snail's pace for three days, the weather forcing them to take the long way, go some sixty miles around a glen that took mere hours to cross in summer. As the crow flew—if a crow could fly in all this snow—it would be a distance of less than fifteen miles to reach Craigleith, where his bride was hiding, or staying. It wasn't quite clear to him why she hadn't returned to Dundrummie before now. He understood she had been injured somehow. He hoped it wasn't anything disfiguring, or something that would prevent her from breeding. Lady Marjorie's letter hadn't said, just suggested that he come at once.

He looked out the window yet again, bored with the

interminable journey, and saw the hopeful sight of lights and an inn yard. He knocked on the roof to alert his driver. "We'll stop for the night," he said.

"But we're almost at Craigleith, my lord," Devorguilla said. "A few more hours. I have no doubt that they will offer us hot food and warm beds, and you can be reunited with Alanna."

He was far more interested in the inn's hot food and a deep tot of whisky than he was in the girl. She'd keep. Craigleith Castle was still hours away. In truth, he barely even recalled what Alanna McNabb looked like. Not that it mattered. All cats were gray in the dark, as the proverb said.

"No. We'll stop," he insisted. Lady Marjorie's coach was following this one, carrying Lady Eleanor and the youngest McNabb chit, Sorcha. Eleanor had insisted on coming to Craigleith, and bringing the child. Apparently, the girl couldn't be expected to remain alone at Dundrummie if there was to be a wedding and Christmas at Craigleith. Wilfred could not abide children, especially female children. He had insisted in his turn that the girl be confined to the other coach with Eleanor.

He looked at the stunned surprise on Devorguilla's face now as he pronounced his decision. She was apparently far more eager to reach her daughter than he was. He looked away from the sharp disbelief in her gaze. "It's starting to snow," he said peevishly. "There's no point in pressing on, getting stuck somewhere."

"Are you certain you wish to marry my daughter, Lord Merridew?" Devorguilla asked as they sat in a private dining room, eating the miserable fare the dour innkeeper insisted was the best he had to offer. Merridew ignored the stew and downed several glasses of whisky instead.

He stared at the countess. In truth, he didn't *want* to marry at all. It was simply duty. He wanted Alanna McNabb's dowry, and an heir, in that order. She herself scarcely mattered.

"I'm content with the arrangements," he said.

"What's Alanna's favorite color?" Lady Eleanor asked, her eyes as sharp as knitting needles. The child—Sorcha—regarded him from the corner of the room.

"What the devil—" He recalled the company and paused. "*Why* should that matter?"

"Perhaps you wish to give her a Christmas present—or a wedding present. Shouldn't it be something she likes?"

He raised his chin. "I am giving her a title, my lady. Surely that is enough."

"My lord, what color are Alanna's eyes?" the child piped.

"So long as she has two of them, and they both point in the same direction, I don't care in the least," he quipped, annoyed.

"Her hair?" This prompt came from Devorguilla.

"Blond," he said, since Devorguilla was blond.

Eleanor and Devorguilla exchanged a look, their lips pinching like the strings on a miser's purse. The countess got to her feet. "Come, Sorcha. I think it's time for bed." She left the room without so much as a good night.

Lady Eleanor rose as well and leaned on her walking stick for a moment, scanning his face.

"My niece's eyes are hazel, with flecks of silver and soft brown, my lord. Her hair is dark, with a touch of auburn. Her favorite color is red, like the roses that grow here in the Highlands in summer. She loves books, and she has a romantic heart."

And just what did any of that have to do with anything? Wilfred wondered. He watched as Eleanor Fraser left without another word. Then he ordered another whisky, just to ward off the sudden chill that filled the room.

Chapter Forty-Four

THE WIND WAS growing stronger, and it was getting dark. Iain followed the faint indents of Alanna's footsteps in the snow, prayed that new snow would hold off until he found her.

Alanna seemed to have a knack for taking long walks in the wrong direction. There were no farmsteads in this direction, no inns or roads, just moor and hills for miles, until the land dropped into Glen Dorian. From there, if she should reach it, it was barely ten miles to Dundrummie—but that was in good weather, with a fair wind at your back.

Not in deep snow.

He scanned the horizon, looking for a glimpse of her red cloak. It would be easy to wander off track, fall into a gully the way she had before, and this time—

Iain's heart clenched in his chest. If she still wished to marry her marquess, he could live with that. If she went home to Glenlorne and made her life there, he could accept that, too, but he could not picture the world without Alanna in it.

He loved her. It was why he could never settle for marrying Penelope, or anyone else he didn't love. In a few short weeks, he'd grown used to the feeling of his breath catching and his heart skipping a beat every time Alanna entered a room.

Craigleith Castle felt different with her in it. She made everyone smile, brought joy and laughter when there might have been tears. Even after the fire, she had done what she could to give everyone a sense of hope. She'd given him hope. He'd begun to picture being an English earl with less dread. He knew that with Alanna by his side as his wife, his countess, there was nothing he couldn't accomplish. She'd charm all of England once they met her.

The first thing he intended to do when he found her was to shake some sense into her. Then he planned to propose. This time, he was eager to speak the words, even if he wasn't sure of the answer.

The garron snorted, and Iain looked up. He felt a rush of relief as he saw her red cloak flapping in the wind, her slender body bent against the gale. He frowned.

If she meant to go to Dundrummie, she was going the wrong way.

And just ahead of her, there was a deep ravine, and she was heading toward it. Iain kicked the horse and rode faster.

Chapter Forty-Five

SHE WAS LOST.

Alanna wrapped her cloak against her cheeks, trying to ignore the stinging wind. She was a Highlander, born and bred in hills like these. Perhaps she should have spent more time outdoors, walking with Megan, instead of reading books.

She looked around at the white wilderness. She might get lost for good this time, and Iain would not be there to rescue her. She felt fear bite into her bones, every bit as cold as the wind. She felt regret too. She might have done things differently, been braver. She could have said no when her mother insisted she wed Lord Merridew in Megan's place. Did Merridew wish she was Megan? She pinched her frozen lips together. Well, she wished he was someone else as well. The match was doomed before it had even begun.

She wanted someone who loved her for herself, just her, someone she loved too.

She wanted Iain.

She felt tears freeze against her cheeks, and she brushed them away impatiently. She should have told Iain that she—

"Told me what?"

Alanna spun. Iain sat on his garron, wrapped in his plaid. She was talking to herself. Hallucinating. Did hallucinations answer back? She blinked. He stayed right where he was, as real as she was, his gray eyes crinkled at the corners, fixed on her.

Her heart soared. He'd come for her.

Then she remembered Penelope, naked, in bed, and her heart dropped like a dead bird. She turned away, kept walking. "This is a private conversation, Iain MacGillivray."

"Carry on then. I'll wait. What were you saying?" She heard the crunch of the garron's hooves in the snow, knew he was following her.

She really was glad to see him. "I was wishing—" *Penelope, naked.* "Oh, never mind."

"Let me guess then. Were you wishing it would snow? You have your wish, my lady."

She looked up, saw the thick fluffy flakes falling.

"It will be a lovely Christmas with all this snow," he continued. "Craigleith is lovely in the snow. Mind you, it's lovely in the spring as well, and in the summer. Roses grow up around the kitchen door so thick you can smell them for miles," he said.

She glanced at him. There was snow on his hair, white on copper, and on his eyelashes, and coating the garron's shaggy mane. She would remember him this way, not in spring or summer, with roses rambling over the sturdy walls of his castle. She would not be here then.

He dismounted from the horse and came toward her. "Or perhaps you were wishing to be rescued?"

"I felt like a walk. Surely there's something you should be doing back at Craigleith." She pointed a finger toward the castle. *With Penelope, naked.*

He pointed the opposite direction. "It's that way, Alanna. Over there."

She gaped, scanned the horizon.

He took her hand in his and swung it to point behind her. "Dundrummie is that way, if you planned to go through Glen Dorian, though it's impassable with all the snow. If you keep going the way you're walking, you'll reach England eventually. Of course, there's a steep drop not twenty paces in front of you." She felt her face heat. He was close beside her, blocking the wind. "Were you running away, or running toward something?" he asked.

"Can a person not go out for a walk?"

"Good," he said. He marched beside her through the snow, and the garron followed. "Did you know that Sandy thought I should keep you when I brought you back the last time?"

"Keep me?" she asked, breathless from trying to outpace him. He kept up effortlessly.

"Aye, in the old Highland way. A hundred years ago, the MacGillivrays were reivers, like most Highlanders. We stole cattle from our neighbors, and they stole them back again, with a few of ours for good measure. We stole our brides too, on occasion. Now, if I'd captured a fine cow, sleek and sweet with soft hazel eyes, I'd keep her."

Alanna stopped walking to glare at him. "Are you comparing me to a cow?"

"Not at all. I was just considering the situation we find ourselves in. A stray cow, or a stray lass, is fair game, wouldn't you say?" He smiled at her, and she felt her heart trip over itself, even as indignation rose in her breast. "We're civilized now, of course, but I do miss the old ways, especially since I met you. You bring out the damnedest emotions in me, lass."

Before she could reply, he scooped her up and tossed her over his shoulder. She whooped with surprise, and tried to free herself, but his arm was like an iron band across her bottom. "What are you doing?" she demanded.

"Claiming you," he said.

She went still for an instant. "You're betrothed to Penelope. Is this a new tradition—Scottish harems?"

He laughed. "I love a woman who is well read." He began walking, and she stared at a world where the sky was down and the ground was up.

"I doubt Penelope would find this amusing."

"Ah, but Penelope isn't here."

Alanna struggled again, to no avail. His grip was like iron. "Of course she isn't here—she's back at Craigleith, in your bed."

"You're the only woman who's been in my bed."

She thumped a fist against his back, felt it bounce off solid muscle. "Put me down at once," she said, using her very best lady-of-the-manor English. "I will not have a conversation with your—your *backside*!"

"I don't think I will," he said, his tone light. He wasn't even winded from carrying her. "I like the feel of you in my arms, more than I've ever liked anything, in fact. I've grown used to you there. And I'm talking to your backside as well, and very much enjoying the view."

She gasped, felt the breath cut off by his shoulder pressed to her belly. "Where are you taking me?"

"Ewan MacGillivray's cottage."

"Why?" she demanded, feeling heat course through her.

"Because it's nearly dark, and it's starting to snow. We'll be safer here tonight."

She didn't feel safe. She felt the pull of her own desire. This time she wasn't unconscious, and being alone in a room with this man made her think of kisses, and love, and—

"Take me back to Craigleith," she insisted.

"Are you afraid?" he asked.

"Yes," she said.

"Of me?"

"Of myself," she muttered, but it was muffled in the folds of his plaid.

He kicked open the door of the cottage and carried her inside.

He slid her down the length of his body until she was standing in front of him, dizzy and light-headed. He held her there, his arms around her. She looked up at him, met his eyes.

"There are a few things I wish to set straight," he said. "First of all, I am not betrothed to Penelope or anyone else. I've told her I did not wish to marry her."

"But I saw—"

"Aye, I know what you saw, or at least what you think you saw. Penelope was trying her best to convince me to propose."

The warmth of his body spread through her own. "But you didn't?"

He shook his head. "We wouldn't suit. I wish her well, of course, and as head of the family I will do all in my power to see she marries well, and is happy, but I love someone else."

She felt her throat close. "You do?" she squeaked.

"Aye. You see, I was raised to believe there were two kinds of men. The first kind takes care of the ones in his charge, cares for them, puts their needs above his own."

"And the other kind?" she asked.

"He takes what he wants, and worries about the consequences of his actions later. For twenty-seven years I've been the first kind of man, the laird I was raised to be. I've done my duty to my clan. I never wanted to be the second kind of man until I met you."

"Oh." She lowered her eyes. She had never considered herself the kind of woman that would drive any man off the straight and narrow path of duty and honor.

"Do you understand?" he asked.

"I didn't mean to—"

He pushed back the hood of her cloak. "I want you, Alana McNabb. You made me realize that a man cannot be one or the other. He must be both, or risk losing everything, and being unhappy to the end of his days. I thought inheriting Purbrick was just another duty, more sacrifice. I can see now that with you beside me, it will be a privilege." He slid to his knees. "Marry me, Alanna."

Her breath stopped. Her heart stopped. She put her hands on his shoulders and stared down at him, read hope and love in his eyes, saw her own reflection there. She wanted this, wanted him. More than anything. Or almost.

She thought of the pain, the scandal, the unhappiness she would cause if she dared to say yes, to choose this path instead. And she thought about the joy it would bring her to marry Iain. She shut her eyes. She was not free. She could not promise something new when she had not set aside the old promise, and to do that, she must see Lord Merridew. Surely it had hurt and embarrassed him when Megan had run away, and he had offered her an honorable marriage. She owed him an explanation, if nothing else, in person.

"I'm afraid I might be the first type of person, Iain. I'm not brave or bold."

His face fell. "Will you still marry your marquess?"

"I don't know." Desperation and longing made her bold. She took a breath. "I do know that we have now, Iain, tonight. I can promise you that."

"And after?" he asked.

She shook her head and slowly sank to her knees too, facing him. She ran her hand over his hair, brushed away melting snow. "Must we think of that? Kiss me."

He looked at her, stunned, and she pressed her mouth to his, felt him resist a moment before giving in, kissing her back. He pulled her closer, groaned.

"The first kind of man would not do this—" he began.

"Then be the second," she said.

He lowered his lips to hers, and she met him halfway. How had she lived without kisses? He nipped at her lips until she drew a breath and opened. His tongue tangled with hers, lapped the inside of her lower lip. His hand cupped the back of her head, pulled her closer still, and he pressed his body to hers. He kissed her cheeks, her eyes, her forehead. She sighed, reveled in the sensation. It was like stars coursing through her veins, warming her blood, making it sing. She kissed him back, running her lips over the stubble on his jaw, found the pulse point under his ear, and felt his heart beating under her mouth.

He pulled back and searched her face, his eyes dark, unreadable. "We'd best stop, or—" He got to his feet. "I must go out and see to the garron."

He rose and walked out the door, shutting it behind him, and the room was silent. Alanna bit her lip. What if he did not return, took the garron, and rode away? He might leave her here, knowing she'd be safe inside the cottage. But he wouldn't leave her. He was, after all, the first kind of man.

She found a basket of kindling and laid the fire. She watched the flames lick the dry moss before she fed it some twigs.

She put a hand to her lips, which were sensitive and buzzing. Her whole body buzzed with anticipation. She stared at the door. Was it wrong to want to know what kisses felt like, to understand what it meant to lie with a man she loved, desired? She looked around the room, at the familiar fireplace, at the clothesline strung between the roof beams, at the kettle, and the hearth rug, where he had kept her warm through the night the last time they'd shared a night here.

She didn't want to think, to worry about tomorrow. She picked up his plaid, folded it, and laid it down by the fire.

She undid the buttons of her gown and let it drop to the floor. Then she slipped out of her shift, then her stockings, and laid them over the bench. Naked, she glanced at the door before she slid into the thick warm folds of the plaid and closed her eyes to wait for him.

Chapter Forty-Six

IAIN STOOD IN the lean-to with the garron, staring into the snow. He was not a man who gave in to whims, or desires, or passion. He thought things through before he spoke, considered the drawbacks as well as the benefits of any plan. This time he had allowed his desire to speak for him, had blurted out a clumsy, ham-handed proposal. It had felt right. But it wasn't.

She had more honor than he did, more sense, perhaps. She'd made a promise, and she intended to keep it. He wished he was a reiver, had the right to steal another man's bride. But he was a laird, an earl and a gentleman. And Alanna was a lady. Love did not, could not, enter into this.

He waited for the cold to drive some sense into him, but it didn't.

He shouldn't have brought her here. If he hurried, they could still make it back to Craigleith, if not before dark, then soon after, though the wind was against them, and the snow was thickening. But that would be every bit as foolhardy and dangerous as staying. Could he keep from kissing her if they remained here alone? If he kissed her again, it would lead to more, far more. Did she understand that? He leaned on the animal's broad flank. Would it make it better or worse to love her now, then let her go and marry another man?

"Worse," he told the horse. The animal snorted and shifted its feet.

"Aye, you're right. I'm afraid it must be the honorable thing, the wise thing." He collected an armload of peat and went around to the door. The icy wind blew steely shards of snow into his face; it should have cooled his ardor, but it did not. He fought for control as he opened the door.

The faint light of the fire flickered against the cott's stone walls, warm and inviting. He looked around the room, didn't see her immediately. Then he saw her gown on the bench.

She wasn't in it.

His eyes flew to the plaid stretched before the hearth. The firelight reflected in her eyes, warmed her skin to honey. Her hair was loose over her shoulders, and he stared at her. She was the most beautiful woman he'd ever seen. He stood where he was, his arms full of peat, snow melting on his skin, and gaped at her. "Oh, Lass . . . We cannot—shouldn't—" he managed, his throat thick. Had he ever wanted anything more?

She brought one hand out from under the plaid, and it fell away to expose her shoulders. She was naked. "Come here," she said softly. His resolve crumbled.

He dropped the peat and crossed to her in three strides, falling to his knees. He cupped her face in his hands and kissed her, sipping at her lips, drinking her in.

Her hands fell to his coat, unbuttoned it, shoved it off his shoulders, began on his shirt. She kissed the naked vee of skin as the fastenings fell open. He lowered his hands to help her, desperate now to be out of his clothing. He pulled off his coat, and his shirt, and her hands fell to his flies. He put his hand over hers.

"Are you sure?" he asked.

"I am," she said. She caressed his erection through his breeches, met his eyes. "I want this. I want you," she said. She shook her head as hope filled him. "For tonight, Iain. Only for now."

The words shot straight to his groin, and desire rushed through him like a herd of wild horses. He shut his eyes, fought for control. He turned and went to the fire to add the peat, to slow things.

"That was how I first saw you, crouched by the fire like that. Only then you were naked." Iain groaned, and she grinned at him, sweet, saucy.

The memory had him instantly hard. He rose and undid his flies with one hand, pushed his breeches off, tossed them aside, and stood naked before her. Her eyes roamed over him like a touch, and stopped at his erection. It leaped hopefully under her gaze, making him harder still. He gritted his teeth, made a silent vow that he would stop if she wanted to, no matter how desperately he wanted her.

"You're a braw, bonnie man, Iain MacGillivray," she said. She opened the plaid, folded it back so he could look at her. He knew her body by touch, but not by sight. It had tormented him, haunted his dreams. She was even more lovely than his hands and his imagination had painted her. He swallowed, unable to say a word. The firelight gilded her limbs, the long, supple length of her legs, the slim curves of her hips. Her breasts were rose tipped, perfect. He had held her body against his the night he had rescued her, felt her icy flesh warm slowly, heard her sighs of pain and fear. Now she sighed with longing, and this time, they were both warm, and awake, and they had the whole night together. One night, and he was wasting time.

He lay down beside her, drew her body against his. No icy, marble body this time. She made a soft sound of pleasure, and she wrapped her arms around him, tangled her fingers in his hair, drew him down. He kissed her, and she opened her lips with a sigh of need. He deepened the kiss, touching his tongue to hers, as he skimmed his hands over the softness of her body—her back, her hips, her bottom. He felt her nipples harden against his chest as she pressed closer. He gasped as she brushed her hip against his erection. Her hand dipped down to caress him. He caught her fingers, held her still. "We should go slowly," he said.

She gazed up at him, her eyes glazed. "I don't want to go slowly. Is that a wicked thing to admit? Show me what to do, how to please you," she whispered, and kissed his ear as she swirled her hips against him.

He swallowed. "No, not wicked at all. You are a lady to your fingertips, Alanna, and a woman who deserves pleasure. I want to please you as well. 'Tis best to go carefully."

"Because I'm a virgin? My mother warned me it would hurt. I can't imagine pain amid such delight." She glided her fingertips over the naked plains of his chest, slowly descending across his hips, over his belly. He drew a sharp breath as her hand found his erection again, closed on it. He stifled a groan and let her explore. Beads of sweat popped out on his brow.

He drew his fingertips over the silken skin of her shoulders, cupped her breast, ran his thumb over the pert peak. "Oh," she sighed, as if she'd discovered a hidden secret. She moved restlessly, held him to her, caressing his legs with her own, her body arching up to meet his.

He slid his hands down to the soft curls between her thighs and she gasped as he slid his finger into the hot center of her. He stroked her, and she turned her face into the light, her lips parted, her eyes closed, her skin flushed with desire. Iain gazed down at her, watched the firelight play over her features, and his heart tightened in his breast. This was how he wanted to remember this woman, this moment, forever. One night, just one. He wanted to be perfect—for her, and for himself. Would she remember? He'd do his damnedest to make sure she never, ever forgot him or this night.

Alanna was on fire. Every kiss, every caress drove her higher, into a secret, delicious realm of pleasure. The whole universe centered on this place, and them—Iain and Alanna, and no one else existed. His fingers, his lips, his body, were driving her mad, and she dug her fingernails into his shoulder, wanting more, everything, all at once. Yet she must wait for him to show her, take her there.

Infuriatingly, he lay on his side, appeared to be considering the situation as he touched her softly, carefully, when she wanted heat and friction. He watched her with half-lidded eyes, as passion and sensation spread through her limbs—his doing. She made a soft sound of need, and he kissed her, sipping at her lips. She pressed her tongue to his, urged him on, wordlessly begged for more. Her fingers pressed into his flesh, drawing him nearer.

He whispered in her ear, soft, sweet words she barely heard. She was too aware of his hands on her body, hers on his, and the maddening, burgeoning need that kept on rising, until she was breathless with longing. At last the pressure of his fingers between her thighs increased, driving her higher still, her need unbearable now. She dug her fingernails into his shoulders, a wordless plea. Then the night exploded around her. He caught her cries with his mouth, kissing her, murmuring endearments as his fingers slowed, then moved faster, driving her up all over again, and still again, until she was boneless and weightless and scarcely able to breathe.

"More," she whispered, her voice a husky moan. "Is there more?"

He grinned and kissed her, and she felt him shift, felt hot bluntness where his fingers had been. "Much, much more," he murmured. He slid inside a little way into her body.

New pleasure rippled through her body. "Oh," she sighed.

He paused. "Am I hurting you?" he asked, his voice strained.

She shook her head and slid her arms around his neck. "Don't stop."

He moved carefully, slid deeper, and she gasped at the

invasion, more the wonder of it than the slight pain. She arched her hips, wanting the sensations that his fingers had created, sensing this pleasure would be greater still. He was holding back. She saw it in his eyes, in the strain of his muscles. He was more afraid of her pain than she was, it seemed.

She wrapped her ankles around his hips pressing her body to his, driving him deeper into her body. He swore softly, thrust forward, and filled her completely.

"Lass—" he whispered, his voice strangled in his throat, but she arched again, and he stopped talking, began to move faster, plunging deeper with every stroke. She shut her eyes. This is what she wanted, his body joined to hers, the unbearable pleasure.

She felt her own climax building again, and she cried out as he thrust into her again and again, groaning her name, muttering guttural endearments in Gaelic until he finally found his own release.

He collapsed against her, and she felt the heavy beat of his heart against her own. She smiled, staring up at the dark beams that crossed the ceiling, stroking his hair, reveling in the weight of his body on hers. The warm glow of satisfaction filled her. And love. Was it possible that she loved him more than she had an hour ago? She never wanted this moment to end.

"Is there more?" she asked again, whispering into his ear, kissing it.

He lifted his head and looked at her. "You never cease to amaze me, lass. There's no more for a little while, I'm afraid." He rolled off her, lay beside her, and she leaned up on her elbow, kissed the pebbled male nipple. He drew a sharp breath and she smiled, drawing circles on his chest with her fingernail.

"I meant more—ways," she said, lacking a better explanation.

He laughed, and the sound vibrated through her. "Enough that we could spend a whole lifetime discovering them."

She saw the hope in his eyes. She lowered her own and cuddled into his side.

"Marry me," he said again.

Alanna shut her eyes. She wanted to. She shook her head wordlessly. "You know I can't," she said. He turned onto his side, looked into her eyes, his forehead against hers, his lips an inch from her own.

"Then we had better make the most of every moment we have, don't you think?"

She smiled and he kissed her again, and pulled her on top of him.

Chapter Forty-Seven

Three days before Christmas

CAROLINE REGARDED ALEC across the width of the coach. He was staring out the window, and she knew he was replaying the conversation with Sandy MacGillivray in his mind, because his complexion turned from red, to scarlet, to plum, to pea green.

He'd received Sandy MacGillivray with a scowl. The old gamekeeper had done his best to soothe Alec's fury, swearing that Alanna had not been kidnapped and was certainly not being held against her will.

Caroline saw something in the old man's eyes that Alec did not—affection. He obviously had a soft spot for Lady Alanna McNabb, described her as an angel who had arrived on Craigleith Moor as if by magic.

"Magic?" Alec flushed, two bright spots of angry color in his cheeks. "Just what is that supposed to mean? Is she a prisoner?"

Sandy's white brows flew up to meet the fringe of his hair. "A prisoner? She's an honored guest. I can assure you she's come to no harm from Iain or any other MacGillivray. Why, if not for her, the fire might have been much worse—"

"Fire?" Alec turned red. "What fire?"

Sandy MacGillivray twisted his gnarled hands together. "We had a wee accident, a lantern left burning in the night . . . not intentionally, of course."

"Was Alanna hurt?" Alec demanded.

Sandy blinked, his eyes shining with tears. "No one was injured, thanks to the laird—and Lady Alanna. She saved Donal MacGillivray's pig and his pipes. We lost the barn and several cottages," the old man said. Tears sprang to his eyes. "Tragic enough, but if it hadn't been for the lass—Lady Alanna—it could have been even worse."

"Alanna saved a pig?" Caroline asked, feeling a little flushed herself. Alanna was quiet, shy, and listened more than she spoke. Megan was the bold sister.

Sandy MacGillivray puffed out his chest like a bantam rooster. "Aye. Lady Alanna not only saved Nessa—that's the pig—she saved five cottages, dousing them herself. And she also rescued our piper—that's Donal—and saved a dozen bairns from certain—"

"A dozen bairns? What on earth was your laird doing, your clansmen?" Alec demanded. "At Glenlorne, honored guests—and ladies—are not expected to put out fires and rescue livestock."

Sandy put his thumbs in his belt. "I was the one who saved the livestock. You've got to understand that Nessa is more than just a pig to Donal. He raised her from a piglet. No one forced the lass to be there. In fact, Iain told her to stay at the castle, but she has a way with folk." He gave

Alec a sweet-eyed look that made Alanna's brother turn a
deep shade of scarlet. Caroline noted the vein on his forehead was bulging.

"Are we talking about the same Alanna McNabb?"
Alec asked.

Sandy squinted. "She's about so tall—just up to the laird's
chin when he's not carrying her, hair like dark silk, eyes the
color of frost lying over the hills in autumn, soft lips—"

Alec turned purple. "Carrying her? Soft lips?"

Sandy started at Alec's fierce look and took a step back.
Caroline laid a hand on her husband's arm. The muscles
were like corded iron under her grip.

"There's no need to fret, Chief—no one means the lass
any harm, quite the opposite, I'd say," Sandy said.

Alec's jaw opened, then closed again when Caroline dug
her nails into his flesh. "What do you mean, the opposite?"
she demanded. "I think you'd best start at the beginning. My
husband is not a forgiving man, and if anyone has been—
interfering—with his sister, then there will be hell to pay.
We've heard some shocking tales, Mister MacGillivray."

Sandy winced. "I know—but they aren't true tales. Not
really."

"Did Iain MacGillivray find my sister in a storm, carry
her back to his home wrapped in his plaid?" Alec asked.

Sandy McGillivray scratched his head. "Aye, that part's
true. The laird found her in the snow on the moor. She was
injured, and he took her to a cottage to keep her safe for
the night. It was a cold night, and the lass was half frozen.
More than half."

That was when her husband turned green. "Lost?

Injured? *Keep her for the night?*" He rose to tower over Craigleith's gamekeeper.

Sandy held up his hand. "Now, Chief, it's not what you think, though some did suggest he *should* keep her longer than just the one night—"

Alec bunched his fists in the man's plaid, lifted him half off his feet. "Where the devil is my sister?" he demanded.

MacGillivray turned as green as Alec, and his eyes popped as his shaking hands scrabbled over Alec's fists. "Safe at Craigleith, I swear she's safe. She's awaiting her betrothed, the English marquess. We've shown her every kindness in the old Highland way. We aren't barbarians like some—"

Alec was now a dangerous shade of plum. "Betrothed? What marquess?" he spluttered. Caroline felt her own face heat.

"I don't understand. Alanna's the quiet one," Caroline said. "Put Mister MacGillivray down, Alec."

"Perhaps I haven't explained myself well," Sandy Mac-Gillivray said, straightening his clothes. "Our laird only did what was necessary. Her leg was injured, and she couldn't walk. He brought her home, put her in his bed, and—" He winced. "Not that he was in it of course—not at the same time," he spluttered.

Caroline clutched her shawl to her throat. "What kind of barbarian is this Iain MacGillivray?"

"What about the marquess? Who is he?" Alec said.

Sandy ignored that question. "I'll have you know that Laird Iain is a fine gentleman, the finest anywhere." He raised his chin. "Alanna told me you were a kind gentle-man, a good laird to your own folk. It was she who sent me here, said you'd be inclined to provide us with supplies to see us through the winter if I asked, since the fire—" His chin quivered. "She's a kind lady, and I thought . . ."

Alec softened. "Is she still at Craigleith?"

"Aye," Sandy said. "Unless her English lord has come for her."

"The marquess?" Caroline asked.

"Aye. Iain saved her on the eve of her wedding day. There was some suggestion she might have run away . . ."

"Wedding? Ran away?" Alec's voice went up two octaves. "I haven't even met the man, or given my permission for anyone to marry Alanna. She's far too young—"

"She's a woman grown," Caroline said softly. "Perhaps she's in love."

"With Iain?" Sandy asked hopefully.

"If she's in love with Iain, then who is the marquess?" Alec demanded.

No one answered.

"I'll leave at once for Craigleith, within the hour," Alec said. He looked at Sandy MacGillivray. "You'll take me there."

"I'm going with you," Caroline said, rising to her feet.

"No, you're not. You'll stay here, where it's safe."

She set her hands on her hips, broader now with the babe she was carrying. "I will not spend our first Christmas together alone, Alec McNabb," she insisted. "We'll find Alanna and bring her home." She rolled up her sleeves, then rolled them down again. "I'll tell Muira to pack a few things."

"There could be bloodshed," Alec warned, and for a moment she wondered if he was serious. His expression was flat, calm, dangerous.

"Bloodshed?" Sandy MacGillivray squeaked, stepping back. "But surely there's no need for that—"

Alec fixed their visitor with a glare as sharp as a dirk. "If the MacGillivray—or anyone else—has harmed a hair on Alanna's head, I will kill them with my own bare hands." He held those hands up before Sandy's eyes, and the gamekeeper paled as he stared at them.

Alec's expression softened at the sight of the old man's fear. "You'd best go and have a meal in the kitchen while we prepare for the journey. Give Leith Rennie the list of the supplies you need, and he'll see to it." Alec and Caroline watched him go.

Caroline clutched her husband's arm. "Alec, I'm sure everything is all right. Who would harm Alanna?"

Alec frowned. "When I last heard from her, she was at Dundrummie, safe with her mother and her aunt. I haven't forgotten the trouble Megan got herself into."

Caroline smiled. "But Megan is now happily married. You said you liked Kit Rossington."

"This is different. How many English lords are there in the Scottish Highlands, and how did Alanna get herself betrothed to one without my even meeting the man? She ran away from her wedding, was kidnapped by a reiver." He looked at her, the worry in his eyes softening as he laid his hand on her rounded belly. "I only hope that this child is not a girl. I couldn't go through this again."

She put her hand on his and smiled back. "Ah, but that's years away. You still have one more sister to see married long before then."

He groaned. "Sorcha. How could I have forgotten?"

Chapter Forty-Eight

Two days before Christmas

LADY SORCHA McNABB looked at her mother across the width of the coach from where she sat beside her aunt, bundled into blankets. Her mother had been travelling with Lord Merridew but had gotten into this coach this morning, without even bidding his lordship good morning.

Sorcha had been dreadfully afraid something awful had happened to Alanna. She'd been glad to hear that her sister was safe, and she saw this journey as a grand adventure. She understood by the whispers and the speaking looks that there was much about Alanna's own adventure that Sorcha wasn't being told and didn't entirely understand, but still, Alanna was alive, and at least mostly well, and her wedding to Lord Merridew had been postponed. Sorcha didn't like Lord Merridew, and despite Alanna's quiet acceptance of the marquess's proposal, Sorcha suspected Alanna didn't like him much either. Alec loved Caroline, and Megan loved her English lord too. Love was very important to Alanna, and Sorcha knew her sister would suffer without it. It was obvious that Lord Merridew didn't love Alanna. He had been more annoyed at the necessity of having to go and fetch her than he was glad to hear she was safe.

His lordship wasn't a very kind man. Nor was he smart—Sorcha could best him at chess, and cards, and even stump him by speaking French. He had insisted she be banished to the nursery, out of sight and mind. Eleanor had insisted that Sorcha be allowed to come to Craigleith, just in case they were gone over Christmas, and in case Lord Merridew insisted on marrying Alanna as soon as they found her. She was, after all, the second McNabb bride who had managed to slip through his fat fingers. When her turn came to choose, Sorcha vowed she would pick a better husband, and marry for love. She hoped Mama wouldn't mind too much.

Sorcha clung to Aunt Eleanor for warmth under the heavy swaddling of blankets while her mother yelled at the coachman through the hole in the roof. Lord Merridew followed in his heavy, luxurious coach, slowing them down with constant stops.

"Can't you go any faster?" Mama said to their own coachman.

"He's doing his best," Eleanor said. "We're fortunate we can get there at all in this snow. We might as well arrive safely. Tomorrow's Christmas Eve. We'll be there by then, a fine Christmas surprise for Alanna."

"I heard the most wonderful story at the inn," Sorcha said, bored by the long journey, even if she was eager to see Alanna.

"Oh? What was it?" Eleanor asked.

"They say the Laird of Craigleith has a new bride. He found her in the hills, frozen in the ice, and thawed her out. She's twice as fair as the hills in spring. The laird carried her home to his castle, stark naked, and—"

"Sorcha!" Devorguilla put a dismayed hand to her cheek. "Not another word!"

But Sorcha was not to be deterred. "But they say the laird's bride came to him by magic, carried there by a powerful spell. It was she who brought all this snow to Craigleith. Perhaps the story is true, or maybe it isn't, but don't you think it's odd there's so much snow here? Much, much more than at Dundrummie."

"Well, magic or not, I must admit I've never seen so much snow," Eleanor said. "Perhaps it is magic."

"Magic?" Devorguilla scoffed. "The snow is an inconvenience, but nothing more sinister than that. Have you forgotten Alanna was caught in a snowstorm, might have frozen to death if not for the kindness of a stranger?"

"And after all, Craigleith is exactly where we're going. I wonder if Alanna will know the story?" Sorcha said.

She watched her mother's face bloom with color and her eyes widen. "Magic," she muttered. "Sorcha—what's the rest of the story?"

"There isn't any more," Sorcha said.

Her mother leaned toward her. "A name, a description of the lass in the ice?"

Sorcha frowned and considered. "I don't think anyone mentioned her name."

The three ladies stared at each other. "Alanna," Eleanor murmured. "Could it be?"

"Naked?" Sorcha gasped.

Her mother tossed aside the blanket, opened the window, and thrust her head out into the snow. She bellowed into the wind, ordering the driver to whip the horses to a gallop.

Chapter Forty-Nine

ALANNA WOKE AND STRETCHED. Every muscle in her body was pleasantly sore. She turned toward the fire and smiled. Iain was crouched there, stark naked, his back to her. This time, her heart sang in her breast at the sight of him. She wished they could stay here forever.

"Is it morning?" she asked, and he turned.

"Almost. It's still early."

She lay back. "Then come back to bed."

"How can I resist an offer like that?" he said, sliding back under the plaid. "You're an insatiable lass, Alanna McNabb." He kissed her again, pulled her close to his side.

She curled against him, felt the fire warmth of his skin, and dipped her hand beneath the blankets to find what she was looking for. He groaned as her hand closed on his erection.

"We should get dressed, go home—back—to Craigleith," he said.

She smiled at him. "Not just yet," she said, and he laughed and kissed her, before he rolled her beneath him one more time.

"Marry me," he said afterward, as they lay in each other's arms, limbs tangled, hearts pounding. "We can announce it when we return to Craigleith."

She frowned. "I can't—there is still Lord Merridew to consider. I made a promise to him. How can I make another to you now?"

"And what will you tell him, that we spent the night together, that you and I—" She put a finger against his lips.

"Of course not," she said, blushing, imagining that conversation. She would go home, find Lord Merridew if he was still at Dundrummie, and tell him she could not marry him. He would be angry—furious no doubt, just the way he'd been when Megan had rejected him, but the choice was hers. She would not allow him, or her mother, to blame anyone else, especially Iain, for this.

She'd fallen in love with Iain MacGillivray. Spending the night in his arms had made that unbreakable, indelible. Was this how Caroline felt when she looked at Alec, how Megan felt with Kit? Then it was indeed magic. She opened her lips to tell him, to say the words, but he got up slowly, left her, avoiding her eyes. His expression was closed, cool. She watched him stalk around the room, picking up his clothing. He turned away, began to dress, his motions crisp and angry—or hurt.

He'd mistaken her silence for stubbornness, or worse, cowardice. It took more courage not to say yes, to give him hope for happiness where none may exist. A future together might still be impossible, and if that turned out to be so, then the heartbreak would be hers alone to bear. She would not cause Iain pain by speaking now, before she'd made her peace with Lord Merridew and her mother—and there was Alec's blessing to gain as well.

"I'll see to the garron," he said and went out the door.

She picked up his plaid and wrapped it around her body, smelled heather and smoke and sex. She loved Iain with all her heart, wished it could be different. Perhaps in the future, when she was free, she would find him again, and tell him, ask him . . .

But not yet.

IAIN LEANED ON the wall, let the wind scrub the scent of her body away from his hair, his hands, his lips. He'd been right. Loving her, knowing he must give her up now, had made it much worse indeed. His hands curled against his sides. He wanted to throw her over his shoulder yet again and carry her off, go—where?

She had made her choice. She had chosen a marquess over a laird, an earl. Over him.

She had made a promise, and he respected that. He had to. Was that noble of her, or stupid? She loved him—he was sure of that. And he loved her. Would she now condemn them both to a life of loss and longing? He walked around the side of the cottage to the lean-to and patted the horse.

There was nothing to do but take her back to Dundrummie as soon as possible, let her go on with her own life, and get on with his own. Honor, duty and responsibility were damnable inconveniences.

So was love.

Chapter Fifty

FIONA STARED OUT the window of the library at the swirling snow. It had begun in the late hours of yesterday afternoon, as the early winter darkness had been falling. Iain had ridden out to look for Alanna. The snow had grown thicker throughout the night, and they had not returned. Now it was morning, and the sky had subsided to a grumbling gray pout.

Tonight was Christmas Eve, and she worried that Iain—and Alanna—would not be here. She had never celebrated Christmas without her brother, and even with the rest of the clan here, it wouldn't be the same. Was he lost, or hurt? Perhaps he'd taken Alanna home, all the way to Dundrummie, and would not return in time for Christmas here at Craigleith. She wished she'd had the opportunity to say good-bye to Alanna McNabb. She had made Craigleith merry indeed, and it felt almost gloomy without her.

Elizabeth entered the room and climbed up on the window seat beside Fiona.

"Any sign of them yet?" she asked.

"No, not yet," Fiona said through tight lips.

Elizabeth sighed. "Aren't we supposed to go out today, gather greens, get ready for Christmas? That's what we'd be doing in England, anyway."

Fiona turned on her cousin. "This isn't England, Elizabeth. Alanna left without a word to anyone, and Iain had to go after her."

"Is that another Highland tradition?" Elizabeth asked.

"It's simple kindness."

"Oh. I thought perhaps it was a chase of some sort. He loves her, doesn't he?"

Fiona nodded. "Yes, I think he does."

"Is it magic?" Elizabeth whispered. She bit her lip. "I mean, it wasn't our spell, was it?" She hesitated, picking at her nails. "Tell me, what would—could—happen if another spell was cast, with the best of intentions, of course, but it went wrong?"

Her voice fell away, and Fiona looked at her, noted her cousin's flushed cheeks, felt her stomach sink. "Oh, Elizabeth, what did you do?"

Elizabeth shrugged uneasily. "Nothing really—I may have taken a little bit of Alanna's hair after all. And I might have stolen some of Penelope's too. I might have said the words and tossed them into the fireplace at the stroke of midnight. But I had to know—Penelope is so sure Iain will marry her, but he only ever looks at Alanna. Penelope and Mama whisper and plot and decide things and never tell me what's happening. I wanted to be the first to know this time."

Fiona stared at her. "What happened?"

"Penelope's burned up at once. But Alanna's burned slowly. There were sparks, then it burst into flames. The ashes floated, Fee. They swooped over the flames, still burning at the edges, like red lace. They hovered, then drifted down to land on the hearth. A gust of wind came down the chimney and blew them right into the room. What does that mean?"

"It means you're lucky you didn't set the house on fire," Fiona said tartly.

Elizabeth looked contrite, and Fiona grabbed her hand.

"Come on—we'd better ask Annie."

"THEY'VE BEEN GONE all night—what if they've eloped?" Penelope asked her mother.

Marjorie frowned and crossed her sitting room to peer out the window. Was it necessary to go to Gretna Green if one was already in Scotland, she wondered, or would any anvil do for a hasty wedding? She shook the thought away. "Don't be silly, Penelope. Of course they haven't."

Penelope paced the rug of her mother's room. "The whole castle is in an uproar because she's gone, left without a word of farewell, without wishing anyone a Merry Christmas. Children are crying for her, the men are talking about mounting a search party. And Iain—he went after her."

Marjorie frowned. What would become of Purbrick if Iain was lost in the storm, injured or killed? On the other hand, Alanna McNabb's departure was welcome news indeed.

"I thought I'd convinced her that Iain didn't want her."

Marjorie turned to her daughter. "Convinced her? How did you convince her?"

Penelope stopped pacing, and her face flamed scarlet. "She saw me, with Iain. I was in bed, naked." She gave her mother a sharp, nasty little smile. "The look on her face . . ."

Marjorie's limbs turned to water, and she gaped at her daughter. "You seduced Iain, let him—"

Penelope tossed her chin. "You said I should do anything—*anything*—to make him propose. It wasn't Alanna who was supposed to find us together. It was supposed to be my maid. She was to scream, and draw everyone, make them think . . . well, once they saw me, and Iain, he would have no choice but to marry me."

Marjorie felt her chest constrict. "Perhaps I should have been more clear. That isn't what I meant, Penelope. What happened?"

"He took one look at me and told me he would not propose, that he had decided we would not suit. He did not *want* me. It was most humiliating."

"He refused to b-bed you, or to marry you?"

"Both," Penelope said. She had tears glittering in her eyes now. "Oh mama, is there something wrong with me?"

Marjorie began pacing the rug herself, fury rising like a bonfire. "He refused? A bumpkin, a lout, a fool like Iain MacGillivray *dared* to refuse my daughter?"

"What will you do, Mama?" Penelope asked. "How

can we fix this, make him marry me? I told him I didn't care, but I do. I will not let her—"

Marjorie considered. "You say Lady Alanna saw you with Iain?"

"Yes. She came through the door and turned white as snow when she saw me in bed, with Iain looking at me, as if we had actually been—"

Marjorie rang the bell. "We need her back after all."

"Why?"

Marjorie smiled at her daughter. "She will have to admit what she saw. Then Iain will be forced to marry you. He will have no choice. We will have won."

Penelope smiled, though it didn't reach her eyes. She didn't look like a happy bride. She looked hateful. For an instant, Marjorie's throat closed. What had she done?

But Penelope was turning toward the door. "Then we will announce our betrothal tonight after all. If— when—he comes back, with Alanna or without her. I do hope she's there. If I had one Christmas wish, that would be it."

"Penelope," Marjorie began, but Penelope opened the door.

"I'll have my maid work the creases out of my blue silk after all," she said. "I want to look like a countess tonight."

Chapter Fifty-One

WILFRED ESMOND, MARQUESS of Merridew, sniffed as his coach finally pulled up at the door of Craigleith Castle. He stared up at the cold gray stones and they stared back at him, suspicious and unwelcoming. It was an unimpressive place, a forbidding stone tower with a pointed turret, half buried in snow.

Wilfred longed for the comforts of his father's estates, the grand ducal palace set in the hospitable English countryside. He tightened his fist on the head of his walking stick, angry, and threw back the mountain of furs that protected him from the wolfish teeth of the Highland winter. He would have been at Lyall this very moment, sitting in the elegant salon drinking hot rum punch, if it wasn't for the silly chit who had delayed him, ruined his plans.

Now he would be forced to spend a miserable Christmas here, in the middle of nowhere, among people who were little better than barbarians, if the exterior of their home was any indication. Castle indeed. They did not know the meaning of the word. He'd make his bride pay for her sins against him.

"I hope they have claret in the cellar," he muttered as he waited for the coachman to open the door and let down the steps. Or brandy.

People began to crowd around the coach as if they'd never seen a modern vehicle before. Rosy-cheeked urchins, broad-backed women, and squint-eyed men regarded the crest on the door as if it was a declaration of nefarious intent—or superiority.

Wilfred waited until the footman let down the steps and opened the door before he descended among the peasants, his nose in the air, his stick at the ready, demonstrating he was better than they were in every possible way, offering them a brief glimpse of his impressive dignity and power as he swept past them, toward the steps.

They didn't say a word—until he set his foot on a patch of ice. He felt his boot slip out from beneath him, betraying him. His arms flailed, and he toppled backward, landed hard on his broad backside. He watched his beaver hat shoot up into the air above him and come down again to land on his chest.

For a long moment, no one moved. Wilfred lay in the snow and stared up at the leaden sky. One by one, faces appeared above him, peered down at him, their eyes filled more with curiosity than concern.

Worse was to come. His footman offered a hand, and Wilfred clasped it, only to pull the servant down on top of him. His hat was crushed. Then the peasants themselves set upon him, men, women, and children, laying hands upon him, tugging at him, pushing, prodding, and pulling until he was finally back on his feet. Hands brushed at the clinging snow on his coat, and someone held out his broken hat and his walking stick. They had not dared to laugh outright, but merriment had replaced simple curiosity. Wilfred felt his face flush despite the cold.

"I wish to go inside," he said to no one in particular. As if by magic the door opened. He climbed the steps, moving carefully.

"Welcome to Craigleith," said a crone wrapped in a ragged plaid.

"Lady Alanna McNabb?" he said, not bothering with a greeting.

"Lord Wilfred!" The crone was pushed aside. "I saw your arrival from the window. Welcome to Craigleith Castle."

"Lady Marjorie," he said, nodding. Her gaze took in the snow crusted on his coat, and his damaged hat, and her welcoming smile wavered. He smoothed a hand over his rumpled hair and walked in.

The Scottish crone appraised him boldly as he passed, her eyes lighting with a sharp flare. "You're the English lord, Lady Alanna's marquess." She jerked her head. "You'd best come away into the library."

She led the way along an ancient hall, barbarically decked with swords and shields, the floor made of thick, unadorned flagstones. It appeared the place was as gray inside as out. Marjorie took his arm. "I see you received my letter," she said. "How is your dear mother?" The crone opened a set of double doors, and he stepped into the library.

This room was at least reminiscent of a fine English room, well-appointed with books and comfortable furniture. A fire blazed merrily in the fireplace. "Whisky or tea?" the crone asked, her tone suggesting a distinct lack of deference or enthusiasm.

"Lady Alanna?" Wilfred demanded instead, keeping his tone bland and insistent.

The crone looked bemused as she shook her head. "She isn't here."

He turned to Marjorie. "She is . . . out," she said.

"Out? It is freezing, and snowing, and there is a high wind," Wilfred said, making his tone as chilly as the weather.

The door burst open, and a pretty young woman hurried in. Her gown rustled, shimmered, and she came to a stop in a deep curtsy at his feet. He looked down on golden lashes over blue eyes, as well as an ample bosom, displayed to advantage in the low-cut gown. Was this his bride? He regarded her hopefully.

"May I present my daughter, Lady Penelope Curry?" Lady Marjorie said, and Wilfred felt a frisson of disappointment.

He took Lady Penelope's hand and kissed it. She smiled with pleasure, a natural flirt. "Good afternoon, my lord," she purred.

"Oh no—you're Alanna's marquess," another girl said behind her. Surely this one was too young to be his bride, and too plain, Wilfred thought.

"My younger daughter, Elizabeth," Lady Marjorie

said, her tone flat. Merridew inclined his head—slightly—instead of bowing. The child appraised him boldly.

The door opened again, and the ladies of Dumdrummie flew into the room. Devorguilla's eyes darted into the corners, searching for her daughter. "She isn't here," Wilfred said disdainfully, not bothering to greet her. Lady Eleanor's brows rose. Young Sorcha stood behind her, gaping like a fish.

"Then where is she?" Devorguilla asked, looking at the other women in the room. No one replied.

"Out, apparently," Wilfred said.

The door opened again. He cringed as Sorcha shrieked like a banshee and flew across the room and threw herself into the arms of a red-haired beauty.

Wilfred swallowed. Perhaps this, then, was his bride at last? But when Sorcha stepped back, he took note of the woman's rounded belly. Not his bride then—he hoped.

"Alanna's not here," the child told the tall, broad, angry-looking Scotsman who appeared next.

The man fixed his eyes on Wilfred, a glare sharp enough to pierce skin. "Where's my sister, MacGillivray?" he demanded, advancing on him.

Wilfred raised his chin. "I'm not—" he began, but the Scot merely took advantage of the target and let his fist connect with Wilfred's jaw. Wilfred reeled backward and landed in a chair, white-hot pain filling the room.

"Lord Wilfred!" Marjorie and her daughter fluttered above him. Lacy handkerchiefs were deployed, pressed to his bleeding lip.

"This isn't Iain MacGillivray. This is the Marquess of Merridew," Lady Marjorie said.

"*The* marquess?" the man demanded. "*Alanna's marquess?*" He raised his fist again. Devorguilla got between them. "Alec, please!"

"Who the devil are you?" Wilfred asked the man, cringing.

"Glenlorne," the Scot said, regarding Wilfred coldly. Wilfred looked away first.

"Good day, Alec," Lady Eleanor said, and embraced the redheaded woman. "Caroline—you're absolutely blooming! It appears we have a family reunion, and at Christmas, too. How wonderful—"

"Where is Alanna?" Glenlorne demanded again.

Devorguilla raised her chin. "I don't know," she said coolly. "We were told she was out."

"In the snow," Wilfred added, still not believing it.

"All night," Elizabeth murmured, and everyone turned to look at her in surprise.

"What on earth does that mean?" Glenlorne's countess demanded, but the door opened again. Everyone turned to look. The crone was back with tea. Behind her, another young woman entered the room, limping. Merridew felt his heart sink as he stared at her leg, hoping this crippled creature wasn't Lady Alanna.

She stopped and regarded them all. "Good day, I'm Fiona MacGillivray," she said, scanning the faces. "Welcome to Craigleith."

Merridew surprised a sigh of relief.

"Where's my daughter?" Devorguilla demanded, advancing on the girl.

"Where's Iain MacGillivray?" Glenlorne demanded.

The girl blinked, paling. "Iain isn't here. Nor is Alanna."

"They'll be back," the old woman murmured, setting the tray down. "It's going to snow, but they'll be back before it thickens."

Everyone began to talk at once, demanding answers, asking questions. Wilfred's jaw ached. He stared at the door, tempted to bolt, to climb back into his coach and order the coachman south as fast as possible. He would never set foot in Scotland again . . .

Another woman appeared in the doorway. Wilfred's mouth dried. She had dark hair, wide, hazel eyes. Her cheeks were flushed. She was tall and slim, a beauty. She was wearing a length of plaid over her head and shoulders. She reached up to unwind it, let it fall around her shoulders in graceful folds. No one had noticed her arrival but himself. She stood gazing around the room at the assembly, her cheeks flushing further, her lush lips falling open in surprise. If this was his bride, he was pleased indeed. He barely looked at the person behind her, until the man spoke.

"Good afternoon." His firm voice cut through the din, and everyone spun. He was as tall and wide as Glenlorne.

"Alanna!" Half the folk in the room raced toward her and swept her up.

"Iain!" Fiona MacGillivray cried.

Glenlorne turned. "Iain? Iain MacGillivray?" he

demanded. Wilfred winced as the man's fist flew once more.

To his credit, MacGillivray didn't topple; he simply took a step back as Glenlorne's fist connected with his mouth. MacGillivray blinked, put a hand to the injury—a split lip—and looked flatly at his assailant.

Chapter Fifty-Two

"ALEC, STOP IT!" Alanna stepped between her brother and Iain. Iain's lip was bleeding. He ignored it.

"It's all right, Alanna." Iain put his hands on her shoulders and moved her gently aside. "Welcome to Craigleith. I assume you're Alanna's brother."

Alanna moved back where she'd been and stood up to Alec. "It's not all right. You can't come here and punch people," she said fiercely, glaring at her brother.

"I heartily agree." Alanna looked up as another man spoke, and she felt her stomach sink as she recognized Lord Merridew. He was moving toward her. She felt her cheeks heat, and she looked at the floor and dipped a curtsy.

Alec grabbed her arm. "Come, Alanna."

"What are you doing?" she demanded.

"I'm rescuing you," Alec said. "We're leaving."

Lord Merridew got to his feet. He was sporting a fresh bruise on his jaw, and she glanced balefully at her brother.

"If the lady is going anywhere, it will be with me. She's my wife—or she soon will be."

Alanna watched Alec's fist bunch again, and she reached out to grab his arm before he could take a step.

"No!" She shoved him back toward Iain. "This is my fight, Alec. You will not do this, do you understand?"

He paused, and regarded her with surprise. He had never seen her this way, fierce and bold.

She turned back to Merridew. He was shorter than she remembered, broader. He gave her a smile that did not reach his eyes. "Shall we go?" he asked, crossing the room toward her. "I see no reason to linger here."

"It's Christmas Eve," Fiona began, but Merridew ignored her.

"I wish to be over the border as soon as possible, home before the New Year." He held out his hand, and Alanna stared at it for a moment. She didn't look at her mother, or her sister, or at Iain. She shook her head.

"I cannot marry you, my lord."

His face became hard and sharp. There was no sorrow, or disappointment. Just proud anger. "Why not?" he demanded.

"You don't have my permission, for one thing," Alec began. "I'm Alanna's guardian, and—"

Alanna looked at him. "I can do this, Alec," she said. She could feel Iain standing beside her brother, felt his eyes on her like a touch, a caress, felt her skin heat.

"Alanna," her mother began, her tone pleading, but Alanna raised her chin.

"I must insist that you honor your word, my lady," Merridew said, but she shook her head again, clasped her hands together.

"I am honored that you asked me to be your wife, but I—I love someone else, you see. It would not be fair to you to expect you to—"

With an impatient grunt, Merridew closed his hand on her wrist. "I'll risk it," he said tartly.

Iain's hand closed on the marquess's. "No," he said.

Alec pushed both of them away. "Alanna is not going anywhere but home to Glenlorne."

She looked at her brother and smiled. "I *am* home, Alec," she said. "I'm in love with—"

"My fiancé?" Penelope demanded.

Alanna looked at the smug young woman. Penelope came forward and put her arm through Iain's, pressed herself close to his side, looked down her nose at Alanna. "You can't have Iain, Alanna. He's going to marry me."

Alanna felt her chest cave in. Iain was staring at his cousin in surprise. "Penelope," he began.

"Two women?" Alec demanded, glaring at Iain. "Is this some kind of Highland harem?" he unknowingly parroted Alanna. "Alanna, exactly which gentleman are you betrothed to?"

She bit her lip, looked around the room. "At the moment—well, I was betrothed to Lord Merridew, but I can't—"

"And have you also agreed to marry MacGillivray?" Alec demanded.

Her throat closed. She lowered her gaze and shook her head.

"That will be impossible," Penelope said, fixing Alanna with a sharp blue glare. "He must marry me."

"Penelope, we discussed this. I am not going to marry you," Iain began, but Penelope's eyes remained on Alanna.

"You know why he must marry me, don't you, my lady? You saw." She turned to Iain with a smirk. "We can announce our betrothal tonight, at the party. In fact, I insist we do."

Iain's face fell, and he closed his eyes.

Alanna remembered Penelope in bed, Iain staring at the English beauty, her hair tumbled over her shoulders, her eyes alight. Alanna felt her knees turn to water. She couldn't breathe. She looked around her, heard the small sound of sympathy that Caroline made, saw Sorcha blink at her, not understanding what was happening. Fiona had tears in her eyes, and Elizabeth was frowning. Lady Marjorie's expression was unreadable. Eleanor's lips were pursed. And her mother stood where she was, uncertain. There was no anger in her eyes, no insistence that she marry Lord Merridew. Alanna turned away from all of them. She could not bear their pity.

Alec put his arm around her. "I think we should be going," he said quietly. She stood in the shelter of his arms. He unwound Iain's plaid from her shoulders, tossed it aside, put his own greatcoat over her, a heavy weight that nearly swallowed her. Good. She wanted to be swallowed.

She clutched the edges, pulled it closer to her chin. The scent of her brother's skin replaced Iain's.

"Alanna—" Iain began, but Penelope held him fast, clung to his sleeve, triumph clear on her face. Alanna couldn't look at him now. She turned away.

"I'll help you gather your things," Caroline said.

Alanna considered for a moment. "I have nothing to gather. All my belongings are at Dundrummie, or at Glenlorne." It didn't matter. All the fine clothes and luxuries in the world could never be enough now. She had lost what she most wanted.

Merridew turned to Devorguilla. "Have you nothing to say to this, my lady? Despite your daughter's foolishness, I am still willing to marry her."

Devorguilla met her daughter's eyes. "It's Alanna's choice to make, my lord, and I believe she has made it. I was wrong to make it for her, to insist. Will you forgive me, Alanna?"

Alanna went to hug her. "Of course, Mama."

"You are rejecting a *marquess*?" Penelope gasped.

"I am choosing not to marry him," Alanna said. She didn't look at Iain, didn't want to. There was nothing left to say. "Can I come home to Glenlorne for a little while, Alec?"

"Of course," he said. He looked coldly at Iain. "We'll take our leave now, I believe, let you get on with your Christmas celebrations."

Annie returned. "I'm afraid no one will be going anywhere tonight," she said. "The snow has started again, and it's so thick you can't see a hand before your face."

Everyone rushed to the windows, crowded together to look out at the snow. The entire world was white.

"You're all welcome to stay, though quarters will be tight, to say the least. But it's Christmas Eve, and there will be plenty of cheer to go around," Iain said, his tone flat.

Fiona forced a smile. "It won't be so bad. Our folk are decorating the hall—please join us."

The group regarded each other soberly, without a shred of merriment.

Marjorie linked her arm through Merridew's. "Come, Wilfred. It won't be quite like Christmas at Lyall Castle, but I have insisted upon some English touches. Would you like some ice for your poor jaw?"

"There's plenty in the loch," Elizabeth quipped. Sorcha snickered, and Fiona hid a smile. Lady Marjorie sent her youngest daughter a quelling glare.

"We're all but too old now, of course, but the children are going to ride the *Cailleach Nollaigh* around the hall, since it's too stormy to go outside. Shall we join them?" Fiona said. Sorcha nodded eagerly, and the three girls went out, chattering.

Caroline put her arm around Alanna's shoulders. "Come. It's my first Christmas in Scotland, and next year we'll have a babe to share it with. Muira is already predicting it will be a boy . . ." She babbled happily. Alec followed them out, flanking Alanna's other side, protecting her. It was too late for that. Alanna cast a glance over her shoulder at Iain. He looked stricken, his eyes on hers, and she felt her heart freeze in her breast, and stop beating. She turned away and clung to Caroline as she silently wished him happy and tried not to cry.

Chapter Fifty-Three

PENELOPE WAITED UNTIL everyone else left the room. "Well?" she said, folding her arms over her chest, fixing Iain with a cold glare. "Ask me. We will announce our betrothal tonight whether you do or not, but let's observe some of the niceties—the English ones, at least."

"Are you so desperate to marry that you'd take a man who loves someone else?" Iain asked. She looked into his eyes, expecting anger or defeat, but saw pity instead.

It made her hesitate. She had been raised to marry a title. She'd been educated, outfitted, trained, and pampered. The only thing she lacked was a dowry. While a gentleman might be attracted by her face and figure, he would be repelled by her lack of fortune. She might manage to snag a baronet, or perhaps a titled lord's second son, but she could not aim higher without money. She could not even count on men courting a connection to the new Earl of Purbrick, since he was a Scot, a foreigner, a nobody. Worse, he had chosen another woman over her, fallen in love. It was not to be borne.

She raised her chin. "I wish to be the Countess of Purbrick, Iain, and I intend to be. Perhaps you can make Alanna your mistress." She waited for him to speak, to fall to his knees, resigned, but he stood stubbornly still, regarding her. "Well, if you aren't going to ask me—"

"I'm not," he insisted.

"Well, we can make the announcement without it, then. I think I'll go upstairs and find something fetching to wear," she said, and left him alone.

Chapter Fifty-Four

IF ANY OF the MacGillivrays making the hall ready for Christmas suspected that Alanna's heart lay broken in her chest, they gave no sign of it.

They welcomed her family, even if they looked at Lord Merridew with reticent curiosity. Eleanor found a place amid the grandmothers by the fire, where she joined in the gossiping and the stitching and sipping of tea well laced with whisky in honor of Christmas.

Caroline was given another lesson on making a proper black bun, and she made Alec swear not to tell Muira. Annie placed a hand on Caroline's belly and grinned. "A lass," she said. "And a lad."

Alec blanched. "Twins?"

Alanna smiled at the bemused expression on her brother's face, and Caroline kissed his cheek, delighted.

Sorcha joined Fiona and Elizabeth and the children, and helped decorate the hall while the snow swirled outside.

Alanna forced herself to smile gaily, to laugh as if nothing at all was wrong. She sampled the treats coming out of the kitchen and did her best to ignore the whispers among the MacGillivrays as they hung the mistletoe and cast sly glances in her direction. They had hopes, perhaps, that she and Iain might have— She put it out of her mind. It was impossible. They would learn to love Penelope as well. Even now, knowing it would not come until the party later that evening, Alanna steeled herself for the announcement of their betrothal. She would not allow one hint of sorrow to show on her face on such a happy occasion. Her family would be watching her, and Lord Merridew, and Penelope. And Iain—her breath hitched. She put a steadying hand to her chest and continued doing what she was doing, tying a length of MacGillivray plaid around a bouquet of fragrant greens. In a few days, she would go home to Glenlorne and never see Iain MacGillivray again.

She could do this. She must.

Alanna helped Seonag find rooms for the new guests—the lord's chamber for Lord Merridew, and the lady's chamber for Alec and Caroline. Sorcha happily accepted space in Fiona and Elizabeth's room. Devorguilla and Eleanor agreed to share a room. Alanna could not bear the idea of returning to Iain's room, not now, not after the events of last night and today, so she put a pallet in the corner of her mother's room. Iain was upstairs in the tower. Would Penelope join him there tonight, and every night from now on? Alanna found more things to do, constantly moving, helping, laughing, if only to keep from thinking or feeling. Alec knew what she was doing, how she felt, and so did her mother, and Eleanor. She saw it in their eyes. Her family wanted to be her fortress, to protect her, but she was an adult. She had her own armor.

Of Iain, she saw nothing at all. He did not join the merry preparations. Nor did Penelope. She tried not to wonder where they were, what they were doing. Images of Iain's body on hers, his caresses, his kisses drove her half mad, and still Alanna whirled through the day, twice as bright and gay and merry as anyone else.

MARJORIE SAT WITH Lord Merridew and watched the hullabaloo from a safe distance. All had worked out as planned, yet there was a feeling in her belly, an uncertainty that made her uneasy. She kept Wilfred company, attempted to engage him in conversation, but he offered only short, terse replies and indulged in glass after glass of whisky punch. "It's not quite like Christmas in England, is it?" Marjorie said sympathetically.

Merridew filled his glass again. "I planned to be at Lyall Castle, at my father's table, tonight. I expected I'd be married by now—to her." He pointed to Alanna, who was hanging greens.

"Did you love her very much, Wilfred?" Marjorie asked.

"Love her? I barely know her. I loved her dowry, though. Passionately." He clasped his hand to his chest and regarded Alanna balefully. "Now I shall have to court another dowry—bride—in London, come spring." He glanced at Marjorie and grinned. "It's a pity your daughter is already spoken for." Marjorie's heart lurched. "What is it about Iain MacGillivray and men like him that make women love them?" Merridew slurred.

"Not all women, Wilfred." Marjorie said, thinking of her daughter, She filled the marquess's glass again, and forced herself to smile.

AN HOUR LATER, Marjorie found Iain in the solar, staring down at the wooden figure of an angel that stood amid curls of wood.

"You're not even dressed yet," she said, regarding the kilt he wore. "I mean, surely you don't intend to wear that." The laird's brooch he wore glittered in the candlelight, a symbol of an age gone by. The kilt made him look broad and dangerous, and devastatingly handsome.

He met her eye only briefly, then looked away. "If you've come to give me a lecture, or instruct me, you needn't bother."

She folded her arms over her chest. "I won't even ask what that means."

"It means I won't shame any woman, even for a lie."

Marjorie drew nearer. "That's why I've come, Iain. Not to lie, to tell you the truth."

He looked up at her. "Oh?"

"My husband, Viscount Aldridge, was the handsomest man I'd ever set eyes on. Every debutant of my Season wished to marry Aldridge. So I set my cap for him, won him. I was once as beautiful as Penelope, a diamond of the first water. I was the daughter of the Earl of Purbrick, wealthy, connected, esteemed. My friends let their parents marry them off to elderly dukes, or stodgy earls, but I wanted Aldridge. I would have done anything to get him."

She looked at her hands. "I didn't discover until after the wedding that he had only married me for my money. He liked to gamble, you see. He wagered everything that wasn't entailed, including my jewels, even my wedding rings." She rubbed her naked finger. "It broke my heart. When he died, he left us penniless, me and Penelope and Elizabeth. We had no choice but to return to Purbrick. My uncle was the earl by then, and he needed a hostess. I had expected—counted on—him to leave money in trust for the girls, for dowries, so they could make suitable matches. He didn't. So, it became essential that Penelope marry the next earl—you." He was looking at her now. "But you are in love with Alanna McNabb." He didn't speak. "If you were to provide Penelope with a dowry, I have no doubt she would release you."

Iain folded his arms over his chest. "All this is because of money?"

"Perhaps it's more important in England than in Scotland," Marjorie said carefully. "I want my daughters to know security in their marriages, and love, if they are fortunate enough to find it. Money often substitutes for love among our class, I'm afraid. My youngest brother—your father—married for love. My father thought him a fool."

"I would have offered Penelope a dowry the day you arrived if you'd asked," he said. "Elizabeth as well."

She smiled, took a breath, and laid her hand over her nephew's. She was not a demonstrative woman—she kept her emotions to herself—but it seemed appropriate now.

He caught her fingers in his and squeezed them. She smiled at him. "I trust there will be a betrothal announcement tonight after all?" she asked. "I think every single one of your clan expects it."

He rose to his feet and kissed his aunt's forehead. "Thank you, Aunt. This is a fine Christmas present."

"Oh, it will still cost you rather dearly, but I think this is a price you'd much rather pay. Merry Christmas, Iain," she said. "For what it's worth, I think you'll make a very fine earl, and Alanna will be a . . . worthy . . . countess."

He smiled at her faint praise of Alanna. "She will," he said, and Lady Marjorie Curry smiled back and felt a thrill of Christmas joy she hadn't known since she was a girl.

"I WISH TO ask for Alanna's hand in marriage," Iain said, standing before Glenlorne in the sitting room that had once been his mother's. It would eventually be Alanna's, if all went well.

"No," Glenlorne growled.

"Alec," Caroline said. "Be reasonable. Alanna loves him."

"You may come and court her in the spring—next spring, the one after this one," Alec insisted.

"I have already asked her to marry me, and we've already—" He shifted his stance. He would not use their night at the cottage to barter for her. It was too close to what Penelope had done.

Still, he heard Glenlorne's intake of breath, watched as the earl turned a dangerous shade of red.

"I've heard the tales, MacGillivray—stories about handkerchiefs, and Alanna being carried here over your shoulder, wrapped in nothing but your plaid, kept in your bed."

Iain couldn't resist. He grinned. "I'm afraid they're all true," he said. "Every one."

He heard Caroline McNabb cry out as her husband's fist flew, and he watched it coming, felt it land hard on his jaw. The pain was excruciating, and stars exploded in his head. Iain put a hand to his chin and grinned again. "I'll take that as your permission."

Chapter Fifty-Five

CHRISTMAS EVE OFFICIALLY arrived as night fell, though the sky was still bright with falling snow. The ancient hall of Craigleith Castle had been magically transformed for the celebration of *Nollaig Beag*. The MacGillivray plaid draped tables and wrapped bundles of greens, and the fragrance of pine and fir filled the room. Candles were placed in the windows to light the way for travellers, and the golden light reflected on the frosty windowpanes and in the eyes of every joyful member of Clan MacGillivray. The pipes played, and Alanna clapped and smiled until her face hurt.

She watched as Iain entered the room with Lady Marjorie and the party officially began. He looked braw in his bonnet and kilt, so handsome that he stole the air from the room and left her breathless.

She looked behind him, seeking Penelope, but Iain's betrothed was nowhere to be seen. Surely she would arrive soon. Perhaps Penelope wished to make a more dramatic entrance, would come in on a chariot of ice pulled by seven magic stags. Nothing could surprise Alanna now, or hurt her—or so she hoped. Her spine was so stiff it ached, and her jaw was sore from smiling. But her heart was numb, frozen and dead in her breast.

Iain's gaze roamed the room until he found her. Alanna felt as if lightning had struck her. Just one look made her heart pound, her body burn. She dragged her eyes away and tightened her grip on the cup in her hand. She took a bracing sip of whisky, felt it burn a path to her belly, and forced her smile back into place. She must be ready when the announcement came. There would be a toast to Christmas, one to the *Cailleach Nollaigh,* and then another to the betrothal of Laird Iain MacGillivray and Lady Penelope.

Alanna wondered if anyone would notice if she slipped away or sank through the floor.

The *Cailleach Nollaigh* was carried out of the armory, and ropes were tied to it. Since they could not go outside in the storm, children climbed astride the log in the hall, and it was dragged around the perimeter of the room three times for luck, men taking turns hauling it, making it a good-natured test of strength. The children shrieked with laughter.

With a final flourish of pipe music, the *Cailleach Nollaigh* came to a stop before the fireplace, and the children were lifted off the great log. Five strong men made ready to raise the tree on its end to stand before the fireplace. The *Cailleach Nollaigh*'s carved face would look out upon the assembly. Everyone would raise a toast to the winter goddess, take a moment to admire the laird's carving skills, and then the log would be rolled into the fire to burn throughout the night.

"Alanna."

She spun at the sound of his voice, found Iain standing behind her. "Iain, what are you doing? They're waiting for you to raise the toast," she said. She clenched her hands around her own cup to keep from touching him, then noticed he didn't have a cup. She thrust it into his hands. "Take mine," she said. But his fingers curled around hers, holding the cup between them.

"Come outside for a moment," he whispered. She swayed a little, surrounded by the smell of him—the wool of his kilt, the wind in his hair, the scent of his body. She closed her eyes. Would he kiss her? Bid her a formal farewell? How foolish.

"I can't, Iain. It isn't right. I wish you and Pe—your bride—all the happiness in the world, truly I do," she said. She couldn't look at him. If she did, she'd cry.

"I'm glad to hear it." There was the soft burr of humor in his voice, and she met his eyes. He was smiling at her. Was he daft? What if Penelope saw?

"Go—they're raising the *Cailleach Nollaigh*!" she whispered. The great log was already being picked up, set upright. In a moment, there would be a great cheer. She waited for it.

Instead of a cheer, there was a gasp. Alanna looked up.

Above the crowd, the *Cailleach Nollaigh* stared back at her. She blinked. It wasn't the face of a crone. The face was mischievous, fey, sweet, a young woman.

"It's me," she murmured, stunned.

Faces turned to look at her. Her heart lurched. She looked at Iain. "What does this mean? Oh, Iain, what will Penelope say?"

He grinned and tilted his head. "I believe she'd say it's a fair likeness of the woman I love."

Her face heated. She looked down at the cup in her hands—their hands, still clasped together around the vessel—and tried to pull away. He held her still. "But you can't—"

"I'm not going to marry Penelope. I've spoken to her, made her understand that we—she and I—wouldn't suit. Not when I love someone else."

The warmth of the room made Alanna's head spin. Perhaps she'd misheard him. It was noisy in the hall. She looked around, realized that the whole room had fallen silent, and everyone was staring at her.

"Will you kiss her, Laird?" someone asked. "Will there be a wedding?"

He looked at the faces that surrounded them, took the cup, and handed it to someone in the crowd. "I think we'd best ask Lady Alanna," he said. She watched in stunned surprise as he dropped to his knee. "Alanna McNabb, will you marry me, be my wife and Lady of Craigleith and Countess of Purbrick?"

She stared at him, her tongue knotted around her tonsils.

His hands tightened around hers. "I hope you're not going to say no again, lass."

Alanna felt her heart melt. Tears filled her eyes. A rush went through her, a bolt of light and joy. It felt like sparks, shooting through her veins, filling the room. She looked into Iain's eyes, saw her own face reflected there. "Yes," she said.

"What?" Sandy called from the front of the room, putting a hand to his ear. "I didn't hear."

"She said yes," Iain yelled, his eyes on Alanna's. "She said yes." Now the cheer rose, shaking the rafters of the ancient hall.

Sandy raised his glass. "Here's to the *Cailleach Nollaigh* and *Nollaig Beag,* and to the fair face of Lady Alanna McNabb, the angel of Craigleith."

Iain took the cup back again and held it to her lips. She sipped, laughing, then helped Iain drink. Then he passed the cup to the nearest MacGillivray and drew Alanna into his arms. His mouth met hers, hot and whisky-sweet. Could a kiss make a lass drunk? She didn't care. She clung to him, kissed him back, let him lift her off her feet and spin her around, still kissing her.

She put her hands on his face as he lowered her to the floor, his arms still around her. "Yes," she said again, laughing. "Yes."

She scanned the crowds. Alec and Caroline were grinning. Her mother had happy tears in her eyes. Auld Annie and Fiona and Sandy were smiling. Seonag was crying sentimental tears on Wee Janet's shoulder. Donal winked at her as he set his pipes to his lips and began to play a merry tune. Ian was swept up by his merry clan.

Alanna saw Penelope standing in the doorway, her expression cool, but serene. She was, as always, dressed like a princess. Alanna crossed to her.

"I suppose you've come for my congratulations," Penelope said blandly. I wish you well of him—it cost him a great deal of money to change my mind. I could still insist . . ." She raised her chin, but Alanna squeezed her rival's hand and smiled.

"Thank you, Penelope. Merry Christmas," Alanna said.

Penelope tossed her head and looked away. "I have dozens of other suitors, you know. I'll have my choice of title now. Oh, look. Lord Merridew has fallen asleep in his cups. I think I will go and wake him, wish him a Merry Christmas." She looked back at Alanna Any objections?" Alanna shook her head.

"I wish you well, Penelope." She watched as Penelope moved off toward the head table and the sleeping marquess.

Iain grabbed Alanna's hand and dragged her over to the mistletoe. He pulled her into his arms and kissed her again.

The pipes struck up a reel and couples paired off, laughing, the mood all the merrier for the happiness between the laird and his lady.

"D'you think it's magic?" Elizabeth asked breathlessly, catching Fiona's sleeve. Auld Annie leaned in.

"Of course it was magic. Love is always magical, and doubly so at Christmas."

Epilogue

To EVERYONE'S SURPRISE, the weather broke the very next day—Christmas Day, and the sun shone.

Lord Merridew offered to escort Lady Marjorie and Penelope home to Woodford Park, where they would prepare for the new Earl of Purbrick's spring wedding.

His English wedding, that is. His Scottish one took place on Christmas Day, before the assembled crowd of MacGillivrays, McNabbs, MacIntoshes, Currys, and Frasers. The bride wore a blue silk gown, borrowed from Lady Penelope, and a sash of MacGillivray plaid. Lord Glenlorne placed his sister's hand in Laird Iain's, and when everyone saw the love and the joy in the happy couple's eyes, there wasn't a dry eye in the castle.

There was waltzing in the great hall that night, and the laird danced with his young sister, who wore special dancing slippers that made it look like she floated on air—more of the magic that Lady Alanna had brought to Craigleith, folk said. Magic, Auld Annie predicted, that would last as long as the love the laird had found, like his father before him, or in other words, forever, since it was now an old Highland tradition that the lairds of the MacGillivrays always married for love.

Even the very oldest folk said it was the happiest Christmas they could ever remember. When the wedding ceremony ended, under a clear sky of vibrant blue, the laird's garron was brought forward, decorated with ribbons, much to the valiant beast's chagrin. The laird helped his bride onto the creature's back, and they set off.

"Where are they going?" Sorcha asked as she waved farewell.

"Old Ewan's cott," Fiona said.

Sorcha wrinkled her nose. "That doesn't sound very romantic."

Auld Annie just smiled. "Come away inside, little one, and I'll tell your fortune. Do you believe in magic?"

"Of course not," Sorcha replied.

Annie chuckled. "You will, lass. You will."

About the Author

LECIA CORNWALL lives and writes in Calgary, Canada, in the beautiful foothills of the Canadian Rockies, with five cats, two teenagers, a crazy chocolate Lab, and one very patient husband.

Discover great authors, exclusive offers, and more at hc.com.

Give in to your impulses . . .
Read on for a sneak peek at six brand-new
e-book original tales of romance
from Avon Impulse.
Available now wherever e-books are sold.

AN HEIRESS FOR ALL SEASONS
A Debutante Files Christmas Novella
By Sophie Jordan

INTRUSION
An Under the Skin Novel
By Charlotte Stein

CAN'T WAIT
A Christmas Novella
By Jennifer Ryan

THE LAWS OF SEDUCTION
A French Kiss Novel
By Gwen Jones

SINFUL REWARDS 1
A Billionaires and Bikers Novella
By Cynthia Sax

SWEET COWBOY CHRISTMAS
A Sweet, Texas Novella
By Candis Terry

An Excerpt from

AN HEIRESS FOR ALL SEASONS

A Debutante Files Christmas Novella

by Sophie Jordan

Feisty American heiress Violet Howard swears she'll never wed a crusty British aristocrat. Will, the Earl of Moreton, is determined to salvage his family's fortune without succumbing to a marriage of convenience. But when a snowstorm strands Violet and Will together, their sudden chemistry will challenge good intentions. They're seized by a desire that burns through the night, but will their passion survive the storm? Will they realize they've found a love to last them through all seasons?

HIS EYES FLASHED, appearing darker in that moment, the blue as deep and stormy as the waters she had crossed to arrive in this country. "Who are you?"

"I'm a guest here." She motioned in the direction of the house. "My name is V—"

"Are you indeed?" His expression altered then, sliding over her with something bordering belligerence. "No one mentioned that you were an American."

Before she could process that statement—or why he should be told of anything—she felt a hot puff of breath on her neck.

The insolent man released a shout and lunged. Hard hands grabbed her shoulders. She resisted, struggling and twisting until they both lost their balance.

Then they were falling. She registered this with a sick sense of dread. He grunted, turning slightly so that he took the brunt of the fall. They landed with her body sprawled over his.

Her nose was practically buried in his chest. *A pleasant smelling chest.* She inhaled leather and horseflesh and the warm saltiness of male skin.

He released a small moan of pain. She lifted her face to observe his grimace and felt a stab of worry. Absolutely misplaced considering this situation was his fault, but there it was nonetheless. "Are you hurt?"

"Crippled. But alive."

Scowling, she tried to clamber off him, but his hands shot up and seized her arms, holding fast.

"Unhand me! Serves you right if you are hurt. Why did you accost me?"

"Devil was about to take a chunk from that lovely neck of yours."

Lovely? He thinks she is lovely? Or rather her neck is lovely? This bold specimen of a man in front of her, who looks as though he has stepped from the pages of a Radcliffe novel, thinks that plain, in-between Violet is lovely.

She shook off the distracting thought. Virile stable hands like him did not look twice at females like her. No. Scholarly bookish types with kind eyes and soft smiles looked at her. Men such as Mr. Weston who saw beyond a woman's face and other physical attributes.

"I am certain you overreacted."

He snorted.

She arched, jerking away from him, but still he did not budge. His hands tightened around her. She glared down at him, feeling utterly discombobulated. There was so *much* of him—all hard male and it was pressed against her in a way that was entirely inappropriate and did strange, fluttery things to her stomach. "Are you planning to let me up any time soon?"

His gaze crawled over her face. "Perhaps I'll stay like this forever. I rather like the feel of you on top of me."

She gasped.

He grinned then and that smile stole her breath and made all her intimate parts heat and loosen to the consistency of pudding. His teeth were blinding white and straight set against features that were young and strong and much too handsome. And there were his eyes. So bright a blue their brilliance was no less powerful in the dimness of the stables.

Was this how girls lost their virtue? She'd heard the stories and always thought them weak and addle-headed creatures. How did a sensible female of good family cast aside all sense and thought to propriety?

His voice rumbled out from his chest, vibrating against her own body, shooting sensation along every nerve, driving home the realization that she wore nothing beyond her cloak and night rail. No corset. No chemise. Her breasts rose on a deep inhale. They felt tight and aching. Her skin felt like it was suddenly stretched too thin over her bones. "You are not precisely what I expected."

His words sank in, penetrating through the fog swirling around her mind. Why would he expect anything from her? He did not know her.

His gaze traveled her face and she felt it like a touch—a caress. "I shall have to pay closer attention to my mother when she says she's found someone for me to wed."

Violet's gaze shot up from the mesmerizing movement of his lips to his eyes. "Your *mother?*"

He nodded. "Indeed. Lady Merlton."

"Are you . . ." she choked on halting words. *He couldn't be.* "You're the—"

"The Earl of Merlton," he finished, that smile back again, wrapping around the words as though he was supremely amused. As though she were the butt of some grand jest. He was the Earl of Merlton, and she was the heiress brought here to tempt him.

A jest indeed. It was laughable. Especially considering the way he looked. Temptation incarnate. She was not the sort of female to tempt a man like him. At least not without a dowry, and that's what her mother was relying upon.

"And you're the heiress I've been avoiding," he finished.

If the earth opened up to swallow her in that moment, she would have gladly surrendered to its depths.

An Excerpt from

INTRUSION
An Under the Skin Novel
by Charlotte Stein

I believed I would never be able to trust any man again. I thought so with every fiber of my being—and then I met Noah Gideon Grant. Everyone says he's dangerous. But the thing is . . . I think something happened to him too. I know the chemistry between us isn't just in my head. I know he feels it, but he's holding back. He's made a labyrinth of himself. Now all I need to do is dare to find my way through.

An Avon Red Novel

HE SAID NO sexual contact, and a handshake apparently counts. I should respect that—I do respect that, I swear. I can respect it, no matter how much my heart sinks or my eyes sting at a rejection that isn't a rejection at all.

I can do without. I'm sure I can do without, all the way up to the point where he says words that make my heart soar up, up toward the sun that shines right out of him.

"Kissing is perfectly okay with me," he murmurs, and then, oh, God, then he takes my face in his two good hands, roughened by all the patient and careful fixing he does and so tender I could cry, and starts to lean down to me. Slowly at first, and in these hesitant bursts that nearly make my heart explode, before finally, Lord, finally, yes, finally.

He closes that gap between us.

His lips press to mine, so soft I can barely feel them. Yet somehow, I feel them everywhere. That closemouthed bit of pressure tingles outward from that one place, all the way down to the tips of my fingers and the ends of my toes. I think my hair stands on end, and when he pulls away it doesn't go back down again.

No part of me will ever go back down again. I feel dazed in the aftermath, cast adrift on a sensation that shouldn't have happened. For a long moment I can only stand there in stunned silence, sort of afraid to open my eyes in case the spell is broken.

But I needn't have worried—he doesn't break it. His expression is just like mine when I finally dare to look, full of shivering wonder at the idea that something so small could be so powerful. We barely touched and yet everything is suddenly different. My body is alight. I think his body is alight.

How else to explain the hand he suddenly pushes into my hair? Or the way he pulls me to him? He does it like someone lost at sea, finally seeing something he can grab on to. His hand nearly makes a fist in my insane curls, and when he kisses me this time there is absolutely nothing chaste about it. Nothing cautious.

His mouth slants over mine, hot and wet and so incredibly urgent. The pressure this time is almost bruising, and after a second I could swear I feel his tongue. Just a flicker of it, sliding over mine. Barely anything really, but enough to stun me with sensation. I thought my reaction in the movie theater was intense.

Apparently there's another level altogether—one that makes me want to clutch at him. I need to clutch at him. My bones and muscles seem to have abandoned me, and if I don't hold on to something I'm going to end up on the floor. Grabbing him is practically necessary, even though I have no idea where to grab.

He put his hand in my hair. Does that make it all right to put mine in his? I suspect not, but have no clue where that leaves me. Is an elbow any better? What about his upper arm? His upper arm is hardly suggestive at all, yet I can't quite bring myself to do it. If I do he might break this kiss, and I'm just not ready for that.

I probably won't be ready for that tomorrow. His stubble is burning me just a little and the excitement is making me so shaky I could pass for a cement mixer, but I still want it to carry on. Every new thing he does is just such a revelation—like when he turns a little and just sort of catches my lower lip between his, or caresses my jaw with the side of his thumb.

I didn't think he had it in him.

It could be that he doesn't. When he finally comes up for air he has to kind of rest his forehead against mine for a second. His breathing comes in erratic bursts, as though he just ran up a hill that isn't really there. Those hands in my hair are trembling, unable to let go, and his first words to me blunder out in guttural rush.

"I wasn't expecting that to be so intense," he says, and I get it then. He didn't mean for things to go that way. They just got out of control. All of that passion and urgency isn't who he is, and now he wants to go back to being the real him. He even steps back, and straightens, and breathes long and slow until that man returns.

Now he is the person he wants to be: stoic and cool. Or at least, that's what I think until he turns to leave. He tells me good-bye and I accept it; he touches my shoulder and I process this as all I might reasonably expect in the future. And then just as he's almost gone I happen to glance down, and see something that suggests that the idea of a real him may not be so clear-cut:

The outline of his erection, hard and heavy against the material of his jeans.

An Excerpt from

CAN'T WAIT
A Christmas Novella
by Jennifer Ryan

**(Previously appeared in the anthology
All I Want for Christmas Is a Cowboy)**

*Before The Hunted Series, Caleb and Summer
had a whirlwind romance not to be forgotten . . .*

Caleb Bowden has a lot to thank his best
friend, Jack, for—saving his life in Iraq and
giving him a job helping to run his family's
ranch. Jack also introduced Caleb to the most
incredible woman he's ever met. Too bad he can't
ask her out. You do not date your best friend's
sister. Summer and Caleb share a closeness
she's never felt with anyone, but the stubborn
man refuses to turn the flirtatious friendship
into something meaningful. Frustrated
and tired of merely wishing to be happy,
Caleb tells Jack how he feels about Summer.
With his friend's help, he plans a surprise
Christmas proposal she'll never forget—
because he can't wait to make her his wife.

CALEB OPENED HIS mouth to yell, *Where the hell do you think you're going?*

He snapped his jaw shut, thinking better of it. He couldn't afford to let Jack see how much Summer meant to him. He'd thought he'd kept his need for her under wraps, but the too-observant woman had his number. Over the last few months, the easy friendship they'd shared from the moment he stepped foot on Stargazer Ranch turned into a fun flirtation he secretly wished could turn into something more. The week leading up to Thanksgiving brought that flirtation dangerously close to crossing the line when he walked through the barn door and didn't see her coming out due to the changing light. They crashed into each other. Her sweetly soft body slammed full-length into his and everything in him went hot and hard. Their faces remained close when he grabbed her shoulders to steady her. For a moment, they stood plastered to each other, eyes locked. Her breath stopped along with his and he nearly kissed her strawberry-colored lips to see if she tasted as sweet as she smelled.

Instead of giving in to his baser need, he leashed the beast and gently set her away, walking away without even a single word. She'd called after him, but he never turned back.

Thanksgiving nearly undid him. She'd sat alone in the

dining room and all he'd wanted to do was be with her. But how could he? You do not date your best friend's sister. Worse, you do not have dangerous thoughts of sleeping with her, let alone dreaming of a life with a woman kinder than anyone he'd ever met. Just being around her made him feel lighter. She brightened the dark world he'd lived in for too long.

He needed to stay firmly planted on this side of the line. Adhere to the best-bro code. This thing went beyond friendship. Jack was his boss and had saved his life. He owed Jack more than he could ever repay.

"Can you believe her?" Jack pulled him out of his thoughts. He dragged his gaze from Summer's retreating sweet backside.

"Who's the guy?" He kept his tone casual.

Jack glared. "Ex-boyfriend from high school," he said, irritated. "He's home from grad school for the holiday."

"Probably looking for a good time."

Caleb tried not to smile when Jack growled, fisted his hands, and stepped off the curb, following after his sister. He'd counted on Jack's protective streak to allow him to chase Summer himself. Caleb didn't want anyone to hurt her. He sure as hell didn't want her rekindling an old flame with some ex-lover.

He and Jack walked into the park square just as everyone counted down, three, two, one, and the multicolored lights blinked on, lighting the fourteen-foot tree in the center of the huge gazebo, and sparking the carolers to sing "O Christmas Tree."

Tiny white lights circled up the posts and nearby trees,

casting a glow over everything. The soft light made Summer's golden hair shine. She smiled with her head tipped back, her bright blue eyes glowing as she stared at the tree.

His temper flared when the guy hooked his arm around her neck and pulled her close, nearly spilling his beer down the front of her. She laughed and playfully shoved him away. The guy smiled and put his hand to her back, guiding her toward everyone's favorite bar. Several other people joined their small group.

Caleb tapped Jack's shoulder and pointed to Summer's back. Her long hair was bundled into a loose braid he wanted to unravel and then run his fingers through the silky strands.

"There she goes."

"What the . . . Let's go get her."

Caleb grabbed Jack's shoulder. "If you go in there and demand she leaves, it'll only embarrass her in front of all her friends. Let's scout the situation. Lie low."

"You're right. She'll only fight harder if we demand she come home. Let's get a beer."

Caleb grimaced. Hell yes, he wanted to drag Summer home, but fought the compulsion.

He did not want to watch her with some other guy.

Why did he torture himself like this?

An Excerpt from

THE LAWS OF SEDUCTION
A French Kiss Novel
by Gwen Jones

**In the final fun and sexy French Kiss novel,
sparks fly as sassy lawyer Charlotte Andreko
and Rex Renaud, the COO of Mercier
Shipping, race to clear his name after he's
arrested for a crime he didn't commit.**

IN HER FIFTEEN years as an attorney, Charlotte had never let anyone throw her off her game, and she wasn't about to let it happen now.

So why was she shaking in her Louboutins?

"Put your briefcase and purse on the belt, keys in the tray, and step through," the officer said, waving her into the metal detector.

She complied, cold washing through her as the gate behind her clanged shut. She glanced over her shoulder, thinking how much better she liked it when her interpretation of "bar" remained figurative.

"Name . . . ?" asked the other cop at the desk.

"Charlotte Andreko."

He ran down the list, checking her off, then held out his hand, waggling it. "Photo ID and attorney card."

She grabbed her purse from the other side of the metal detector and dug into it, producing both. After the officer examined them, he sat back with a smirk. "So you're here for that Frenchie dude, huh? What's he—some kinda big deal?"

She eyed him coolly, hefting her briefcase from the belt. "They're all just clients to me."

"That so?" He dropped his gaze, fingering her IDs. "How come he don't have to sit in a cell? Why'd he get a private room?"

Why are you scoping my legs, you big douche? "It's *your* jail. Why'd you give him one?"

He cocked a brow. "You're pretty sassy, ain't you?"

"And you're wasting my time," she said, swiping back her IDs. *God, it's times like these I really hate men.* "Are you going to let me through or what?"

He didn't answer. He just leered at her with that simpering grin as he handed her a visitor's badge, reaching back to open the next gate.

"Thank you." She clipped it on, following the other cop to one more door at the other side of the vestibule.

"It's late," the officer said, pressing a code into a keypad, "so we can't give you much time."

"I won't need much." After all, how long could it take to say *no fucking way?*

"Then just ring the buzzer by the door when you're ready to leave." When he opened the door and she stepped in, her breath immediately caught at the sight of the man behind it. She clutched her briefcase so tightly she could feel the blood rushing from her fingers.

"*Bonsoir*, Mademoiselle Andreko," Rex Renaud said.

Even with his large body cramped behind a metal table, the Mercier Shipping COO had never looked more imposing—and, in spite of his circumstances, never more elegant. The last time they'd met had been in Boston, negotiating the separation terms of his company's lone female captain, Dani Lloyd, who had recently become Marcel Mercier's wife. With his cashmere Kiton bespoke now replaced by Gucci black tie, he struck an odd contrast in that concrete room, yet still exuded a coiled and barely contained strength. He folded his arms across his chest as his black eyes fixed on hers, Charlotte getting the distinct impression he more or less regarded her as cornered prey.

All at once the door behind her slammed shut, and her heart beat so violently she nearly called the officer back. Instead she planted her heels and forced herself to focus, staring the Frenchman down. "All right, I'm here," she said *en français*. "Not that I know why."

If there was anything she remembered about Rex Renaud—and he wasn't easy to forget—it was how lethally he wielded his physicality. How he worked those inky eyes, jet-black hair and Greek-statue handsomeness into a kind of immobilizing presence, leaving her weak in the knees every time his gaze locked on hers. Which meant she needed to work twice as hard to keep her wits sharp enough to match his, as no way would she allow him the upper hand.

An Excerpt from

SINFUL REWARDS 1
A Billionaires and Bikers Novella
by Cynthia Sax

Belinda "Bee" Carter is a good girl; at least,
that's what she tells herself. And a good girl
deserves a nice guy—just like the gorgeous
and moody billionaire Nicolas Rainer. Or
so she thinks, until she takes a look through
her telescope and sees a naked, tattooed man
on the balcony across the courtyard. He has
been watching her, and that makes him all
the more enticing. But when a mysterious
and anonymous text message dares her to
do something bad, she must decide if she is
really the good girl she has always claimed
to be, or if she's willing to risk everything
for her secret fantasy of being watched.

An Avon Red Novella

I'D TOLD CYNDI I'd never use it, that it was an instrument purchased by perverts to spy on their neighbors. She'd laughed and called me a prude, not knowing that I was one of those perverts, that I secretly yearned to watch and be watched, to care and be cared for.

If I'm cautious, and I'm always cautious, she'll never realize I used her telescope this morning. I swing the tube toward the bench and adjust the knob, bringing the mysterious object into focus.

It's a phone. Nicolas's phone. I bounce on the balls of my feet. This is a sign, another declaration from fate that we belong together. I'll return Nicolas's much-needed device to him. As a thank you, he'll invite me to dinner. We'll talk. He'll realize how perfect I am for him, fall in love with me, marry me.

Cyndi will find a fiancé also—everyone loves her—and we'll have a double wedding, as sisters of the heart often do. It'll be the first wedding my family has had in generations.

Everyone will watch us as we walk down the aisle. I'll wear a strapless white Vera Wang mermaid gown with organza and lace details, crystal and pearl embroidery accents, the bodice fitted, and the skirt hemmed for my shorter height. My hair will be swept up. My shoes—

Voices murmur outside the condo's door, the sound

piercing my delightful daydream. I swing the telescope upward, not wanting to be caught using it. The snippets of conversation drift away.

I don't relax. If the telescope isn't positioned in the same way as it was last night, Cyndi will realize I've been using it. She'll tease me about being a fellow pervert, sharing the story, embellished for dramatic effect, with her stern, serious dad—or, worse, with Angel, that snobby friend of hers.

I'll die. It'll be worse than being the butt of jokes in high school because that ridicule was about my clothes and this will center on the part of my soul I've always kept hidden. It'll also be the truth, and I won't be able to deny it. I am a pervert.

I have to return the telescope to its original position. This is the only acceptable solution. I tap the metal tube.

Last night, my man-crazy roommate was giggling over the new guy in three-eleven north. The previous occupant was a gray-haired, bowtie-wearing tax auditor, his luxurious accommodations supplied by Nicolas. The most exciting thing he ever did was drink his tea on the balcony.

According to Cyndi, the new occupant is a delicious piece of man candy—tattooed, buff, and head-to-toe lickable. He was completing armcurls outside, and she enthusiastically counted his reps, oohing and aahing over his bulging biceps, calling to me to take a look.

I resisted that temptation, focusing on making macaroni and cheese for the two of us, the recipe snagged from the diner my mom works in. After we scarfed down dinner, Cyndi licking her plate clean, she left for the club and hasn't returned.

Three-eleven north is the mirror condo to ours. I straighten the telescope. That position looks about right, but then, the imitation UGGs I bought in my second year of college looked about right also. The first time I wore the boots in the rain, the sheepskin fell apart, leaving me barefoot in Economics 201.

Unwilling to risk Cyndi's friendship on "about right," I gaze through the eyepiece. The view consists of rippling golden planes, almost like . . .

Tanned skin pulled over defined abs.

I blink. It can't be. I take another look. A perfect pearl of perspiration clings to a puckered scar. The drop elongates more and more, stretching, snapping. It trickles downward, navigating the swells and valleys of a man's honed torso.

No. I straighten. This is wrong. I shouldn't watch our sexy neighbor as he stands on his balcony. If anyone catches me . . .

Parts 1, 2, 3, 4, and 5 available now!

An Excerpt from

SWEET COWBOY CHRISTMAS
A Sweet, Texas Novella
by Candis Terry

**Years ago, Chase Morgan gave up his Texas
life for the fame and fortune of New York
City, and he never planned on coming
back—especially not for Christmas. But
when his life is turned upside down, he finds
himself at the door of sexy Faith Walker's
Magic Box Guest Ranch. Chase is home for
Christmas, and it's never been sweeter.**

CHASE HAD COME up to stand beside her and hand her more ornaments. While most of the influential men who visited the ranch usually reeked of overpowering aftershave, Chase wore the scent of warm man and clean cotton. Tonight, when he'd shown up in a pair of black slacks and a black T-shirt, she'd had to find a composure that had nothing to do with his rescuing her.

She'd taken a fall all right.

For him.

Broken her own damn rules is what she'd done. Hadn't she learned her lesson? Men with pockets full of change they threw around like penny candy at a parade weren't the kind she could ever be interested in.

At least never again.

Trouble was, Chase Morgan was an extremely sexy man with bedroom eyes and a smile that said he could deliver on anything he'd promise in that direction. Broad shoulders that confirmed he could carry the weight of the world if need be. And big, capable hands that had already proven they could catch her if she fell.

He was trouble.

And she had no doubt she was in trouble.

Best to keep to the subject of the charity work and leave the drooling for some yummy, untouchable movie star like Chris Hemsworth or Mark Wahlberg.

Discreetly, she moved to the other side of the tree and hung a pinecone Santa on a higher branch. "We also hold a winter fund-raiser, which is what I'm preparing for now."

"What kind of fund-raiser?" he asked from right beside her again, with that delicious male scent tickling her nostrils.

"We hold it the week before Christmas. It's a barn dance, bake sale, auction, and craft fair all rolled into one." She escaped to the other side of the tree, but he showed up again, hands full of dangling ornaments. "Last year we raised $25,000. I'd like to top that this year if possible."

"You must have a large committee to handle all that planning."

She laughed.

Dark brows came together over those green eyes that had flashes of gold and copper near their centers. "So I gather you're not just the receptionist-slash–tree decorator."

"I have a few other talents I put to good use around here."

"Now you've really caught my interest."

To get away from the intensity in his gaze, she climbed up the stepstool and placed a beaded-heart ornament on the tree. She could only imagine how he probably used that intensity to cut through the boardroom bullshit.

As a rule, she never liked the clientele to know she was the sole owner of the ranch. Even though society should be living in this more open-minded century, there were those who believed it was still a man's world.

"Oh, it's really nothing that special," she said. "Just some odds and ends here and there."

When she came down the stepstool, his hands went to

her waist to provide stability. At least that's what she told herself, even after those big warm palms lingered when she'd turned around to face him.

"Fibber," he said while they were practically nose to nose.

"I beg your pardon?"

"You know what I do for a living, Faith? How I've been so successful? I read people. I come up with an idea, then I read people for how they're going to respond. Going into a pitch, I know whether they're likely to jump on board or whether I need to go straight to plan B."

His grip around her waist tightened, and the fervor with which he studied her face sent a shiver racing down her spine. There was nothing threatening in his eyes or the way his thumbs gently caressed the area just above the waistband of her Wranglers.

Quite the opposite.

"You have the most expressive face I've ever seen," he declared. "And when you're stretching the truth, you can't look someone in the eye. Dead giveaway."

"And you've known me for what? All of five minutes?" she protested.

One corner of his masculine lips slowly curved into a smile. "Guess that's just me being presumptuous again."

Everything female in Faith's body awakened from the death sleep she'd put it in after she'd discovered the man she'd been just weeks away from marrying, hadn't been the man she'd thought him to be at all.

"Looks like we're both a little too trigger-happy in the jumping-the-gun department," she said, while deftly extricating herself from his grasp even as her body begged her to stay put.

"Maybe."

Backing away, she figured she'd tempted herself enough for one night. Best they get dinner over with before she made some grievous error in judgment she'd never allow herself to forget.

She clapped her hands together. "So . . . how about we get to that dinner?"

"Sounds great." His gaze wandered all over her face and body. "I'm getting hungrier by the second."

Whoo boy.